MANOLIS

Titles available in this series

Yannis
Anna
Giovanni
Joseph
Christabelle
Saffron
Manolis

MANOLIS

Beryl Darby

JACH

ISBN 978-0-9554278-6-2

Printed and bound in Great Britain by
MPG Books Group, Bodmin and King's Lynn

First published in the UK in 2010 by

JACH Publishing
92 Upper North Street, Brighton, East Sussex, England BN1 3FJ

website: www.beryldarbybooks.com

For my father, who survived his ship
being bombed in Heraklion harbour.

Author's Note

All the characters in this novel are entirely fictitious. Any resemblance to actual persons, living or dead, is entirely coincidental.

The events that Manolis and Vasilis are credited to have participated in are based on various true incidents that occurred during the occupation of Crete 20th May 1941 to 11th October 1944.

This book about Manolis the fisherman, who first appears in *Yannis*, relates what happened to him during the Second World War, when the Germans and Italians occupied Greece, and takes his story up to 1953.

Although *Manolis* is the seventh book to be published in the continuing saga, it does not actually follow *Saffron* in the overall timescale. It was written really at the insistence of many readers who wanted to know more about Manolis and his activities. The next book, *Cathy*, is a sequel to *Manolis*.

1930

Manolis raised the sail of the fishing boat and sat at the tiller. He manoeuvred the sail by pulling on the ropes until he felt confident that he would be able to do so whilst out at sea. He was nervous about making his first trip alone.

'You won't get far like that, Manolis. You're still tied to the quay.'

Manolis looked up and grinned. 'I'm not planning to go anywhere today. I just want to make sure the sails are in one piece and I know what I'm doing.'

Lambros looked down at him. 'You're going to be a fisherman, then? Like your father?'

'I don't have a choice.'

Lambros looked at him doubtfully. 'Your father had years of experience and considerably more strength than you have.'

'I know. I'll have to take it easy and learn as I go along.'

'How do you expect to manage that boat on your own? A boy your size hasn't the strength.'

'I'll soon build up my muscles,' Manolis answered, and flexed his arm.

'You don't even know where the best fishing is to be had.'

'I can always follow you.'

'You'd have a job to keep up with me. I'll be on my way back with full nets by the time you reach the end of the jetty. I have a man who helps with the rowing.'

'And by the time I'm your age I'll have a fleet of boats and men to row them,' Manolis replied cheerfully

Lambros turned on his heel. 'Cheeky brat,' he muttered.

Manolis had spoken with far more confidence than he felt. Although he had accompanied his father regularly at the weekends, he had never taken a good deal of notice where they headed. He had not planned to be a fisherman. He dreamed of being a grocer. The smell of the herbs and spices delighted him whenever he passed a shop and he would have been happy surrounded by the aroma all day. He also dreamed of Maria, the chemist's daughter, with her long black hair and laughing eyes. If he had been working in a grocer's shop, her family might have considered him as a suitor but they would not accept a penniless fisherman.

He could ask his uncle to take him into his leather business, but he disliked the smell of the leather even more than he disliked the smell of stale fish. The tanners lived on the outskirts of the small town. No one wanted to live close to them. The smell that emanated from their backyards was repulsive with the stale urine that they stored to cure the leather and make it supple. All the workers had a permanent cough and none of them lived to be old men.

Manolis lowered the sail and stowed it carefully. He could not afford to get it damaged. When he had opened the small wooden box his father had kept beside his mattress there had been forty-eight drachmas and a few leptas hidden inside. He wanted to repay his aunt the cost of his father's funeral and he must ask her how much she expected each week for his keep.

He checked the moorings and stepped ashore. He needed to go to the Town Hall and ask them to add his name to the list of boatmen who took supplies out to the island regularly. He would need a permit and no doubt that would cost him some drachmas and take time as he would be shuffled from one department to another. He must also go to the fish market and see if he could work out how much he was likely to earn in a week from fishing.

If neither option was available to him his only alternative was to sell his father's fishing boat and hire himself out as a rower.

As he walked along the waterfront he scrutinised the other boats carefully. They were all much about the same size as his own, only a couple were considerably larger. Yiorgo had a particularly large boat and he wondered how the man had managed to purchase such an expensive craft. He would not be any competition for them. He would be sensible, he decided. Tomorrow, when he took the boat out for the first time on his own, he would not go far, just out in the bay. He hoped the other fishermen would be engrossed in their own tasks so they would not observe his first clumsy efforts to raise the sail or throw his net over board.

Manolis stood in line at the Town Hall waiting for directions to the correct desk to apply for an island permit. The clerk glanced at him sourly.

'How big is your boat?'

Manolis shrugged. 'It's my father's fishing boat.'

The man pulled a form towards him. 'Can you write?

'Of course,' answered Manolis indignantly.

'Fill that in. When you've completed it bring it back to me and I'll tell you the regulations.'

'Why can't you tell me now?'

The clerk sighed heavily. 'You collect a consignment each morning. You off-load at the jetty. You don't go on the island.'

Manolis nodded. 'How much do I get paid?'

'Fifty leptas for each container, no difference between a sack or a box. Don't get greedy and overload your boat. If you lose anything overboard you'll have to pay for it.'

'What am I carrying?'

'Bread, cheese, vegetables, rice, olives.' The clerk shrugged. 'The usual food stuffs.'

'How do you know how much I'm carrying?'

'The amount you're taking will be entered on a form when

you collect it. You'll be paid at the end of each week. Any more questions or are you going to fill in that form?'

Manolis smiled happily. 'I'll be back in a few minutes. Can I start on Monday?'

'You'll be told when you can start. You need your permit before you can carry anything. If it's granted look after it. If you lose it you'll be charged for us issuing you with another – if we do.'

Manolis completed the simple form rapidly, supplying his name, address and the name of his boat. He handed it back to the clerk who scrutinized it for so long Manolis began to feel that he must have made a mistake; finally the clerk placed a rubber stamp on it and handed it back.

'Take it to the desk over there. They'll add your name to the list.'

Manolis rowed strongly away from the jetty. Once clear, he raised the sail and he was pleasantly surprised as the wind filled it and took him swiftly out into the bay. He sat and looked back at Aghios Nikolaos. He would be on view to the whole town. Cautiously he moved the tiller and felt the boat change direction beneath him. Feeling more confident, he continued until he had sailed away from the cluster of boats that were making their way further out to sea. Probably the fish were more plentiful out there, but this was as far as he cared to venture on his first trip, and he did not want to be accused of poaching on another's fishing area.

He lowered the sail, the boat's progress halted immediately. He threw the net over the side and raised the sail once more, pleased that he had accomplished the manoeuvre without losing his balance at all. It would be far more difficult when he hauled the net back in, hopefully full of fish, the weight of which would make the craft unstable.

For half an hour he allowed the wind to carry him forward, then once again he lowered the sail and began to haul in the net, pulling on the ropes to close the mouth. At first it was relatively easy, the water taking the weight, but as it came nearer to the surface his arms were straining, the boat was rocking uncontrollably and the sweat was pouring from him. He needed to take a rest, but if he released the net it would sink to the sea floor and he would have to start hauling it up again.

How had his father managed? No doubt with his superior strength it had been no problem. Desperately he looked around. He took the ends of the rope used to close the neck of the net and wound it around the mast before tying it securely. Holding onto the mast whilst he regained his breath he checked the knots were secure. He now had two hands free to pull the net aboard and stabilise the craft so that it was not swamped. Already it was leaning with the side perilously close to the sea. He would then be able to take a brief rest before continuing.

He leaned back against the small cabin and wedged his feet against the side, hauling on the net with all the strength he possessed. With a sudden rush it came over the side and landed in a heap on top of him. Pushing his way free he pulled the dripping, wriggling mass to the stern of the boat before rinsing his dry mouth with some water from his bottle and spitting it out. He looked around cautiously. Had any of the seasoned fishermen seen his inexpert and ungainly recovery of his net?

Anxious though he was to see what his catch contained he knew he must work carefully. It was rare not to damage a net whilst fishing, but he did not need to make it any worse by tearing at it thoughtlessly. From the small cabin he brought out the buckets and placed them within easy reach. He pulled the mouth of the net open, folding it back on itself as he worked. The fish were slippery and flipped as he tried to pick them up, often sliding straight through his grasp, making him curse. He banged their heads against the wooden planking to kill them, often with more force than was necessary as he vented his bad temper on them, and threw them into the buckets.

Disappointed that he did not have a larger catch to show for his exertions, he folded the net carefully and stowed it back in the cabin. Now he realised he had forgotten to put water in the buckets. With a sigh he tipped a bucket of fish out on the deck and swung the bucket over the side bringing it up almost full of water. He tipped enough into each bucket to cover the catch and lowered it again. He added more water and then had the arduous task of picking up the fish from the bottom of the boat and replacing them in the bucket.

He remembered to soak some old sacks in the sea and placed them across the top of each bucket. If he left the fish exposed to the hot sun, even immersed in water, the contents of the buckets would be stinking by the time he reached the jetty and no one would want to buy his catch. Manolis looked at the position of the sun in the sky and judged that it was well past mid-day. He drank half his bottle of water and stretched his limbs. His back was beginning to ache and feel stiff from his unaccustomed exertion. He must raise the sail again and hope he would not have to row back to the shore. Once there he would have to visit the fish market, then return to inspect his net and make any repairs that were necessary.

Manolis sat at the table with his aunt and uncle. His mother had died when their house in Mohlos had burnt to the ground. Despite suffering some bad burns whilst rescuing his son and attempting to save his wife, Manolis senior had rowed across the bay to Aghios Nikolaos, throwing himself upon the mercy of his sister. She and her husband had made room for them in their cramped cottage, providing them with a mattress each up in the loft area. Manolis knew no other home and he hoped she and his uncle would be willing for him to continue to live with them.

'Aunt Eirini, Uncle Thanassis, I need to talk seriously with you.' He pushed some coins towards them. 'You paid for Pappa's funeral and I know it cost forty drachmas. I'd like to pay you back.'

'Where did you get that from?' Eirini asked suspiciously.

'It was in Pappa's box.'

Eirini stretched out her hand and counted the coins carefully. She could not read or write but she knew how to count money. She struggled with her conscience. 'How much did he have in there?' she asked.

'Forty eight drachmas and a few lepta.'

'What are you going to do Manolis? You can't live for long on a few drachmas,' asked Thanassis, sucking on his cigarette greedily, taking the acrid smoke down into his lungs.

Manolis shifted uncomfortably in his chair. 'I'd like to stay living here. This is the only home I can remember. I'll pay for my keep, the same as Pappa did.'

'What are you going to pay with? Your Pappa paid fifteen drachmas a week. I'll need ten from you, that's only fair.'

'I've got his boat and I went fishing today. I sold my catch for four drachmas. I should manage to make enough to pay you each week, and I'll bring you fish whenever you want.'

Eirini hesitated before pocketing the coins. She looked at her husband who had been struck with a paroxysm of coughing. 'What about the days when you can't go out or you have a bad catch? You could have been lucky today.'

Manolis nodded sombrely. 'I know. That's why I've bought a permit.'

'A permit?'

Manolis nodded. 'It cost me ten drachmas. I'm going to deliver supplies to the island. It will give me a guaranteed income. I earn fifty lepta for each container, so I shall have paid for it within a few days.'

Eirini shook her head. 'I don't think you should go there. You could end up being infected. You don't want to be sent to live there.'

'According to the Town Hall we don't go onto the island. We off-load the goods onto the jetty. We don't mix with the lepers. Have you heard of any of the boatmen catching leprosy? I haven't.'

'I still don't like the idea. What do you say, Thanassis?'

Thanassis shrugged and removed the cigarette from his mouth. 'He has to earn enough to pay for his keep. Fishing for a living is pretty unreliable. You could sell the boat and come into the tanners' yard.'

'I'd rather be a fisherman. Having a guaranteed income from the island deliveries should mean I have enough money each week to pay you and some saved for the weeks when I can't go out.'

Eirini pursed her lips. 'Your father never went there.'

'That's no reason why I shouldn't. Anyway, I've paid for the permit now. They told me to start next week. I'll deliver any goods I'm asked and then fish on the way back. However small my catch I shall have some money in my pocket.'

Manolis ignored his aunt's concern. Whatever the risk to his person it would be worth it to him financially. If he could take eight containers to Spinalonga each day, he would earn at least twenty drachmas a week. Ten drachmas would go to his aunt for his food and lodging and the remaining amount was his to spend or save.

If he saved the money he would make from fishing, in a few years time he would be able to afford to rent a room in one of the fishermen's cottages away from the smell of the tanners' yard, maybe purchase a larger boat and employ a rower. He might even make enough money to be able to buy a cottage of his own, then maybe Maria would look at him. He smiled to himself and shook his head. Daydreams. By the time he could afford to buy a home of his own Maria would no doubt be married and have a family. There was no way the beautiful chemist's daughter was ever going to look at him.

Flora sat on the quay and waited until a boat bringing supplies drew close. She moved a little further away and waved to the man. He raised his hand to her; then ignored her as he began to manhandle the boxes and sacks from his boat onto the land.

Flora moved closer once he was engrossed in his work. 'Could you bring a hammer to us?' she called.

Dimitris looked up. 'What's that?'

'Yannis needs a hammer. Could you bring one for us, please?'

'What do you need a hammer for? You can't eat that!'

Flora smiled. 'Yannis is trying to do some repairs. He needs a hammer.'

Dimitris frowned. From the quay all that was visible of the island were the high Venetian walls. 'What's he repairing?'

'The roof of a house. He's trying to make it dry for the winter.'

'If I give him a hammer for his repairs everyone else will be asking for things to repair theirs.'

Flora moved a little closer. 'All the houses need to be repaired. No one would do it until Yannis came. He managed to build a house and show them it was possible, but he needs a hammer to knock the nails home. He has to use a stone at the moment.'

Dimitris threw back his head and laughed. 'What's he using for nails?'

'We're taking out the old ones from some of the timbers. He'd love to have some new ones. The old ones have to be straightened out and they often bend again when he tries to knock them in.'

Dimitris shook his head and untied his boat. A hammer and nails! What would they be asking for next? He rowed away from the island before raising his sail and letting the wind take him out into the bay. Sitting at the tiller, he looked back across the expanse of water. From the distance he could see there were buildings behind the Venetian walls that he had never noticed before and someone appeared to be moving around on a roof.

Flora resumed her position on the quay. She would ask the next boat that arrived for a hammer.

Manolis loaded the eight boxes he had been allocated for the island onto his boat. He felt as nervous about visiting the island as he had about venturing out to fish alone the previous week. As he approached Spinalonga he looked at the island curiously. What must it be like to live there in such isolation? He shivered, despite the warm sunshine, desperately hoping he would not have to see any of the inhabitants. He tied his boat securely and turned his attention towards the boxes.

'Hello. You're a new boatman.'

Manolis spun round. Looking at him from a short distance away was a young girl. Her skirt and blouse hung on her small frame, with her face almost hidden by her mass of long dark hair. She pushed it back from her eyes as she spoke to him.

'Could you bring a hammer to us?' she asked.

'A hammer? What for?'

Flora smiled. 'Yannis is trying to do some repairs. He needs a hammer.' She repeated her story about repairing the houses.

'Hammers and nails cost money,' replied Manolis as he lifted the last box ashore. 'How much can you afford?'

Flora shook her head. 'We haven't any money.'

'Then you've not much chance of getting a hammer.' Manolis raised his hand to her and untied his boat.

'Please,' entreated Flora and held out her hands to him as he rowed away.

Feeling distinctly uncomfortable Manolis pretended to be engrossed in raising the sail. Once at a safe distance he looked back. She was sitting dejectedly on the quay, obviously waiting for the next boat to make a similar request.

Dimitris looked around his cottage. He felt a pang of guilt. His roof was sound, he had a warm bed and a plentiful supply of good food. Would it cause him any hardship to buy a hammer and give it to the girl on the island? Each time he delivered to the island Flora made her same request until he finally gave in to his conscience.

He placed the hammer and a screw of paper with a few nails onto the quay as he was about to untie his boat. 'There you are,' he called to Flora. 'A hammer and nails.'

Flora darted forward and seized upon them as if they would disappear before her eyes. 'Thank you,' she called. 'Thank you, thank you.'

She turned and began to run up the slope. Dimitris could hear her calling 'Yannis! Yannis!' as she disappeared from his view. With a shrug he continued to sail away. His duty was done and his conscience was clear.

Manolis had become used to seeing the waif-like girl on the quay when he delivered and her request for a hammer and nails had become monotonous. He waved and smiled at her, but deliberately closed his ears to her pleas. She moved nearer to him.

'Would you be able to bring us a ladder, please?'

Manolis stopped in the act of pushing a box onto the quay. 'A ladder?'

Flora nodded eagerly. 'Yannis needs a ladder to get up onto the roof. One of the boatmen brought us a hammer and nails and Yannis wants to get the roof finished. It's difficult for him to climb up there without a ladder.'

'Where would I get a ladder from?'

Flora shrugged. 'I don't know, but Yannis needs one.'

Manolis shook his head. 'Tell him to grow wings,' he grinned.

Flora scowled. 'That's not funny. Yannis is trying so hard to make things better for us.'

'Why don't you ask the government to repair your houses?'

'The government? All they do is send us food and water. They don't care how we live.' Flora spoke bitterly.

'Have you asked them?'

'We're not allowed contact with anyone except the boatmen. How can we ask the government for anything?'

'You can't expect poor fishermen to provide for you.' Manolis pushed the box ashore and lifted the next one.

Flora shrugged. 'Compared with us you are millionaires. We're beggars. We have nothing.'

'You have your food for nothing. You don't have to pay for that.'

'Have you seen what they send us? Sometimes it's mouldy or crawling with maggots.'

To Manolis's embarrassment, tears filled Flora's eyes and she brushed them away impatiently. He turned his attention back to the boxes, wondering for the first time what they held.

'I'll see you tomorrow,' he said gruffly.

'With a ladder?' she asked eagerly.

Manolis shook his head. You had to admire the girl's persistence.

The conversation worried at him on his return journey as he waited for his net to fill. Was he really taking out inedible food to the people and receiving payment for doing so? He could do nothing to rectify that as he was not a farmer, but he could find out how much a ladder cost.

He trudged along the path towards the market. The buckets seemed heavier than usual and he placed them on the ground to flex his hands. Lying on the ground a short distance away was a length of dirty ribbon. He looked around. There was no girl or woman in sight who could have dropped it. He picked it up and stuffed it into his pocket. He would give it to the girl on the island.

The price of a ladder horrified him. It would take all of his meagre savings to buy one. Despite thinking he would have plenty of money in his pocket each week it was not so. He had needed to buy more twine to repair his nets, one of his buckets had sprung a leak and had to be replaced, his uncle had charged him two drachmas to patch his boots, and he had given his aunt a further five drachmas so she could visit the doctor to have her ulcerated leg treated.

He shrugged. Why was he even considering it? The plight of the islanders was nothing to do with him. The vision of the thin little girl with her bandaged arm and tears in her eyes came to him, making him feel uncomfortable. Maybe he would be able to persuade some of the other boatmen to contribute. If they were willing to give a drachma each, or even fifty lepta, between them they should be able to send out a ladder.

Manolis went from boat to boat, explaining why the islanders needed a ladder, only to be met with a shake of the head and derisive comments. At the end of two hours he had accrued six leptas. He put them aside from his other money in the wooden box he had inherited from his father. He would call it the ladder fund and add to it when he was able. He hoped that his gift of the ribbon to the girl would stop her from asking him for anything else.

Manolis tossed the ribbon onto the quay. 'There you are. A present for you.'

Flora looked at him in disbelief. 'A present? For me?'

Manolis nodded. 'I found it yesterday. I thought you might like it.'

Flora picked up the grubby strip and looked at it lovingly. 'It's beautiful. Thank you. What's your name?'

'Manolis. What's yours?'

'Flora. Thank you, Manolis.'

'You're welcome, Flora.'

'Have you managed to get a ladder?' she asked eagerly.

Manolis threw back his head and laughed. 'You don't find ladders lying around in the street.' He sailed away, a warm glow inside him, which he could only attribute to the delight Flora had shown over the gift of the dirty piece of ribbon.

Flora left the jetty and made her way to the small area of beach. She stripped off her clothes and lay at the edge of the water. She could not swim and bathed infrequently, frightened she would be swept away by the ripples and small waves created by the boats. After a few minutes she decided she must be clean enough and returned to the shelter of the Venetian wall, hoping the sun would dry her before she needed to replace her blouse and skirt. She looked at the piece of ribbon she still had tightly clutched in her hand. It looked cleaner than when Manolis had given it to her. She pulled her wet hair back from her face and tied it securely with the ribbon, wishing she had a mirror so she could see the effect.

Manolis counted his savings and added the six lepta. He made his way to the local hardware store and stood outside hesitantly. There were a number of ladders of various lengths stacked outside of the shop. He tried to imagine how high a roof would be and counted the number of rungs each one had. He tried to lift the longest and he could not move it more than an inch from the ground.

'You'll not run away with that one in a hurry.'

He turned to see the shopkeeper standing in the doorway.

'I want to buy a ladder,' he assured him. 'I'm just not sure of the length I need.'

'What do you want to use it for?'

Manolis shrugged. 'I need to get up to a roof.'

'How high is it?'

'I don't know.'

The shopkeeper frowned. 'Is it two or three storeys?'

'I don't know,' repeated Manolis, feeling foolish. 'A friend just asked me to buy a ladder long enough to get to his roof.'

'Best to buy the longest one. Can't go wrong then. Better to have it too long than too short.'

'That one's far too heavy.' Manolis pointed to the one he had tried to lift.

'Try that one, then.' The shopkeeper indicated one that was a few feet shorter.

Manolis again attempted to lift it and found it extremely heavy and unwieldy. 'What about that one? Would that reach up to a roof?'

'It might. It all depends how high the roof is.' The shopkeeper smiled smugly.

Manolis grasped the rungs of the ladder and pulled it towards him. It was at least twice his height, but he was able to lift it off the ground. 'I'll take this one.' He leaned the ladder back against its fellows and handed over the notes.

The shopkeeper smiled in amusement as he watched Manolis try to move the ladder in an upright position, swinging it from leg to leg. 'You'll not get very far if you try to move it like that. Turn it on its side and carry it.'

'I will, as soon as there is enough space.' Manolis did not wish to show his ignorance, continuing to move the ladder awkwardly, finally lowering it to the ground and lifting the end.

'Are you going to drag it home? Hold it in the middle and put it over your shoulder. Like this.' The shopkeeper finally took pity on him, lifted the ladder and slipped the centre rung over Manolis's shoulder. 'Put your hand up to steady it and be careful how you go round corners.' He moved rapidly out of the way as Manolis turned to thank him, the ladder swinging around dangerously. He smiled and shook his head as he followed Manolis's wavering progress down the street towards the waterfront.

Manolis relieved himself of the cumbersome burden when he reached his boat. He was not at all sure how to get it aboard and keep it safe. If he lashed it to the cabin he would be unable to swing the sail round to take advantage of the wind and if he laid it flat he would be unable to use one of the oars. He sighed. He really did need a bigger boat.

A bigger boat! That was the answer. He would ask one of the fishermen who had a larger boat if they would take it across for him. He tied the ladder to the bollard with the end of the rope that was securing his boat and began to walk along the quay. He discounted many of the boats that he passed, they were only marginally larger than his own. He stopped at Yiorgo's and hailed him.

Yiorgo looked up from stowing his nets. 'Are you wanting me?'

Manolis nodded. 'I wanted to ask a favour. Would you take something out to the island for me the next time you go there?'

Yiorgo shook his head. 'I don't take supplies over. Why can't you take it yourself?'

'My boat isn't big enough.'

'What are you taking them? An elephant?'

Manolis grinned. 'A ladder.'

Yiorgo frowned. 'A ladder? Why do they want a ladder?'

Manolis shrugged. 'Something to do with repairing a roof before the winter.'

Yiorgo jerked his thumb. 'Ask Dimitris. He goes over regularly and he has a fair size boat.'

'Thanks. I will.'

Flora could not believe it when she saw Dimitris lift the ladder and push it on the jetty.

'A ladder,' she breathed. 'Yannis will be so happy.'

'Well, I'm glad someone is.' Dimitris mopped his brow. 'It's heavy. I hope he'll be strong enough to carry it.'

'Yannis will be able to carry it,' Flora answered confidently. 'How long can we keep it?'

'It's yours. Keep it as long as you like.'

'Do you mean it?' Flora's face lit up with a smile. 'It's really ours to keep?'

'As far as I know. Move back, I need to get the boxes off.'

'I'll go and tell Yannis.' Flora ran up the slope towards the interior of the island.

As Dimitris rowed away he saw two men approach the jetty and look at the ladder, one clapped the other on the back, and between them they lifted it and began to walk up towards the Venetian walls.

'We've got a ladder,' Flora declared as Manolis moored. 'One of the boatmen has given us a ladder. Yannis is so happy.'

Manolis smiled at the delighted girl. He did not admit that he had bought it, using all his savings and still owing his aunt that week's money for his keep. 'That's good. I like your hair tied back. It shows off your pretty face.'

Flora flushed and raised her hand self-consciously to her hair. 'I tied it with the ribbon you brought me. You haven't got any nails with you, have you?'

'Only those on my fingers and toes,' he grinned and then felt embarrassed. He looked down at Flora's bare feet and was relieved to see that she appeared to have all her toes.

Flora's face fell and she shrugged. 'Yannis will have to continue to use the old ones then. We really do need some new ones, long ones for roofing, and some hinges to fix the shutters and doors. Yannis says we need screws and a screw driver for those.'

'Who is this Yannis you keep talking about?'

Flora's eyes lit up. 'He came over from the hospital. He decided the houses could be repaired and persuaded some of us to help him. He built a house all by himself to prove to them that it could be done. Do you want to meet him?'

Manolis shook his head. 'I don't need to meet him.' If the man had been in hospital he was probably badly disfigured. 'How do you help with the building?' he asked. The girl did not look strong enough to cope with manual labour.

'I talk to the boatmen and ask them if they will bring us the things we need. After they've delivered the boxes I take some food up to Yannis and Spiro. If they need more water I fetch it for them.'

'Why can't they get their own food and water?'

'Yannis likes to work as long as possible.'

'A real slave driver.'

'No he isn't,' Flora answered indignantly. 'He doesn't make people work. They can come and go as they please.' She gave a small smile. 'It just makes them feel guilty when they see that Yannis is still working hard when they have gone off for a rest.

He says that if they want somewhere decent to live they have to help him.'

Manolis frowned. 'Where do the people live now? In the old fortress?'

Flora shook her head. 'That's just walls. The new arrivals live in the church or shelter in the tunnel. The people who have lived here for years have taken over the old houses that the Turks built when they were here.'

'So how many need to be repaired?'

'Lots. They have holes in the roof, the shutters have fallen off, sometimes a wall has fallen down.'

'How many is lots? Ten? Twenty? A hundred?'

Flora shrugged. 'I don't know. I can't count.'

'You can't count?' Manolis was aghast.

'I didn't go to school and then I became sick.'

'I'll teach you to count.' Manolis regretted the words as soon as he had spoken them.

'You will? When?'

'When I have the time.' Manolis looked up through the archway, but he could see no sign of any buildings at all. 'I'm off. There's another boat on the way and he'll need my space. Keep your hair tied back. I like it that way.'

Colour suffused Flora's cheeks and she touched her hair self-consciously again as she waved the boatman away.

1931

Father Minos was elated. After badgering Doctor Kandakis for over a year requesting permission to visit the island of Spinalonga, finally threatening to approach the authorities, the doctor had at last relented. He had travelled down to Aghios Nikolaos and was now looking for the fisherman who had given him hospitality on his first visit. He hoped to beg a bed for the night. He would be able to give them the name of the hospital where their nephew had been taken in Athens, although he had no other news of the man. He wondered if the young man who wanted to be a priest was still determined about his calling.

The waterfront was deserted of fishing boats and Father Minos wandered up into the huddle of cottages, hoping he would remember correctly where he had stayed the previous year. There was no answer to his knock and he turned away disconsolately. Maybe the doctor would be willing for him to stay in his house.

He trudged up over the hill to where the doctor's house was situated and entered the hallway where people sat and waited to be called in for their consultation. He waited until the last of the patients had left, then knocked and asked permission to enter.

'Good morning, doctor. I am Father Minos. I have your letter giving me permission to visit Spinalonga. I was hoping you might be able to give me some information about the conditions I can expect over there.'

Doctor Kandakis shrugged. 'I can tell you nothing.'

'You mean you don't visit them?'

'I go over once a year and leave a supply of medicine and bandages for them.' The doctor did not mention that the government gave him an additional allowance to treat the islanders on a regular basis.

'But you don't actually examine the patients?'

'There is no need to see them. They are incurables.'

'They are also people,' Father Minos pointed out gently.

'They are lepers. They have to live in isolation. It is the only way to contain the disease and prevent it from spreading. How would my patients feel if they knew I was visiting them and possibly bringing the disease back to the mainland?' The doctor glowered at the priest.

'Don't you feel you have a duty?'

'I have a duty to keep the people of Aghios Nikolaos healthy.' The doctor rose and opened the door. 'I will arrange for a boatman to take you across tomorrow. Be on the quay at eight in the morning.'

Father Minos looked steadily at the man. 'Thank you. I will report my findings to you,' he promised. He would certainly not ask the doctor for a bed for the night, convinced that his request would be refused.

He returned to the waterfront, again there was no sign of Yiorgo's boat. With a sigh he turned into the taverna and ordered a moussaka. He begrudged the money when he knew a piece of bread and cheese would have sufficed, but he knew the taverna owner was more likely to be forthcoming with the information he needed if he bought a meal.

He mopped his plate with the remains of his bread and smiled at the man who was hovering nearby. 'That was very good. Thank you.'

The man sat down in the chair opposite. 'You're a stranger round here, aren't you? Are you visiting the church?'

'I certainly plan to do so. I was actually looking for a fisherman who is an acquaintance of mine.'

The owner squinted through the window. 'Most of the boats are back now. Who did you want?'

'Yiorgo.'

'He and his wife went off in the boat yesterday. Probably gone to visit their relatives who live in Plaka. Their son would know. He'll be at the church. He's one of the novices. Always thought he'd be a fisherman like his father.' The man shrugged. 'No telling with these youngsters. Thought my daughter would be willing to stay here and help her mother, but, no, off she went to Heraklion. Said she wanted to be a dressmaker.'

'And did she succeed in her ambition?'

The taverna owner looked at the priest sourly. 'No. She says she's working in a taverna.'

'I come from Heraklion. Would you like me to speak to her? Tell her you would appreciate a visit from her.'

'Do no harm, I suppose. Doubt if she'll take much notice, though.'

'Tell me the taverna where she works and I'll pay her a visit,' promised Father Minos. 'I can at least tell her you are both well and missing her.' He pulled out his small notebook and wrote down the address the man reeled off to him. 'Now, I must make my way to the church and see if I am able to speak to Yiorgo's son.'

Andreas's face lit up with pleasure when he saw Father Minos. When told he had a visitor he had expected it to be his father saying that had returned early for some reason. He explained to Father Minos that his parents had left for Plaka the previous day.

'It's easier for them to go down by boat than for my uncle to leave his wife and walk up. Pappa always goes down once a week. Sometimes he takes Mamma with him and then they usually stay the night and Pappa does some fishing on the way back.'

'Why does he go so often?'

Andreas shrugged. 'I think he likes to know they are managing all right. It will be easier for Anna when Stelios comes to Aghios

Nikolaos. One less person for her to look after. Will you be able to wait and see them when they return?'

'I'm not sure. Much depends upon my visit tomorrow.'

Andreas looked at him curiously. 'Where are you going?'

'Spinalonga.'

Andreas drew in his breath. 'Do you have permission? Yes, of course you have. You couldn't go otherwise. May I come with you?'

'Why would you want to come?'

Andreas shrugged. 'I'm not sure I can answer that. I just want to be with you when you visit.'

Father Minos frowned. 'I have a letter giving me permission. It doesn't mention a companion. Besides, what would your parents say?'

'They wouldn't object to me going anywhere with you.'

'They might object very strongly to you going to Spinalonga.'

'Please let me go with you.'

Father Minos sighed, won over by the pleading in the boy's eyes. 'We'll see what the boatman says.'

'Thank you, Father. Now, how would you like to spend the remainder of your day? Would you like me to show you the town or we could walk up the hill above the pool and look at the view? Whilst I gain permission to go out with you I'll also ask if they can provide you with a bed for the night.'

Father Minos found the climb up the steep hill tiring and it left him breathless. He was relieved when Andreas stopped climbing and they both stood and drank in the panoramic view that spread out before them. Finally Andreas began to lead the way back down the hill.

'Shall we find a taverna?' asked Father Minos. 'I could do with a drink after such unaccustomed exercise and I want to hear about the family in Plaka and your sister, Annita. Did she go to Athens as she planned?'

Andreas nodded. 'I'll tell you everything whilst we're having a drink. You need almost as much breath to climb down as you do to climb up. It's quite steep in places. Be careful.'

They sat in the taverna until the bell tolled from a nearby church announcing an imminent service. Both men rose and walked over to the church, both lighting a candle as they entered and kneeling to say their private prayers. Father Minos realised with a guilty shock that he was not listening to the exhortations of the priest, but thinking about his impending visit the following day. He asked forgiveness for his inattention and waited until Andreas rose from his knees.

'Now where?' asked the priest.

'Back to the taverna for a meal and then I would like to go to bed. I plan to go to the early service so I shall have to be up at five.'

Father Minos nodded. 'I'm not used to getting up that early nowadays. I'd like to join you, so please wake me.'

Father Minos and Andreas were waiting on the quay before Manolis arrived. Father Minos was worried that the doctor would have forgotten his promise to arrange a boatman for him and his journey to Aghios Nikolaos would have been in vain. Manolis frowned when he saw the two men.

'Doctor Kandakis told me there was a priest I was to take to Spinalonga for the day. Which one of you is my passenger?'

'We both are,' replied Father Minos firmly. 'As I went alone to visit the doctor he cannot have realised that I had a companion.'

Manolis pursed his lips. 'I've only been paid for one passenger.'

'I'm sure the doctor will make up the difference when you point out his mistake to him,' smiled Father Minos.

Manolis grimaced. He would not dare to ask the doctor for any more money, having charged him five drachmas to ferry the priest each way. He had his quota of boxes, for which he would be paid, and knew he could spend the day fishing until the time he arranged to collect the men. He wished each day was as profitable.

As the boat rounded the side of the island and began to nose its way towards the jetty it took Flora by surprise. It was far too early for Manolis to arrive. The first boats came over from Plaka, just a short distance away across the water; those from Aghios Nikolaos had a far longer journey. Her usual greeting to Manolis died on her lips when she saw he was not alone.

She ran up the uneven path shouting loudly. 'Yannis! Yannis!'

Yannis looked down from the top of the wall he was attempting to repair. 'What's wrong?'

'There's a boat arriving and it has two priests in it.'

Yannis climbed down carefully to the ground. 'Are you sure they're priests?'

Flora nodded vigorously. 'They must have come from Aghios Nikolaos. Come quickly, Yannis.'

Yannis rubbed his hands down his trousers to remove some of the dust. He wished he had received more warning and could have washed before they arrived. He stood at the top of the steps leading down to the jetty and waited as the two men alighted from the boat, the younger jumping ashore easily, holding his hand out to assist the older. Their heads bowed and their eyes downcast the priests walked slowly to the archway before either of them looked up.

'Andreas!'

Flora and Father Minos watched as the two men were locked in each other's arms. Father Minos pursed his lips. He had not expected to find Yannis on the island.

'Have you come to stay?' asked Flora.

Father Minos shook his head. 'I have been given permission to visit for the day. Maybe you could let the people know I am here. I think Yannis and his cousin need some private time together.'

Flora nodded happily and began to hurry down the main path, calling out as she went, whilst Father Minos stood with Yannis and Andreas.

Manolis off-loaded his boxes and waited for Flora to return to the quay. He could see a small pile of pebbles that she had collected at his behest. Although he had regretted his impulsive offer, she had begged him week after week to teach her how to count until he had finally relented. Having started out earlier than usual, he would have been quite willing to spend an hour with her before going fishing. He continually looked up towards the archway, hoping to see her returning. He also had a small length of blue wool in his pocket. He had no idea what use she would have for it but he had found it blowing along the road and picked it up. In recent weeks he had taken to wandering around the town during the early evening looking for discarded items and scraps that had been dropped.

Her delight had been evident when he had given her a pair of mis-matched hinges, but the two glass beads he had given her four days ago had sent her into raptures. She turned them over and over between her fingers and kept saying how beautiful they were.

Finally realising that Flora was not going to return to the quay and feeling aggrieved he rowed away. He could not waste his day sitting there. He had solved the problem of raising his net. He usually dragged it for no longer than ten minutes a couple of times on his way out. That way he was able to haul it aboard without capsizing his boat. After off loading the boxes or sacks onto the jetty he would return to the open sea and cast it many more times to ensure he had a reasonable catch to take to the market. He would give Flora the piece of wool when he returned at the allotted time to collect the two men.

When he returned to the quay the press of people was far too great for him to see Flora. It appeared that they all wanted to touch the hem of Father Minos's cassock before Andreas helped him back into the boat. Father Minos stood, holding onto the mast, as Manolis rowed away, his hand raised in farewell and the islanders waving back to him.

Both men sat silently during the journey and although Manolis was longing to ask questions of them, he respected their silence.

No doubt the experience had been traumatic for both of them. Once back at Aghios Nikolaos they both thanked him and walked away before holding a quiet conversation together and parting company.

Manolis placed his bottle of water, a hunk of bread, piece of cheese and handful of olives, wrapped in a cloth, in the damaged bucket. He had found it made an ideal container and as he no longer used it to store his fish his meal did not become tainted. He was still feeling annoyed that Flora had not bothered to return to the quay to speak to him the previous day. He began to unwind the rope that held his boat securely at its mooring.

'Good morning.'

Manolis looked up to see the priest standing a short distance away.

Father Minos's face creased into a smile. 'I thought it was you, but I needed to make sure. Would you be able to take me out in your boat again today?'

'To the island?'

Father Minos shook his head. 'I need to visit a family in Plaka. How much is your fare?'

Manolis thought quickly. He had no scruples about overcharging the doctor, but to overcharge a priest would be considered sinful. 'Two drachmas.'

Clumsily Father Minos climbed aboard. 'I'm not sure how long I shall spend with them.'

Manolis frowned. 'If I have to sit and wait for you I shall have to charge you more. I can't afford to lose a day's fishing.'

'Of course not. I would not expect it of you. We will have a good deal to talk about, but if you tell me the time of your return I will be ready for you.'

'Is the other priest coming with you?'

'Not today.' Father Minos settled himself as comfortably as he was able on the hard wooden seat. 'Do you go out to the island every day?'

'I get paid to take out supplies.' He grinned. 'It gives me plenty of time to go fishing.'

'What happens when the weather is bad and you're unable to get over?'

'They have to wait until it clears.'

'So at those times they are without food or water?'

Manolis shrugged. 'They're bound to have some stored for emergencies.'

'Do you know how many people live on the island?'

'No idea. They know they have to wait for us to finish unloading before they come down to collect the boxes. I don't hang around to find out.'

'I'm sure I saw more than three hundred men and women yesterday.' Father Minos appeared to be thinking aloud. 'They made me welcome. They respected my calling, but they made no concessions. They shared their food with me as if I was one of them. They live in the most comfortless surroundings I have ever seen and something has to be done about it.' Father Minos brought his fist down on the seat.

Manolis shipped his oars and proceeded to raise the sail. Was the priest blaming him for the hardships the islanders suffered? It was nothing to do with him.

He concentrated on steering the boat, wishing the priest would stop muttering. Was he praying or talking to himself? It was unnerving. No wonder many of the fishermen refused to carry a priest on their boat.

Manolis helped Father Minos ashore at Plaka and sailed across to Spinalonga where he could see Flora sitting on the quay.

'Where did you get to yesterday?' he asked.

'I was with Yannis and the priests.'

'Why did they come to see him? Was he a priest?'

Flora shook her head. 'They didn't come 'specially to see him. They didn't know he was here. Yannis knew Father Minos when he was in Heraklion and the younger man is his cousin.'

Manolis raised his eyebrows. 'Is that why the priest has gone over to Plaka?'

'I expect so. Yannis's family live there.'

Manolis looked back towards the mainland, but he could no longer see the priest.

'It was wonderful to have them here.' Flora's eyes glowed at the memory.

'Are you religious?'

Flora shrugged. 'I used to go to church regularly. Don't you go?'

Manolis nodded. 'I go on a Sunday with my aunt and uncle.'

'What about your parents?'

'They're both dead.'

'I'm sorry.'

'I don't remember my mother. She died when I was a baby. My father died last year. He'd been drinking and got into a brawl with some other fishermen. What about you? Where are your parents?'

Flora shrugged. 'Still in Maronia as far as I know.'

'Where's that?'

Flora shrugged. 'I don't know. It was in the country. We had olive trees and a few animals.'

'Where do they think you are now?'

'Probably in the hospital.'

'Suppose they try to visit you?'

Flora looked at him in surprise. 'Visit me? You don't visit lepers. Besides, once they knew I was sick they were only too glad to be rid of me.'

'Why should they want to be rid of you? You're their daughter.'

'I have two older sisters. They're beautiful, not like me. My father wants them to make good marriages.'

'You're beautiful,' Manolis insisted.

Flora blushed. 'Don't be silly. I'm the runt of the litter.'

'What does that mean?'

'We use that expression with the animals. The last one of a litter to be born is usually the smallest, it often has a defect of some sort. That's me. I'm the runt.'

'Why didn't you go to the hospital?'

'I was supposed to, but then I was sent here instead. Yannis says they sent a lot of them over here as a punishment. He blames himself. He and Spiro and some of the others caused a lot of trouble.' Flora dropped her voice.

'Yes? What kind of trouble?'

'They had a fight with the hospital orderlies.'

'What were they fighting for? Were they trying to get out?'

Flora shook her head. 'It was over the way they were treated. Yannis says it was much worse in the hospital than it is over here.'

'I can't believe that. In a hospital you have treatment and regular meals.'

'Yannis says they didn't have any treatment. When their food was sent in and they had to fight for a share. He says it was even more mouldy and rancid than some that's sent over here and there was never enough water.'

'It sounds to me as if this Yannis of yours is trying to make excuses for his behaviour.'

'He wouldn't do that,' Flora answered indignantly.

Manolis raised his eyebrows. 'I suggest you watch out for him. He sounds like a trouble maker.'

'If you met him you'd realise what a fine man he is. He's working so hard to make things better for us over here. Have you brought any nails or screws today?'

Manolis grinned. 'I couldn't find any lying around. I brought you this.' He handed Flora the length of blue wool.

'Oh, that's pretty.' Flora began to wind it around her fingers, making intricate patterns.

'What are you doing?' Manolis was intrigued.

'Cat's Cradle. Look.' She turned her hands over to show a

different pattern. 'I used to play it when I was a little girl.' She frowned. 'I can't remember all the rhyme that went with it.'

'Maybe one of the others will know. Do you want to do some counting?'

Flora nodded eagerly. 'I've collected some pebbles from the beach as you told me. I don't know if I've got enough.' She pointed to the pile of well over a hundred small stones.

'There's plenty there for the time being. Bring some over here and we'll make a start.'

Flora picked up a handful of pebbles and placed them on the quay within Manolis's reach.

Manolis picked up ten pebbles and laid them out in a line. 'Put those others back over there. This is more than enough for today. Now, say after me, one.'

'One.'

Manolis pushed another to join the first. 'One and one are two.'

'One and one are two.'

Manolis separated the pebbles. He held up the first. 'One.' He picked up the second. 'One. Now I put them together and there are two.'

Flora looked at him puzzled. 'One,' she said again.

'No,' Manolis shook his head. 'One and one make two.' He picked up another and added it to the first two. He pointed to each pebble, 'One, two, three. You need to know the names of the numbers. Maybe I should try to teach you those first?'

Flora pushed at the pebbles and finally selected one. 'One,' she said and smiled.

Manolis nodded eagerly. 'That's right.'

She picked up another. 'One,' she said again and put them next to each other before picking up the third and adding it. 'One.'

Manolis shook his head. 'No. One and one are two and another one makes three.'

Flora frowned. 'You said it was one.'

36

'The first pebble is one, as you add more you call them different names.' He stretched out his hand to move the pebbles back and their fingers touched.

Flora drew her hand away as if she had been burnt. 'Don't touch me.'

'I won't hurt you.' Manolis felt upset that the idea should have entered her head.

Flora looked into his concerned brown eyes. 'I mean you mustn't touch me. You don't want to become ill like me.'

'I'm sure touching your fingers won't make me ill.'

'You don't know.'

'I'll take a chance.' Manolis smiled and touched her hand again. 'It might be easier if we start to count by using your fingers. Put your hand out.'

Flora extended her hand and Manolis took it gently in his own large fist. 'What tiny hands you have,' he remarked. 'I've never seen anyone with hands this small.'

'I told you I was the runt of the litter.' Flora tried to pull her hand away.

'No, they're perfect.' He held her firmly. 'Now, this is your thumb.'

'I know that!'

Manolis nodded. 'So how many fingers do you have?'

Flora looked at him. 'Those that are on my hand.'

'That's not the answer. You have four fingers. One, two, three, four.' He touched each one as he numbered them. 'Now find me four pebbles.'

He released her hand and Flora pushed the stones to one side, laying her fingers on them when she had done so. 'Is that right?' she asked.

'Absolutely. Now, take one away and tell me how many pebbles there are.'

Flora frowned. She laid her fingers on the pebbles; then removed one. She looked at her fingers. 'I still have four,' she announced.

'You still have four fingers, but how many pebbles do you have?'

Flora hung her head. 'I don't remember the word,' she admitted.

'Don't worry. We'll count your fingers again.'

Dutifully Flora extended her hand and Manolis took it in his without hesitation. He stood in his boat, patiently repeating the numbers to her until she suddenly smiled. She picked up a handful of pebbles and began to lay them in a line.

'One, two, three, four, five,' she announced proudly.

Manolis smiled with her. 'You see, it's not difficult, is it? Remember that until the next time and then we'll count to ten. The more we do it the easier you will find it to remember. I'm off now. My fish are calling.'

'Your fish are calling? What are they saying?' Flora looked mystified.

'It's just an expression. Fish can't speak. It means I must go and catch some before I collect the priest from Plaka. I have to earn my living.' Manolis untied the rope that had been holding his boat at the quay. 'I'll see you tomorrow.'

'With some screws and to do some counting?' asked Flora eagerly.

'No promises.' Manolis waved his hand to her as he rowed away. He always spent far longer talking to her than he intended.

Anna stood on the shore waving her red scarf towards the island. Despite her father's protestations she had defied him, accompanying the priest down to where Manolis was waiting for him. He accepted the fisherman's hand to help him aboard, whilst he kept his other clamped to the side of his cassock where there was a deep pocket. He did not want the bag of money that Yannis's father had given him to fall into the water.

Father Minos sat engrossed in his thoughts. He needed someone he could trust to take the supplies he planned to purchase out to the island. The doctor was out of the question and although Andreas could complete the purchases he could not transport them. Maybe his father, Yiorgo, would be willing, although Andreas had asserted that his father never went over there.

The priest suddenly realised they were sailing far closer to the island than was necessary. He watched as Manolis raised his hand to the girl who sat on the jetty and blew a kiss to her, grinning self-consciously at the priest afterwards.

'A friend of yours?'

Manolis shrugged. 'She's always there, asking the boatmen to bring things over to the island. She asked for a ladder a while ago. Sometimes I take her a little present when I deliver.'

Father Minos shifted his position on the wooden seat, his hand still clamped to his pocket. 'If I bought some supplies would you be willing to deliver them for me?'

'How much would you pay me to deliver them?'

'I hoped you would not charge as you have to go there anyway.'

Manolis frowned. 'That's not business. Whilst I'm loading and off-loading goods for you I can't be fishing.'

'How much do you get paid by the government?'

'Fifty lepta for each container.'

Father Minos sighed. 'I can't possibly afford that.' He begrudged spending any money on transportation as the boatman would be going to the island daily.

'What are you sending out to them?'

'Blankets, bandages and disinfectant at first. Then I'll start to send the sand, cement and lime.' Father Minos smiled at the amazed look on Manolis's face. 'They need it to repair their houses.'

Manolis considered. There was nothing on his permit for delivering to the island that said he could not take out other goods. There was often room on his boat for a few more sacks or boxes. 'Maybe I could manage to take some out for you, if I have the space.'

'For nothing?'

Manolis shook his head. 'It would probably mean leaving a couple of containers behind. How about if I charged you a drachma for each delivery I make?'

Father Minos eyes him suspiciously. No doubt the boatman was going to get the better bargain, but if he approached another he might well ask for more. 'Very well. I will expect you to go to the church each morning,' continued Father Minos. 'There will be boxes or sacks of bandages, disinfectant and blankets waiting for you to take over to the island. I expect you to take as much as possible each trip. The people are in urgent need of these supplies. In some cases their lives may depend upon them. Can you give someone over there a message from me?'

'Who?'

'You could tell the girl on the jetty. Ask her to tell Yannis that Anna is waving.'

Manolis nodded. He longed to ask the priest who Anna was and why she should wave to this man Yannis he seemed to be continually hearing about.

Father Minos counted the money given to him by Yannis's father. There was more than a thousand drachmas in the bag. Despite Yannis senior's assurances that it was not his life savings Father Minos was concerned. He visited Andreas's father and tried to suggest tactfully that most of the money should be returned. Yiorgo shook his head.

'He can spare it. There's more where that came from. Better to use it beneficially than give it to the government.' Yiorgo went over to the cupboard in the corner of the room and returned with a bottle and glasses, along with a small bag similar to the one Yannis senior had given to the priest. 'You'd better have this to add to it. Building materials are not cheap. If all you've told me is true they are going to need more than just sand and cement.'

'I had thought you might be willing to transport my purchases, but I understand from Andreas that you don't go over there.'

Yiorgo looked at the priest suspiciously. Had Yannis senior told him about their profitable business that necessitated a visit from him to the farm each week and his own surreptitious visits to the island under the cover of darkness?

'I catch fish. I don't want to catch a disease.'

'Of course not. I have made an arrangement with the boatman I used. He is willing to deliver for me. My first priority is to send them bandages and disinfectant, followed by blankets and clothing. I hope to have some tools and building materials sent within a few weeks.' Father Minos smiled happily. He had sat up far into the night making a list of the items he felt were necessities and a second list of building materials and tools. 'Provided you have no objection, I plan to leave the balance of the money that has been donated with your son. The islanders can send their requests through the boatman and he can relay them to Andreas. Once the items have been paid for they can be shipped out.'

Yiorgo nodded. He did not mind how the arrangement worked provided it did not involve him.

Doctor Stavros strolled along the waterfront. His week's holiday in Sitia had not refreshed him as he had hoped. He had returned to Aghios Nikolaos and dropped back into his routine as if he had never been away, seeing his patients at his house in the morning and visiting the hospital cases during the afternoon. Had it not been for his encounter with Doctor Kandakis that afternoon he would consider himself a happy and contented man.

Two days before he left for Sitia he had received a letter from the medical authorities containing instructions to visit Spinalonga. There had to be some mistake. He was not the doctor in charge of the island so why would he be expected to go out there? The letter had obviously been meant for Doctor Kandakis. The authorities would no doubt contact him when they realised their error. He decided to ignore it.

Doctor Stavros had erased the letter from his memory until

he encountered Doctor Kandakis at the hospital. It would obviously be a courtesy on his part to mention it.

'Excuse me, Doctor. May I have a quick word?'

Doctor Kandakis grunted. 'I'm in a hurry.'

'I wished to ask you about a letter I received from the Medical Authorities asking me to visit Spinalonga. I understood you were the doctor in charge of the island.'

'I have resigned.' The doctor pushed his way through the door and hurried away. If that meddling priest had not appeared, he could still be the doctor in charge of the island and receiving the additional salary. He was certain that the priest would write a very adverse report of his medical care for the islanders and he was not prepared to face an enquiry into his negligence. A letter of resignation had been the obvious solution to the problem.

Doctor Stavros had looked after the doctor in annoyance. His plan to spend the remainder of the afternoon reading had been ruined; now he would have to compose an answer to the letter.

However hard he tried the appropriate words would not come to his mind and eventually he threw aside his pen in disgust. He would take a stroll along the waterfront. The fresh air would clear his brain and he might meet a fisherman who was willing to give him a fish for his supper.

His eye alighted on a young man hauling sacks aboard his fishing boat. They seemed extremely heavy and it was not the usual time for a boat to set sail if they were fishing.

'What's in there?' he asked, curiosity getting the better of him.

'Sand and cement for the island. The priest pays to have it taken over regularly. The forecast is bad for tomorrow, so I thought I'd do a special run with it now. It has to be kept dry, you see.' Manolis enjoyed showing off his newfound knowledge.

'What do they want that for?'

'I don't know. The priest pays for it to be sent over.'

'Do you go on to the island?'

Manolis shook his head. 'I only unload at the jetty.'

'So you don't see the people who live there?'

'I see Flora. She's usually there waiting to ask the boatmen to bring things out to them.' Manolis heaved the last sack aboard. 'Do you want me to give a message to anyone? I can tell Flora. She'll pass it on.'

'No, I've no message for anyone.' Doctor Stavros watched as Manolis sailed out into the bay. The priest must be sending building materials out to the island for the people to build a church. If they were capable of manual labour, they could not be particularly sick or disabled. Maybe Doctor Kandakis had been right when he said it was not necessary to visit them.

He continued on his way, raising his hand to the various men he was acquainted with, but not one of them offered him a fish. He entered the general store to make his weekly purchase of a bottle of raki and the owner handed him a brown envelope.

'Good holiday, Doctor? This has been sitting here for you since last Wednesday.'

'Thank you.' As Doctor Stavros saw the medical authorities stamp across the back of the envelope his heart sank. A quick glance at the contents confirmed his initial misgivings. He would have to read the missive carefully.

Manolis had been correct with his forecast of the weather. There was a stiff wind running and the boats did not venture away from the quay. He checked to ensure his moorings were fast and he wandered aimlessly along the waterfront.

'Manolis.' A voice hailed him and he smiled at the fellow fisherman.

'What can I do for you?'

'Wondered if you fancied a game of cards?'

Manolis hesitated. He had no aversion to playing cards to while away the time. 'What are the stakes?' he asked.

Makkis shrugged. 'High as you like.'

Manolis shook his head and dug his hand into his pocket. 'I've two drachmas and seventeen lepta,' he announced.

'You could have four drachmas by the end of the morning,' Makkis tried to tempt him.

'I could,' grinned Manolis, 'But I could also have empty pockets. Thanks for the offer. Another day, maybe, besides, I've jobs I need to do.'

Makkis scowled and retreated into the small cabin. He had hoped the young man would accept so he could relieve him of as much money as possible. He doubted if any of the other men would join him. They all knew his reputation too well.

Manolis continued on his way. When he returned from fishing in the late afternoon he checked and mended his nets as necessary. In the remaining daylight he would wander through the streets, looking for any discarded items he thought might be useful to the islanders. On a day when he was unable to sail he would walk to the far outskirts of the town where the gypsies camped when they visited and people would dump their rubbish. During the day a few goats were tethered there to clear any food debris and eat the grass. Here he had found a variety of old nails, screws, a couple of handles and the mis-matched hinges that Flora had seized upon with delight. Now supplies of building materials were going to be sent out on a regular basis they would have no need of his meagre offerings. He kicked at a stone disconsolately. How was he going to occupy his time?

It had become a habit for him to walk looking down at the ground, swivelling his eyes from side to side in the hope of espying a nail glinting in the sun. The roadway was bare, the only shining object that caught his attention today was a piece of broken glass. The goats ignored him as he walked across the scrubland, only one looked up, a red flower hanging from her mouth.

Manolis looked at her in surprise. No flowers grew on the rough ground; they would have been trampled by the goats or eaten as the first sign of greenery appeared. Cautiously Manolis moved forward and saw the flower was artificial. Between her legs were three more. Manolis waved his arms and shooed her away. He gathered up the faded imitations. They would be something to take out to Flora the next time he delivered. Mentally he shook himself. He was becoming obsessed with the girl on the island.

Manolis tossed the artificial flowers on to the quay beside Flora. She snatched them up and held them to her nose, then looked disappointed. 'They have no smell,' she said sadly.

'Of course they don't. They're not real flowers.'

'They're lovely anyway.' Flora tried to hide her disappointment. 'Thank you, Manolis. Can you bring us a spade?' she asked.

'What for? To plant the flowers?'

'Don't be silly, Manolis,' she giggled. 'Yannis needs a spade to mix the sand and cement you've brought. He also asked if you could bring him some instructions. He needs to know that he's mixing it right.'

'I thought this Yannis knew everything.'

'Of course he doesn't. He's never done any building work before and Christos isn't any help.'

'Who's Christos?' asked Manolis.

'One of the men over here. He used to be a builder, but he doesn't seem to like Yannis.'

Manolis made no reply. He had an idea he would not like Yannis either. 'Where am I supposed to get a spade and instructions from?'

'Yannis said...' Flora wrinkled her brow. 'Wait a moment. I'll go and fetch Yannis.'

Manolis frowned. He was happy to talk to Flora but he was not sure about meeting other members of the community. 'I can't wait for long,' he called after her.

It was only a matter of moments before Manolis saw a man hurrying down the ramp towards the jetty. This must be the Yannis that Flora kept talking about. He studied him carefully. He was younger than he had imagined and walked easily, obviously the disease had not yet attacked his feet.

Yannis stood a short distance away from Manolis's boat. 'Pleased to meet you,' he called, his voice harsh and rasping. 'I'm Yannis. I understand Father Minos has arranged for you to bring over building materials for us.'

Manolis nodded. 'Flora said you wanted a spade. She also said you wanted some instructions.'

'That's right. You see, only a few men were builders before they came here, and only Christos would be capable of any practical help and he's being difficult. I need to know what quantity of sand I use to the amount of cement and how stiff the mix should be. I also need a spade and a trowel. We need some saws to cut the timber. They'll need to be various sizes depending upon the job we're doing. Then we'll need screws and screwdrivers.' Yannis frowned. 'A chisel. We'll definitely need a chisel so I can fit the hinges properly.'

'And where am I expected to find these things? They won't be lying around in the rubbish like the bits I bring for Flora.'

'You can buy them from the hardware shop or builders merchants.'

Manolis looked at Yannis in amazement. 'Buy them? What am I supposed to buy them with? I'm only a poor fisherman. Where am I going to get the money from; and why should I buy them for you anyway?'

Yannis smiled and squatted down on the quay. 'Didn't Father Minos explain? He's left a sum of money with Andreas. He'll pay you for anything you buy for us.'

Manolis pursed his lips. 'How do I know he'll pay? I could buy something and when I ask for the money he could refuse or say I've bought the wrong tools.'

Yannis sighed. 'Any tools would be useful. We'd not refuse them. I'll give you a list. Take it to Andreas and he'll give you some money. You take the bills back to him and he'll either make up the difference or you give him back the change.'

Manolis considered. The proposal seemed reasonable enough. He had been instructed by Father Minos to visit the church each day and collect whatever was being sent out to the island. The first sacks had been soft and reasonably light, holding blankets and clothes, but the last few days he had been expected to carry sacks of sand and cement down to his boat. 'Give me a list and I'll see what I can do.'

'Instructions for mixing the cement, a spade, trowel, a large saw, two smaller ones, a chisel, hinges of various sizes, screws, again various sizes, nails ...'

Manolis held up his hand and stopped him. 'I'll never remember all that lot. You'll have to write it down for me.'

'I can't. I haven't any writing materials.'

'Surely someone must have some paper and a pencil.'

Yannis shrugged. 'They might have, but I doubt if they'd let me use it. It would be too precious to them. Besides, I'm not allowed to give you anything. If you could bring a pencil and paper out with you tomorrow I could give you a list. You can write, can't you?' asked Yannis as an afterthought.

Manolis looked at him sourly. 'Of course I can write. I've been to school.'

Yannis smiled. 'I didn't mean to offend, but I know a number of the fishermen can't read or write. My uncle has a struggle.'

Manolis sighed. 'I'll go and see Andreas when I return tonight. I can ask him about buying things for you then.' He felt the word of the novice priest would be more reliable than that of the man on the quay. He would obviously say anything to get what he wanted. He wondered just how much longer the priest would be able to afford to send out the vast quantities. He was either a very rich man or he was accessing church funds in a way that was probably illegal.

Doctor Stavros paced up and down on the quay as he waited for the fishing boat to reach the shore. He had been told by the fishermen to speak to Manolis. They only delivered food to the island to supplement their income, whilst he appeared to be employed by the priest for all other transactions. It was one thing to off-load the goods, but they did not want to be carrying someone back and forth who had been mixing with the lepers.

Manolis greeted the doctor with a grin. 'Decided you would like me to take a message to someone?'

'No. I told you, I know no one on the island. I've come to ask if you will take me out there.'

Manolis raised his eyebrows. 'I thought Doctor Kandakis was in charge of the island. He commissioned me the first time to take the priest out there.'

'Doctor Kandakis has resigned. I have been asked to take his place.'

Manolis shrugged. 'Makes no difference to me which doctor goes out there. I charge a drachma each way.'

Doctor Stavros frowned. 'That's a considerable amount. You're already going out to the island with goods for the people.'

'True,' Manolis smiled again. 'I take over the goods, off-load and go away and fish for the rest of the day, gradually making my way back to Aghios Nikolaos. If I have to return for you that's half my fishing time wasted.'

Doctor Stavros sighed. 'Very well. Would it suit you if I visited on Wednesday?'

Manolis shrugged. 'Whatever day you like.'

'Then we'll agree on Wednesday. Will you be ready to leave by seven?'

'I'm usually well out to sea by then,' lied Manolis, 'But I'll make an exception and wait for you.'

The Doctor looked across the bay in trepidation. The strong winds of the previous two days had died down, but there was still a stiff breeze blowing. He hoped the fisherman would say it was too rough for them to make the journey to the island.

Manolis greeted him with a wide smile. 'I'm just about ready to sail. I suggest you sit just behind the cabin. You'll be sheltered from the wind there.'

Nervously Doctor Stavros climbed aboard and made his way unsteadily to the area indicated. 'How long does it take to sail to the island?'

Manolis shrugged. 'With this wind blowing we should make it in about an hour or hour and a half.' He manned the oars and rowed strongly away from the jetty before raising the sail. The small boat shot forwards and Doctor Stavros clutched at the wooden seat, his knuckles white. Yiorgo passed them, his larger boat making a wash that sent the smaller craft rolling from side to side

'Can you swim?' asked Manolis.

'Not very well. Why? Are we going to capsize?' Doctor Stavros looked back anxiously to where the land was receding quickly.

Manolis grinned cheerfully. 'Just asking. You're holding on to that seat as if your life depended upon it.'

'Couldn't we go through the canal?' asked the doctor miserably.

'We could, but it would mean I had to moor and take down the mast, row through and moor again to put it up. It would probably take longer than sailing round. It would be a different matter if I had a motor.'

'It wouldn't be so rough, though.'

'Rough? This isn't a rough sea. Relax. You're quite safe with me.'

Doctor Stavros disagreed. To him each time the boat lurched he was convinced he would be pitched overboard. It was a relief when Manolis rounded the headland and the water calmed as he lowered the sail and rowed the final few yards to the island.

Flora returned Manolis's wave before running back through the archway.

'She's gone to tell someone they have a visitor. I expect she thinks you've come to stay.'

'How many people are there on the island?' asked Doctor Stavros as he released his grip on the seat and flexed his numb fingers.

Manolis shrugged. 'Two or three hundred according to the priest.'

'I'll never be able to see everyone in a day, let alone examine them. That's more patients than I have in Aghios Nikolaos.' He picked up his bag and clambered clumsily out of the boat. 'Will you wait for me?'

Manolis nodded. 'I'll chat to Flora and do some fishing. I'll be here when you're ready to leave.'

He watched as the doctor walked uncertainly through the archway to where Yannis stood ready to greet him.

Flora returned to the quay. 'Who's that?' she asked of Manolis.

'He's a doctor.'

'What's he going to do?'

Manolis shrugged. 'He talked about examining people. Maybe he could have a look at your arm.' It was the first time Manolis had mentioned Flora's bandaged arm.

Flora shook her head. 'He can't do anything about that.'

'Does it hurt?'

'Sometimes, but I'm used to it.' Flora refused to admit, even to herself, that her arm was getting worse. It throbbed continually and she had formed the habit of holding it pressed against her side for support and a modicum of relief.

'Why do you have it bandaged?'

'That was Spiro's idea. He said I shouldn't get any dirt in it.'

'Who's Spiro?'

'He came from the hospital. He's one of Yannis's friends. He's nice, like Yannis. I'm not frightened of either of them.'

Manolis frowned. 'Are you frightened of some of the others?'

'Sometimes.'

'Why? What do they do to you?'

Flora shrugged. 'It's the way I hear them talk about the women over here. I try to avoid them and hope they won't notice me.'

'If anyone frightens you or hurts you in any way, you let me know.' Manolis spoke fiercely.

'What could you do about it?'

'I'd give them a beating they'd remember for the rest of their lives,' promised Manolis.

'How would you?' Flora raised her eyebrows. 'You're not allowed on the island.'

'If I thought you were in trouble I'd take no notice of that order. When you think about it, it's pretty stupid anyway. I talk to you whilst I'm sitting in my boat. I could just as well talk to you sitting on the jetty.' Manolis swung himself over the side of his boat and sat down beside the girl.

Doctor Stavros finally returned to the jetty where Manolis was waiting for him. He had eaten sparingly of the food he had been offered, but he had been forced to drink from the jug of water that had been passed to him. Despite wiping the rim carefully on his sleeve, he was sure it would still be contaminated. In future he would must remember to bring his own food and drink with him.

Manolis grinned and helped him aboard. 'Did you manage to see everyone?'

Doctor Stavros shook his head. 'I'll need to come out again. When can you bring me?'

'Whenever you like, provided we don't have a storm blowing. I come every day.'

Doctor Stavros nodded miserably. He would have to make the trip on a number of occasions before he would be in possession of the full facts regarding the condition of the islanders. Once he had investigated thoroughly he would write to the authorities and demand medicines and better treatment for the men and women over there. The way they lived at present was deplorable.

Yannis now came down with Flora to meet Manolis as he arrived at the island each morning, greeting him with appreciation and delight as he examined the goods that Manolis lifted onto the quay. As Yannis expressed his humble and genuine gratitude, Manolis revised his preconceived opinion of the young man. He was not forcing the people to work for him; he was a leader by example and Manolis began to look forward to Yannis giving him an update on the progress of the buildings

Flora was as excited with the different goods that were arriving as she was with the little gifts that Manolis took to her. As each sack or box was unloaded she asked Yannis or Manolis what it contained, and would rush back up to the village asking people to help move the items into a safe storage place.

'Yannis says the cement must be kept dry,' she explained to Manolis. 'It would probably be quite safe lying on the quay for a few days, but a heavy dew or sudden downpour and it would all be spoilt. Yannis says we mustn't waste the materials. If we did we probably wouldn't have them given to us again.' Flora supported her bandaged arm with her hand. It was hurting her so much today.

'Well, if that's what Yannis says, that's what we must do. According to you he's always right.'

Flora frowned. 'What's the matter, Manolis? Why don't you like Yannis?'

'I don't dislike him. I just get sick of hearing you tell me how wonderful he is.' Manolis pulled the rope off the bollard and began to row away, whilst Flora looked after him, puzzled by his attitude, but feeling far too ill to call after him.

Manolis threw the fish violently into the buckets. He was

determined not to spend any more time with the girl. He would off-load and sail away, not spend his time talking to her. He would tell her tomorrow that he needed to spend the time fishing to make his living. He stowed his net and headed back to Aghios Nikolaos. An unexpected gust of wind filled his sail and almost capsized him before he could alter his course to account for it. He cursed roundly as seawater slopped on board. If he had not been thinking about Flora he would have been paying attention to his sails and the wind.

To his surprise when he reached the quay both Doctor Stavros and Father Minos were waiting for him. 'What's wrong?' he asked immediately.

'Nothing. I merely wished to arrange for you to take me over to the island every Thursday. Weather permitting, of course.'

'Of course. I'll have to charge you a drachma each time.'

'I can't afford that. I have only limited funds at my disposal.'

Manolis frowned and did a rapid calculation in his head. He was making thirty drachmas a week from the island transportation and at least another thirty from his fishing. 'I'll take you there and back for nothing and charge you fifty leptas for my waiting time.'

Doctor Stavros sighed heavily. 'Very well. You leave me no option.' He knew Manolis could easily have insisted on more, and he also knew that the authorities would not object to him claiming a couple of drachmas each week for travelling back and forth to the island.

Father Minos smiled to himself, hoping he could negotiate the same deal for himself and Andreas. 'I would like to take advantage of your boat tomorrow. I presume the same fare holds good for me?'

Manolis spread his hands. 'You men drive hard bargains. How are we poor fishermen expected to make an honest living?'

'I'll see you at seven. By the way, my young friend will be with me. Will you be charging me extra for him?

Manolis rolled his eyes and shook his head. 'I shall pretend I did not see him.'

Father Minos and Andreas stepped ashore, leaving Manolis to unload the supplies for the island. Flora was not on the jetty to greet him as usual and he took his time unloading the sacks and boxes, hoping someone would appear and he could ask them to tell Flora he had arrived. He felt guilty about his churlish attitude the previous day, and tried to persuade himself that he was not jealous of the high opinion with which Flora regarded Yannis. No doubt now the priest was here, neither Yannis or Flora would be interested in the goods he had brought that day. Feeling decidedly aggrieved he began to cast off.

'Manolis! Manolis! We need the doctor urgently. You must fetch him.' Andreas called frantically from the quayside.

Manolis raised his hand in acknowledgement, slipped his mooring rope, and began to row away from the island. He changed direction abruptly and began to make his way towards the shore. If he went through the canal it would save a considerable amount of time on the journey as there was only a light wind blowing. He struggled, cursing, as he lowered the mast to enable him to pole the craft through the narrow canal and beneath the low bridge. Once through he had to repeat the procedure. He hoped he would be able to find the doctor at his house and not have to search the town for him.

He tried to curb his impatience as he waited for the doctor to collect a parcel of morphine, methylated spirit and aspirin from the hospital.

'Who's my patient?' asked Doctor Stavros as he finally settled himself into Manolis's boat.

'I've no idea, but they said it was urgent.'

'Probably an accident, most likely Yannis fallen off a roof.'

Manolis made no comment. If Yannis had suffered an accident that could explain Flora's absence from the quay. He headed for the canal and Doctor Stavros sat and watched as Manolis struggled to lower the mast again.

'I wish you would always come this way.'

Manolis glared at him. 'I've only come this way today because there's hardly any wind. It took me nearly two hours to get out to the island this morning.' He shipped the oars and poled carefully between the narrow concrete sides of the short canal. Spinalonga came into view and Manolis continued to row, rather than wrestle with the mast and sails again.

Phaedra was watching from the headland and as she saw the boat approaching she rushed down to where Yannis was working. Without hesitation he abandoned his tools and followed her down to the quay.

'Who's my patient?' asked Doctor Stavros of Yannis as he scrambled ashore and waited for Manolis to hand up the box he had collected from the hospital.

'Flora. Her arm has turned gangrenous.'

'Flora!' Manolis jumped ashore. 'Where is she? Why didn't anyone tell me she was ill?'

'You can't do anything,' Yannis remonstrated with the distraught young man. 'The doctor will help her.'

'I want to go to her.'

Yannis shook his head. 'You can't. You're not allowed on the island.'

Manolis's mouth set in a grim line. 'If the priests and the doctor are allowed over here, there's no reason why I shouldn't be.'

'I'll take you.' Phaedra stepped forward. 'Follow me.'

Manolis set off after Phaedra, leaving Yannis and Doctor Stavros to follow.

'She's in there.' Phaedra indicated to the dark interior of a house.

Manolis entered and knelt beside the delirious girl on the mattress. Spiro looked at him in surprise as he mopped at Flora's forehead with a damp rag.

'Flora, oh, Flora. You mustn't die.' Manolis took her hand. 'Please, please don't die.' The strength of the emotion that flooded through him took him by surprise and he could feel hot tears coursing their way down his cheeks. 'You have to do something, doctor, please.'

Doctor Stavros stood in the doorway, blocking the meagre amount of light that penetrated. 'She'll have to be brought out. I can't see anything in there.'

Yannis nodded. He picked up the end of the mattress and Spiro took the head. Still holding Flora's hand, Manolis placed his free arm beneath and helped them to haul the mattress out into the daylight. He continued to kneel beside Flora, holding her hand and smoothing her hair whilst Doctor Stavros unwrapped her arm. He could not help an involuntary shudder go through him as he saw the blackened flesh.

Pursing his lips, Doctor Stavros rose and beckoned Yannis, Spiro and Father Minos to one side where they held a quiet conversation.

Father Minos laid his hand on Manolis's shoulder. 'Come with me. We are going to pray for Flora.'

'I must stay with her,' protested Manolis.

'The doctor is going to operate on her arm. You'll be no help to him. Come with me. I promise you can come back and be with her again when he has finished.'

Reluctantly Manolis released Flora's hand and allowed the priest to escort him down to the square along with most of the other inhabitants. Manolis stood to one side, just behind Father Minos. He found it difficult to focus his mind on prayer, continually turning his head to where he had left Flora. A piercing scream rent the air and Manolis felt the firm hand of Father Minos on his shoulder. He struggled to shake it off, but the priest bore down on him with all his weight.

'You stay here,' he said quietly. 'The doctor knows his business.'

The people who had been joining in with the prayers began to look warily in the direction of the sound. Another scream came and Manolis pushed the priest away from him and began to run to where the doctor was attending to Flora. The villagers followed him and Father Minos gathered his robes in his hand and hurried after them. Sweat was standing out on Manolis's forehead. Flora's screams and sobs were making him tremble. Father Minos effectively held him back and he was unable to see what the doctor was doing to the poor girl. Gradually her screams abated and he wriggled from the priest's grasp and forced himself through the silent crowd of onlookers.

Doctor Stavros was covered in blood, beside him was the blackened arm that had belonged to Flora. Yannis still knelt beside her where she gripped his hand too tightly for him to move. Manolis began to prise her fingers loose and placed her hand in his own.

'What have you done to her?' he asked.

'I had to amputate. I've done my best.'

'You hurt her,' he said accusingly.

'I had no choice. I didn't have enough morphine.' Doctor Stavros's shoulders slumped. He wrapped Flora's amputated arm in a piece of cloth and looked at Spiro. 'Can you dispose of that for me?'

Spiro nodded. 'I'll wait until things have quietened down a bit and then throw it into the tower.'

Doctor Stavros regained his feet. 'I'm going to get washed, then I will be ready to go back to Aghios Nikolaos.' He looked at his ruined suit. It was unlikely the government would be willing to reimburse him. He would bring it back with him the next time he visited and leave it on the island. He could then wear it again should a similar situation occur.

'We'll return with you,' Father Minos announced. 'I'm sure Manolis will not want to make yet another journey out here today.' The priest looked at Manolis, daring him to contradict him. 'We will be waiting on the jetty in ten minutes.'

Phaedra looked at Manolis sympathetically. 'I'm sure the doctor really did do his best. Ritsa and I will look after her. We'll ask the men to move her back into the house when they return.'

'I'll carry her. Is there a mattress in there she can have? This one is ruined.'

Phaedra nodded. 'She can have mine. Can you manage her?'

Manolis lifted the light form from the ground. 'She weighs next to nothing. Hold her shoulder. I don't want to bang her arm.'

Flora moaned softly as Manolis moved her and he hushed her like a baby. He laid her gently on the mattress that Phaedra indicated and placed a light kiss on her forehead. 'Get well, Flora. Please get well.'

Manolis brushed the tears from his eyes impatiently as he returned to the sunlight and walked back down to the jetty. The islanders were gathered around Father Minos as he said a final prayer before leaving them for the day. Manolis joined them, saying his own private entreaties, before walking through the arch and down to his boat.

There was hardly a breeze as he cast off and he sighed. It would mean either going through the canal again and the lowering of the mast or a long haul around the spit of land, with a boat that was carrying four men. Andreas seemed to sense his dilemma.

'If we went through the canal I could help you lower the mast,' he offered. 'Let me take an oar. It will be quicker if two of us row.'

'Can you row?' asked Manolis.

'You're forgetting my father is a fisherman. Before he bought the motor I helped him row every weekend.'

Manolis nodded and moved over, allowing Andreas the space to sit beside him. 'How much did his motor cost?' he asked.

'I've no idea. You'd have to ask him. Why? Are you thinking of getting one?'

Manolis glanced sideways at the doctor. 'I have a regular passenger who is not very fond of the sea. If I had a motor I'd be able to use the canal on every trip. It would certainly save some long and rough journeys when the winter sets in.'

Doctor Stavros ignored the remark, but it was not lost on him. It would save a considerable amount of time if they made the boat trip from Aghios Nikolaos to the canal and through to Elounda. He had already been dreading his regular Thursday trips when the weather worsened.

'Are you wanting to go out to the island tomorrow?' asked Manolis.

Doctor Stavros shook his head. 'I have my patients on the mainland. There's nothing more I can do over there at present.'

'Flora will get better, won't she?' asked Manolis anxiously.

The doctor regarded him gravely. 'I don't know. It will depend upon a number of things. If I haven't cleared the infection completely it will return, she is doubtless suffering from shock and she will be in pain. I have no idea how strong she is physically, whether her body will be able to cope with such trauma.' He shrugged. 'You can find out how she is tomorrow and let me know when you return.' He gathered up his ruined jacket and held it against his stained shirt, hoping he would be able to reach his house and wash and change before anyone saw his dishevelled state.

Manolis nodded. He understood what the doctor was trying to tell him. There was little hope of Flora surviving her ordeal. He turned his distressed eyes to Father Minos.

'Please say a prayer and light a candle for her, Father.'

Manolis left Aghios Nikolaos as soon as he had collected his government consignment and the packages from the church courtyard. Despite the fact that the wind was blowing in the right direction he used his oars also, convinced that he would make the journey in half the time. He moored at the deserted jetty and without waiting to off-load he rushed up through the archway to the house where he had last seen Flora. At the doorway he hesitated.

He knocked tentatively and waited, there was no response and he knocked again a little louder, his heart beating rapidly and a feeling of desolation overtaking him. What would he do if she had died during the night? Maybe they had already placed her in the tower they used for the disposal of the dead and he would have no chance then to tell her that he loved her or even say goodbye.

'Good morning, Manolis. You're early.'

He spun round to see Phaedra standing behind him, a bowl of water in her hands.

'Flora. How's Flora?' His throat was so dry he could hardly utter the words.

'There's no change. She seems to drift in and out of consciousness.'

'Can I see her?'

'I was just about to give her a wash. Do you want to wait?'

'I'd rather see her now.'

'Don't be too long or I'll have to heat the water up again.' Phaedra set the bowl on the ground and sat beside it.

Manolis pushed open the door and waited for his eyes to become accustomed to the dark interior. He walked carefully to the mattress where Flora was lying and knelt down beside her, taking her hand and deliberately averting his eyes from the bandaged remains of her left arm.

'Flora.' His voice caught in his throat and he felt tears at the back of his eyes. He never cried. He had not cried over the death of his father. 'Oh, Flora, please get well. I love you, Flora. We can have a life together, I know we can, but first you must get well.'

Flora opened her eyes at the sound of his voice and closed them again, tossing her head restlessly, her lips moved, but no sound came from them. Manolis stroked her hair, matted with sweat, away from her eyes. He kissed her forehead and released her hand 'I don't know if you can hear me, Flora, but if you can, remember I love you.'

He regained his feet and returned to where Phaedra was waiting patiently for him. 'You'll look after her, won't you?' he asked anxiously.

'Of course I will, Manolis. As soon as she comes round properly I'll tell her you visited.'

'I'll be back tomorrow,' he assured her.

'I'm sure you will,' smiled Phaedra as she lifted the bowl of water. 'Can you let Yannis know that you're here? He can arrange for the supplies to be brought up then.'

'Where is he?'

Phaedra shrugged. 'He'll be working somewhere. Go back down to the arch and walk on towards the square. If you can't see him stand there and shout his name. Someone will find him for you.'

Manolis walked slowly back down to the archway that led to the jetty. He felt rather self-conscious walking around alone. He gazed curiously at the buildings he passed, all of them seemed to be in a ruinous state, yet he would catch occasional glimpses of a figure inside. Did people live in these apologies for houses or were they in there repairing the damaged walls and roofs?

'Hey, you.' A voice hailed him from nowhere.

He stopped and looked around, the hairs on the back of his neck rising.

'I'm up here. Look up.'

Manolis lifted his eyes and saw a man sitting on a patch of concrete, his back against a ruined wall.

'I'm Kyriakos, Kyriakos the legless. You must be new over here. I've not seen you before.'

Manolis swallowed. 'My name's Manolis. I don't live over here. I'm a boatman. I'm looking for Yannis.'

'Everyone is always looking for Yannis,' grumbled Kyriakos to himself.

'Do you know where I could find him?'

'Try down at the square. Someone down there is bound to know where he's working. Whilst you're there could you bring me back a jug of water?'

'Where do I get it from?' Manolis scrambled up the bank to the man and took the jug that was held out to him.

'There's a water fountain set into the wall just before the tunnel. I expect there'll be a queue. There usually is.'

'I'll be as quick as I can.'

Kyriakos shrugged. 'There's no rush. I'm not going anywhere.'

Manolis waited amongst the people waiting to fill their containers at the water fountain. They looked at him curiously.

'You're new here. What's your name?' asked an elderly man

'I'm not living here. Kyriakos,' Manolis jerked his thumb, 'he asked me to take him some water.'

The man frowned. 'Why are you on the island, then?'

'The doctor asked me to find out how Flora was and I came down this way to look for Yannis.'

'He's up there.' The man indicated a path leading off from the square. 'Leave the jug with me. I'll take it back to Kyriakos.'

Manolis handed it over, thankful that he did not have to stand and wait with the other men and women. None of them appeared to be in any particular hurry and would stand and chat before they began to collect their water, also none of them appeared to be particularly ill. He walked up the path that rose steeply from the square, flanked on either side by semi-ruined buildings. No wonder Flora had been unable to tell him how many houses there were.

Yannis stared at him in surprise. 'What are you doing over here?'

Manolis grinned. 'Doctor Stavros asked me to see how Flora was today. I wanted to let you know I'd arrived so you could get the boxes moved from the jetty.'

Yannis nodded. 'Pass me that hammer, can you?'

Manolis handed the tool to him and watched whilst Yannis knocked in half a dozen nails and gave the hammer back to him. Slightly nonplussed, Manolis replaced it on the grass.

'I shall need it again,' remonstrated Yannis.

'I can't stand here all day holding your tools for you,' complained Manolis.

Yannis did not appear to hear him. 'Does that look straight to you?'

Manolis squinted at the doorframe. 'Needs to be a bit higher on the left I would say.'

Yannis held out his hand for the hammer and proceeded to remove the nails he had so recently hammered home. He moved the piece of timber higher on the left hand side. 'How does that look?'

'About right.'

'You hold it whilst I fix it, otherwise it will probably slip again.'

Bemused, Manolis held the timber in place until Yannis had nailed it firmly. He stepped back and scrutinized his handiwork, before nodding in satisfaction and turning to Manolis.

'I'll walk back down with you and see if I can pick up a few helpers on the way.' He felt his pocket. 'I've got the rule. Can you bring us out a few more? It's always being left in different places and then we have to spend time searching.'

Manolis nodded. 'Anything else?'

'Timber and hinges, more screws and another screwdriver would be a help, along with the sand and cement, of course. If you can bring that over within a week we should be able to get a couple more houses finished pretty soon.'

'Do you plan to rebuild all of them?'

Yannis shook his head. 'That's not possible. Some of them are just a pile of stones. Provided we can make enough of them habitable to house everyone I shall be happy. A number of the islanders are working on the hospital ready for the winter.'

'The hospital?' This was the first Manolis had heard about the project.

'It was Spiro's idea. There was a hospital way back when the Turks lived here. It's just as much a ruin as everything else, of course. Spiro reckoned we could build up on the foundations and those who couldn't look after themselves could be housed in there.'

'Who'd look after them?'

Yannis waved his arm airily. 'Spiro's volunteered and I expect some of the others will help him.'

Flora recovered slowly. Her missing arm throbbed painfully. She could not understand how this could be. It was not there, so how could it hurt so much? Doctor Stavros explained gently to her that it was quite normal after the removal of a limb and that with time the pain would lessen. He assured her the operation he had performed to remove the gangrene had been both necessary and successful.

Manolis left his boat tied up at the jetty every day and visited her. He was greeted now by the islanders as a familiar face and no longer felt uncomfortable and self-conscious when he met them. Each day he took a small gift for Flora and she would thank him profusely. The bunches of wild flowers that he collected first thing in the morning she was particularly delighted with and Manolis decided that he would take her some plants.

'Don't be silly, Manolis,' she laughed at him. 'There's no soil over here to grow plants.'

'Then I'll bring you some that are growing in pots,' he promised. 'What would you like?'

Flora looked pensive. 'I'd like some geraniums. My mother always grew geraniums. They're such a beautiful colour.'

'Geraniums it will be then.' Manolis knew the other fishermen would mock him once they knew he was taking pots of plants out to the barren island, but he could shrug off their derision if the action would make Flora happy.

Father Minos studied his small account book. The money given to him by Yannis's father and uncle he had spent from liberally for the first couple of weeks; then he had deposited the balance in the bank with instructions that Andreas could draw a sum each week to cover the cost of supplies sent out to the island. Andreas was scrupulous in his bookkeeping, insisting that Manolis produced every receipt and every month Andreas would send a brief account to the priest.

During the winter months' the expenses had lessened, no building materials were sent over, but more mattresses, rubber sheeting and blankets were requested. Father Minos tapped his fingertips together. Despite the bank paying generous interest, the funds were dwindling. He had approached the hospital in Heraklion and asked if there were any funds being held on behalf of the patients who had stayed there before being sent on to Athens. He was not surprised when the answer was negative.

He had tried to exert pressure on Pavlos and Louisa to return the money Yannis's father had paid in advance for his son's board and lodging to no avail. Maybe Yiorgo Pavlakis, Yannis's old school teacher and now a prominent politician in Heraklion, would be able and willing to help.

It had taken a considerable amount of time and patience on Father Minos's behalf to persuade Yiorgo to visit Spinalonga with him. He had stressed that to become a benefactor for the island would place him in high esteem with the townspeople. Yiorgo hesitated. The elections were looming and if he could show how caring he was for the unfortunate incurables, doubtless some of them relatives of the local people, it could stand him in good stead.

Yiorgo regarded the weather with trepidation as he and Father Minos sat on the bus. It had been cool and cloudy when they had started from Heraklion, spitting with rain by the time they had reached Malia, but as they reached Aghios Nikolaos there was a strong wind blowing and it was raining hard.

'We might as well take the bus back,' remarked Yiorgo. 'We'll not get over there today.'

Father Minos shrugged. 'The weather often changes very quickly down here. We'll find the boatman and ask his opinion.'

Yiorgo had no option but to trudge after the priest until they found Manolis in the cabin of a neighbouring boat playing cards.

'You're lucky to catch me. I was proposing to leave when I had won this hand,' he lied. 'It was far worse earlier, so I thought I'd play a few games until it improved.'

'Are you fully loaded or do you have room for both of us?' asked the priest.

'I expect I can squeeze you both in. I've only got the government consignment to take today.' Manolis grinned. 'As it's you I'll only charge the usual rate. Anyone else I'd ask double on a day like this.'

Yiorgo looked doubtfully at the choppy sea. 'Are you sure it will be safe to go out in this?'

'No problem for a good boatman like me. We'll go through the canal and it won't be any rougher at Elounda than it is here.' He winked at Father Minos conspiratorially.

Manolis tethered the boat to the jetty and stepped ashore, Father Minos and Yiorgo Pavlakis joining him. He walked confidently up through the arch until he reached the deserted pathway where he called loudly until Ritsa appeared.

'We didn't expect to see you today,' she observed.

'I have brought a visitor for Yannis and no doubt most of you will be pleased to see the Father.'

Ritsa smiled. 'He's always a welcome sight. I expect Yannis is in his house. You know where it is, don't you?'

Father Minos nodded. 'I'll show Yiorgo the way and then visit the occupants in their houses. I can hold a service in the square later if the islanders are brave enough to face the weather.'

Ritsa shrugged. 'We're used to it.'

Manolis turned in the opposite direction and walked up to the house that Flora shared with Phaedra. It was too rough to go fishing and there was no telling how long the men were going to stay on the island. He had an idea that the politician from Heraklion would be eager to make the return journey as soon as possible.

Manolis sat beside Flora on her mattress. He placed his arm round her and pulled her towards him. 'How's my favourite girl today?'

She tried to wriggle away from him. 'You shouldn't, Manolis.'

'I shouldn't what? Say you're my favourite girl. It's true.'

Flora giggled nervously. 'You shouldn't put your arm round me.'

If anything Manolis held her more tightly. 'I want to put my arm round you. I want to put both my arms round you and never let you go.'

'Don't be silly, Manolis. I might be contagious.'

Manolis sighed heavily. 'If you are I hope I catch it. Then I could be over here with you all the time.'

'You wouldn't want to be a leper.'

Manolis took her chin in his hand and turned her face towards him. 'Flora, I love you. I would happily have leprosy and live over here on this island provided I was with you.' He kissed her lips and Flora drew in her breath sharply.

'Manolis, you mustn't.'

'I want to kiss you. Why shouldn't I kiss you?'

'I've told you ...'

Manolis bent his head and kissed her again. He pushed her unkempt hair back from her eyes. 'If I was over here with you or you were on the mainland with me we'd be married.'

Flora shook her head. 'That's not possible.'

'Wouldn't you want to marry me?'

Flora's lip trembled. 'Please, Manolis. I don't want to talk about it. If you want to get married you must find a girl on the mainland. A nice, healthy girl who'll give you lots of children.'

'I don't want lots of children. I'd be content just to have you.' Manolis tried to kiss her again and this time Flora wriggled out of his arms.

MANOLIS

Yiorgo Pavlakis was a relieved man when they finally reached the small port of Aghios Nikolaos. The journey back over the rough sea had been a nightmare to him. The boat had travelled far too fast and been tossed around uncontrollably until Manolis had lowered the sail and taken to the oars. Their progress was slow, as Manolis had to stop continually to ride out a wave. Once they reached the canal Yiorgo suggested the boat moored there and they walked the rest of the distance to Aghios Nikolaos.

Manolis looked at Father Minos and raised his eyebrows. The priest smiled at him encouragingly. 'We have travelled this far unscathed; I suggest we continue. We are in the hands of our Lord and I have confidence that he will hold us safely and take us to our destination.'

Yiorgo staggered ashore. He could still feel the motion of the boat beneath his feet as he tried to walk along the quay. Father Minos seemed unaffected and strolled casually by his side, his head bent against the wind and his cloak clutched firmly round him.

'We will make our way to the bus station,' he announced. 'I think we should have time for a quick snack before the last bus for Heraklion leaves.'

Yiorgo felt his stomach revolt against the thought of food. 'Maybe a coffee or glass of wine. I would not want to miss the bus.' He longed to back home in the taverna, where he would be able to get dry and warm again.

Once on the bus Yiorgo closed his eyes. He wanted to think about the proposal he had made to the islanders for a pension, try to get his thoughts in order, but he could not concentrate. He still felt as if he was being tossed around on the sea and on more than one occasion he could feel the bile rising in him. How could he convince the government that he was making this suggestion for humanitarian reasons and not in the hope of gaining popularity amongst the people ready for the forthcoming mayoral elections?

Doctor Stavros hurried down to the quay. The last trip he had made to the island had decided him and he sought out Yiorgo Mandrakis to ask him where he could purchase a motor suitable for Manolis's fishing boat.

Yiorgo scratched his head. 'You won't get one down here. You'll have to send to Heraklion. They may have to send to Piraeus.'

'Where did you get yours from?'

Yiorgo frowned. 'A friend arranged it for me.' He was not prepared to tell the doctor that he had been given it to assist him in the transportation of smuggled goods.

'Could I meet him? Do you think he could arrange for me to purchase one?'

Yiorgo shook his head. 'He's not local. The best thing would be for you to go to the chandlers and tell them what you want.'

Doctor Stavros hesitated. 'I don't actually know what I want. I'm a doctor, not a sailor. I have to visit the island every week and it would be easier to go through the canal. The problem is that Manolis has to lower the mast and raise it again. Either that or he has to row all the way.'

Yiorgo shrugged. 'Tell them the size of the boat. They should be able to tell you what you need.'

Doctor Stavros sighed. Provided the motor was not exorbitantly expensive it had seemed like a practical idea. Now it meant negotiating for something about which he had no knowledge.

Despite his forebodings, Doctor Stavros found the chandler helpful. He walked along the quay with him to where Manolis's boat was moored.

'The engines are measured in horse power,' he explained. 'It's not a very large boat so you won't need one that's too big. If it were too powerful you'd have no control. You'd be thrown all over the place and probably end up in the sea with the boat racing away from you. Dangerous, that, for you and the other boatmen.'

Doctor Stavros nodded as if he understood. 'So can you get one for me? How much will it cost?'

'Can't say without asking the manufacturers. There'll be a delivery charge, of course, and then I presume you'll want it fitted, that's extra.'

'Three hundred drachmas is my absolute limit,' said the doctor firmly, immediately regretting having mentioned a figure. He should have asked for the price of the motor, the transport and the fitting separately.

'Should get away with it for a bit less than that. Leave it with me and come back in a fortnight. If I hear anything before then I'll let you know.' Savas smirked. He should make a nice profit from the ignorant doctor.

Disconsolately Doctor Stavros walked away. At least two more journeys to be faced across the open sea and he knew the weather would probably be worse each time he made the crossing.

Manolis polished the top of the motor lovingly. He had been unable to believe it when Savas had arrived with the large package, checked he was at the right boat, and proceeded to fit the motor. He watched carefully as the chandler placed it in position and screwed it firmly in place. Savas showed him how to fill it with petrol, check the level, oil the working parts, start and stop it.

'I suggest you go out in the bay and have a practice run before you take the doctor out. You need to be able to recognise the sound when it's running sweetly. If it begins to sound laboured you'll most likely have some weed caught round the propeller. You'll have to stop, haul it up and clean it, otherwise you'll burn the motor out.'

Manolis nodded. He could hardly wait to take the boat out and feel the difference having a motor made to the speed. It should feel like it did when he sailed on a windy day and the boat sped along, but much safer. Unless there was a real gale blowing, he would be able to travel in a direct line and not have to change the direction of the sail continually and tack to cope with the wind. He debated whether he should try to go over to the island

and show it to Flora, but he doubted she would be sitting on the quay at five in the afternoon. He also had a sneaking feeling that she would not be very interested in a motor.

He would take her a special present to celebrate and racked his brains. He had taken her a shawl, apron, ribbons for her hair, a comb, flowers, and plants. Then he remembered the couple of glass beads he had found and given her. Maybe he could purchase a necklace or bracelet of glass beads. He was sure she would enjoy wearing some jewellery.

The boat sped smoothly over the water as he considered a gift for Flora. If she had been Maria, the chemist's daughter, he would not have given her a few worthless glass beads. She would have laughed and thrown them back in his face. He realised he had not thought of Maria for months. He no longer lingered outside the grocer's shop hoping to catch a glimpse of her as she went in or out of the chemist next door. The last time he had seen her he thought she looked fat, rather than voluptuous, not a bit like the fragile form of Flora.

He ought to go to a proper jeweller, he decided. If he gave her something beautiful she might realise he was serious in his wish to court her.

Engrossed in his thoughts he suddenly realised he had travelled far further from the land than he had intended and hoped he would have enough petrol to return to the shore. He did not dare to turn the engine off to check the contents of the petrol tank just in case he could not start it again. He moved the tiller and felt the boat respond, making a graceful arc as it turned and he headed back to Aghios Nikolaos.

Doctor Stavros paid the bill of two hundred and seventy seven drachmas without demur and did not ask for a receipt. Savas smiled happily. The motor had cost one hundred and eighty two drachmas, Costas had charged him ten drachmas to transport it from Heraklion and the fitting had cost him a dozen long screws. He had made almost one hundred drachmas profit.

The doctor found he was almost looking forward to his next journey to the island. He would insist they travelled through the canal, and their journey time would be reduced by at least an hour. Not only did he want to spend less time out at sea, but it would give him more time ashore to visit his patients. He really must see Flora and give her a thorough examination, but the last few times he had been unable to find her.

Manolis counted his savings carefully. He had scoured the local jeweller's shops for a suitable gift for Flora. Most of the goods on offer were way beyond his pocket, those marked 'gold' or 'diamonds' looked small and insignificant. His eye had alighted on a gold coloured necklace, set with red, blue, and green stones. It reminded him of pictures he had seen of royalty wearing their regalia. Tentatively he had entered the shop and asked to inspect the garish jewellery. As soon as he had taken it in his hands he knew it was far too heavy for Flora's slender neck and returned it sadly to the owner.

'What exactly are you looking for?'

'I'm not sure. It mustn't be too weighty, but it must be bright and colourful.'

'Are you looking for gold?'

Manolis shook his head. 'I doubt if I could afford anything that splendid.'

The jeweller pulled a tray from beneath the counter. 'What about silver?'

'No, it has to be gold coloured,' Manolis said firmly.

'Have a look around. See if you can find anything you think would be suitable.' The jeweller stood and watched as Manolis slowly progressed around the small shop, studying some items for some considerable time. Finally he returned to the counter.

'There's a gold cross over there. How heavy is that?'

Obligingly the shopkeeper removed the cross from the protective glass and handed it to the boatman. 'It's not solid gold, you understand, so it won't be as heavy, and the stones are coloured glass.'

Manolis turned it this way and that, watching as the sunlight lit upon the small purple and red stones. He considered carefully. No one could object to Flora wearing a cross, whoever gave it to her. It could be a better choice than a conventional necklace that would look out of place and pretentious on the island. He looked at the price tag, he could afford it; he turned it towards the light again, watching, fascinated, as the glass sparkled and sent coloured rays in all directions.

'I'll have it,' he said firmly and swallowed hard. He had never bought anything so expensive before in his life. He dreaded what his aunt would say if she knew he had spent his hard-earned money on a trinket for a one-armed girl who had leprosy.

Manolis negotiated the canal and began to motor across to the island. Half way there he cut the motor and turned to Doctor Stavros. 'Can I ask you something, Doctor? I've got a bit of a problem.'

Doctor Stavros frowned. 'I can't give medical consultations out here. Come to my surgery tomorrow.'

Manolis shook his head. 'It's not that kind of problem. It's Flora.'

'Flora?'

Manolis leaned forward. 'How contagious is leprosy?'

'Do you think you've caught it?'

Manolis shrugged. 'I don't think so. I haven't seen any marks or found any lumps on me. Flora seems to think I might catch it from her.'

'You might. You might catch it from anyone over on the island.'

'So it wouldn't matter if I touched her?'

'What are you really asking me, Manolis?'

'If I married her, how likely would I be to catch it?'

Doctor Stavros shook his head. 'Lepers are not allowed to marry, you know that, Manolis.'

'But would I be more likely to catch it by - being with her, than just talking to her?'

'Much more likely I should imagine.' Doctor Stavros spoke firmly. 'You must put any ideas like that right out of your mind.'

Manolis scowled. 'Many of the people on the island were married before they were diagnosed. None of them have a husband or wife over there with them.'

'Sometimes it can take a considerable amount of time before the effects show. I would imagine there are a number of people walking around who have the disease and have not consulted a doctor. If they are able to keep the lesions covered with their clothing no one but them is going to know about their condition.' Doctor Stavros looked at the young man keenly. He blamed himself for allowing the relationship to progress. He should have guessed Manolis's feelings for the young girl by his reaction to her amputation and not encouraged him to visit her and report on her progress. 'Besides,' he continued, 'Once it became known on the mainland you'd be shunned. Your permit to deliver would be withdrawn and no one would buy your fish.'

'The way I see it I have nothing to lose. There's no reason anyone should know,' Manolis replied stubbornly. 'You're the only person I've spoken to, and being a doctor whatever I say to you is supposed to be confidential. If anyone began to point a finger at me I would know where they had gained their knowledge.' He glared at the doctor.

Doctor Stavros shrugged and sighed. He was powerless to stop Manolis and Flora meeting and what they did when they met was really none of his business. 'I can only advise you,' he said.

To Manolis's surprise, Phaedra was waiting on the quay for him. 'Where's Flora?' he asked immediately.

'She's busy somewhere,' she replied vaguely.

'Is she feeling all right? I gave her a thorough examination last week and I was very pleased with her progress.' Doctor

Stavros pushed his bag onto the jetty. 'Is there anyone I need to visit, Phaedra, or shall I go straight up to the hospital?'

'That would be best. Spiro can tell you if he has any problems.' Phaedra wanted the doctor to leave so she could talk to Manolis alone. She waited until he had walked through the archway and turned to the boatman.

'Flora has asked me to speak to you.'

Manolis looked at Phaedra suspiciously. 'Why? Why can't she talk to me herself?'

Phaedra looked at him sadly. 'She says you won't listen to her. She keeps telling you that you must forget her and find a healthy girl on the mainland and you take no notice.'

Manolis rested his arms on the box he had placed on the jetty. 'Phaedra, I love Flora. I'm not prepared to wave goodbye to her and look for someone else. I've been talking to the doctor. He says I'm as likely to catch leprosy from talking to you as I am from her.' He bent the truth of the conversation. 'I'm willing to take that risk. If I catch it, I will be able to come over here and live. Until that happens I just continue to come over every day and visit her. Why should we be denied our happiness just because she's sick?'

Phaedra bit her lip. What more could she say? She had promised the unhappy girl that she would speak to Manolis, but he was obviously not going to take any notice of her words. She stood there uncertainly.

'Suppose Yannis spoke to you? Would you listen to him?'

Manolis looked at her scornfully. 'Why should I? Does he know more than the doctor?'

Phaedra shook her head helplessly and turned away. Manolis picked up another box and threw it roughly onto the jetty. Once he had finished unloading he was determined to go in search of Flora. He would take whatever steps were necessary to persuade her to marry him, even if the union was illegal and only in their hearts.

Manolis picked up a box and carried it up to where the food was stored. He strode on through the arch and up the path to the dark, semi-ruined house that Flora shared with Phaedra. He pushed open the door and stood waiting for his eyes to become accustomed to the gloomy interior. 'Flora?'

There was no answer. He leaned against the rotten doorjamb and considered where he was most likely to find her. Probably up at the hospital helping prepare vegetables, or handing tools to Yannis or one of the other men who were repairing a house. He sighed. He did not want to confront her before onlookers and he could not force her to return to her house with him. He looked through the doorway again and a slight movement caught his eye.

'You are in there, Flora. Why didn't you answer me?' He strode inside to where Flora was cowering in a corner. 'Anyone would think you were frightened of me the way you're hiding away in here.' He reached out his hand and Flora shrank away from him. 'Please, come and sit down. I want to talk to you. I've spoken to Doctor Stavros and I want to tell you what he told me.'

Flora looked at him warily, tears welling up in her eyes.

'Please, Flora, at least listen to me,' he begged. He reached his hand out again and this time Flora allowed him to touch her arm. 'Come and sit down,' he cajoled.

Hesitantly Flora walked the few steps to her mattress and sat on the edge. Manolis immediately joined her and placed his arm round her shoulders. Flora shrank away from him.

'No, don't move away from me,' he remonstrated and pulled her closer.

'You're too close to me. You'll get sick like me.'

'Too close? Flora, for the last two years I have held your hand. When you were delirious after your operation I used to stroke your hair and kiss your forehead each time I visited. I haven't become sick. I love you, Flora and I want to marry you. I talked to Doctor Stavros as we were coming over today. I told him I want to marry you...'

'Manolis, you know we can't marry. We're not allowed.'

Manolis placed a finger on her lips. 'Listen to me, Flora. I know we're not allowed to get married. That's the law, but we don't need a piece of paper. The doctor said I was no more likely to catch leprosy from you than from anyone else over here. He said he examined you last week and was very pleased. Do you understand what that means? If you were really ill you wouldn't have recovered so well from the operation.'

'That doesn't mean I'm not contagious,' protested Flora.

'Think about all the men and women over here who were married. They lived with someone for years, but none of them has a sick husband or wife over here with them. There's no reason why you should infect me.' He could feel her slender body trembling against him.

'I love you, Flora. I truly love you and if I could legally marry you, I would. Do you love me? Please say you do, or I'll throw myself off my boat as I sail back.'

'You wouldn't! Please, Manolis, promise me you wouldn't do anything like that.'

'Do you love me, Flora?' Tears began to run down Flora's cheeks and Manolis caught one on his finger. 'I never, ever, want to make you cry, Flora, unless they are tears of happiness.' He kissed her damp cheek. 'Look, I've bought you this.'

Flora looked at the ornate cross wide-eyed. 'It's really for me? You bought it for me?'

'It's real gold on the outside,' he assured her earnestly. 'It won't make your neck go green. Will you accept it in place of a wedding ring? It will be my promise to love you for ever.'

'What will happen to you if the authorities find out?'

'They're not going to find out.'

'But suppose you do become ill?'

'Then I'll be over here with you anyway. Please marry me. You know what that means. I want you, Flora. I want you now.'

He held her tightly with one arm whilst he slipped his other hand beneath her skirt, not surprised to find that she was not wearing any underwear. He heard her quick intake of breath as he began to explore her nakedness. Swiftly he unbuckled his belt, lowered his trousers, and pushed her skirt out of the way.

Flora turned the cross over and over in her hand, admiring the way the sun, coming through the doorway, made the stones shine. She thanked him with tears in her eyes.

'I have nothing to give you,' she said sadly.

'You have already given me yourself. That was a priceless gift.' Manolis kissed her hair.

'Does this mean we are properly married now?'

'As properly as possible. We will know that this means the same as if we had gone to the church, a priest had said a few words and we'd come away with a piece of paper. This is my promise to you, the same as if it was a wedding ring, but it will be our secret.'

'I do love you, Manolis,' she said earnestly. 'I'll wear it always. Can you put it on for me, please.'

Manolis took it from her, placed it around her neck and fastened the clasp. He kissed her passionately. 'I think it's time we went and renewed our marriage vows again,' he suggested.

Flora gave a little giggle and allowed him to push her back on her mattress.

Manolis returned with the doctor to Aghios Nikolaos with a smile on his face. He considered Flora to be his wife now. Flora had waved him off, looking as happy as he felt. Doctor Stavros looked first at one and then the other. He shrugged. There was nothing he could do about the situation. He would just have to let time take its course and hope Flora did not become pregnant or Manolis show signs of leprosy.

Father Minos packed his underclothes carefully in a clean sack. His religious robes he placed in the brand new case he had bought and his precious books into two boxes. He took a last look around his small, but comfortable living room. It was no time for second thoughts. He had made his decision and the necessary arrangements. All that was left now was for him to bid his housekeeper farewell and wish Andreas success with the difficult parish he was handing over to him.

Andreas helped him to carry his belongings to the bus station and Father Minos wondered how he would manage when he reached Aghios Nikolaos if his letter had not been received at the church by Father Dhakanalis. In his usual philosophical fashion he decided not to worry about the problem until it actually arose. Throughout the journey he looked out of the dusty window at the countryside as it passed by.

'I'll not see this again,' he thought sadly. 'I must drink in every moment as I shall have to remember how the mainland looks for the rest of my life.' He raised the cross he wore to his lips. 'It was my decision to carry out Your wishes, Lord. I must be grateful to You for answering my prayer.'

Once at the bus station in Aghios Nikolaos he offered a lad five leptas to help him carry his luggage to the church and was greeted by a sombre Father Dhakanalis.

'You are very welcome, Father.'

'You don't look that pleased to see me.'

'I am always happy to see you, but your letter puzzled me greatly. You have asked for a bed for the night, to which you are more than welcome, but what is this idea you mention about living on Spinalonga? Are you sick?'

Father Minos shook his head. 'Would you refuse me a bed if I was?'

Father Dhakanalis shook his head. 'The church is a sanctuary for all. I would not refuse you.'

'You wouldn't be that anxious to have me stay, though,' the priest observed keenly. 'Rest assured, as far as I am aware I am in perfect health. I feel it is my duty, my calling, to live on the island and give whatever comfort I can to the poor souls who live there.'

'That is very commendable, but is it necessary to live with them?'

'That was a condition imposed upon me by the Bishop. He tried to dissuade me, but I had to persist. He placed various obstacles in my way and I overcame them each time. Finally he understood that it is my destiny.' Father Minos shrugged. 'No mortal man can escape his destiny in life.'

'I will pray each day that you remain healthy.' Father Dhakanalis crossed himself.

'Thank you. I will pray that your prayers are answered. I will be of little use to them if I fall sick. Now, can we sit somewhere? I have various matters I need to discuss with you.'

Father Dhakanalis led the way to his parlour, opened a cupboard and poured each of them a glass of wine. 'What is it you need to talk with me about?'

Father Minos sighed. 'I have agreed to live exactly as they do on the island. You can send a written message to me but I have no way of communicating with you except by giving a verbal message to a boatman. The man I trust is Manolis. I am sure you know him. He is the young man who collects the supplies purchased by the church.'

Father Dhakanalis held up his hand. 'I have to correct you there. We have never purchased any supplies for the island. We have simply been an assembly point.'

Father Minos smiled. 'When I first visited the island I was appalled by their conditions. I visited some local people and they gave me donations to be spent on the islanders' behalf, to better their lot. I entrusted this fund to Andreas, Father Andreas now he is fully ordained and has a parish of his own. He has purchased items, along with medicines and bandages, either under my direction or the direction of Doctor Stavros. Father Andreas opened a bank account and as his address was here, it was assumed it was a church fund and that enabled the bank to pay a higher rate of interest. We did not feel we needed to enlighten them. Now Father Andreas has taken my parish under his wing I propose to put Manolis in charge of the expenditure.'

'A boatman? Are you sure you can trust him? Can he even read and write?'

'I am convinced that he is trustworthy. He can read and write, his spelling sometimes leaves a lot to be desired, but he can also add up and take away accurately. What I should like is for you or one of the other Fathers to act as a signatory on the account. Manolis will present the bills to you as he did to Father Andreas and you will go to the bank and withdraw the correct amount of money for him to either pay the supplier or reimburse himself.'

'And how much of this does he take for himself?' asked Father Dhakanalis suspiciously.

'He takes nothing. He has never asked for payment and I, naturally, have never offered.'

'If you think he is so trustworthy why do you not transfer the fund to his name?'

Father Minos shook his head. 'That would mean we lost the benefit of the extra interest. If you refuse to help me then that is what I would have to do.' He sighed heavily. 'The loss of the additional interest over the course of the year could mean the people are cold in the winter due to lack of blankets, or sleeping on the ground as they are without a mattress.'

'That is blackmail.'

'Not at all.' Father Minos pretended to be hurt at the very idea. 'I am simply stating the obvious.'

Father Dhakanalis raised his glass. 'I think maybe you should have been a politician. You have manoeuvred me into a position from which I cannot escape without a bad conscience and feeling unchristian. You are a devious man.'

Father Minos lifted his own glass. 'You are in agreement then? The account stays where it is in the bank with a signatory from the church and Manolis purchasing and delivering the goods as he does now?'

'You give me no choice.' Father Dhakanalis sighed. 'How long are you expecting this fund to last?'

'I'm not sure. There are a couple of men on the island whom I also trust. When Manolis delivers they tell him their immediate needs. They know they must not waste the money as they will never have this opportunity again. I would have to rely upon you to let me know if the funds were low and I would then have to insist that the money was used for medical purposes only.'

Father Dhakanalis raised his eyebrows. 'By the way you spoke I thought all the money was being spent on medicine.'

Father Minos shook his head. 'The Doctor is able to draw a certain amount of medical supplies from the hospital. He has an allocation each month that he is not able to exceed. By the time he has the Chaulmoogra oil capsules and bandages most of it has gone. The church fund, as I call it, is for bedding, essential cooking utensils and building materials.'

'Building materials?'

Father Minos nodded. 'Most of the buildings they were expected to inhabit were in ruins. An enterprising young man began to repair them. He used the old materials taken from unusable houses. Once I was able to provide them with the sand, cement, timber and the tools they needed they were able to make vast improvements. They have even constructed a building they use as a hospital.'

'Is there a church on the island?'

'Oh, yes. There are two, in fact. One is in reasonable condition and is being used as a shelter for some of the people until there is a suitable building for them to occupy.' A smile spread across Father Minos's face. 'I intend, once I am established over there, to use the church for the purpose for which it was originally built. I cannot wait to hold my first service there and thank our Lord for His goodness.'

Father Dhakanalis drained his glass. 'You have given me a good deal to think about. There is no time to talk longer now. Our service is due shortly.'

'But you are in agreement with my proposal regarding the funds?' Father Minos pressed home his advantage.

Father Dhakanalis smiled at the earnest man before him. 'I understand what you are asking and I do not feel I am in a position to refuse without being uncharitable. Maybe a small addition to the fund from ourselves could make it a legitimate church fund? That could salve my conscience about misleading the bank.'

Father Minos allowed a broad smile to cross his face as he followed Father Dhakanalis from his parlour to the church for the impending service.

Father Minos sat on the quay waiting for Manolis to appear. It was already hot and he wished he could discard his robes and take advantage of the cool sea. No doubt the novelty of sea bathing would soon pall once it became his only means of washing himself thoroughly.

Manolis arrived, carrying four sacks with him, a broad grin spreading across his face when he saw the priest was waiting for him. He placed the sacks on board to join the boxes that were neatly stacked and secured.

'Good job I'm not too loaded. You've brought a good deal more down with you.'

Father Minos held out a coin to the fisherman. Manolis shook his head.

'The usual price for a round trip. I ought to charge you more with that lot.'

'It's a one way trip. I'm not coming back. I have a new parish.'

'What do you mean?' frowned Manolis. 'Are you ill?'

Father Minos shook his head. 'I've been given permission to live on the island. I am going to be their priest.'

'Permanently, you mean?'

'Permanently,' answered the priest firmly. 'Father Andreas has taken my parish and I have made some arrangements regarding the supplies that I shall need to talk to you about.'

Manolis raised his eyebrows. 'Everything is paid up to date,' he assured Father Minos.

Father Minos smiled easily. 'I'm sure it is. When we reach the island we'll have a chat. In the meantime I'll let you concentrate on sailing. I'd like to go the long way round, not through the canal. I want to savour my last moments as a free man.' He sat and watched as they sailed out to sea and round the headland, Aghios Nikolaos disappearing from view. He wondered if he would ever see the town again. He sat quietly until Spinalonga became visible and then he felt his heart leap. He was coming home.

The first week he was on Spinalonga Father Minos spent his time visiting every islander. He assured them he was there to help them both spiritually and practically. Anyone who wished to talk to him privately was welcome and whatever he heard would be confidential. He explained his ambition for opening the church and using it for services, but until that was possible, he would hold a short service every morning and evening in the open air for those who wished to attend.

He was gratified to see the number of people who turned up to participate in the prayers each day. It was ironic that once the church was empty of its current occupants and refurbished, he would have a larger congregation than he had ever achieved in Heraklion.

Once the morning service was over, he replaced his robes with an old pair of trousers and shirt and joined the people who were working on the buildings. Uncomplainingly he moved large stones, searched for timber, and carried out whatever instructions he was given. To his surprise, he found he began to enjoy the manual labour and the sense of accomplishment it brought when a house was finally declared suitable for habitation.

'I would like to think that everyone had suitable shelter before the winter,' said Yannis as he and Father Minos sat in the small house they shared. 'Provided no newcomers are sent over we should be able to manage it. I'd like to start on yours next week.'

Father Minos shook his head. 'You must leave me until the last. It is far more important that the church is made useable again now it is empty.'

Yannis grinned at him. 'Apart from me, you will be the last person housed. I'm sure many of the islanders think we should have repaired one for you the moment you arrived.'

'I am one of you. I do not expect any special treatment.' Father Minos frowned. 'I think you should stop referring to yourselves as 'the islanders'. Thanks to you, there is a community over here, much the same as any village on the mainland.'

'Except that we are all sick people,' exclaimed Yannis bitterly.

'That is not your fault.' Father Minos leaned forward. 'I truly believe that you were inflicted by this illness so you could be sent here and help these unfortunate people. Had you not arrived and decided that rebuilding was possible many of them would be dead by now, or surviving in the most miserable of conditions.'

Yannis shrugged. 'Anyone could have done it.'

'Very true, but they needed someone to lead them, make them see that a better life was possible.'

'Life only became better after your first visit. You are the person they have to thank. No more mouldy food, sufficient mattresses and blankets and no longer having to beg for a nail or screw. I don't know how you did it, Father, but we should all be grateful to you for ever more.'

Father Minos smiled. 'No, you should be grateful to our Lord. I believe He has a purpose for everyone. He guided you to me in the first place. Had I not come down to visit your family I would not have known about this island and paid a visit. Everything that happens to us in our lives is ordained by Him. I'd like to think that you believed that, Yannis, as I do.'

Yannis looked at the priest sceptically. 'I wish my faith was as strong as yours. My mother has a stroke, my sister dies in childbirth; why should that be?'

Father Minos shook his head sadly. 'I cannot answer those questions. I wish I could. I just have to accept it and say it was His will. I pray that in time you will have a peaceful heart that is no longer filled with resentment.'

Manolis was surprised when he collected two sacks of old clothes to take out to the island, and also to be handed a letter by Father Dhakanalis.

'This is to go to Father Minos. It is obviously important as it has the government seal on the envelope.'

Manolis nodded gravely and placed it into the pocket of his jacket. He hoped it was not an order for the priest to return to the mainland. For some weeks he had been trying to pluck up enough courage to approach the priest and ask him for a blessing on his union with Flora.

Father Minos read the letter, a smile spreading over his face, and immediately went in search of Yannis.

'Read this, Yannis. Your friend has managed to pass a bill. You will all receive a pension of thirty drachmas a month.'

Yannis read the letter and frowned.

'I don't see how this is going to benefit us. What would we do with the money over here? We can't go over to the mainland to spend it.'

Father Minos leaned against the doorway. 'Andreas and I discussed this at great length before I left Heraklion. I hope he will have managed to see Mr Pavlakis and convinced him the scheme will work.'

Yannis raised his eyebrows.

'The money will sit in a bank on the mainland. Everyone's name will be entered into a ledger along with the amount they receive each month. When they wish to make a purchase the cost will be deducted from their balance and the money drawn from the bank to pay the supplier.'

Yannis frowned. 'Are they still going to send out our food, or are we going to be expected to pay for it?'

'No, the government will remain responsible for sending you food supplies as they do now.'

'So who is going to do all this buying, paying and book-keeping?'

'Manolis.'

'Manolis! He's a fisherman, not a book-keeper.'

'He's been very capable when dealing with the purchases I arranged on the mainland. There are a couple of book-keepers over here and they can help him with any problems that arise; besides, it will mean he can spend more time on the island with Flora.'

'You approve of him and Flora, then? Doctor Stavros doesn't.'

Father Minos shrugged. 'He's a doctor. He says lepers should not marry because it speeds up the disease. If two people are happy to share their lives together, who am I to say otherwise?'

'Suppose he does become infected and sent over here? What happens then?'

'We will face that obstacle if it arises. Don't be so pessimistic, Yannis. I thought you'd be as delighted as I am.'

Yannis handed the letter back to the priest. 'There is another problem, you know. I have no idea how much Manolis earns as a fisherman, but if he's spending most of his time over here book-keeping and time on the mainland shopping, when is he going to fish? He won't have an income.'

Father Minos frowned, then his face cleared. 'Provided he agrees to the proposal I shall ask Mr Pavlakis to have his name added to the list of government employees. That way he will be guaranteed a regular income. He will no longer be dependent upon his catch each day.'

Yannis sighed. 'I hope you will be successful. I don't think anyone should be told about this until we know that Manolis would be willing and that he will be reimbursed. We don't want to raise peoples' hopes.'

Father Minos pocketed the letter. 'I'll write to Mr Pavlakis immediately and ask Manolis to take it back with him to post.'

'Are you allowed to write letters?' asked Yannis.

Father Minos winked at him. 'Strictly speaking, no. Sometimes I might have to make an exception to the rules governing my stay over here.'

'Would you be able to write a letter for me? I'd like to let my family know how I am and that I appreciate Anna waving to me each day.'

Father Minos shook his head. 'No, Yannis. If I did that for you, I would be obliged to do that for everyone else who asked me to write to their family. You are fortunate. You could always ask Manolis to take a message to them.'

Yannis looked across the short stretch of water that separated the island from the mainland. He could see the farm where he had spent his childhood, and a surge of longing overtook him. There were six wooden bathtubs on the island that Doctor Stavros had insisted were needed to enable the islanders to wash in rainwater, leaving them feeling considerable cleaner than when they washed in the sea. Surely they would float and he would be able to drift over to the small village. The more he thought about it, the more he decided his idea was feasible and worth any risk involved.

He took Spiro and Takkis into his confidence and once darkness fell the men carried a bathtub down to the jetty. He selected a length of wood from the storehouse and climbed carefully into the fragile craft.

'You're taking an awful risk, Yannis. You could drift out to sea,' frowned Spiro.

'It's not likely,' Yannis assured him. 'If the wind or currents change I'm more likely to end up back here.'

'Why don't you wait until tomorrow and ask Manolis to take you?' suggested Phaedra.

Yannis shook his head. 'I couldn't expect that of him. He could have his boat impounded if the authorities found out. He wouldn't be able to come and see Flora then. Give me a push to start me off.'

Manolis sat on his boat. He had been forbidden to leave the harbour until a thorough search of the area had been made. A bathtub had been found, wedged amongst the rocks, a short distance from Plaka. One of the lepers from the island had obviously used it as a makeshift boat to reach the mainland. Until he or his body had been recovered no boat was to leave the harbour.

The morning dragged on. All the fishermen were frustrated and annoyed. They were losing valuable fishing time. Manolis was particularly frustrated. He would have little time to spend with Flora, even if he was finally allowed to leave Aghios Nikolaos that day.

He looked along the waterfront to the source of a noise that had alerted him. There seemed to be a number of people approaching, shouting and brandishing sticks. At their head walked a dejected figure, his head bent. Manolis felt fairly certain it was Yannis and a small smile touched his lips. Over the years his respect and liking for the man had grown. He now counted Yannis as a friend. The two policemen held the vociferous crowd back and Yannis made his way to where Manolis was waiting.

Manolis scowled. 'I might have guessed you'd be the trouble maker. Making us all wait around and lose our fishing time. Get in,' he growled.

Meekly Yannis climbed into the boat and Manolis cast off hurriedly. He waited until they were well out to sea and away from any eyes that might be watching them before he turned to Yannis.

'Where did you get to?' he asked.

'I visited my family.'

'Good for you. It must have been pretty hazardous going over in a bathtub. There was a real panic when it was found. No one was allowed to leave the harbour.'

'Maybe they thought I had arranged with one of you to pick me up.'

'You should have told me your intention and I would have done so.'

Yannis shook his head. 'If they'd found out they would have taken away your boat. That would have been the end of your living as a fisherman and your visits to Flora.'

'We could have brought the bathtub back with us. That way they would probably never have known.' Manolis grinned at him conspiratorially. 'Just let me know the next time you plan a visit.'

1941

Manolis had been the official book-keeper to the islanders for the past four years. At first he had worried about the responsibility, but now he accepted it happily. It enabled him to spend at least two days each week on the island with Flora at his side. She acted as his assistant, finding the various people whose purchases he had accomplished and he needed to sign on their account in the ledger.

He had been surprised when Father Minos had first told him he would be paid for his work. A set rate each week would be deposited in a bank account for him and it was his to do as he pleased with. Manolis decided he would leave it there. He had no immediate need of extra cash in his pocket. He would save it for his old age when he was no longer able to work as a fisherman.

The atmosphere on the island was now much the same as in any village on the mainland. Many of the islanders had taken advantage of their pension to create a small business. Along the main path leading from the square was a dairy, grocer, greengrocer, two tavernas, a barber, dressmaker, cobbler and a general store that stocked a variety of items from Elastoplasts to a tin of paint.

Their ingenuity had impressed Manolis. He had been asked to take over soil and seeds and many of the small houses now had a flourishing garden, growing vegetables that they sold to the greengrocer and he sold on to the islanders. The goat, originally sent over to provide milk for Panicos, had finally been eaten, but in her place were another dozen, providing milk and cheese. Five households kept chickens, selling their eggs to the dairy, and two women ran a laundry for those unable to wash their own clothes.

A small amount of cash circulated regularly between everyone. No longer did they have to depend upon bundles of old clothes to be sent over, but could ask Manolis to buy them a new jumper or shirt. He had frequent requests for bales of material, needles and thread by the dressmaker who made new skirts or blouses for the women, he took leather for the cobbler who patched and mended boots, and each week he took over bottles of local wine for the tavernas.

Yannis no longer spent his time inspecting and supervising building work, but was busy teaching many of the islanders to read and write. Spiro spent all his time up at the hospital, his helpers being paid fifty leptas a day for their services by those who were being nursed. Father Minos continually gave him letters to be sent on to Andreas in Heraklion requesting equipment for the hospital.

The payment he received for his book-keeping services more than made up for the lack of time he spent fishing. He watched his account growing steadily, despite his aunt asking him to contribute more for his keep each week. He accepted that he and Flora could not be officially married, but he was grateful for the blessing Father Minos had given them and thankful that Doctor Stavros had never reported him to the authorities.

Were it not for the news that filtered down to Aghios Nikolaos from Heraklion life would be good. Each day Yannis seized the newspaper he brought eagerly from him and after scanning the headlines would search out Father Minos. Before he left Manolis would ask what the latest news implied.

Yannis shrugged. 'You can read, the same as me.'

'I can read, but I don't understand politics. Where are these places they're talking about? Why should we be threatened with a war?'

'It's to do with Germany. They've a leader there whose name is Hitler. His forces have invaded most of Europe. They're now in Italy and the Italians appear to have joined up with them. The British fought them off when they tried to land in England, but they haven't been able to stop him in any of the other countries.'

'Why should he want to invade Greece? We are a poor country.'

'I don't know. I think he suffers from megalomania and wants to rule the world.'

Manolis nodded, pretending to understand. He had no idea what megalomania was and wondered if it was a painful disease.

'The next few weeks will be crucial. If the Greek mainland capitulates what hope do we have on the islands?'

'We would fight him,' Manolis assured Yannis.

Yannis gave a thin smile. 'I'm sure you'd try. How many men are there living on Crete? I have no idea, but I would expect an invading army to have three times as many.'

Manolis frowned. 'I thought the newspaper said there were British troops over here making the island safe from attack. I've seen some in Aghios Nikolaos.'

'According to this,' Yannis tapped the newspaper with his finger, 'they are strengthening the garrisons and also the sea defences. As the Germans advanced on the mainland the defeated army were transported over here and there are hundreds of soldiers up in Chania, but the British have based their navy over in Egypt. How long would it take them to get over here if the Germans decided to attack Chania? By the time they arrived the Germans could have landed and occupied the town.'

'Surely the soldiers would defend the town and hold them off until reinforcements arrived.'

'I'm sure they would try, but have we got the weaponry?'

'So what can we do?'

Yannis folded the newspaper with a deep sigh. 'There's nothing we can do. We'll just carry on from day to day and see what transpires. If they do invade our country I just hope they restrict themselves to the main towns and don't spread out into the countryside. We certainly don't want them down here.'

'Maybe we could get some guns,' suggested Manolis.

Yannis looked at him in amusement. 'You know it's against the law now to carry one. Where would you buy guns locally anyway? They probably cost more than any of us have saved up, and what would we do with them?'

'If I got hold of some guns and brought them out to you, you'd be able to shoot them if they tried to land.' Manolis thought of the money he had in the bank, sure there would be more than enough there to purchase weapons for the islanders.

This time Yannis laughed outright. 'Why on earth should they want to land on an island occupied by lepers? And if they did and we shot at them they would very soon annihilate all of us. I know you mean well, Manolis, but forget that idea.'

Yannis looked across the bay to where his childhood home was situated. His father had a gun. He had used it to shoot their donkey when she was sick. Would he be able to defend his family if the Germans came to their village? Suppose his father was shot? What would happen to his mother and Anna and the children? Despite Yannis's assurances to Manolis that the Germans would have no interest in the island or surrounding area he felt uneasy. He was enjoying life at the moment, their conditions on the island had improved beyond his wildest expectations, they had money in their pockets to spend as they pleased and he was happily married to Phaedra. The last time he had felt that content his life had been shattered by the diagnosis that he was suffering from leprosy. He tried to shrug off his fears and as the days passed he had almost succeeded in doing so when Anna arrived.

Manolis arrived in the early evening, a child sitting fearfully in his boat. Flora had seen him coming and she greeted him with a smile.

'Find Yannis,' he called and proceeded to take his time fiddling with the ropes and tying up to the jetty, waiting to help the girl from the boat until Flora returned to the jetty with Yannis.

'You go with Flora. She'll look after you and find you something nice to eat and somewhere to sleep. I'm sure I'll be back for you within a couple of days.'

Dubiously Anna looked at him, but allowed Flora to lead her up through the archway. Yannis waited until they were out of hearing and turned to Manolis.

'Where did you find her?'

'I didn't. Nikos, the policeman, found me and told me I was to bring her across tonight. She was caught stealing in the town. She says her mother has gone to Heraklion to get some money. It's more likely she's abandoned the child. Doctor Kandakis diagnosed leprosy.'

'Why not Doctor Stavros?' Yannis frowned.

'I'd left him over in Elounda.'

'Did he take a blood test and scraping?'

Manolis shrugged. 'I don't know. I expect Doctor Stavros will do that if it's necessary. The girl says it's a birthmark. I thought she could stay with Flora until she's taken back. Nikos has offered to take her in until her mother returns, provided she's not ill.'

'It would probably be better if she came to Phaedra and myself. We have more space than Flora at the moment. She took in two newcomers last month.'

Manolis grinned widely. 'I hoped you'd say that. By the way,' his voice took on a sombre tone. 'I heard a bit of news in Aghios Nikolaos, about the Germans.'

Yannis glanced at him keenly. 'You didn't bring a newspaper this morning.'

'They haven't arrived. I'm not sure if there will be any tomorrow, either. There's a rumour that the Germans have taken Chania.'

Yannis frowned. 'How? The soldiers up in Chania were supposed to be defending the island.'

'Someone told me they floated down from the sky. I don't know any details. It might not be true. I'll let you know tomorrow whatever I can find out this evening.' Manolis cast off and waved his hand. It would soon be dark. He would return through the canal. It was far quicker than sailing round the spit of land back to Aghios Nikolaos and he had no lights on his boat.

Basil Hurst sat with his wife in the small house where they lived with his in-laws and baby son. He had spent time the previous evening with the other men from the village discussing the disquieting news from Greece. The allied armies were retreating on the mainland. The comforting news was that they were being sent to Crete to defend the island.

'We shall be safe enough here,' Basil assured Katerina. 'There are hundreds of Australians and New Zealanders in Chania. As soon as the Germans try to land by sea they'll mow them down.'

'Won't they send more Germans?' asked Katerina as she nursed her son of three weeks.

Basil shrugged. 'I expect so, but they'll just keep on fighting them.'

'You won't have to go and fight, will you, Vasilis?' she asked anxiously.

'No call up papers ever arrived for me from Britain. As far as they are concerned I don't exist.'

'Wouldn't they have expected you to contact them and volunteer?'

Basil shook his head. 'Hundreds of English men live abroad. Why should they suddenly want to leave their wives and families and be sent off to fight for a country they no longer consider their home? If I wasn't married to you I would have returned, but I think my first duty is to my family in Crete. As far as I know I've only an elderly aunt in Wales whom I've not seen since I was a boy. I belong here, I'm a Cretan now.'

Katerina sat Vasilis junior up and began to rub his back until he expelled the wind that had been building up inside him. He opened his mouth eagerly as Katerina transferred him to her other breast. Basil looked at him with loving pride. It was every man's desire to have a son as his first child. He would be happy to have a girl or two later, but Vasilis would always have a very special place in his heart.

Basil walked down to the cafe where the men sat drinking raki and coffee and swinging their beads between their fingers. If there was any news to be had this was where he would find it.

'British troops have landed in Suda Bay,' announced Dimitris, the cafe owner.

Basil nodded. 'That's good; there'll be more men to defend us.'

Dimitris shook his head. 'I understand that most of them are wounded. They've been brought here from mainland Greece to get medical treatment.'

'Why weren't they taken to Athens?'

'The Germans have filled the hospitals there. They insist their casualties have priority.'

'I heard the hospital there had been bombed,' remarked Mikaelis. 'If it was I hope it killed all the Germans who were inside.'

'Who bombed it?'

Mikaelis shrugged. 'I don't know. It was only what I heard.'

'If we're treating casualties here the Germans might bomb our hospitals,' Thranassis commented morosely.

'Their bombers won't get through. There are men stationed all along the coast with anti-aircraft guns. They'll shoot them down as soon as they're spotted.' Dimitris spoke confidently.

Basil listened as the talk went back and forth. It was impossible to know the truth of the situation, but he hoped Dimitris was correct and the Germans would be prevented from landing.

Panayiotis arrived in the village. He was dishevelled and distraught. 'The Germans have landed,' he announced.

'How?' asked Basil. 'I understand the coast line was defended.'

Panayiotis nodded sombrely. 'It was. The Germans came in by parachute. They landed at Maleme.'

'Why didn't we fight them?' asked Basil.

'We tried,' Panayiotis assured him. 'They've suffered a tremendous number of casualties. As the parachutists landed we attacked them, but they just kept coming.'

'I thought we had anti-aircraft guns strategically placed along that stretch?' Basil frowned.

'Most of them had been destroyed the day before. Wave after wave of bombers kept flying over. Eventually the guns fell silent. We thought that was the end of it for that day, then the parachutists arrived. They're attacking the airport now, trying to dislodge the British who are defending it. If we lose the airport we're helpless.'

Basil considered the information Panayiotis had brought to the village. There was no reason to expect the Germans to visit them. There was nothing there. The villagers made their living by farming and keeping a few sheep or goats. There was a general store and a cafe; a doctor would visit if you were unable to make the journey to Chania. The village priest schooled the children until they were considered old enough to leave home and live with relatives in a nearby town but most of them joined their families and worked on the farms. Only very basic education was considered necessary for a farmer and certainly not necessary for a girl who would become a farmer's wife. Life there was uneventful and peaceful. Once a week a bus would arrive and you could travel to Chania or stop at the villages en route, but few people had ever journeyed further than Chania.

Panayiotis drank the last of his raki and ran a crust of bread around his plate. 'I'm off,' he announced. 'I want to get back to Chania before dark.'

'I'll take you as far as the lake,' offered Basil. He was one of the few farmers who had a motorised cart.

Panayiotis shook his head. 'I promised to let the people know in Varipetro and Garipas. I'm returning by that route.'

'All right, I'll take you to Garipas and I'll stop at Varipetro on my way back and let the people there know the news you brought. That should save you some time.'

Panayiotis accepted the offer gratefully. He had already walked from the town into the countryside.

Basil drove the three-wheeled cart back from Varipetro deep in thought. Despite telling his wife he considered himself a Cretan he felt guilty. British soldiers were dying to defend his adopted country. Should he now offer to fight with the Cretans or alongside the British forces?

He had never been interested in the armed forces. Having graduated from university as a teacher, he had spent two miserable years trying to instil knowledge into unwilling and disinterested pupils. The boys in the school knew they had a job waiting for them in the Welsh mining pits and saw no point in education.

Deciding he was a bad teacher and unsuited to the occupation, he had left Wales with enough money in his pocket to travel to Greece. He had read of the archaeological discoveries there and had an overwhelming desire to see them. He calculated that he could afford to spend a year in the country before returning to England and applying for a teaching post again, this time somewhere outside of Wales where the pupils would be eager to learn.

His Welsh aunt, who had spoken to her neighbours with pride about her nephew, the teacher, now called him feckless and irresponsible to have thrown away a steady job on a whim. He wrote to her, long letters describing Greece and the sites he had visited, receiving an occasional scant reply from her.

Having reached Crete he volunteered to help excavating a site and whilst doing so he had realised this was his true interest. The indescribable joy of finding small artefacts long hidden in the ground and away from sight for so long thrilled him. The year he had planned in Greece stretched into two and it was with despair that he realised he was running out of money to enable him to stay in the country.

He sought casual work, picking produce for the farmers, moving his way around the country, his Greek language improving until he spoke like a native and making many friends. He had finally ended up at the farm where Katerina lived with her parents and joined them in picking olives. They had invited him to stay for the Christmas festivities and he had agreed willingly, accompanying them to church and joining them in their celebrations.

When Katerina's father had a bad bout of bronchitis he offered to stay until he had recovered, ignoring the cold and damp to work outdoors. Once Elias declared himself fit, Basil realised he did not want to move on again. He had fallen in love with Katerina.

Now he was in a dilemma. Should he stay with his wife and baby in safety at the farm or join the forces trying to defend the country? By the time he returned to the farmhouse he had decided he would do nothing. He would wait and see what unfolded in the next few days. There were British, Australian and New Zealand troops defending them, they would surely be more than a match for the Germans.

Each day Basil visited the taverna and was anxious for any news Panayiotis brought with him, expecting him to say the Germans had been routed and all was well. He could hardly believe it when Panayiotis reported that Maleme had been captured despite the British defending the area vigorously. They had been joined by Cretans who had removed guns and ammunition from the dead and used the olive groves as cover to fire on the German positions. It had been to no avail and now the troops were fighting to hold Chania and deny the Germans access to Suda Bay.

The day that Panayiotis did not arrive at the usual time in the village Basil decided he would drive his cart up towards Chania and see what the situation was for himself. Long before he reached the town he was met by columns of soldiers marching wearily along the road.

He drew his cart in to the side of the road. 'What's happened?'

'They've taken Chania and Suda,' the man replied despondently.

Basil looked at him incredulously. 'Why aren't you up there fighting?' he asked.

'It's hopeless. We've been told to make for Rethymnon. They reckon that's where they'll make for next.'

'You'd be quicker using the coastal route.'

'Yeah, and get bombed by the Germans as they fly over! Our orders are to go cross country. It's safer.'

'Have you got water and rations with you?'

'We should have enough. Rethymnon's not that far away. We reckon we'll be there by tomorrow at the latest.'

Basil nodded sombrely. Just because the men were marching in relatively flat countryside on a dirt road it would not stay like that. They would have steep terrain to cross and have to contend with the heat of the sun during the day and the cold at night. He thought it extremely unlikely they would have reached their destination by the following day, more likely they would be lost in the inhospitable countryside.

He returned to the village, stopping to relay his information at the cafe. Panayiotis was sitting waiting for him.

'I'd all but given you up,' he complained.

Basil shrugged. 'I thought I'd go up myself and see what the situation was.'

'Don't you trust me?'

'Of course, but I didn't think you were coming today.'

'I had to make a detour. There were soldiers everywhere.'

Basil nodded. 'They've been told to make their way to Rethymnon by way of the back roads and join the forces there.'

'No wonder I kept bumping into them. If they're going to walk cross country they'll be too exhausted to fight when they get to Rethymnon.'

'They say it's too dangerous to go by the main road. The Germans will fire on them.'

Panayiotis drank the last of his raki and smacked his lips. 'I was asked to deliver a letter to you.' He pulled the crumpled envelope from his pocket. There was no name and Basil looked at it in surprise.

'How do you know it's for me?'

'Someone asked if I knew your whereabouts and if so would I deliver a letter to you.'

'What did you tell this person?'

Panayiotis gave Basil a crafty look. 'I said I'd ask around in the area and if you could be found I'd pass it on to you. He said it was important.'

Basil slit the envelope open and took out the single sheet of paper.

> *Dear Bas*
>
> *Not heard from you in a while. Trust you are keeping well.*
>
> *I am working on a new project that I think might interest you. I think you could well be suited to be one of the team.*
>
> *I will be at my usual address in Rethymnon next week and hope to have a visit from you as soon as possible.*
>
> *If I am unavailable please contact Doug in Heraklion. He has all the details and relevant equipment.*
>
> *Yours M*

Basil read the cryptic words a second time. They told him nothing. Maurice had lived in Rethymnon and been in charge of various excavations when he had worked with the archaeologists during his early years on the island. He had been enthusiastic and hard working, but had no knowledge or particular expertise that would make them single him out and ask him to work with them again.

Panayiotis was looking at him impatiently. 'Am I to take back an answer?' he asked.

Basil shook his head. 'Not at the moment. I'll need to think about it.'

Basil rode away from the village, taking the country tracks to avoid Chania and Suda Bay. He had no wish to run into a German patrol and have to explain where he was going. At Malaxa he had bought some more petrol from a farmer, telling him he was on urgent business on behalf of the Cretan Government. Grudgingly the farmer had handed him the can he had kept for his own emergency escape, despite Basil having paid twice the amount it had cost initially.

Even at Malaxa there was a smell in the air of smoke, and Basil could see the haze that hung over the coastal area, obscuring the sun. He stopped at the church and spoke briefly to the priest who advised him to take the road to Katohori and continue on the mountain tracks until he reached Filipos. There he would only be a short distance away from the metalled road leading to Georgioupoli and on to Rethymnon and would be able to assess how safe it would be to ride directly down the road or whether he should stay on the cart tracks and mountain passes.

Basil thanked him for his advice, hoping he would have enough petrol in the tank to take him to Rethymnon by the longer route. It was dark by the time he reached the area of Pemonia and he headed for a clump of trees, which would give him shelter and also hide his small cart from anyone who happened to pass by. He sat in the darkness listening to the creaking and sighing of the trees and then realised he was also hearing another sound. It was the sound of breathing. He felt the hairs on the back of his neck standing up. Was he being watched by an animal or had he inadvertently stumbled across a German patrol hiding there?

He sat a while longer and decided if an animal had thought he was their supper that night they would have sprung out at him by now. The breathing he was convinced he could hear must be human. Slowly he rose to his feet and held his hands up.

'I am a farmer,' he called quietly in Greek. 'I am unarmed.'

He heard the click of a safety catch as it was released on a rifle. Convinced he would be shot, he stood unmoving, hoping he would be believed when he said he had no armaments. Dark shapes made their way towards him and he stood his ground. If he ran, they were certain to shoot at him. The men who had emerged from the cover of the trees surrounded him and one walked forward, his rifle on a level with Basil's stomach.

'I am a farmer,' he said again. 'I am unarmed.'

He could hear low voices conversing together and Basil was sure they were speaking English. He took a chance. 'I'm English,' he said. 'Can I put my hands down?'

'No. Which battalion are you from?'

'I'm not. I'm a civilian.

'What's your rank and number?'

'I don't have a rank or number. I've told you, I'm a civilian. I'm a farmer. My name is Basil Hurst. Please take me to your commanding officer – and can I put my hands down now?'

'Stay as you are,' he was ordered.

He sighed. His arms were beginning to ache from being held above his head. It seemed an age before a man finally emerged from the darkness.

'Papers?' he barked at Basil.

'In my pocket. I've assured your men I'm unarmed.'

'Keep your hands up.' The commander spoke to one of his men who stepped forward and began to search Basil. There was no pocket in his shirt, but one each side of his trousers. The soldier removed the contents passing them to his commanding officer, before checking Basil's sleeves, trouser legs and boots for hidden weapons.

By the light of a torch the commander examined Basil's identity papers, finally handing them back to him. 'You can put your hands down now.'

Basil dropped them to his sides in relief.

'Can't be too careful,' observed the commander. 'Tell me about yourself.'

'Not much to tell. I've lived over here for the last six years. I'm married to a Cretan woman and we have a small farm a few kilometres from Chania. I've come to offer my help.'

The commander frowned. 'Help? What help?'

'Do you or your men speak Greek? Can you read the signs? Do you even know where you are?'

The commander hesitated. 'We're on our way to Rethymnon.'

Basil nodded. 'Which direction will you go in when you've rested?'

'That way.' He pointed north east. 'Back up to the road we've been travelling on.'

'Have you got a map?' asked Basil.

The commander eyed him dubiously, finally taking one from the pocket in his uniform.

'May I sit down?' asked Basil. 'I can put it on the ground then.'

'Remember my men still have you covered.'

'I take that as a yes,' replied Basil and knelt down, spreading the map before him. 'Shine your torch about there.' He pointed to an area and the commander obliged. 'Move it back a bit. Stop there. This is where you are, near enough. Pemonia. Now if you rejoin the road you'll eventually come to a Roman bridge. That's where the road forks.' Basil traced the route with his finger. 'Make sure you continue straight on or you'll end up on the other side of the island. Follow that road and you'll eventually end up at Rethymnon.'

The commander frowned. 'How far away is Rethymnon? I was told we were needed there as quickly as possible. There's heavy fighting in the area and they need our support.'

Basil shrugged. 'About a day's march.'

'Isn't there a quicker way?'

Basil shook his head. 'You could try cutting across from Drania, but I wouldn't advise it. There's nothing between Drania and Atsipopoula and some of the terrain is pretty tough going.'

'We'll stick to the road,' the commander said decisively. 'Where are you making for?'

'Rethymnon, the same as you.'

'Why are you going there?' asked the commander suspiciously.

'I know people in the area. I thought I ought to tell them the latest news.'

'Are you taking the same route?'

Basil nodded. 'If I see any German troops I'll go back onto a cart track and avoid them by going through the villages. I'm just a Cretan going about my business.'

The commander considered the situation. 'Would you be willing to come to this bridge you mention? Make sure we take the right road.'

'How long will it take you to get the men mobilised?'

'They'll be ready to move at dawn. Not before. They need some rest.'

Basil drove slowly down the cart track that led back to the road to Rethymnon. He waited for the first of the men to catch up with him and then continued slowly on, looking behind him continuously to ensure they were following him. Once he reached the fork in the road he sat and watched as the weary men began to march past him, all of them carrying heavy back packs, but appearing good humoured and accepting of another gruelling day. Basil waved his hand as they moved to one side to let him overtake them. He wondered just how long it would take the long column of men to reach the town and whether they would be fit to fight when they reached their destination.

As Basil reached the outskirts of Rethymnon he stopped and drove his three wheel cart into an olive grove. He dug a small hole at the root of an olive tree and placed the can of petrol in it, covering it with earth and debris. As an added precaution he tipped the vehicle on its side and mounded up loose earth on the back wheel. He hoped it would be safe there, anyone who spotted it thinking it was defunct, and leaving it alone.

Whilst he walked towards the town he met women and children making for the countryside, they were desperate to get away from the fighting that was taking place and find a sanctuary. The sound of gunfire came to his ears as he drew closer, a group of people fled in his direction and he shrank back against a wall to let them pass.

'The Germans are coming,' one of them gasped at him and Basil promptly joined their number. He ran a short distance with them, then turned and took a side road leading back into the town. Keeping as far away from the centre and the port as he could he took a long meandering route until he came to the house he was looking for. He stopped and looked at it aghast.

The door had been forced off its hinges and lay on the ground along with some of the shutters. The glass was broken in the windows and curtains hung in tatters. As he peered into the damaged building he could see bullet marks on the walls and blood lay in a congealing pool on the floor.

Basil hesitated. It was unlikely there was anyone in the house. Cautiously he entered and peered into the rooms on the ground floor. There was a smell in the air that assaulted his nostrils and made him want to reach. Laying half way up the stairs was the body of the man he had been seeking. Swallowing the bile that was rising in him, Basil stepped forwards, overcame his nausea, and felt for a pulse.

He hesitated. Should he go upstairs and see if there was anyone alive up there? As far as he knew his friend had lived alone, but he could have had visitors at the time of his assassination. Stepping over the prostrate form, he climbed the stairs and looked in each room in turn. They had been ransacked, the furniture virtually destroyed, bedding tumbled to the floor, cupboard doors hanging loose on their hinges. What had they been looking for that was so important or was it just an act of vandalism?

Basil retraced his steps to the ground floor and stepped back into the street. The gunfire seemed to be continuous now, with explosions at intervals. Rethymnon was fighting for its life. He wondered if the troops he had left marching towards the town would arrive in time to make any difference to the situation.

Slinking down side roads, often having to retrace his steps and find another route, Basil finally reached a church that appeared unmolested and entered quietly. He was met by a petrified group of women and children, wild-eyed and desperate. He shook his head at them and forced his way through to where the priest stood helplessly.

'Father, how can I help?' he asked.

Father Elias looked at him sadly. 'There is nothing you can do. The Germans are going through the town, destroying everything in their path, shooting people indiscriminately.'

'There are reinforcements on their way. They should be here by nightfall' Basil told him encouragingly.

The priest wrung his hands. 'They will be too late to save us. By then we will have been annihilated. The people are fighting in the streets, but it is no use.'

An explosion close by rent the air and the women let out involuntary screams whilst the children began to cry, burying their heads in their mother's skirts.

'I'm sure you will be safe in here. They have no reason to bomb a church.'

'They have no reason to ravage the city,' Father Elias replied angrily. 'If these mad men wish to fight they should do it where there are no civilians. Why should innocent women and children suffer?'

Basil had no answer for him. 'Do you know what has happened in Heraklion?'

Father Elias shook his head. 'We heard Maleme had fallen, that the British had sunk a convoy carrying supplies in Suda Bay, but we've had no news from Heraklion.'

'That's encouraging. That could mean the allied troops there are in control. If the city is secure they could send more men up here to assist you in your struggle.'

'If we don't know what is happening in Heraklion, how will they know what is happening to us?'

'I'll let them know,' promised Basil.

Taking the same circuitous route, he returned to the olive grove, retrieved his cart and dug up his can of petrol. He would have to take the back roads to avoid the town, travel through the outlying villages, and rejoin the road that led to Heraklion at Stavromenos.

Each village he passed through someone would call out and stop him, asking for news. He admitted that Rethymnon was the scene of a fierce fight between the invading forces and the allied troops, the allies having been joined by the townsfolk, but that a battalion was on its way to assist them. He heard conflicting reports about the situation in Heraklion, some said the town had fallen, others that it was holding firm.

He had reached Marathos when his petrol ran out and he was forced to abandon the vehicle and continue his journey on foot. He begged a meal and a bed for the night, both of which were given willingly to him and when it was light he asked the farmer if there was a quick route on foot to get to Heraklion.

The farmer pondered. 'There's a track over the fields, but if I were you I'd stick to the road. It's a bit further to walk, but you'll make better time.'

Basil considered his advice, filled his water bottle from the pump, accepted a small bag of olives, and continued on his way. He had no clear idea what he hoped to accomplish, but felt he should ask the troops stationed at Heraklion to make their way to Rethymnon to relieve their desperate situation. When he had done that he would see if he could find Douglas. He should know what Maurice was referring to in his letter.

A rumbling came to his ears and he dived into the ditch beside the road. He would find out who was travelling towards Heraklion before he made himself known to them. He rolled into the sparse cover afforded by the scrub that grew close to the road and peered out. A convoy of lorries were driving at a reckless speed down the road, the dust they were creating making the men travelling in the back of each one cough and choke.

The dust churned up by their wheels gave him no chance to see their markings, he thought they looked like the allied transport, but he was not prepared to declare himself and find he was mistaken. He lay in the grass, a thistle scratching at his face, until the last of them had passed. Basil lifted his head cautiously, but stayed where he was. Finally he took a mouthful of water, sluiced it around his mouth and spat it out to clear the dust.

He decided it had taken him longer to walk from Marathos than he had anticipated, as the sky over the town of Heraklion in the distance was dark. He looked up, the sun was nowhere near setting, and the truth dawned on him. The darkness he could see was actually smoke. Heraklion was in flames.

Basil threaded his way carefully through the olive groves and farmland outside of Heraklion. Everywhere he looked there were battle weary troops sitting under the trees, some were wearing a makeshift bandage, but all had a blank look of utter disbelief on their faces. Their weapons were by their hands, but none of them looked as if they had the strength to use them. Interspersed between them were anti-aircraft guns and machine guns beside their tripods, salvaged, however useless, rather than delivered into enemy hands. A few men raised their hands to him, pleading for food or water and he had to shake his head and move on. He had no food with him and his one bottle of water would go nowhere amongst so many.

Basil continued until the olive groves thinned and he could see the dirt road ahead of him. Poor houses stood in this area outside the old city wall, mostly occupied by the tanners and their families. He made straight for the nearest house and knocked decorously on the door, hoping he would not alarm the occupants. He knocked again when he received no answer and risked calling out.

'I am a fellow Cretan. Please help me.'

The door opened a crack and he smiled at the frightened man who stood there. 'May I come in? I don't feel very safe out here?'

The door did not move. 'Who are you?'

'I am Vasilis. I have travelled down from Rethymnon to tell you that help is on its way, but it appears I am too late.'

The man opened the door wide enough for Basil to enter, closing and bolting it after him. Basil stood in the room that served all purposes. The large bed in the corner took up most of the space, a table and two chairs stood to one side and before the open fireplace were stacked the cooking implements. Most disconcerting was the fact that a woman stood there with a rifle pointed at him. Slowly Basil raised his hands.

'I am unarmed,' he informed her. 'I come to ask for your help.'

'We're in no position to help anyone,' the man stated firmly.

'All I'm asking for is water.'

'So why didn't you help yourself from the pump?'

'I need a container. It's not for me. There are hundreds of allied soldiers in the olive groves. They need water.'

'So why didn't they come for it themselves?'

Basil shook his head. 'They have no idea where they are and most of them look too exhausted to move. If you let me have a bucket to take water to them I can show some of the others where the pump is and they can manage for themselves.'

'If they're Germans they can die of thirst.' The woman spoke for the first time and Basil was taken aback by the hatred in her voice.

Basil shook his head. 'They are part of the allied army.'

She threw the rifle on the table nonchalantly. 'You can put your hands down. It's not loaded.'

Relieved, Basil lowered his hands.

'I'll get you a bucket.' The woman looked out of the window into the yard at the back before unbolting the door and scuttling outside. She returned with two empty buckets and held them out to Basil. 'Tell them to leave them by the pump,' she ordered.

Basil returned to the olive grove carrying two buckets of water. He placed them behind an olive tree and spoke to the first man he saw telling him to call his commanding officer.

'He's over there.'

Basil looked where he pointed and saw the soldier lolling against a tree, his head bandaged and his eyes closed. He turned back to the man. 'He doesn't look fit enough to be in command.'

'He's not. Shrapnel in the head. He's still our commanding officer, though.'

'Are you injured?' asked Basil.

The man shook his head.

'Then get to your feet and find me a couple of other men who are able to walk and carry a bucket.'

The soldier looked at him in surprise and did not move.

'Do these men need water or not?' asked Basil angrily.

'Of course we do.'

'Then do as I say. Have you got a medical officer with you?'

'He was shot.'

'So who's dealing with the injured?'

'Whoever's nearest to them when they fall.' Reluctantly the man rose to his feet. 'I'll find a couple of men to carry buckets.'

The man staggered away and Basil felt guilty for speaking to him so harshly. He appeared to be as dehydrated and exhausted as everyone else. Two men rose from where they had been laying on the ground and walked slowly over to him.

'We've been told you want us.'

Basil nodded. 'Follow me.' He led them the few steps to where the buckets stood. 'That's fresh water. You two can drink your fill, then take them on to the next man in line. When they're empty come back to me here and I'll take you to the pump to refill them.'

Thankfully the men knelt, cupped their hands and began to drink noisily. Word had spread that water was available and the men began to form a queue, accusing those before them of drinking more than their share and pushing to get to the forefront.

Basil held up his hand and shouted at them. 'Wait your turn. There's plenty more. If you have water bottles follow me and I'll show you where you can fill them.'

Basil led a straggling line of men back to the outskirts of Heraklion and showed the men where the pump was situated. He stood and watched whilst they drank and filled their bottles; returning to the shelter of the olives talking cheerfully to each other. Many of them were young boys! The inhabitants of the poor houses watched them also. One by one they left their homes and pressed some food into the hands of the men, being rewarded by a smile of gratitude. There would be little to go round, but it would provide a welcome mouthful for many of them.

Basil left them, he felt he could do no more for the defeated and demoralised army. He needed to find out the truth of the situation in Heraklion.

He skirted the city walls that had been built long ago to defend the town from marauders. They had been no defence against bullets and the bombs that had rained down from the sky. Wherever he looked there were ruined buildings, people either stared at him vacantly or cringed away in fear. He was so thankful that his family were in a small country village that would be of no interest to the invaders.

To his relief the building he sought appeared to be intact and he knocked, hoping the occupants were at home. The man who opened the door looked at him and no flicker of recognition registered on his face.

'Hello, Doug. May I come in?'

'Basil! What the devil brings you here?'

Douglas waved his unexpected visitor into the kitchen. 'It's safer in the back,' he said.

Basil sat down at the kitchen table and accepted the glass of wine that was poured and passed to him. Douglas peered at him over his half-moon glasses. 'So what brings you here? I thought you were a farmer these days. You certainly look like one. I took you for a Cretan.'

'I had a strange letter from Maurice. He asked me to go to Rethymnon to see him.'

'May I see the letter?'

Basil handed over the sheet of paper and Douglas scanned it quickly.

'So why have you come to me? Why didn't you go to Rethymnon?'

'Maurice is dead. I went to his house; it had been ransacked and he was lying dead on the stairs. He'd been shot.'

Douglas paled visibly. 'It was his idea. Someone must have heard about it.'

Basil folded his arms. 'Doug, you obviously know what this is about. What is this project that Maurice wanted to include me in? Under the circumstances I doubt if there'll be any archaeology undertaken for a good long while.'

Douglas shook his head. 'He was so careful. You can tell that by his letter to you, but someone must have known.'

'Known what, Douglas?'

Douglas leant forward so his head was nearly touching Basil's. 'Crete is in a mess, to put it mildly. We thought the British along with the allies would be well able to defend the island, but we were wrong. Chania and Rethymnon have been taken; Heraklion is on the brink and if Heraklion falls,' he spread his hands, 'that's it. Maurice came up with the idea of forming a resistance group. There are a few of us over here who are bi-lingual, even multi-lingual. He thought those who could speak German would be able to infiltrate and gather information. That could be relayed back to the Cretan andartes and they would know where they could ambush the troops or hide out safely. If communication was needed between the British and the Cretans, men like yourself would be able to translate exactly; no guesswork that could be misinterpreted. His letter was asking you to become a member of the club.'

'Some club! If he was killed for an idea what would they do to those who actually tried to resist them?' Basil shook his head. 'I don't think so, Doug. It's a good idea and you can trust me not to breathe a word to anyone, but I've a wife and child to think about. I can't get involved.'

'You're already involved.' Douglas peered at him. 'You came down here to tell me about Maurice. You didn't have to do that. You took a chance going into Rethymnon to look for him and then another when you made your way down here. You consider yourself a Cretan, don't you?'

Basil nodded.

'Then don't you consider that you have a duty to help them?'

'I've not been trained to fight.'

'I'm not asking you to fight them physically, but mentally. Maurice was convinced that those of us who were working over here outmatched them in intelligence. These Germans are brute animals. They follow orders the same way as an animal follows its instinct. If you join this group you'll not be asked to do anything very difficult. Take a message that needs to be translated, warn the andartes that a German force is coming their way so they can vacate the area, simple things like that.'

'If this is all so simple why do you need me?' asked Basil suspiciously.

'You pass as a Cretan. With your dark colouring no one would think you were English.'

'Welsh,' Basil corrected him.

'The Cretans will trust you because you are one of them, married to a countrywoman. The British will trust you because they find it inconceivable that anyone who is British could even contemplate being a traitor.'

'Is that really all I would be asked to do?'

Douglas nodded and looked at Basil expectantly.

'I'll think about it,' he promised.

'If you don't find me here, look in the church,' Douglas replied cryptically as he opened the door for Basil to leave.

Basil walked back to the olive grove on the outskirts of the town deep in thought. The men were still sitting or lying beneath the olive trees and this time he received a smile or a raised hand in greeting.

'How long are you staying here?' he asked.

'No idea. We're waiting for orders. We were told to withdraw from our positions and gather here. They'll probably tell us tomorrow to go back into the town and fight,' the soldier added gloomily.

'And will you?' asked Basil.

'Of course.' The man looked at him incredulously. 'We're soldiers. Wouldn't you?'

The news did not get any better. Rethymnon had fallen, the British had tried to evacuate their troops from Heraklion and many of their ships had been bombed, lost in the bay along with their crew and the soldiers they had been intent on helping. Cretans who had helped to defend Maleme had been rounded up and shot, as an example, the Germans had declared, and the others imprisoned. Panayiotis did not appear in their village any more and Basil feared he had been among the men captured by the Germans. Heraklion had been taken after bitter hand-to-hand fighting in the streets and the Germans had been given the liberty to do as they pleased to both citizens and property. The allied troops had been told to make for the coast on the other side of the island where arrangements would be made to evacuate them from Sfakia to Egypt.

Basil returned to Marathos where he had abandoned his cart and pushed it back onto the road. At the village he asked if anyone had petrol to spare, once again saying he was on urgent government business, and paid an extortionate amount for half a can. He had seen no sign of a bus, all the traffic appeared to be coming towards him, soldiers marching dispiritedly, locals carrying bundles of possessions, even a priest in robes covered in dust and clutching an icon to his chest. At regular intervals a German plane would fly overhead and spray the road indiscriminately with bullets. The people diving for whatever cover they could find.

Having passed Damaista, Basil turned off onto a dirt road, deciding he would be safer on the country roads and be more likely to find some petrol available. Each village he came to he asked to buy a can, filling the tank in the cart to the brim each time and tying any spare cans to the strut of the seat beside him. Even driving the cart all the way he knew it would take him at least two days, maybe longer, to cover the distance between Heraklion and his home village.

The traditional hospitality of the people meant he did not have to beg for food, it was offered to him wherever he stopped. He ate a strange mixture of meals, supplementing them with grapes or any vegetables he found growing on his route. He hoped Katerina had not been concerned about his extended absence. He should have made the journey to and from Rethymnon within two days and now he had been away for over a week.

He was relieved when he saw the familiar landmark of Profitis Ilias and knew that he had only a few more kilometres to cover.

He stopped in Garipas and Varipetro to tell them the latest news of the German advance, then hastened on to the farmhouse.

Katerina heated water for him and he sat in the bathtub in the kitchen. It was a pleasure to shave the stubble from his face and don clean clothes. Vasilis sat on his lap, the small boy kicking his legs and reaching up a hand to explore his father's face.

'I'm so pleased you're back, Vasilis. I was becoming worried. I thought maybe you had to walk back from Rethymnon.'

Basil smiled. It was good that she was only concerned about him having had to walk. He would not tell her about the fighting that was taking place or the plight of the townsfolk. She would be safe down here in the countryside.

Basil sat at the kitchen table and began to make a list of the places where he had worked and the friends he had made in the area. He was torn between considering himself British or Cretan, but Douglas had struck a chord in him. It was his duty to help in whatever way he could. Even if he only communicated with the fleeing soldiers, directing them to the safest and easiest roads and asking his Cretan acquaintances for any help they were able to give. It was doubtful if they were able to read Greek and the sparse signs that were dotted about would be meaningless to them. His decision made, he announced his intention to his wife and her family.

He drove the three-wheeled cart from village to village on the back roads until he finally reached the outskirts of Heraklion. The olive groves where he had found the soldiers sheltering were empty, the ground trampled, evidence of their temporary occupation everywhere. Basil tipped the cart over on its side and continued on foot to the house where Douglas lived.

He was horrified by the sight that met his eyes. The town had been devastated. Whole areas had been laid waste and apart from the patrolling soldiers, there was no one to be seen in the vicinity. Craters in the road bore evidence to the bombing that had taken place, in the harbour the stern of a ship struggled to stay afloat just above the water line. The small boats the fishermen used to make their living were smashed to splinters, their nets tangled amongst the planking, torn and useless.

Longing to leave the stricken town, but feeling he had a duty to find Douglas, Basil returned to the outskirts beyond the old city wall and walked to the other side before slipping back into the town and making his way to the house where he had met his friend.

He was not surprised when he arrived to find it empty, in much the same state as he had found the house in Rethymnon, but this time there was no body lying on the stairs. Basil hoped that meant Douglas had escaped before the marauding soldiers had arrived.

Basil stood in the kitchen where they had sat drinking wine and thought back over their conversation. Douglas had said he would be at his house or the church. Warily Basil picked his way across the rubble that lay in the streets until he came to the church two roads away. The doors stood open, but not in welcome. The building was being used as a shelter for the occupying army. There was no way Douglas would have found safety there.

Basil moved from church to church, hoping to find one that was intact and the priest still in occupation. It was not until late in the afternoon that he found one in the poorest quarter of the town that seemed to have been ignored by the rampaging soldiers.

He knocked on the side door and was relieved when it was opened to him.

'Come in, my son. How can I help?'

Basil drew a breath of relief. 'Father, I do not know if you can help me, but I would appreciate spending a short while on my knees in your church.'

'Of course. Do you wish me to stay and pray with you?'

'No. I have nothing to confess, except the hatred I have in my heart for those who have killed and maimed.'

The priest returned to his own small sanctuary leaving Basil to kneel and let the calm atmosphere wash over him. Feeling more composed he rose and crossed himself, wishing he had been able to put his jumbled thoughts into a semblance of prayer.

'Father, I have come to Heraklion seeking an old acquaintance. I visited him two weeks ago. He said I would find him at his house or the church. His house has been ransacked and this is the first church I have found that has not been damaged or occupied by the invaders. Are you able to give me any news of the Englishman, Douglas?'

A slow smile spread across the countenance of the priest. 'God willing, he is safe. Where have you come from?'

'I live in a village in the countryside near to Chania. I am married to Katerina.'

Father Andreas nodded. 'And your name?'

'I am Basil Hurst. I'm known over here by the Greek form, Vasilis.'

'Welcome, Vasilis. I know Douglas was hoping you would come to offer your help. Fortunately he received a warning that his house was to be targeted and he left in good time. He intended to make his way towards Aghios Nikolaos. I believe he knows the area and has friends there who will offer him shelter. Will you be going that way?'

Basil hesitated and his hesitation was not lost on the priest.

'He left a package with me and requested that I ask you to deliver it to him.'

'He could be anywhere!'

'I am sure if you make enquiries of Father Dhakanalis in Aghios Nikolaos he will be able to help you. Douglas said he would leave word of his destination with him. Do you have some form of transport? The package would be heavy to carry with you.'

Basil nodded. 'I have a cart. I left it hidden in the olive grove.'

'Then it will be safer if I assist you in carrying it there than you bringing the cart to my door.'

'But there are German patrols everywhere!'

'I do not think they will stop a priest and a grieving father whilst he is carrying the coffin of his child,' Father Andreas smiled confidently.

'A coffin!' Basil paled at the thought, a stricken look on his face.

'There is no body inside,' the priest assured him hurriedly. 'Follow me.'

Father Andreas led the way back into the church where a small coffin lay draped with a white cloth. 'If you will carry it we will walk openly through the streets until we reach the cemetery. I will wait there until you return with your cart.'

'What is in there?' asked Basil.

'A wireless.' Father Andreas smiled triumphantly.

Basil felt uncomfortable and self-conscious as he followed Father Andreas with the small, but heavy coffin in his arms. At the graveyard he deposited it on the ground at the feet of the priest and hurried to where he had left his cart. Now he must try to find Douglas at Aghios Nikolaos.

Basil travelled by cart tracks and country roads to reach the town of Aghios Nikolaos. When he reached the outskirts he took a further detour into deserted countryside and his cart laboured up an overgrown track. He pushed his cart as deep into the undergrowth as possible and removed the coffin from the back. He would take the precaution of hiding his important package before entering the town and searching out Father Dhakanalis.

He continued up the track for over an hour before his goal came into sight, by then the track had disappeared into a steep, boulder-strewn hillside. He continually had to place the coffin ahead of himself, scramble up to it and repeat the procedure. By the time he reached the cave he was dripping with sweat from his exertions.

He entered the dark opening and began to inch his way

forwards, wishing he had brought a torch with him. The cold metal of a gun pressed between his shoulder blades and he almost dropped the coffin in alarm.

'I cannot raise my hands, or I will drop what I am carrying. I am unarmed.'

Rough hands ran over his body verifying the truth of his statement. A torch shone in his eyes, momentarily blinding him.

'Basil! I'm sorry. I didn't realise it was you arriving.'

Basil placed his burden on the floor of the cave, opened his arms and embraced Douglas.

'I didn't expect to find you up here.'

'I found Aghios Nikolaos wasn't safe. I left a message with Father Dhakanalis that I was up here, but I didn't expect you to carry this up with you.'

Basil grinned. 'I haven't been into the town yet. I thought this could be a safe hiding place until I found out the situation there.'

Douglas shook his head. 'It's not good. Come and sit outside. It's considerably warmer and more pleasant out there.'

Basil sat beside him on the rocky hillside. 'So, what have I got myself into?'

Douglas grinned. 'Only a little bit of espionage. Luckily I've lived in Crete long enough to have friends. They warned me that foreigners were being rounded up for questioning. After what happened to Maurice I decided not to hang around. I took my wireless to Father Andreas and walked down here. I had hoped the Germans hadn't reached the area, but I was wrong. Not only are they here, but the Italians also.'

'So what are your plans now?'

'I was hoping if you got through you'd be willing to deliver it to Toplou for me.'

Basil considered his words. 'If the Germans and Italians are in the area what hope do I have of getting down there carrying it? So far I've not been stopped. My luck can't hold for ever.'

'It would be safest to take it by sea. Father Dhakanalis said he knew a boatman who could be trusted. Italians have occupied Aghios Nikolaos and they appear t be waiting for the Germans to join them. Once that happens they will probably put the harbour under guard and either stop the fishing boats going out or start escorting them.' Douglas frowned. 'They can't be watching every cove and inlet. Maybe you could move down the coast to a more deserted spot and be picked up from there.'

'Where do you suggest?' Basil did not relish taking the coffin back down the steep hillside.

'What about Pahia Amnos? It's not that much further for you to travel and they shouldn't have found anything to interest them in that area. If you have a problem move on to Mohlos.'

Basil nodded. 'Are you able to get a message to Father Dhakanalis? It would be more sensible for me to go straight there rather than risk entering the town. My cart's hidden down below.'

'I'll help you back down the hill and I'll beg a ride in return. Give me a few minutes to collect my belongings, such as they are.'

'Where are you making for?'

'Kapsa Monastery.'

Basil raised his eyebrows.

'Arthur is due to be dropped off at Koufonisi Island. When you've delivered the wireless I'm relying on you to persuade the boatman to sail round there and collect him.' Douglas handed Basil his revolver and some rounds of ammunition. 'You might need this,' he said. 'I have a spare.'

JUNE 1941

Father Andreas walked through the ravaged streets of Heraklion. Piles of rubble stood everywhere, dust swirling up into the air as a surviving resident would search for a member of the family they believed might be buried underneath or a few meagre possessions they hoped to salvage.

The Germans had marched into the town despite the heroic attempts of the men and women to prevent the occupation and now they were paying the cost. He had watched in horror as the government were marched along the main road and out into the countryside, from where they did not return.

For days the Germans had looted, raped, pillaged and destroyed whatever they found in their path. The main area of the town and the waterfront had been set on fire and the residents had run for their lives. Those who were able had fled to the countryside, believing they would be safer there.

Now the survivors walked silently with their heads bent. They were cowed and petrified. If they saw a soldier coming in their direction they would scuttle away and hide as best they could.

Father Andreas had prayed for their safety and relief from their oppressors with no avail. He had provided sanctuary and succour in his church, thankful that he lived in a poor area of the town that had been spared. The Germans seemed to ignore his insignificant church whilst they looted shamelessly from the larger, more magnificent edifices, removing anything they considered valuable and destroying wantonly age-old icons and artefacts.

He was thankful his parents and sister were in America and spared the horrors that Crete was suffering. He wondered how his aunt and uncle were faring, but thought the Germans would not be interested in the insignificant little village of Plaka.

Yannis watched in disbelief. There were soldiers marching down the main street of Plaka, the men of the village amongst them. He was not sure if he could make out Yiorgo, but one of them was limping and Yannis felt certain it was his father. The women and children stood in a frightened group, surrounded by soldiers with rifles pointing at them. As he watched, the soldiers carried a boat down to the sea, waited until an officer had climbed in, then began to row strongly towards the island.

A short distance from the jetty the boat stopped. Yannis, along with many of the others had made his way down to the sea. He wanted to ask them what was happening on the mainland.

The German commander stood up in the boat as the small crowd watched him silently. Two of the soldiers in the boat trained their rifles on the group and Yannis felt Phaedra slip her hand into his. He squeezed it reassuringly and placed his arm protectively around Anna.

Father Minos stepped forward and the German regarded him coldly. 'I have given orders that no boats are to come to this island. You are a devious people. I cannot trust you. You could bring men out here to form resistance groups, believing that my soldiers would be too scared to search them out and shoot them. I can assure you they would not be frightened to go amongst you. They would shoot you all. Feel grateful that I have spared your lives today.'

Father Minos looked at him in disbelief. 'You cannot be so inhumane. These people over here are sick. They need medicine as well as food. It is necessary for the people from the mainland to bring supplies out to us.'

'I see no people over here. All I see is a verminous populace of lepers. You spread your filthy sickness wherever you go. I would like to exterminate all of you. If you were in my beautiful country you would be sent to be cleansed, and your relatives with you. We know how to deal with unwanted humanity. You have heard my orders.' He raised his hand, indicating to the rowers that he was ready to leave.

'I beg you,' Father Minos fell to his knees and held his hands up imploringly, 'please allow food and medicine to be sent out to us. We are not criminals. We cannot help being sick. Please, do not treat us in this way. Have some compassion for your fellow.'

The German Commander curled his lip derisively, making the white scar that ran down his face show up more clearly. A shot rang out, followed by an uncanny silence as Father Minos stopped abruptly.

'If I have to order my man to shoot again he will be more accurate,' warned the German. 'Enough of this hysteria.' He pointed his finger at the islanders generally. 'Any fishing boat that leaves the harbour will be accompanied by soldiers. If it should come to my ears that you have given sanctuary to anyone on this island the repercussions on the mainland will not bear thinking about. There will be no one left to bring you supplies or know your fate.'

Father Minos continued to pray loudly and another shot was fired, this time landing very close to the priest. Yannis seized him by the arm.

'Please, Father, there's nothing you can do. Come and lead us in a prayer. We will need all our mental and physical strength to stay alive if that German carries out his threat.'

Manolis loaded up his boat, two boxes of bandages, twenty blankets to replace those that had become too soiled or worn to be of any further use, two sacks one of bread, the other of cheese and a bale of black material that Despina had requested. She had agreed to make trousers for the men who wanted to keep to the traditional style and not wear the new designs that were sold in the shops of Aghios Nikolaos. Their deformed and damaged fingers could not cope with the buttons. He wondered idly if he should call at Doctor Stavros's house and ask him if the girl he had taken over had been officially diagnosed. If she was free from leprosy he could collect her and take her back to Nikos and his wife.

He looked up at the sun. There was plenty of time; he had all day at his disposal. He walked up the hill rounded the corner and knocked on the door of the doctor's house. He stood patiently, then knocked again. The woman who lived opposite opened her door.

'He's not there. Went off early. Saw him go.'

Manolis raised his hand in thanks. He would not wait around. The doctor could be anywhere. He could always seek him out when he returned that evening and ask about the girl. Manolis frowned. Yannis had appeared quite reluctant for him and Phaedra to care for her in the first place, but now his attitude had changed, he seemed almost possessive. Maybe it had to do with the terrible news that Doctor Stavros had taken the previous week. According to Anna, her father was Yiorgo Pavlakis, the Mayor of Heraklion and Yannis's old school teacher. Yiorgo Pavlakis along with the other members of the government had been shot when Heraklion finally capitulated to the Germans.

Manolis heard the sound of marching feet. It sent a shiver down his spine. A woman opened her door and beckoned to him.

'Come in,' she urged.

'What's happening?'

'I've no idea, but you could be safer in here than on the street.'

The tramping feet drew nearer and Manolis hesitated no longer. He entered the woman's house and she locked the door behind him. An elderly man sat at the table, before him was a rifle and he was cleaning and reassembling it carefully.

'Are you going to fight?' Manolis asked him.

Sadly he shook his head. 'I'm too old, besides I haven't any bullets. I thought I'd give it to one of the young ones who are going off to join the resistance. Are you going to Lassithi?'

Manolis frowned. 'I'm a fisherman. I don't know how to handle a gun.'

'Might be a good time for you to find out,' he remarked dourly, wrapped the rifle in a piece of cloth and pushed it towards Manolis.

'I'm needed here,' Manolis said firmly. 'I take supplies to Spinalonga. I would be on my way there now if I hadn't come up to speak to the doctor.'

The woman held up her hand and all three stood in silence, the noise of the soldiers marching came closer, then began to recede. Manolis drew in his breath sharply. They had obviously continued up to the main square and were not entering the side streets. Cautiously he peered out of the window; the street appeared deserted.

'They've moved on. It should be safe enough for me to make my way back down to the harbour. Thank you for sheltering me.'

'Don't forget the gun,' the old man said.

Manolis looked at the woman uncertainly and she nodded.

She unlocked the door and bent her head close to Manolis. 'Please take it. If the Germans find it here they'll probably shoot him, even if he hasn't any bullets.'

Manolis took a swift glance up and down the deserted street. He moved from doorway to doorway, conscious of the rifle beneath his arm. He was puzzled. Had the woman panicked? Maybe they were British soldiers he had heard marching through the town, in which case he had nothing to fear. He reached the village square and stopped, his knees buckling beneath him at the sight that met his eyes.

Tied to each palm tree was a man. Standing in the back of an open jeep was a man haranguing them in Greek. As he finished his speech he gave a signal to the soldiers. Each one lifted his rifle and aimed at the helpless victims. A crescendo of noise erupted from the watching villagers and the soldiers shot into the crowd indiscriminately to quieten them.

Manolis found he was trembling and had an overwhelming desire to vomit. Slowly he walked backwards for a few steps, then began to run back down the road he had walked up a short while earlier. He would have to take the long way round to reach the harbour.

Reaching his boat safely Manolis stowed the rifle in the middle of the bale of cloth and cast off hurriedly. He sailed out to sea, deliberately making his way to where Dimitris was casting his nets.

'There are soldiers in the town.' he called. 'They've shot some people up in the square.'

Dimitris nodded sombrely. 'The Germans have marched down from Heraklion and joined up with the Italians.'

'Why have they come down here?'

'Who knows!'

'They may just be passing through,' said Manolis hopefully.

Dimitris shrugged and returned to his nets. He was thankful he did not have a wife or children. He planned to stay out at sea until it was dark. He would then slip back into the harbour and see if there were any soldiers still in the vicinity.

Manolis sailed out of the bay and along the arm of land before turning into the inlet that led to Spinalonga. He had formulated a plan in his head. He would sail round Spinalonga on the seaward side and after depositing his supplies and seeing Flora he would sail over to Plaka and moor up there for a few days.

As he began to tack towards the island he saw there was another boat standing off a short distance from the jetty. The occupants appeared to be in conversation with the islanders. He froze in horror as he realised the men were wearing a uniform and a rifle was pointed towards the gathering of people on the quay.

A shot rang out and he ducked instinctively. He raised himself on his hands and looked again at the boatload of soldiers. They had not even noticed him. Deftly he turned his sails to catch the wind and allowed it to carry him back out to sea.

Manolis cast his nets overboard automatically. He might as well fish whilst he waited until he considered it would be safe to return to the island. He continually looked back at Spinalonga, he was on the far side from the mainland, where the cliffs ran down sheer to the sea. There was no sign of movement, but that was not unusual. The islanders had little reason to go around to that bleak and inhospitable area.

He sailed further along, where he had a view of Plaka. All seemed quiet there, there were no sign of any soldiers and he could see someone working up in the fields; obviously the Germans had not found a reason to stay in the area. He changed the direction of his sails. He would call at the island and deposit the goods he was carrying, then go over to Plaka and moor up for a few days until he knew what the situation was in Aghios Nikolaos. The sight of the men tied to the trees had unnerved him.

He began to negotiate the wide inlet between the headland on the far side of Plaka and the island. He would have to be careful, there were submerged rocks and he did not know the waters on that side of the island. The wind began to drop and he furled in the sails, taking to the oars. Concentrating on avoiding the rocks he was taken by surprise when a shot rang out. He looked up in surprise.

There was no one in evidence on the island, but that did not mean that the Germans had not landed and slaughtered all the occupants. He sat there, his boat rocking gently in the swell. Another shot came and this time he looked at the headland, seeing the glint of binoculars. Hurriedly he began to row back towards the open sea.

He tacked along the length of the island and began to scan the other, much closer headland. If they decided to shoot at him from there they could hardly miss. Once again he saw the sun shining on binoculars. As he raised his sails a shot rang out and landed close to him in the water. He hesitated no longer, he started the motor and sped out to sea until he was sure he was out of their range. Once there he cut the motor and sat and considered his position.

His idea of staying at Plaka was obviously out of the question. He did not know why the Germans should guard the headlands and shoot at him, but nor was he going to go in any closer to find out. He calculated that they would be able to see him quite clearly through their binoculars and his best option was to continue with his fishing as if it were a normal day. He hoped they would realise he was no threat to them and leave him alone.

As he trawled his nets he inched closer and closer to the inlet, keeping a wary eye on the headland. As he came on a level with the land a shot landed in the water just ahead of him. Once again he started his motor and headed back out to sea. For whatever reason he was not going to be allowed near the island or in the sheltered bay at Plaka.

Perplexed and unhappy he allowed the wind to take him back towards Aghios Nikolaos. He stayed well away from the arm of land that jutted out, although he could see no sign of any soldiers on the seaward side. Once in view of the harbour he lowered his sails and began to row slowly towards the jetty where he moored his boat. He could see soldiers moving up and down on the waterfront and he frowned. He would have to land, he could not stay out in the harbour mouth forever.

As he tied the rope around the bollard a soldier stepped forward pointing a rifle at him. Slowly Manolis raised his hands. A second soldier stepped forward and jumped aboard, making the small craft rock wildly.

'You. Fish? Show.'

Manolis lowered his hands and pulled back the wet sacking that covered the buckets. The soldier wrinkled his nose and took a step backwards. He indicated that Manolis should place the buckets on the harbour wall and Manolis scowled at him. If they thought he was going to spend his time catching them fish for their supper they were mistaken.

He dumped the first three buckets up on the wall, making sure that as he placed the fourth one up there he misjudged the distance and it fell back into the harbour, taking its neighbour with it. He exclaimed in dismay and let out a torrent of abuse at himself for being so clumsy. The soldier sniggered and called to his companion.

'Come and collect these. This idiot has already knocked two back into the sea.'

The soldier slung his rifle over his back and lifted the buckets. 'What kind of fish are they?'

'No idea, but if he's bothered to bring them back they must be good to eat. Take them up and give them to Otto and Hans. They'll know what to do with them.'

Manolis watched resentfully as he saw his catch being taken away to feed the German army. He placed the remaining four buckets up on the wall, not daring to knock them into the sea again. The German clambered back onto the jetty and waited until his companion returned, then between them they carried away the remainder of Manolis's catch.

Manolis shook his fist at their retreating backs. He took some comfort in the knowledge that they had not searched his boat and taken away the bread, cheese and blankets he had stowed in the small cabin. He frowned. They could well come back for those later. He looked around and saw Lambros sitting disconsolately in his boat. No doubt the Germans had helped themselves to his catch also.

He climbed ashore and went over to him. 'Robbed you, did they?'

Lambros nodded. 'Held a rifle at me and demanded I gave it to them.'

Manolis stroked his chin. 'I was shot at whilst I was fishing,' he confided. 'I was up by the island. They've stationed soldiers on the headlands.'

'What for?'

'No idea. Have you heard anything down here?'

'I was told I wouldn't be allowed to go out again without an armed soldier on board. The same rule is going to apply to all of us.'

Manolis rolled his eyes. 'I wonder if any of them have been out in a fishing boat before? We could always throw them overboard,' he grinned.

Lambros shook his head. 'I imagine they'll make us stick close together. They'd see if we did anything like that.'

'So what are you going to do?' asked Manolis.

'There's nothing I can do,' he replied despondently. 'I've a wife and mother in law to think about. I can't leave them.'

'What about your son?"

'He's gone up towards Lassithi.'

'What's he going to do up there?'

'Resistance groups are forming. He plans to be a part of them. What about you?'

Manolis shrugged. 'I don't know.'

'I went up into the town when I first arrived back. They've shot the government, the shops are closed, and the people have barricaded themselves into their houses.'

'I saw they'd tied men to the palm trees up in the square. I didn't know it was the government, but I saw the soldiers shoot them.' Manolis looked around the small harbour, the fishermen were talking quietly together, keeping a wary eye on the watchful soldiers.

'Father Dhakanalis was up there trying to comfort their widows. He asked me to tell you he wanted to see you.'

Manolis raised his eyebrows, but Lambros had no further information. Maybe the priest would be able to give him some reassurance about the situation in the town or tell him where it would be safe for him to go.

He knocked on the side door and a novice peered out nervously at him.

'Good evening. May I see Father Dhakanalis, please? He left a message that he would like to speak to me.'

'The Father is at prayers. He is praying for the souls of the unfortunate men who were shot today.' The novice spoke in a whisper.

'I understand. I can wait for him until he feels he has completed his duty. May I come in? I would feel safer inside.' Manolis pushed at the door.

Uncertain the novice hesitated. 'I'm not sure. I ought to ask a superior.'

'I am requesting sanctuary.' Manolis knew the young man would not refuse such a demand.

Still the novice did not open the door any wider and Manolis felt annoyed. The priest had asked him to visit and now having asked for sanctuary he should have been admitted immediately and questions asked afterwards. 'I will wait just inside the door until Father Dhakanalis has time to speak to me. Please, let me in.'

Reluctantly the door was opened wider and Manolis slipped inside. He stood with his back to the door and the novice stood a short distance up the stone passage not taking his eyes off the fisherman.

'You will have to wait.'

'I understand that,' sighed Manolis. He sat on the wooden chair in the hall, but the novice made no move to leave the passage, effectively barring the way.

Finally the door to the Abbot's private room opened and he looked out warily. He relaxed visibly when he saw it was Manolis waiting and smiled at the novice. 'Thank you, Alexandros. I am available to visitors now.'

Manolis rose to his feet. 'Forgive me for intruding upon your prayers, Father.'

Father Dhakanalis smiled. 'You are not intruding, my son. Come in,' he held open the door of his parlour and Manolis entered cautiously. 'Please sit down. Do you have any news?'

Manolis felt embarrassed. 'Lambros said you had asked me to call on you. I wanted to ask if you had any news.' He swallowed. 'I saw what happened to the men this morning. When I tried to make my delivery to Spinalonga someone shot at me. I brought my catch back to the harbour and some German soldiers took it from me. Lambros told me that any boat that goes out will have an armed soldier aboard.' The words tumbled from him.

Father Dhakanalis sat on the hard chair before a small table. He placed his fingers together and looked at Manolis thoughtfully. 'I understand that the Germans have declared the island of Spinalonga to be under armed guard. They are concerned that it could be a gathering place for rebels. That is why they shot at you and why they will not let a fishing boat go out of the harbour without an armed escort.'

Manolis's face paled. 'But the people on Spinalonga; what will happen to them? They need food and water, their medical supplies. What about Doctor Stavros? Will he be allowed to visit his patients?'

Father Dhakanalis crossed himself. 'I will pray that the restrictions do not last very long.'

'There must be something we can do?'

Father Dhakanalis shook his head. 'We have to obey them. If we go against their instructions they could be vindictive.'

'We have to fight them.' Manolis spoke vehemently. He leant forward confidentially. 'I have a rifle on my boat. It was given to me this morning by an old man. I have some money in the bank. I could get some ammunition for it and some more guns and we could fight them.'

Father Dhakanalis shook his head. 'I trust you not to do

anything foolhardy, Manolis. You could lose your own life and endanger the lives of other innocent people.'

'You mean they might shoot them – as they did the government?'

'Exactly. There are often other more effective ways to fight them than shooting a rifle.'

'How?'

Father Dhakanalis regarded Manolis steadily. 'How far can I trust you? Can I trust you with my life? Can I trust you with the lives of others? Answer me honestly, please. Remember you are in the sight of God. He will know if you are lying, even if I don't.'

'I don't know what you want me to answer. I would never hurt anyone intentionally, but if I had to defend myself I would do so.'

'Suppose you were in excruciating pain, the only way of relieving yourself of this pain would be to expose others to it. What would you do?'

Manolis shook his head. 'I don't know.' He leant forward earnestly. 'If it was someone I cared about a great deal I would do everything in my power to spare them pain, but if they were strangers to me I would probably be a coward.'

'An honest answer,' Father Dhakanalis smiled for the first time. 'So if I asked you to do something for me that could end up with you suffering pain what would your answer be?'

'I would ask first what it was that you wanted me to do. Would it be worth suffering for?'

'Would you be willing to take a message for me?'

'Of course,' Manolis replied unhesitatingly.

'It could be difficult. I believe the person I need to contact is at Pahia Amnos. I have no idea if the Germans or Italians are in the area. If they are, the person may well have moved elsewhere. You will need to sail into the bay, make your way to the church and ask for Father Constantine. You would tell him I have sent you.'

'If you give me the message I will do my best to deliver it,' promised Manolis.

'That is the message.' Father Dhakanalis smiled at the puzzled look on Manolis's face. 'He will know he can trust you. He may give you a message for someone else, ask you to deliver a package if it is in his possession, or take a passenger aboard your boat.'

'Suppose I'm stopped by a German patrol?'

Father Dhakanalis shrugged. 'You are a simple fisherman, trying to continue with your livelihood. You have lost your way, been blown off course, sailed further than you intended. Whatever little fabrication seems the most believable at the time.'

Manolis looked at the priest dubiously. 'I doubt that they would believe me. Fishermen do not get lost.'

'They are not going to be familiar with the weather conditions or currents for some months. We need to take advantage of their ignorance whilst we can. Can I rely on you, Manolis? The sooner we manage to rid our country of these infidels the sooner you will be able to resume your duties to the island. Any package you will be given is very important, if you are stopped once you have collected it you must dispose of it. Do not let it fall into the enemies' hands.'

Manolis frowned. 'What's in this package?'

'A small piece of equipment that is vital. Someone is waiting for it. No doubt Father Constantine will tell you where to deliver it.' Father Dhakanalis sat back in his chair and watched Manolis carefully. He knew of the young man's association with a girl on the island and did not doubt that he would be anxious to relieve the situation and continue his daily visits.

'When do you want me to leave?'

'I think tonight would be best. The troops are still somewhat disorganised. It should be simple enough for you to slip back to your home and collect a change of clothing. I would prefer it if you did not tell your relatives about our conversation.'

Manolis returned to the harbour with his spare shirts and trousers rolled up beneath his arm. He had slipped on his jacket, despite the warmth of the evening. There had been no sign of his aunt or uncle and he hoped they were spending the evening with neighbours, gossiping over the events of the day. He had left the money due to his aunt for his keep on the table, and placed his remaining few drachmas in his pocket. Deciding that to take his bankbook was unnecessary, he left it safely in its hiding place under a floorboard beneath his mattress.

He pushed his clothes into the small hold and hoped they would not smell too strongly of fish when he needed them and looked around cautiously. There were only two other boats in the harbour that had a motor, one had belonged to Yiorgo before he had left for America and it now sat sadly at its moorings. He looked at it longingly. It was sad to see the once proud craft chained up and neglected.

Manolis decided he would delay leaving the harbour no longer. He would take advantage of the clouds that were drifting across the night sky and obscuring the light from the moon intermittently. He had tied two sacks to the oars, hoping they would serve to muffle the sound of his rowing until he was far enough out that bullets would not reach him. He was not prepared to risk raising his white sails and drawing attention to himself, and he dared not use the motor as the sound would travel across the water in the quiet night.

Manolis untied his mooring rope and laid it carefully on the quay rather than letting it drop into the water as usual. He pushed himself away slowly from the wall of the jetty, then began to row with long, deep strokes, allowing the boat to glide as far as possible before taking another pull. The whole time he strained his eyes to see if anyone was pursuing him, although certain he would have heard some shouting and probably gunfire.

It was not until he was well out in the bay that he felt he could relax for a short while. He wiped the sweat from his brow on the sleeve of his shirt and proceeded to raise his sails. It should be safe enough now to take advantage of the breeze and go further out to sea. He was suddenly hungry, realising that he had not eaten since early that morning. He opened the sack of bread and took out the loaf that was hardening at the top. With his fishing knife he cut a thick slice and poured a little of his water on to moisten it. He added a generous slice from a round of cheese and began to munch contentedly.

In the darkness he had no idea of his direction. For all he knew he could be drifting out into the middle of the sea, out of the sight of land, and then he would have no idea which way to head. The thought sobered him and he took in his sails rapidly and threw his anchor overboard. It would make sense to stay where he was and get some sleep. When the sun rose he would be able to ascertain a rough bearing, he might even be able to see some land and he could make his way in that direction.

Thankful that he had been taking blankets to Spinalonga, he placed one beneath his head and rolled himself in another. At least he would be warm and it would certainly be no more uncomfortable than the thin and lumpy mattress he slept on at his aunt and uncle's house. He felt a pang of guilt. They would have no idea what had happened to him. He doubted that they would be concerned for a few days, and he could well have returned by the end of a week.

The sun rose, painting the sky a vivid red streaked with navy clouds. Manolis opened his eyes, squinting in the brightness and wondering at first where he was. He took a couple of mouthfuls of water. He must make it last until he made land and was able to replenish his supplies. He softened another piece of the hard bread and chewed at it slowly, before throwing the remainder of the loaf overboard. It was too hard to be of any use and he hoped that if he delved into the centre of the sack later in the day he would find one that was softer.

He wished he had seen Doctor Stavros before leaving and could have asked him to pass a message to Flora for him. Deciding he must sit no longer; he raised his sails and set a course that should take him across the mouth of the bay towards Pahia Amnos. He had no clear idea where he was, but he could see the coastline clearly and was sure he could make out some buildings in a fold of the hills.

He drew into a small, deserted bay and walked up the path that led to the top of the low cliff. From there he could see the straggle of stone cottages that made up the village. At the far end and standing a little apart was a small church. As he approached a man barred his way.

'Where have you come from?'

'I've sailed from Aghios Nikolaos. Father Dhakanalis asked me to visit Father Constantine.'

The man frowned. 'Why would he want you to do that?'

'He didn't give a reason.' Manolis shrugged. 'I assume he just wanted to know his colleague was keeping well.'

The priest appeared in the doorway of the church. He had obviously been standing there listening to the interchange between the two men. He stepped forward and extended his hand to Manolis.

'Thank you, Christos.' He waved his hand in dismissal to the villager. 'So, Father Dhakanalis sent you?'

'Yes, Father.'

'What was his message for me?'

Manolis frowned. 'I asked him and he said I was his message. That you would know you could trust me as I had come from him.'

Father Constantine nodded. 'I presume as you are a fisherman you have your boat with you?'

'It's down in the bay at the bottom of the cliffs.'

'I am sorry you have had a wasted journey.'

Manolis frowned. 'What do you mean? A wasted journey.'

'The package could not be left here. The Germans were patrolling the area and it was decided to take it on to Mohlos. It should be there awaiting collection.'

'What do you want me to do when I reach Mohlos?'

'Make yourself known to the priest. He will be able to advise you of the whereabouts of the package. Do you know where Mohlos is situated?' asked Father Constantine.

'Further round the bay. I was born there.'

'Really? So you know the area?' The priest raised his eyebrows in surprise.

Manolis shook his head. 'My father took me to Aghios Nikolaos when I was a baby. My mother had died. We went to live with my aunt and uncle.'

Father Constantine crossed himself. 'Very sad,' he murmured.

Manolis bade Father Constantine farewell, filled his water bottles from the village pump and returned to his boat. Once there he cursed himself for a fool. He should have asked for some fresh bread to take on his journey, but no doubt he would be able to buy some when he reached Mohlos. The journey should take no more than a few hours and he would not starve in the meantime.

Basil drove along warily. He motored through vineyards, olive groves and orchards, keeping as close to the coast as he was able, knowing he would have to make long detours if he went inland and also wishing to save his precious petrol. He did not relish having to walk with the unwieldy coffin in his arms. He emerged from amongst some orange trees carefully, looking for any sign that there were Germans patrolling that stretch of the coast.

He had almost reached the dirt road that ran up to the fishing village when he spotted the uniformed men gathered together beneath a clump of trees. They had a map spread out and were looking at it, obviously trying to decide exactly where they were.

Basil drove back the way he had come and abandoned his cart. He approached briskly on foot until he reached the group of soldiers. 'Good Morning,' he called and they turned and looked at him. A hurried conversation took place between them and one approached him as he began to walk away.

He shook the map at Basil. 'Mohlos,' he said.

Basil pretended to consider, then took the map from the man's hand and placed it on the ground. He pointed to the village, then at the soldier and down the track he had just traversed and back again at the map. He hoped the foreigner would understand he was being told he had missed the turn off and would need to retrace a considerable part of his journey. After Basil had repeated himself a number of times and left some very dirty marks on the map, partially obliterating the names of the villages, the soldier appeared to understand. He called to his companions and they shouldered their arms and began to walk off in the direction Basil had indicated.

Basil watched them go with a smile on his face. Once they were out of sight he hurried up the dirt road and entered Mohlos. He made his way to the church and sought out Father Yiannis. He advised him that the soldiers were planning a visit, and also asked him to relay a message to any boatman that put in an appearance. He would drive on to Liopetra, provided the area was safe he would hide up there until the boatman arrived.

As his boat sped easily across the water Manolis screwed up his eyes and squinted into the distance. He could see land a short distance away and began to steer towards it. A few small fishing boats were pulled up on the rocky shore and Manolis nosed his craft in behind them and hoped no one would notice his. A steep path ran up the cliffs and he could only guess that it led eventually to a village. Idly he wondered if he would pass the ruins of the house where he had been born and if there was a cemetery where he would see a headstone in memory of his mother. He checked his mooring line was firm, attached his water bottle to his belt, said a silent prayer for his safety, and jumped ashore.

His boots slipped on the stony surface and the sun beat down relentlessly on his back as he climbed. He stopped frequently to mop his brown and have a mouthful of water before the path began to level out and in the distance he could see a scattering of small buildings. The area appeared to be deserted and he wondered what he should do if he did not find the priest at the church. From where he was standing he could not even see a sign of the religious building and he thought he must have landed in the wrong area.

Manolis walked on doggedly. He would ask at the first occupied house he came to, rather than turn back now and have to climb another cliff path. Each house he approached had their shutters closed and no one answered his knock on the door. Disconsolately he continued on his way, although not convinced he was at his intended destination.

He rounded another corner and another small group of houses came into view. Standing alone on a small rise was the church and his hopes soared. He rubbed his arm across his sweaty face and had another mouthful of water before striding out towards it. As he passed the houses he had the distinct impression that he was being watched, but he saw no one. Arriving at the church he was relieved to find the door opened at his touch and he was able to enter the cool interior. He stood there, revelling in the coolness and allowing his eyes to become accustomed to the dimness. There was no sign of the priest, but there was the smell of burnt candle wax and he touched the blackened wick, convinced it still felt warm to his fingers. He sat on a wooden chair to rest and also to wait, convinced that someone would enter eventually.

Half an hour later he was still sitting there, wishing he had brought some cheese with him and another bottle of water. He no longer appreciated the coolness of the church but was beginning to feel chilled. It could make more sense to sit outside in the sunshine until he was warm again. He would be able to see if anyone approached and ask directions to Mohlos. He rose to his feet and walked quietly to the door and back out into the glare of the sun.

Before his eyes had a chance to adjust to the brightness, he found he was looking into the barrel of a rifle. Slowly he lifted his hands. Four men surrounded him, one with a rifle, two with knives and the other with a length of wood. They had obviously seen him arrive and been waiting for him to leave the church.

'I'm looking for the priest,' Manolis managed to say, hoping the fear he felt did not manifest itself in his voice.

The man with the rifle tilted his head towards the man holding the wooden club, who nodded and walked off towards one of the houses.

'Can I put my hands down, please?'

'Are you carrying any weapons?'

'My fishing knife.'

Again the man nodded to one of his companions who stepped forward and removed the knife from the leather sheath that was attached to Manolis's belt.

'You can put your hands down now.'

Manolis lowered them gratefully. His mouth felt dry, but he did not want to risk asking if he could have a drink. The man might think he was attempting to reach a hidden weapon and he had no desire to be shot, particularly at such close quarters.

It seemed an age before Manolis saw the man accompanied by an elderly priest walking towards the church. He heaved a sigh of relief, hoping this was Father Yiannis. The priest stood a short distance away and scrutinized Manolis carefully, finally he smiled and held out his hand.

'You are welcome. Please come with me to the house for some refreshment.'

The men relinquished their threatening positions, but Manolis's fishing knife was not returned to him. Together the small group walked from the church to the nearest house and the door was opened for Manolis to enter. The priest indicated that he should sit, whilst he busied himself with finding glasses and a bottle of raki. He poured a generous measure for each man, then raised his glass.

'To freedom,' he said and the men repeated his words, including Manolis, and drained the glasses in one swallow.

The men placed their glasses on the table and left the room, leaving Manolis and the priest alone, although Manolis was convinced they were waiting outside.

The priest leaned forward confidentially. 'I am Father Yiannis. I understand you were expecting to collect a package from Pahia Amnos.'

Manolis nodded. 'I was told it had been sent here as Pahia Amnos was not safe.'

'I regret I do not have it. Fortunately the carrier learnt that the Germans planned to make a visit to the town. He decided it was too risky to remain here. He is hoping to find a safe bay between here and Liopetra where he can rest and wait for you. There you will collect him and the package.'

'How will I know where he is?'

'You will have to wait at the mouth of a bay and if he is there he will give you a signal. If there is no sign after a reasonable amount of time you will have to sail on to the next one.'

'How far away is Liopetra?'

The priest shrugged. 'I do not know. I have never been there. I understand that you need to sail across this bay and also across the next large one. You then reach Liopetra. I have been given a rough map to pass on to you.'

'Why haven't you sent one of the fishermen from your village?'

'Did you examine the boats that were on the beach?'

Manolis shook his head.

'A detachment of soldiers visited us earlier; they holed the boats.'

'Why did they do that?'

'They thought we might take andartes out to Psira Island. They were also taking out their spite on us as they had been directed away from the village by a farmer.' The priest chuckled.

'Suppose the soldiers have found him at Liopetra?'

'That is most unlikely. They had already passed through the area on their way here and found no one. If you do not receive a signal from one of the bays it could be worth your while to make your way up to the old fortress. He could be waiting for you there.'

'And if there is no one?'

Father Yiannis smiled confidently. 'I am quite sure you will find him eventually.'

Manolis slipped and slithered back down the path towards the beach where he had left his boat. Once the priest had vouched for him, the men who had held him captive were friendly, returned his fishing knife, and invited him to stay and share a meal with them. He was tempted, but refused, accepting a loaf of bread and some olives to carry on his journey. It was early afternoon and one of the men had drawn him a rough map, assuring him it should be possible for him to reach Liopetra before dark. Curiously he examined the boats that lay abandoned on the beach before he cast off. Each one had a row of bullet holes along the side.

Manolis sailed for the remainder of the afternoon. He moored and waited at the mouth of every small inlet or cleft between the rocks that he saw, but no one signalled to him. He continued to sail whilst the sun moved round in the sky until it was at his back. He looked at the rough map again. It was devoid of landmarks and having sailed in and out of small bays he was not at all sure where he was. He was certain he had not sailed around the promontory that the man had indicated, so obviously he had not reached Liopetra yet, the fortress was further away than he had realised.

He chewed disconsolately on some fresh bread and a piece of cheese, washing it down with a long draught of water. He would have liked to pour some over his head to cool himself down, but dared not waste a drop. He had three quarters of a bottle left and that would have to last him until he made land and he was able to replenish his supply.

The sun was dipping in the sky and Manolis knew he would have no more than half an hour of light left in which to search. He reconciled himself to spending another night at sea; he had no lights and would not have dared to use them for fear of being spotted by soldiers on the mainland. He had not seen any other craft in the area, but there was always the danger that another fisherman would be travelling at night and he would be mown down. He pulled a couple of blankets from the hold and once again proceeded to make himself as comfortable as he could.

Basil chuckled to himself as he drove towards Liopetra. He had sent the Germans half way back to Pahia Amnos, smudged the map with the dirt from his finger and torn a small hole with his fingernail as he had folded it and handed it back. It was quite possible they would take the path that led to Tholos rather than Mohlos.

He continued on his way, riding slowly over the rough ground. There were hardly any cart tracks to use and he did not want to have to divert to the mountain passes, not at all sure if the motor on the cart would be capable of tackling the steep inclines.

The whole area appeared to be deserted and he had almost reached Liopetra, congratulating himself that he was making good time and would be able to find a safe place to spend the night, when the front wheel of the cart hit a stone and buckled. Basil looked at it in dismay. There was no way he could straighten it without tools, nor could he expect to drive it until it had been repaired. Disgusted with himself for his momentary lapse of concentration he hauled the coffin off the back, balanced it on his shoulder and began to walk.

At first he strode out purposefully, but within half an hour his pace had slowed. It was hot and the ground he was walking over was covered in prickly scrub, catching at his boots and tripping him. He began to count his paces before he would stop, mop his brow, have a sip of water and shift the coffin to the other shoulder. By the time he reached the ruins of Liopetra fortress he decided he could certainly not carry the coffin any further. He pushed and pulled it up a steep incline where a ruined wall stood as high as his head. Beneath it lay a scattering of stones that had fallen from higher up. Basil placed the coffin next to the wall and began the tedious job of collecting the stones and covering it completely.

An hour later he stood back and admired his handiwork. The heap of debris looked natural. He shook his water bottle, depressed to find that there was hardly anything left and he knew of nowhere in the vicinity where he could replenish it. With a deep sigh he made the decision to walk on to Sitia. He could not sit and wait at Liopetra without water for an indefinite period of time. The boatman might never turn up.

Father Michaelis in Sitia had known Basil when he and Douglas had worked in the area. He sent for food and wine and allowed Basil to eat and drink his fill before he asked what had brought him to the area. Tired and dispirited Basil related the events of the last few days, admitted he was trying to deliver a wireless to Toplou and depressed that he had not yet managed to liaise with the boatman that Father Dhakanalis had assured him would be willing to help.

Father Michaelis frowned. 'Do you think he is reliable? Maybe he has decided to hole up in a deserted bay and will eventually return to Aghios Nikolaos and say he could not find you.'

Basil sighed. 'That could well be the case. Would one of your fishermen be willing to take me?'

'I'm sure they would – if they had a serviceable boat. The harbour is being strictly guarded. The whole area has been put off limits. No one is even allowed on the water front. Any boats the soldiers found hidden away they holed.'

'So I have no choice but to walk the rest of the way.' Basil spoke despondently.

'You say the wireless is well hidden at Liopetra?'

Basil nodded.

'Then I suggest you remain here over night, get some rest. I will send a couple of trustworthy men out to scout the coast line and see if there is any sign of a fishing boat in the area. If this boatman has still not turned up by the following morning then I fear you have no choice.'

Reluctantly Basil had to agree that the priest was being practical. He was exhausted. The thought of having to walk back to Liopetra the following morning and then make the journey on to Toplou carrying the wireless was daunting. He would have to travel cross country, probably having to take cover and needing to hide his burden frequently. Father Michaelis had informed him the whole area was swarming with Italian troops, some had moved towards Aghios Nikolaos, but hundreds were billeted in the area guarding the bay at Sitia.

When the sun rose Manolis scanned the coastline hoping he would see some sign of a fortress, even ruins would be comforting and he would know he was in the right area. He sailed closer to the shore, hoping he would see an inlet and find someone waiting for him. From the corner of his eye he caught a flash of light. The man he was to collect must have been looking out for him and was sending him a signal. He had almost reached the small beach when a shot rang out, narrowly missing his sails. Soldiers suddenly emerged from behind the rocks, their rifles pointed in his direction. For a moment he stood transfixed, then started his motor and headed back out to sea. Shots followed him, but although they landed close to his vessel, they did not find their mark.

Once having reached what he considered to be a safe distance from the shore he cut the motor, and sat and considered his position. The priest had assured him that the soldiers had already moved through the area of Liopetra. He had obviously not yet reached his intended destination. Keeping well out at sea and praying that no patrol would follow him he sailed on down the coast.

Within an hour a finger of land pointing out to sea came into view and he smiled and looked at the crude map again. The time he had taken searching all the inlets had made him misjudge the distance he had travelled. He was obviously nowhere near Liopetra yet. He sailed out and round the headland and into another bay. Cautiously he crept in closer to the shore, rugged cliffs came down into the water, with no sign of a safe landing place and also no sign of human habitation. Manolis shrugged in frustration. The men obviously had no idea how far away Liopetra was from Mohlos. He sipped a little more water; he must be very sparing with it now as there was so little remaining.

Steering a steady course, he studied the coastline for an area of comparative safety where he could land. The sun was rising higher in the sky and the heat of the day was increasing. It was essential that he went ashore and found somewhere to land and refill his water bottles as quickly as possible. He rounded another headland and immediately the area looked a little more hospitable.

With his hopes rising he looked for a small town or village where he would be able to moor, ask directions of a local fisherman and buy some more fresh bread. He had a sudden longing to add a tomato to his mid-day meal. Scanning the coast anxiously he finally saw a small inlet and made his way towards it, lowering his sails and rowing the remaining distance, watching for submerged rocks. His boat grounded on the sand and he jumped ashore, pulling the craft as far onto the beach as he was able and dropping the anchor.

For a while he watched to ensure that it did not begin to drift back into the sea, and once he was certain that it was as safe as possible he made his way towards the path that ran up between the low cliffs.

He had not covered more than a few yards when he heard a

noise behind him. He spun round, his hand on his fishing knife, to see a man holding a rifle barring his path. Slowly Manolis raised his hands.

'Who are you?'

'I'm a fisherman.'

The man lowered his gun. 'What's your name?'

'Manolis, Manolis the fisherman.'

'I'm Tassos. Sit down and we'll talk.'

'I only came ashore to look for some water.' Manolis held up his empty bottle.

Tassos handed Manolis the bottle that hung from his belt and he took a long drink, wiping his mouth with the back of his hand and sighing with relief before handing it back. Tassos lowered himself to the ground and sat with his rifle across his knees. Manolis went to sit beside him and as he did so he saw the man had a companion who was blocking his route back to the beach, a hunting knife in his hand.

'Who's that?' asked Manolis.

'My brother, Kyriakos.'

Manolis inclined his head by way of a greeting. 'I really only want to fill my water bottle.'

'All in good time. Where have you come from?'

'Aghios Nikolaos.'

'What made you come here? The Italians took over the town three days ago.'

'Father Dhakanalis in Aghios Nikolaos asked me to carry a message for him. Each time I've tried to deliver it I've been asked to go elsewhere. I don't actually know where I am now. I was making for Liopetra. Could I have some more water, please?'

The man handed over his water bottle again. 'This is Sitia, you're just a short distance from the town.'

'So which way is Liopetra from here?'

'Back there somewhere.' Tassos jerked his thumb.

Manolis frowned. 'I obviously sailed out too far.'

'Why were you going there anyway?'

'I was told I would definitely be able to deliver my message there. The area was safe. The Germans had already searched it and moved on.'

The man holding the hunting knife spoke for the first time. 'Are you coming with us to fight?'

'Fight? Fight where?'

'We're going up into the mountains to join the other men. You could come with us.'

Manolis shook his head. 'I can't leave my boat. It's all I have in the world. If I lose that I can't make my living as a fisherman.'

'So you're going to stay here and catch fish to keep the German's bellies filled?'

Manolis spoke scornfully. 'If I'd wanted to do that I could have stayed in Aghios Nikolaos. I'm happy to supply the villagers with fish, but not the Germans. Do you have a priest here I could speak with?'

The two men exchanged glances, and Tassos nodded. 'Father Michaelis would probably like to see you.'

'Where is he?' asked Manolis eagerly.

'At the church.'

'Can you take me there?'

Tassos rose to his feet. 'We'll take you as far as we can. If we run into trouble you're on your own,' he warned.

Manolis swallowed nervously. He was not sure if he trusted these two men, but he felt he had little choice except to follow where they led. If they did plan to steal his boat he would be powerless to stop them.

Tassos placed a finger on his lips and Manolis nodded. He felt like a prisoner as he walked in single file between the two of them up the hillside. At the brow of the hill Tassos held up his hand for them to stop. Manolis felt pressure on his shoulder and obediently dropped to the ground. Tassos wriggled forward on his stomach whilst Kyriakos kept his hand on Manolis's shoulder indicating that he should stay where he was. Finally Tassos rose to his feet again and beckoned to them to follow.

They walked a considerably distance into the countryside before Tassos halted and turned to face Manolis. 'Wait here,' he ordered. 'I'll go and speak to Father Michaelis.' He passed his rifle to Kyriakos and indicated that both men should sit in the shade of the low stone wall.

Manolis sank onto the grass; he was not used to walking over rough countryside. He wiped his forehead with his arm and grinned at Kyriakos. Kyriakos did not return the smile, but sat with the rifle pointing towards Manolis, giving him even less confidence in his companions. He rested his head down on his arms, trying to suppress a yawn. He was beginning to wish that he had never left Aghios Nikolaos. He gave a deep sigh and stretched his aching legs.

'If you try to run away I shall shoot you,' warned Kyriakos.

'Why should I want to run away and where would I run to?' asked Manolis.

Kyriakos shrugged. 'I'm just warning you.'

'How long will it be before your brother returns?'

'When he has spoken with Father Michaelis.'

'Can I lie down and sleep for a while?'

Kyriakos regarded him scornfully. 'If a short walk like that tires you out you'd be useless in the mountains.'

'I didn't get much sleep last night,' Manolis answered sulkily, 'and I'm not used to walking over the hills,' he added, turned his back on Kyriakos and settled himself as comfortably as possible. Tassos finally reappeared as the sun was dropping in the sky. He tapped the sole of Manolis's boot with his foot. 'We'll go now.'

Manolis looked up in surprise. He had obviously been asleep for some while. Kyriakos was nowhere to be seen and Tassos now had the rifle slung over his shoulder.

'Where are you taking me?'

'To Father Michaelis,' answered Tassos impatiently.

Manolis rose to his feet and brushed his trousers down. 'Is it far?' As he stood he realised his feet were hurting from the unaccustomed exercise and he hoped they were not blistered.

Tassos sniggered. 'If you can't walk I'm not carrying you.'

'I can walk,' Manolis assured him. 'I'd like some more water before we start, though.'

Tassos handed over his water bottle again. It was full and Manolis guessed that he had taken the time to fill it whilst searching out the priest. He went to hand it back and Tassos waved his hand. 'Keep it. I have another.'

He began to walk away as Manolis attached the bottle to his belt and Manolis forced himself to hurry after him. After a short distance they turned into a dry river bed with rounded boulders and sharp stones interspersed between them. Tassos appeared to have no problem striding from boulder to boulder, but Manolis found himself slipping and slithering, often ending up walking on the stones that cut into his boots and aggravated his sore feet further. By the time they reached a small bridge he was limping and pleased to see that signs of habitation were appearing in the distance.

From beneath the bridge Kyriakos emerged and beckoned Manolis forward. 'Follow me,' he directed. 'Not a word and keep your head down. If we're stopped I shall say you are my deaf and dumb brother.'

Manolis nodded. He really did not care very much any more. His feet were throbbing and he wanted desperately to remove his boots. He walked beside Kyriakos in silence for a further ten minutes before his escort pointed and began to scramble up the bank towards the stone wall, behind which he could espy the dome of a small church surmounted with a cross. Slowly and carefully Kyriakos inched his way along the wall until he came to an archway with a wooden gate. He pushed it open and signalled to Manolis to follow him. Once inside the courtyard he seemed to relax a little.

'Father Michaelis is waiting for you in the church,' he whispered.

'How will I find my way back to my boat?' asked Manolis anxiously, but Kyriakos had disappeared back through the gate.

Tentatively Manolis walked across the courtyard and entered the small church. He crossed himself automatically and waited for his eyes to become accustomed to the dim light that penetrated from the open door and small windows. Eventually he was able to make out the shape of a priest in his black robes standing before the altar and he approached him hesitantly.

'You are welcome, my son.' The priest spoke hardly above a whisper. 'Follow me.'

Feeling far more confident in the presence of the priest Manolis followed him to a side door that he unlocked with a key from the pocket in his cassock. The room was sparsely furnished with a wooden table and chairs and the priest indicated that he was to sit. Gratefully Manolis did so and was surprised when a glass of wine was pressed into his hand.

'Thank you, Father.'

'No doubt you are hungry.' The priest pointed to some covered dishes on the table. 'Please eat your fill and we will talk afterwards.'

Manolis realised that he was indeed very hungry. He lifted the covers from the plates and heaped food onto a plate, eating ravenously. Whilst he ate he tried to calculate how long he had gone without food. You could hardly count half a stale loaf and round of cheese. He sipped slowly at the wine. He did not want it to go to his head and make him disgrace himself before the priest. Finally he sat back, trying to suppress a belch.

The priest regarded him gravely. 'I am Father Michaelis. I understand from Tassos that you are a fisherman. Where have you come from?'

'Aghios Nikolaos.'

'That is a very long way to sail,' observed Father Michaelis and raised his eyebrows. 'Please tell me exactly why you left there and sailed here.'

'I deliver goods to the island just off the shore from Aghios Nikolaos and fish on the way back. I walked up to the doctor's house to see if he wanted me to take anything over, but he wasn't there. As I walked back down to the harbour I saw there were men tied to the palm trees in the square. I found out later they had been shot.'

Father Michaelis crossed himself. 'May their souls rest in peace.' The priest replenished Manolis's wine and poured a glass for himself. 'Tell me about yourself,' he commanded softly.

Manolis shrugged. 'I'm a fisherman.'

'And were you delivering fish to this island when shots were fired at you?'

Manolis shook his head. 'They could catch their own fish if they wanted. I take other supplies; bandages, mattresses, blankets, whatever they have asked for or the doctor says they need.'

'And what were you trying to deliver on this occasion?'

'Some fresh bread, cheese, blankets and material.'

'Material?'

'One of the women has offered to make trousers in the old style for the men.'

Father Michaelis raised eyebrows. 'What is the name of this island where you make these deliveries?'

Manolis swallowed. 'Spinalonga.'

The priest crossed himself again. 'May the Lord have pity on their plight.' He frowned. 'I am at a loss to know why you should be shot at if you were only making a delivery of everyday items.'

'I don't know either, Father. Another fisherman said they were not going to let anyone go to sea without an armed escort. Father Constantine at Pahia Amnos told me the Germans were concerned that the island would be used by andartes.'

Father Michaelis waved his hand. 'We will talk more about

that later. I wish to have more information about you. How long have you been visiting the island?'

'Some years now.'

'And you go ashore?'

Manolis hoped the priest was not going to ask him if he had a particular liking for any of the women. 'Every day. They were awarded a small pension by the government and I act as their book-keeper. I make a list of the goods they request, purchase them on the mainland, keep the receipts and deduct the amount from their individual accounts.'

'And one of them had requested some blankets?'

'No,' Manolis shook his head. 'Spiro, the man who runs the hospital over there said he needed some more. Those come from the fund held by the church.'

'And he had also asked for the bandages?'

'No,' again Manolis shook his head. 'Doctor Stavros had ordered those to be taken out. I take him out each week to visit the islanders.'

'You have no qualms about dealing with these people? You do not fear that you too may become sick?'

'I am very careful when I deal with them.'

The priest nodded. 'Very wise. So, in fact, you are more than a simple fisherman or delivery boy. You have been given a position of trust by the doctor and the church.'

'And the government,' added Manolis. 'I get a weekly wage for acting as their book-keeper.'

'So three very important bodies have placed their trust in you. Am I able to trust you?'

Manolis looked hurt. 'Of course. Father Dhakanalis trusted me to go to Father Constantine and I was sailing to Liopetra at the request of Father Yiannis.'

Father Michaelis raised his eyebrows. 'Why should he ask you to go there?'

'I understood I was to collect a passenger with a package.'

'And where were you to take this passenger?'

'I have no idea. I was told he had moved on from Pahia Amnos to Mohlos and then to Liopetra. Father Yiannis told me the soldiers had moved through Liopetra and the area was safe. I thought I saw a signal from a cove, but when I made for the beach there were soldiers everywhere and they shot at me. I decided I hadn't reached Liopetra, but the men told me I had sailed past it.' Manolis frowned. 'I don't know what to do now.'

Father Michaelis smiled. 'Are you still willing to take this person to wherever he wishes to go?'

'If I can find him,' replied Manolis gloomily.

Father Michaelis nodded. 'It could end up saving the lives of many gallant men. Men who have fought unsuccessfully to defend Crete from these barbarians who have invaded us. They deserve to be delivered to safety, either to die in peace from their wounds or be reunited again eventually with their families.'

'Where do you want me to take them?'

'No, I am not asking you to take them anywhere. I know where your intended passenger is waiting for you. I am asking you to take him to his destination. He has a very important delivery to make. If either of you are caught with it in your possession you will be shot immediately or tortured until you reveal who gave it to you.'

Manolis felt his mouth go dry with fear. He took another mouthful of the wine. 'What is it?'

'A wireless,' Father Michaelis whispered.

Manolis frowned. 'A wireless? What for?'

Father Michaelis leaned forward. 'I am trusting you with this information. If there are repercussions I will know who is to blame.'

'You can trust me, Father.'

The priest relaxed back in his chair. 'Where are you?'

Manolis looked surprised. 'In your room at the church.'

'And where is that? What is the name of the church? The name of the village?'

Manolis shook his head. 'I don't know.'

'Good. That is as it should be. You cannot give information that you do not possess. Your passenger has a wireless that needs to be moved to a safe destination.'

'Where's that?'

The priest waved his arm airily. 'Further round from Sitia.'

'Are there Germans or Italians there?'

'I would expect them to be in the vicinity, which is why I am asking you to take it.'

'So that I can get shot!' Manolis shook his head. 'I don't think so, Father.'

Father Michaelis held up his hand. 'I am asking you to take it by sea. The hiding place is no great distance from here, but it is too dangerous for the carrier to take it any further overland. We do not know where the invaders are hiding. He could walk straight into a trap. The wireless is essential. We need to be in contact with the British in Egypt. They will send ships to rescue the stranded troops, but we need to know when they will come and be ready to embark immediately. Many lives are at risk and the wireless is needed as quickly as possible.'

Manolis sat back, finished his glass of wine, and shook his head. 'I don't know,' he said doubtfully.

'What don't you know? Whether you have the courage to make a simple journey by sea for the sake of others?'

'No. It's not that, really. I have no idea where I am or to where I would have to sail. I'm not familiar with these waters. I could end up hitting rocks and losing your precious wireless overboard.'

'Your companion will be able to direct you.'

'Why don't you ask one of your local fishermen to take him?'

'They are under the same restrictions as you would be had you stayed at Aghios Nikolaos. The harbour is closed to them and any boats they have found hidden have been wrecked. When you make landfall your companion will go ashore with the wireless and you will wait for him to return. He will then request that you to take him a short distance further along the coast.'

Manolis shrugged. 'And if I refuse?'

Father Michaelis regarded him sadly. 'Then many brave men will be sacrificed.' He sighed deeply. 'He will have to try to carry it through the countryside and hope he is not detected.'

'You only want me to sail around to a bay to offload it?'

The priest nodded and waited, he could see Manolis was struggling with his conscience.

'And when he returns to take him a bit further along the coast?'

'He needs to meet with important person whom he will find waiting there for him.'

'Oh, very well.' Manolis sighed. 'When do I leave?'

A broad smile spread over the countenance of the priest. 'When I was told a fisherman had landed unexpectedly in the bay I prayed you were the one that had been sent from Aghios Nikolaos.' He filled Manolis's glass again. 'Arrangements will be made for you to leave tomorrow.'

'Will my boat be safe? I left it beached. There was nothing to moor to.'

'Perfectly safe. Someone is watching it. We would not want to lose it now under any circumstances. I understand that you found the walk from the bay very tiring. No doubt you would appreciate a night's sleep. I have arranged for a cell to be prepared for you.'

'I'm used to sitting on a boat, not walking. My feet are hurting.'

'I will give you a salve to apply to them. It will ease the soreness. I am sure you will not find the journey so arduous tomorrow.' The priest raised his glass, then replaced it on the table. 'Just one more thing; why do you have a rifle hidden amongst the bale of material?'

Manolis's jaw dropped; evidently his boat had been searched. 'I was given it by an old man in Aghios Nikolaos.'

'Do you know how to use it?'

Manolis shook his head. 'I've never handled a gun and there's no ammunition for it.'

Basil Hurst sat with Father Michaelis and listened whilst the priest told him about the boatman who had arrived unexpectedly in the bay.

'I am sure this is the man sent by Father Dhakanalis, Vasilis. He was supposed to collect you from Pahia Amnos, then Mohlos and later Liopetra. When he tried to land at Liopetra he saw soldiers and was fired upon. That will have convinced them there is something happening in the area and they'll intensify their activities there and leave the surrounding area alone. He appears to be more intelligent than most fishermen.' The priest smiled. 'It was a fortunate coincidence that he does not know this area and ended up here.'

'Will we be sailing at night?'

Father Michaelis shook his head. 'You will leave tomorrow morning. I am afraid that if the boat sits in the bay for very much longer a patrol could spot it. We don't want to lose it now. I will ask Tassos to return to Liopetra with you to collect your burden. Carrying it between you should not be too arduous and it should be safe here. I am suggesting you sail out to sea and stand off until dark before you go into the nearest bay to Toplou. I will send a messenger ahead to tell them to expect you and it should be a straight run in. Once you are ashore the young man will wait for you and take you down the coast to Kato Zakros. Theo should be able to tell you if Arthur has arrived on Koufonisi and you will have to persuade the boatman to take a second passenger aboard.'

'We could run straight into a patrol.'

'That is a chance we have to take, Vasilis. I can rely on your ingenuity. All the boatman will be able to tell them is that he carried a man from one place to another and he had a wireless. He does not know the area and he does not even know that he has been on the outskirts of Sitia. He believes the town to be further along the coast. He knows he has spoken with a Father Michaelis, but that is a very common name amongst the priesthood. I suggest you impress upon him that if you are apprehended he should throw that rifle overboard and insist that he lost his way in the night.'

'Maybe I could relieve him of the rifle.'

'Good idea. I think he would be only too pleased to be rid of it. He says he has never handled a firearm. They can be dangerous things in the hands of a novice. I will arrange for Tassos to take him back to the bay tomorrow and you can meet him there. Kyriakos is watching the boat tonight to ensure that it does not drift away and it is very unlikely that a patrol would go along there in the darkness or be able to see it if they did. Tassos will escort our young friend to his boat tomorrow and you can meet him there a short while later with the wireless.' Father Michaelis smiled. 'The poor chap is complaining of sore feet. Tassos certainly brought him to me the long way round and will take him back the same way.'

Basil threw back his head and laughed. 'I hope he never finds out that it was no more than a fifteen minute stroll over the hill.'

'Better to be cautious. More wine?'

Basil shook his head. 'Not if I have to walk to Liopetra and back tonight!' He stroked his unshaven chin. 'In the event that this young man turned out to be – unreliable – I assume I should deal with the situation appropriately?'

Father Michaelis nodded sombrely.

Manolis lay in the tiny cell that had been prepared as a bedroom for him. He had never been in a room that was so dark or so silent. When he had lived with his aunt and uncle his father had a mattress next to him and he could hear him moving and snoring during the night. After he had died Manolis had still been conscious of the various noises from outside the house and any movement by his aunt and uncle. There was no curtain over the window and the moon or sun would shine in and it was never completely dark.

The nights he had slept on his boat there had been the continual sound of the sea, and although sometimes the moon had been obscured by clouds it was never entirely dark. The complete blackness and silence that surrounded him now he found unnerving. He held his hand up before his face and could not see it. He debated whether he should re-light the oil lamp that had earlier been burning in the room, but was worried that he would knock it over.

He sighed deeply. If Flora were with him, he would not have been concerned about the darkness. He would have felt the warmth of her body against his and he could have held her close, nuzzling in her neck until she laughed and tried to wriggle away from him. Then he would hold her even tighter and pull her closer, until her desire became as great as his own. Thinking of Flora he could feel a pain in his heart and tears were not far away. If something happened to him whilst he was taking this man wherever he had to go Flora would not know. She would simply think he had deserted her.

He tried to tell himself he was being maudlin due to tiredness, but the nagging feeling remained. He shifted his position and tried to ignore his aching leg muscles and the soreness of his feet. The salve had certainly helped them, but he was dreading the long walk again in the morning. He wished he knew his destination. He would feel far more confident if he knew exactly where he was going in the first place and where he was supposed to take the man afterwards. He hoped it was not Tassos or Kyriakos who was sailing with him. Despite the fact that they had shared their water with him he had not taken to either man and did not relish being on his boat alone with them for any length of time.

His thoughts drifted away from Flora, and he began to think of the sparse information the priest had imparted to him. With something of a shock he realised he had agreed to a very hazardous undertaking. Should he end up being captured by either invading army he would not be able to bargain his way out of trouble by giving them information. He did not have any. He shivered, despite the warm blanket that covered him. He had been a fool to agree to transport the man and his wireless.

He tried to recall everything the priest had said to him, their conversation going round in his head and becoming muddled and confused, until he finally dropped into a troubled sleep as exhaustion took over his body and mind.

Manolis felt someone shake his arm and when he opened his eyes he saw a glimmer of light penetrating through a small window set high up in the wall. The monk smiled at him as he lit the oil lamp.

'I hope you slept well. I have been asked to wake you now as you need to make an early start. I will wait outside until you are ready and show you the way to the kitchen where you can eat. Please do not be too long.'

The monk withdrew, leaving the door ajar. Manolis lay on the mattress for a moment longer, then swung his legs over the side and placed his feet on the ground. To his surprise and relief his feet did not hurt as he stood up and he saw someone had placed a pair of thick woollen socks on top of his boots. He donned his shirt and trousers before he pulled the socks on, followed by his boots, and wriggled his toes. He never usually wore socks as he generally removed his boots once he was on board and worked in bare feet, his trousers rolled up above the knee.

Manolis followed the monk down a passage and into a light and airy kitchen. On a scrubbed wooden table was a loaf and jar containing olive oil. He wondered if he was expected to say a grace before he began to eat and hesitated to help himself. As if sensing his problem the monk stood beside him, clasped his hands, and said a short prayer. Manolis followed suit and said a fervent 'amen' at the end.

'I will make you some coffee. Before you leave here I will

give you a package of food that has been prepared for you and your companion. There should be sufficient for your journey. Whilst you are eating I will fill some water bottles for you.'

The monk placed a small cup of coffee and a glass of water before Manolis and hurried outside with four water containers. Manolis could hear the sound of a pump working as he ate the fresh bread drizzled with oil. Before he had finished his coffee Tassos appeared in the kitchen.

'Are you ready?'

Manolis swallowed his mouthful and nodded. He would have liked another slice of the delicious bread. 'I'm just waiting for the water bottles and a pack of food.'

Tassos stood by the door to the courtyard and watched impatiently as the monk finished filling the bottles, put the cap in place, and tested each one for leakage. He placed a leather thong through the handles and helped Manolis to tie them to his belt before handing him a cloth bundle.

The monk smiled at him. 'I pray you will have a safe journey.'

'So do I,' thought Manolis, but he smiled back and said 'Thank you. Thank you for the food and water also.'

'Travellers are always welcome.' The monk folded his hands into his sleeves and stood aside as Tassos led the way across the courtyard and out of the small door where Manolis had entered the night before.

Despite being led across the dry river bed and the low hills for over an hour Manolis was relieved to find that his feet did not hurt as they had the previous day. They walked in silence and at last Manolis recognised the path that led to the beach and he could see his boat safely in the bay. Kyriakos sat on the sand, a rope tied to the boat and loosely attached to his leg. He nodded to the two men as they approached, unwound the rope from his leg and handed it to Manolis.

'Safe journey,' he said, turned his back and began to walk towards the path.

Tassos sat on the beach, his back to the sea, and indicated that Manolis should sit also. 'We may as well sit whilst we wait for Vasilis. You watch the sea and I'll make sure no one approaches from the land.' He rolled a cigarette and offered it to Manolis who shook his head.

'How long will it be before my companion arrives?'

Tassos shrugged. 'I've no idea. Are you in a rush to go somewhere?'

Manolis shook his head. 'I don't know where I'm going, but I feel safer when I'm afloat.'

'No one is safe any more.' Tassos spoke morosely. 'I know the countryside and could probably hide out for some days, but they'd flush me out eventually.'

'Why would they be interested in you?'

'They'd see me as a threat to them.'

'And are you?'

Tassos nodded, a smile on his lips. 'I'd like to shoot the lot of them. They have no right to be in our country.'

'Have you shot anyone yet?' asked Manolis curiously.

'No, but I hope I will when I join the others. We've just got to get properly organised. Form an army, get some more arms and ammunition, then we'll show them.'

'Aren't you frightened?'

Tassos considered the question. 'I'm not frightened of dying provided it's quick and I'm not laying around in agony for days. What about you?'

'I don't want to die,' replied Manolis firmly. 'I just want to be able to return to my home town and continue my life as a fisherman. The doctor needs me to take him to the island, the islanders need their supplies, people rely on me.'

'Is that what you plan to do when you have made this delivery? Return to your home.'

'I don't know if it's safe to return and I don't have any way to find out.' Manolis sighed deeply. 'Until then I'll just wander around, do a bit of fishing, enough to sell to local people so I can buy a bit of food and see what happens.'

Tassos considered Manolis's words. 'Talk to the man who will be travelling with you. He might be able to help.'

'Do you think he could?' asked Manolis eagerly.

'He would probably have some ideas. You'll have plenty of time to talk to him whilst you're out at sea.' Tassos rose. 'He's here.'

Manolis scrambled to his feet and saw a poorly dressed man making his way towards them, carrying a large, unwieldy box. He nodded a greeting to Manolis.

'That needs to be safely stowed. It mustn't get water in it.'

'I'll see to it.' Manolis waded into the shallow water and climbed aboard. He removed the sack of stale bread and threw it ashore, placed the sack of cheese to one side and moved the blankets. Vasilis passed the box to Tassos whilst he also climbed aboard and Tassos handed it up to him.

'Put it there,' Manolis indicated the space he had cleared. 'The blankets can be packed round it. They should stop any damp getting in.'

'What's in that sack you threw ashore?'

'Stale bread. It's useless.'

Vasilis frowned. 'You can't just throw things like that onto the beach. If it's found the soldiers will want to know where it has come from. They'll guess someone has been here. Tassos,' he called, 'throw that sack back up to us.'

Tassos obliged and Manolis scowled. 'What are you planning to do with it?'

'We'll dispose of it later. No doubt the fish will appreciate a meal. Are we off?'

Manolis nodded. 'Where am I headed?'

'Out to sea.'

Manolis did not argue. He raised the sails and hoped a breeze would come up to fill them by the time he had rowed away from the shore. Vasilis raised his hand to Tassos and settled himself on the wooden deck, his eyes alternately scanning the coast line and the open water as they left the shelter of the small inlet.

The shoreline receded and Manolis was beginning to wonder just how far into the ocean they were going. His boat was not built for deep sea fishing and he preferred to be within the sight of land, confident that if an accident did occur he would be able to swim and make a landfall. Once well away from the shore Vasilis seemed to relax. He lit a cigarette and threw the empty packet overboard.

'I'm called Vasilis,' he said and held out his hand. 'I understand your name is Manolis. I'm grateful you decided to come along. That box is somewhat heavy. I didn't fancy having to carry it over the mountains.'

'Couldn't you have hired a donkey?'

Vasilis looked at Manolis with amusement. 'I could, and if I had bumped into a patrol I would have had the problem of hiding a donkey along with myself. Not very practical.'

'How do you know there are patrols around?'

'I don't, but it isn't worth taking a chance. If we lose this package it could take a while to get another. By then it could be too late for the men.'

Manolis nodded, remembering Father Michaelis has said the wireless was to liaise with Egypt and evacuate the allied troops from the area. If the Germans reached them before they were taken off from Crete they would no doubt be massacred.

'Where are you taking it to?'

'Somewhere safe. You don't need to know the details.' Vasilis looked up at the sun. 'About another half an hour and we should be able to see an island. There are two of them lying parallel with each other. We'll slip in between and sit there until the sun begins to go down. It will give us a chance to snatch some sleep. We'll move again at sunset and it should be a straight run in to make our delivery.'

'What happens after that?'

'We'll go back to the islands.'

'Is that where you leave me?'

Vasilis shook his head. 'I hope not. I don't want to be marooned out there. I understood from Father Michaelis that you would take me round to Kato Zakros.'

'Where's that?'

'Around the headland and a short distance down the coast.'

Manolis looked at him dubiously. 'Remember I don't know my way around these waters.'

'Don't worry. I have no desire to be shipwrecked and have to swim for it.'

'Are there Germans or Italians around there?'

Vasilis shrugged. 'They're everywhere.'

'Why do you want to go down there then?'

'I need to meet with someone.'

'Is that where you'll leave me?'

Vasilis shook his head. 'I can't say at the moment. I may ask you to take me somewhere else. It will depend on the information I receive. Now, that's enough about me. Tell me about yourself. If you don't know this coast what brings you down here?'

Manolis launched into an account of his departure from Aghios Nikolaos. Vasilis listened carefully, continually scanning the sea around them.

'So why do you think they shot at you when you tried to get to Spinalonga?'

Manolis shrugged. 'I've no idea. I can only think it was because I was alone. According to Lambros every boat that goes out will be escorted by soldiers. Father Constantine said the Germans were worried that it could be used as a base by the andartes.'

'Interesting.'

Manolis snorted. 'Annoying. All I want to do is continue to deliver their supplies.'

'So why don't you go back and do so?'

'I'm frightened. I don't want to end up tied to a tree and shot.'

'What about your family?'

'I've an aunt and uncle. They should be safe enough. He's a tanner. No doubt soldiers will want their boots patched up.'

Vasilis nodded. 'What do you plan to do?'

Manolis frowned. 'I don't really know. Tassos suggested I spoke to you to see if you had any ideas.'

Vasilis threw back his head and laughed. 'Why should I have any ideas for your future?'

'I'm only repeating what Tassos said to me,' replied Manolis sulkily. 'Maybe you know somewhere I could stay and fish safely. All I want is enough to buy a bit of food.'

'I'll think about it,' Vasilis smiled. This young man could be very useful.

Once in the shelter afforded by the islands Manolis lowered his sails and anchored. Vasilis yawned widely and announced his intention of having a sleep. 'I can rely on you to keep awake, I trust?'

Manolis nodded. 'How long do you plan to sleep for?'

Vasilis squinted up at the sun and pointed to a hill on the island. 'When it looks as if the sun is above that hill you can wake me. If you see any sign of activity wake me immediately.'

'What kind of activity are you expecting?'

'You never know. If a plane goes over it could spot us and send out a sea patrol. We'd need to move swiftly then to hide the wireless before they located us.'

Manolis nodded, hoping there would be no sign of any aeroplane. The two small islands looked inhospitable and he knew they were a considerable distance from the mainland. He looked up at the empty sky and was about to ask his companion another question when he realised the man was already asleep.

It seemed an eternity before the sun moved around and appeared to be over the summit of the hill on the island. Manolis's eyes felt sore from continually looking up at the sky and around at the sea. He was just about to wake Vasilis when the man sat up. He rubbed his hand over his unshaven face and yawned.

'I needed that. I gather you brought some food with you for us. We'll eat now and leave enough for a snack before we set off.'

Manolis pulled the bundle towards him and opened it. The bread was no longer fresh, but not too hard to eat, and there were tomatoes, olives and a small chicken. 'I've some cheese,' Manolis offered. 'I was supposed to take it to the island, but we may as well eat it.'

Vasilis nodded, breaking a loaf in half and apportioning everything out scrupulously. He wrapped the remaining food back in the cloth. 'That has to last us for tomorrow and maybe the next day as well. There'll be no chance to get anything more tonight.'

Manolis nodded soberly. He had never been hungry before a few days ago and it was a very unpleasant feeling. He ate eagerly, savouring every mouthful, finally licking his finger to pick up any stray crumbs. He uncapped his water bottle and began to drink.

'Go easy on your water,' warned Vasilis. 'That will probably have to last as well.'

Reluctantly Manolis recapped the bottle and re-attached it to his belt. 'What do we do now?' he asked.

'If you want a sleep I'll keep watch,' offered Vasilis and Manolis accepted gratefully.

Vasilis shook Manolis awake as the sun began to slide down the sky. 'Time to move,' he announced.

Manolis took a couple of mouthfuls of water before pulling up his anchor and raising the sails. There was very little wind and the sails hung limply in the last of the light. He looked at them in frustration.

'I'll use the motor. I'm not sure if I've enough petrol to take us all the way in, though.'

Vasilis shook his head. 'We don't want to announce our arrival. I'll help you row. Save the motor for an emergency.'

Manolis shrugged. They were way out at sea. Who was going to hear the small motor out here? He did not relish rowing to wherever the shore was and no doubt he would be expected to row back out to sea again. He sighed heavily.

'We might pick up some wind when we're away from these islands,' he said hopefully.

Vasilis looked at him steadily. 'If we do we'll sail if we can for a while. I'll tell you when to take the sails down and after that we row as quietly as we can. No unnecessary noise at all. The sounds carry at night.'

'Do you know where we're heading?'

'I will once I can see the stars. Until then we'll follow my instinct.' He grinned at Manolis. 'Trust me.'

'I don't have much choice,' grumbled Manolis as Vasilis sat beside him and took an oar.

To Manolis's relief once they were back out of the shelter of the islands the sails filled and they were able to rest their oars and take advantage of the breeze.

Vasilis pointed to the sky, which was now dark and pinpricks of light from the stars were beginning to appear. 'Keep that star over your right shoulder and just steer straight ahead until I tell you to stop,' he said quietly.

Manolis nodded. He had never taken very much notice of the night sky before, but now he wished he had more knowledge. He would ask Vasilis to give him a lesson when the opportunity arose.

Eventually Vasilis tapped him on the shoulder. 'Sails down,' he whispered and Manolis hurried to comply. He took a glance up at the star they had been steering by, it was still over his right shoulder, but appeared to be further away in the sky. He had a moment of misgiving. Had he sailed off course? He pointed to it and Vasilis nodded as he lifted an oar and waited for Manolis to do the same.

The two men rowing travelled almost as quickly as they had with the sails up. Vasilis placed his mouth close to Manolis's ear. 'Quiet as you can. We're nearly there.'

With long, slow strokes they inched their way forwards, Manolis straining his eyes in the darkness until he saw a pin point of light. It was gone so quickly that for a moment he thought he had imagined it; then he saw it once more. Vasilis touched his hand and indicated that he should take the oar from him, before he scrambled back to the small sheltered area where the box was hidden, wrapped in blankets. As Vasilis eased it forwards, Manolis felt the boat ground and heaved a sigh of relief.

Vasilis removed his boots and rolled up his trousers. 'Anchor and wait for me,' he ordered before he placed his revolver between his teeth.

Manolis would have liked to ask how long he was expecting to be ashore, but Vasilis had slipped noiselessly over the side into waist deep water. He indicated that Manolis should pass the box down to him, and holding it above the rippling waves he began to wade the last few feet to the shore.

Vasilis disappeared from Manolis's view into the darkness; now he could hear nothing except the sound of the sea lapping gently at the sides of his boat and the occasional movement of the sand beneath him. He decided he would study the stars and looked upwards. With his head tilted back he began to feel dizzy, but he also knew that if he laid down in the boat he would not be able to watch for Vasilis's return and the man would probably think he was sleeping. The thought of sleeping made him yawn and he rubbed his eyes. He decided he would have a few mouthfuls of water in the hope of refreshing himself and detached the bottle from his belt.

Just as he was about to remove the cap he heard a shot ring out, followed swiftly by two more. Manolis sat there, frozen with fear, feeling the hairs rise on his arms as he heard running footsteps and a splashing in the water. Frantically he pulled the anchor aboard as he heard the sound of something being thrown into the boat, followed by Vasilis scrambling aboard.

'Use the motor,' ordered Vasilis and Manolis pulled at the starter, praying that it was primed and he would not have to remove the cover and fiddle around with it as sometimes happened. As the engine turned over he thrust it into reverse and they shot away from the shore so quickly that Vasilis landed once more in a heap at the bottom of the boat. Manolis heard him curse, eased back on the throttle, then turned and headed out to sea.

'Where are we making for?' he called over the noise of the motor. There was no need for silence now.

'Keep going until I tell you to stop.' Vasilis seemed to be struggling with the piece of leather that had tied his water bottle to his belt, one end was in his mouth and the other in his hand. He seemed to be breathing hard, doubled over in an effort to get his breath. Manolis assumed they were making for the shelter of the islands where they had spent the daylight hours and remembered Vasilis's instructions to keep the star over his right shoulder. They were returning and it should now be over his left shoulder. He looked up and realised with dismay that low clouds had come over and he was no longer able to see any stars.

As quickly as the clouds had come, they dispersed and a pale moon appeared allowing Manolis a glimpse of the dark outline of land ahead of them before they returned to cover the moon again. Feeling heartened Manolis reduced the speed of the engine and looked towards Vasilis who was still bent double.

'Are you all right?' he asked.

'I need some help from you. Cut the engine and sit quietly so I can listen for a few minutes.'

Manolis did as Vasilis ordered; the sudden silence unnerving after the steady hum of the engine. Finally Vasilis spoke to him.

'Help me to get my shirt off. I need to stop the bleeding.'

Manolis stepped towards him, nearly losing his balance as his bare feet came into contact with something hard, irregular and cold.

'What am I treading on?'

'Their guns, I expect.' Vasilis's voice was muffled due to the piece of leather he had clamped between his teeth

'What happened?'

'A couple of soldiers out for an evening stroll.'

'Was that the shooting I heard?'

Vasilis tried to shrug and winced. 'Never mind that, help me.'

'I can't see what I'm doing. Can't you wait until it's lighter?'

'Just get my shirt off, damn you.'

Manolis fumbled at the buttons, and began to tug at the shirt. Vasilis released his grip on the leather temporarily to allow him to remove his arm from the sleeve. Manolis pulled it around his back ready for him to slip his other arm out.

'Wait.' Vasilis spat the leather from his mouth and released the end he was holding. He pulled the sleeve down his arm and tried to look at his wound. 'Help me to tie that round. I don't want to sit holding it in my mouth for hours.'

Manolis tied the strip of leather tightly around Vasilis's bicep and the blood ceased to flow down his arm.

'That will have to do for now. Can you pass me a water bottle?'

Manolis removed his own bottle from his belt and held it out. Vasilis had straightened up, his injured arm up across his chest so his hand could rest on his shoulder.

'Are we making for the islands?' asked Manolis. 'I think they're just a short way ahead.'

'No. We'll wait here until it's light enough to see. We need to make for the lighthouse.'

'Surely we'd see the light from that better in the dark?'

'Not from where we are.'

'Can you tell me what happened?' asked Manolis.

Vasilis sighed. 'I was just about to return to the boat when I heard someone coming. I'm pretty sure they weren't part of a patrol as they were smoking and laughing, not worrying about being seen. The clouds parted at the wrong moment and they caught sight of me. One of them took a shot at me and it clipped my arm.'

'How did you get away?'

'I'm a better shot than they were.'

'You mean you killed them?' Manolis spoke wonderingly.

'Of course. We are at war. They were quite prepared to kill me, and for all they knew I was an innocent fisherman. Even if they had captured me alive they would have killed me eventually, and they would probably have made sure that I took a considerable amount of time to die.'

Manolis swallowed hard. 'What will happen when they don't return?'

'No doubt they'll search for them. They might even find them eventually.'

'But you didn't have time to hide them?' Manolis spoke accusingly.

'I only relieved them of their guns. Others will dispose of their bodies. You don't have to worry about them.'

Manolis snorted. 'Of course I do. If you're found with me they'll probably shoot me as well as you.'

Vasilis grinned in the darkness. 'Good reason not to be found, then.'

Manolis sat and mulled over Vasilis's words. This man was dangerous company. The sooner they parted the happier he would be.

As soon as the sun began to rise, Vasilis rose and looked around. The islands were a short distance behind them. He nodded, satisfied. 'Head diagonally towards the sun,' he ordered Manolis.

'Do you want me to have a look at your arm first?'

Vasilis hesitated. It was only a flesh wound, but it was sore and he feared it would become infected. He was also unsure how much blood he would lose if he released the tourniquet.

'What can you do about it?'

Manolis shrugged. 'Not much. I've watched the doctor bandage wounds. I could bandage it up for you. It would be more comfortable than held up like that.'

'What are you going use for bandage?' Vasilis looked at Manolis's dirty, stained shirt apprehensively.

'I've a box of bandages. I was supposed to deliver them to Spinalonga, but no doubt they've had some more sent out now. I can use a couple of those.'

Vasilis nodded wearily. He longed to lie down and sleep for an hour or two, but knew he must stay alert to adjust the tourniquet on his arm as necessary.

Manolis rummaged in the box and brought out some rolls of bandage. He stood and thought carefully. The doctor had always insisted that a wound should be clean before it was covered or you were harbouring dirt and germs ready to multiply. Manolis pulled his fishing knife from his belt and Vasilis eyed him warily. He had pushed and prodded his arm and was certain there was no bullet lodged in there. He was not going to let this fisherman fillet his arm as if it were a fish.

'There's no need for that,' he said firmly.

Manolis looked at him in surprise. 'How am I going to cut a length of bandage, then?'

Vasilis glanced at him sourly. Manolis cut two large strips from the bandage and rolled them both up carefully. He moistened one with water and began to dab at Vasilis's arm.

'Stop tickling it, man. Give it a good scrub.'

'I don't want to hurt you. Would you rather do it yourself?'

Vasilis took the moist cloth from him and rubbed at his arm, wincing as he did so, but unwilling to treat it as tenderly as Manolis had. He threw the soiled rag overboard and held out his arm to Manolis. The second roll of bandage Manolis placed over the wound, pressed hard with his fingers and instructed Vasilis to release the tourniquet slowly. He lifted the edge and peered at the raw flesh.

'You ought to see a doctor as soon as possible. I think it will need to be stitched.'

'Just wrap it up,' Vasilis ordered.

Manolis shrugged. He had given the man his advice. He took a second roll of bandage and placed it over the first, then wound a third around Vasilis's arm to keep the pads in place. 'That's the best I can do,' he said.

Vasilis nodded. 'Thanks,' he said abruptly. 'Keep on course as I said. Wake me up when you can see land.'

'Should I sail or use the motor?' asked Manolis.

'Sail, but keep a good watch out for any other craft or aeroplanes. Wake me immediately if you see either. We ought to save the petrol for emergencies.'

Manolis raised his eyebrows. What other emergencies was Vasilis expecting?

They sailed for over an hour before Manolis thought he could see land in the distance and he touched Vasilis's shoulder. The man was awake in an instant, his hand going to his revolver. He grinned when he saw Manolis's look of alarm.

'Old habits die hard,' he explained. 'It's as well to be prepared immediately.' He scanned the horizon in the direction Manolis had indicated. 'Change course,' he ordered. 'Run parallel until I say otherwise.' Vasilis continued to watch the as they sailed along. 'Turn west,' he commanded suddenly and Manolis hastened to turn the sails.

It seemed he had no sooner fixed them into position than Vasilis countermanded the order. 'Original course, run parallel to the land.'

Manolis complied. Over by the shore he could see flecks of white foam where the sea was running fast into a collection of jagged rocks and realised why Vasilis had ordered him to sail further out from the land. A lighthouse at the very edge of the rocky promontory stood proudly and Vasilis smiled contentedly.

'We're on course. Take a wide berth. Those rocks are lethal

and there are currents and eddies. If you begin to feel the boat being taken off course start the motor.'

Manolis nodded. His mouth felt dry. If the area was dangerous enough to warrant a lighthouse it was indeed treacherous. Vasilis picked up the two rifles that still lay in the bottom of the boat and examined them. He opened the mouth of the sack of stale bread and began to throw the loaves overboard until the sack was almost empty. Manolis watched as a shoal of fish immediately attacked the unexpected meal. Vasilis placed the two rifles inside the sack and packed the remainder of the loaves around them before pushing the sack back inside the hold.

Vasilis was now watching the sea again. 'Sail round the headland past the lighthouse,' he directed. Once we're safely round we need a northerly course and we should end up by another island. There's bound to be an inlet there where we can lay up for a while and get some rest.'

Manolis nodded wearily. Despite sleeping well at the monastery, he had spent the last thirty hours at sea with only a few hours sleep. He longed to lie down and sleep until he could wake naturally and feel refreshed. If the wind dropped or changed course he would not be able to rely on Vasilis to help and take an oar. He forced himself to concentrate and was thankful when the waters calmed and they were away from the headland surrounded by the jagged rocks.

It was no more than an hour later when the small island hove into view and Vasilis directed him to the northern side and they began to search for a suitable cove to moor the boat.

'We should be safe enough here for a few hours,' stated Vasilis. 'You can sleep first. I snatched an hour or so this morning.'

Manolis felt he should protest. 'You're injured, I'm not.'

Vasilis shrugged. 'It's no more than a scratch and I'm the one giving the orders.'

The reprimand made Manolis feel like a small boy. 'If you say so,' he replied sulkily.

'I do. Get your head down. I'll wake you in a few hours.'

Gratefully Manolis rolled a blanket beneath his head and closed his eyes against the glare of the sun.

When Manolis woke his stomach was rumbling through lack of food and his tongue felt swollen and furred. 'Can I have a drink?' he asked.

Vasilis nodded. 'Make sure you save some for after we've eaten. Don't forget we've got tonight to get through.'

'What happens then?'

'We'll sail down the coast whilst it's dark and try to slip into the harbour. Provided we avoid any soldiers we should be able to find a decent meal and somewhere to stay.' Vasilis smiled in anticipation. 'I'll share out the food. When we've eaten I'd like to sleep until the sun goes down.'

Manolis agreed eagerly. He was ravenous and felt quite light headed, not sure whether that was due to hunger or sleeping in the mid-day sun. He seized upon the remainder of the chicken, ate half a round of cheese and some olives before belching loudly and apologizing.

'You ate too fast,' observed Vasilis, as he munched his own portion of food slowly.

'I was hungry,' Manolis defended himself.

'However hungry you might be if you eat slowly it satisfies the body more.'

Manolis considered his companion's words. Was that why Cretan people tended to sit over their meals, sometimes for hours on end? He had never thought about it particularly, just feeling frustrated as a small boy when he had wished to leave the table and go out to play in the street with his friends.

Vasilis settled himself as comfortably as he could, reminded Manolis to wake him as the sun began to set, and was soon asleep. Manolis sat looking alternately at the coastline of the island and the sea. He wished he knew where he was and wondered where he should go after he had parted company with Vasilis. The small area of the mainland he had seen that day looked deserted and they had sailed too far out at sea for him to espy any villages nestling on the shoreline.

He would have liked to go ashore to see if the island showed any signs of habitation, but dared not leave the boat. Vasilis had reminded him to keep a watch and he was sure if when he awoke Manolis had ventured onto the island, the man would be most displeased. He would have disobeyed his orders. Manolis felt a surge of resentment flood through him. Who was this man to give him orders? It was his boat. He should be able to do as he pleased.

He realised he was incredibly bored. Until the last few days he had been busy, spending as much time as possible on Spinalonga with Flora, purchasing the items requested by the islanders and keeping the accounts. He had fished on his return from the island and spent the evening making a list of purchases for the following day. All he was doing now was looking at the sun or the sea, without even the distraction of sorting a net of fish occasionally. He had no idea where he was headed, or what he would do when Vasilis waved him goodbye.

Manolis looked at the sleeping man with annoyance. The blood from the wound on his arm was seeping through the bandage that he had applied. Manolis considered, should he wake Vasilis now or wait until the sun was lower as instructed? He watched as the staining on the bandage increased and decided to incur Vasilis's wrath and wake him early.

He whispered Vasilis's name, but received no response. He tried again a little louder and Vasilis opened his eyes. 'What is it?' He began to look around him as he sat up.

'Your bandage needs changing. Your arm is bleeding again.'

Vasilis grunted and look at his arm. 'I've told you, it's nothing. Just a flesh wound.'

'You need a fresh bandage,' insisted Manolis. 'I don't want

you bleeding all over my boat or dying on me from loss of blood. How would I explain a dead man to the harbour authorities?'

'I hope you'd have the sense to throw me overboard!'

Manolis looked at him, horrified. 'I couldn't do that. Father Michaelis would probably think I had killed you.'

'Why would you want to kill me?'

Manolis shrugged. 'I don't, but he might not believe me. Let me get to the bandages.' He stepped over Vasilis's legs and pulled a fresh roll of bandage from the box. 'Can you put that tourniquet round your arm again?'

Vasilis picked up the strip of leather and handed it to Manolis. 'It will be easier if you do it. You've got two hands.'

Manolis placed it around Vasilis's arm and tightened it as far as he dared before removing the soaking bandage and tossing it into the sea. The edges of the wound looked a little red, but Manolis had no way of knowing whether that was natural or from an infection. He rolled the bandages into pads as before and bound them firmly into place before releasing the tourniquet.

'Thanks,' Vasilis said quietly. He inspected Manolis's handiwork. 'Not bad for a fisherman,' he grinned.

'I've watched the doctor so many times that I know what to do,' Manolis said proudly.

'Did you want to be a doctor?'

Manolis shook his head. 'No, I wanted to be a grocer.'

Vasilis looked at him in disbelief. 'A grocer? Whatever for?'

'I like the smell of the herbs and spices. What do you do when you're not carrying a wireless around and shooting people?'

Vasilis shrugged. 'This and that. I help on the farm most of the time.'

'Is that what you wanted to do? Be a farmer?'

'I trained as a history teacher. There's not a lot of call in the countryside for my services.'

'Why don't you move to one of the large towns? They probably need teachers there and you'd earn a lot more money.'

'I'm happy where I am. Money isn't everything.'

'It is when you haven't got any,' remarked Manolis morosely. 'I've only got a few drachmas in my pocket and at the moment I don't see how I'm going to earn any more.'

Vasilis studied the sky where the sun was travelling in an arc towards the point where it would set behind the island. 'You could fish for an hour if you wanted.'

Manolis shook his head. 'I need to be sailing and dragging the net. It's no good just sitting here and hoping the fish will swim in.'

'There's no pleasing you, is there? Sail around behind the island until the sun sets and cast your nets whilst I go back to sleep.' Vasilis lay back down and closed his eyes again.

Manolis looked at him in exasperation. What was the point of catching fish unless he was able to take them ashore whilst they were still fresh?

'We can take them ashore when we arrive,' said Vasilis without opening his eyes, as if reading the fisherman's mind.

As the sun disappeared behind the island, Manolis hauled in his net. He was surprised to see he had a reasonable catch of small fish and tossed them into a bucket, pouring sea water over them and covering them with a wet sack. Vasilis watched him curiously.

'How does that compare with your usual catch?' he asked.

Manolis shrugged. 'Not bad for one netting. Some of these are a bit small. Are we leaving now?'

Vasilis nodded. 'We'll be sailing most of the night. Do you want anything to eat?'

Manolis took the wedge of cheese he was offered and chewed it slowly, remembering Vasilis's advice. 'Where are we headed?' he asked.

'Due north. The star above your head. I'll tell you when to alter course.'

Manolis looked up at the star Vasilis indicated. 'Do you know all the stars?'

'No. Only the ones that help you to find your way at night. It's the same whether you're on the land or sea.'

'But if you were in a different part of Crete wouldn't the stars be in different places?'

'No,' Vasilis smiled. 'It's you that's in a different place. You decide on your direction and look for a star that is near your destination. If you keep that star in sight you'll end up fairly close to where you want to be. It's different if you have proper navigation tools. The ocean going ships can plot their course exactly.'

Manolis looked up at the star again. 'So if you wanted me to go east or west you'd tell me to keep that star over one of my shoulders?'

'That's right. Like you did last night.'

'That's useful to know.'

Vasilis shrugged. 'I would have thought as a fisherman you would have known about steering by the stars.'

'I'd never sailed at night until I left Aghios Nikolaos,' admitted Manolis. 'If I'd known about the stars I wouldn't have sailed past Liopetra.'

'Which would have been my loss. I would have had to struggle over the mountain pass with a heavy wireless and then spend two or three days walking across country to get to Kato Zakros.'

'What would have happened if you'd been shot and I wasn't there to take you off by boat?' asked Manolis curiously.

'My friends would have taken care of me.'

'Suppose you had been shot after your friends had left? By one of those patrols you said you would have to hide from?'

'Then I would have walked on, holding one end of that piece of leather and the other piece in my mouth until I found someone to help me.'

'Wouldn't they have wanted to know what had happened to you?'

Vasilis shrugged. 'Probably, and I would have told them, but not what I was doing when it happened. It's better that people don't know too much about your business. If they don't know, they can't tell.'

'But I know what you were doing.'

'Father Michaelis decided you could be trusted. I hope his faith was not misplaced.' Vasilis raised his eyebrows.

'You fell over in the boat when I started the engine and we moved suddenly,' Manolis reminded him.

'So I did.' Vasilis nodded. 'I'll bear that in mind.' He clapped Manolis on the back. 'You're a decent chap and you know how to handle a boat. I may rely on you for some considerable time.'

JULY 1941

Dawn was just breaking when they crept into the small, secluded bay at Kato Zakros and Manolis beached his boat on the pebbles. 'Put your rifle in the sack with the others and bring the fish,' ordered Vasilis.

'Will we need the rifles?'

'I hope not! We don't want to leave them behind for the curious, besides, if we're seen it will look more natural, a couple of fishermen coming ashore with a sack and a bucket.'

Manolis did not argue. He moved the loaves that were now as hard as rocks and pushed the rifle down as far as he could. 'How's your arm?'

Vasilis looked at the bandage that was oozing blood again. 'Wrap another bit round and I'll pull my shirt sleeve down. No one will take any notice of the stains, but fresh blood could draw attention, if only from the flies.'

Manolis cut another strip and bandaged Vasilis's arm as tightly as he could. 'Will you be able to carry the sack or shall I?'

'I'll have it over my shoulder. You can carry the fish.'

Vasilis climbed overboard and took the bucket of fish from Manolis. Manolis followed him, holding the sack containing the rifles above his head along with their boots and they splashed their way to the shore together. Once there they replaced their footwear and swapped their burdens.

'It's not far to walk and I doubt if we'll meet anyone on the way. If we're stopped we're just a couple of fishermen bringing in their catch to sell.'

Nervously Manolis fell into step beside him, as they tramped up the stones and into a narrow valley where they followed a winding path, lined with shrubs and low bushes. As the greenery thinned, Manolis could see a church in the distance, the blue and white of the Greek flag fluttering in the light breeze, and guessed they were making their way in that direction. Before they reached it, a cluster of houses came into sight and Vasilis led the way unerringly to the third house where he unlatched the door and entered.

'Theo?'

'Welcome, Vasilis. What news do you bring?'

'Only bad, my friend. Have you any news for me?'

'All seems well, but ...' The elderly man spread his hands and looked at Manolis.

Vasilis nodded understandingly. 'This is my travelling companion, Manolis. We've come to beg a meal and a bed.'

'Of course. My house is yours.' The man rose and shook hands gravely with Manolis. He wrinkled his nose. 'I think you would both appreciate a bath. It would help if you could draw some water whilst I start the fire.'

'Do we stink that badly or is it the fish Manolis had brought you as a present?'

Theo shrugged. 'Whatever. I still think a bath for each of you would not come amiss. If you place the bucket outside that will be one smell less to assault the nostrils.'

Manolis went through the door leading to the yard at the rear of the house. He saw a patch of shade and placed the bucket there, taking the sacking with him. He walked a few yards along the pathway until he reached the village pump and removed his shirt. He yanked the handle vigorously, plunging his head beneath the stream of cold water and letting it run down his back and chest. He rubbed his hands over his hair and across the stubble on his cheeks and chin, hoping he had not left streaks of dirt. He soaked the piece of sacking, replaced his shirt, and walked back to the house where he covered the bucket before entering the living room. The smell of freshly made coffee greeted him and he smiled in anticipation.

Vasilis was already sitting at the table, sipping the steaming mug and chewing on a piece of fresh bread. He indicated that Manolis should join him and he did so with alacrity, remembering Vasilis's advice to eat slowly, despite being ravenously hungry and longing to cram his mouth full.

Their hunger satiated, both men relaxed back in their chairs and Vasilis grinned at Manolis. 'We will be safe here,' he said. 'We will collect the water for Theo so we can both have a bath.'

'I had a wash under the pump,' volunteered Manolis.

'Theo is somewhat fastidious.'

Manolis nodded wearily. Now he had satisfied his hunger he desperately wanted to sleep. As if reading his mind Vasilis yawned. 'After our bath we can sleep, my friend. Whilst we rest Theo will take some fish to the villagers and let them know we are here. I've no doubt Despina will insist on returning with him to have a look at my arm.'

'We should have brought some cheese with us.'

Vasilis shook his head. 'Cheese will keep. Fish will not. Besides, the villagers make their own cheese.'

'Don't they go fishing?'

'Sometimes, if they feel inclined.'

'Maybe I could stay here and be a fisherman. I could supply them with as much fish as they wanted,' suggested Manolis.

Vasilis shook his head. 'There are few people living here. If they have a fancy for fish they catch what they need and eat it the same day. You are more useful as a boatman than a fisherman.'

Manolis sighed. 'Where do you want me to take you now?'

Vasilis shrugged. 'Today and tonight we will stay here. I am expecting a visitor. When I have spoken with him I shall know where I go next. Come, let us get the water, the sooner we are bathed the sooner we can sleep.'

Manolis wanted to ask who the visitor would be and where Vasilis planned to move to, but he knew it would be useless. Vasilis would only evade the question or refuse outright to answer it.

It seemed to Manolis that he had no sooner laid his head on the mattress than someone was shaking his arm to waken him. He muttered crossly and tried to turn away, but Theo shook his arm more vigorously.

'Wake up, Manolis. You have slept long enough.'

Manolis opened his eyes and glared at the man.

'Come, the food is ready and the villagers are waiting to greet you and thank you for giving them your catch.'

Reluctantly Manolis rose to his feet, rubbing the sleep from his eyes. He followed Theo from the house and a short distance along the rough road. In the small square tables had been laid out and the villagers were gathered. Manolis allowed Theo to guide him to a table at one side where Vasilis was already sitting. A glass of the local wine was pushed into his hand and he raised it to the villagers generally.

'What are they celebrating?' asked Manolis.

Theo shrugged. 'The arrival of Vasilis, a good fish meal, there are no Germans or Italians here at present, our own good health, the sun is shining. We have no need of an event as an excuse to celebrate.'

Vasilis rose and held his glass aloft. The villagers fell silent and waited for him to speak. 'To freedom,' he said and they echoed him wholeheartedly. 'Now,' he turned to Manolis, 'bring your plate and find out how good your fish taste now they are cooked.'

Manolis followed him to a long table where steaming plates of fish stood, along with mounds of freshly baked bread, sliced tomatoes, cucumber, olives and cheese. The villagers stood to one side, many of them smiling shyly at the stranger in their midst, and allowed he and Vasilis to serve themselves first. He helped himself liberally and returned to the table. The aroma from the fish had made him feel ravenous yet again and he began to eat eagerly.

During their meal many of the men came up to their table and raised their glass to both men. Manolis felt rather embarrassed, he was not used to being the centre of attention or drinking so much wine. 'Why do they keep coming up to us?' he asked Vasilis quietly.

'To make us feel welcome. Enjoy yourself. You may not have the opportunity again for a considerable amount of time.'

Manolis would have liked to ask him the meaning behind his words, but before he had the chance, Theo spoke to Vasilis, who immediately rose and followed him to the church.

Both men were gone for a considerable amount of time and Manolis was beginning to wonder if anyone would notice if he sneaked back to the house and returned to the comfortable mattress. He felt self conscious and uncomfortable sitting there alone. When Vasilis finally returned he was smiling happily.

'We will move on tomorrow at dawn,' he announced to Manolis. 'My visitor has arrived.'

'Where are we going?' asked Manolis.

'Koufonisi Island.'

'Where's that?'

'A short way down the coast.'

'You keep telling me that, but I still have no idea where I am,' grumbled Manolis.

Vasilis sighed. 'Why is it so important for you to know where you are?'

'Eventually it would be good to know the way back to my home, besides, as I keep telling you, I don't know this coast.'

'Do you trust me?' asked Vasilis.

Manolis nodded.

'When the time comes I will make sure someone guides you

safely home. In the meantime you are probably safer with me than if you were alone. Do you think you would have had a welcome like this if you had arrived at Zakros without me? It is unlikely the villagers would have trusted you. They would have given you food and water and waved you on your way. It would be the same in any village.'

Manolis considered Vasilis's words. 'What you're saying is that I would not be welcome anywhere.'

'If you had a relative in the village who could speak on your behalf they would accept you, of course. Unfortunately the days are gone now when a stranger was welcomed into a village. They are suspicious that you have been sent by the Germans to spy on them or steal their belongings.'

'So I really have no choice but to stay with you.'

'You can leave me any time you wish. You are not a slave or employed by me. Once we have completed our business on Koufonisi you are at liberty to start on your journey back to Aghios Nikolaos.'

Manolis shook his head. 'That isn't what I meant.'

'Explain yourself, then.'

'I would like to know where we are going and more importantly, why we are going there. I could then decide for myself if I was walking headlong into danger with you.'

Vasilis shook his head sympathetically. 'I will always do my best to avoid a dangerous situation. I value my life as you value yours. We need to go to Koufonisi to collect someone very important who has been dropped there. We will then take him to Kapsa Monastery. Now, if you have finished worrying your head over these trivialities I suggest you have another glass of wine and we retire to bed before the villagers start to dance. They would expect us to join in with them, and much as I would like to, I need my sleep.'

'Has someone looked at your arm?' Manolis suddenly remembered that Vasilis had been wounded.

Vasilis nodded. 'Despina sewed the edges of the wound together for me and gave me a clean bandage. She said to tell you that you had done well.'

Manolis shrugged with embarrassment. 'It was nothing.'

Once again Manolis found he was being shaken awake. His head felt heavy and he wished he had not partaken so freely of the wine the night before. He pulled on his boots, accepted a parcel of food from Theo, and shook his hand before following Vasilis back down the winding pathway to the beach. They walked in silence, and Manolis wanted to ask why Vasilis was carrying the sack containing the rifles back to the boat. He had expected Vasilis to leave them in the village. He watched as he placed them carefully in the hold, placing the bale of material and the blankets in front of them. He straightened up and gave Manolis an encouraging smile.

'Once out of the bay keep heading out to sea. I'll tell you when to turn and then we'll run down the coast to Koufonisi. If we make good time we may even be able to take our passenger to Kapsa tonight.'

Manolis rowed away from the shore, then raised the sails and ascertained the direction of the wind. Most of the time he had been fortunate with the wind in his favour. He would certainly not have wanted to row the distance he had covered during the past week. So far they had been lucky with the weather, and it should hold for at least three more months. After that the possibility of rain became more likely and often for days on end. He hoped when that happened that Vasilis had decided to stop moving around and he would be able to stay in a village and fish when the weather was favourable.

Manolis followed Vasilis's directions and their sail to Koufonisi was uneventful. Vasilis instructed Manolis to sail through the inlet between the small island of Stronglion and the larger land mass, keeping as close to the shore as possible. All the while Vasilis stood in the prow and looked anxiously ahead, finally lifting his arm and ordering Manolis to make for the land.

As Manolis inched his way in to the small inlet a man rose from behind the rocks and cautiously began to climb towards them. Vasilis stretched out his hands and helped their passenger aboard.

'Where shall I sit?' he asked and Manolis looked at him in surprise. He did not understand a word the man had said.

'Wherever you like, just give Manolis space to manoeuvre the sails,' replied Vasilis in the same language. He laughed as he saw the look on Manolis's face. 'Arthur comes from Australia,' he explained.

'Do you speak Australian?' asked Manolis as he slipped the rope off the spar where he had tied it.

'Australians speak English, after a fashion.' He grinned at Arthur, who had not understood the exchange. 'He speaks a little Greek, but not much. Now, over to Kapsa as speedily as possible. By the way,' added Vasilis, 'Arthur has to keep his wooden leg stretched out so tell me if he's in the way and I'll get him to move.'

Manolis knew better than to question Vasilis's plans. 'Any chance of having something to eat?' he asked hopefully.

Vasilis turned to Arthur. 'All this man thinks about is his stomach! When did you last eat, Arthur?'

'Yesterday.'

Vasilis opened a sack and broke a piece off from a round of cheese, handing a piece to both men. 'Do you think you can survive on that until we reach Kapsa?' he asked Manolis.

'I'll try,' Manolis grinned at him. 'I'm sure I've lost weight since I've been sailing around with you. My trousers are loose.'

'Then tighten your belt,' replied Vasilis as he watched the shore coming closer.

They sailed for the next few hours in silence; Arthur sat reading a book, his wooden leg stretched out before him and the other crossed over it. He turned the pages slowly, often referring back to a page he had read before. At intervals he would close his eyes and mutter words under his breath that Manolis did not comprehend and found unnerving. He was relieved when Vasilis finally stood up and scrutinized the coast as it slid slowly past them.

He shaded his eyes as he looked into the distance, then bent and spoke to Arthur. Arthur also shaded his eyes and looked in the direction Vasilis pointed, before nodding in agreement.

'Make for the shore, Manolis. No need to lower the sails.'

Manolis changed his course and began to sail directly towards the land. There was no sign of habitation and Manolis drew up on a deserted beach allowing Vasilis to jump ashore.

'Wait here for me. It should be safe enough, but you never know. If you see any soldiers put to sea immediately and return to Koufonisi.'

'What about you?'

'I'll just have to take my chance. Arthur is far more important than I am.'

In less than half an hour Vasilis returned, his face wreathed in smiles. 'No messenger has arrived yet, but the priest told me all is quiet in the area. We can go ashore and have a meal and a wash whilst we wait for Yiorgo to arrive.' He spoke first to Manolis in Greek, then repeated his message to Arthur in English.

They followed Vasilis across the beach and along a country path to the monastery where a priest stood waiting for them. Once inside the cool building Manolis felt he could relax. He felt far safer here than he had on the exposed beach or at Koufonisi where they had collected Arthur.

The priest led them through to a small washroom at the rear of the building where a tin bath already stood, half full of steaming water. The priest withdrew, Arthur sat to one side and began to study his book again, whilst Vasilis and Manolis stripped off their clothes thankfully and stepped into the bath alternately.

'What's the book he's reading?' asked Manolis as they towelled themselves dry.

'He's learning the German codes. If we can pick up a broadcast it doesn't always make sense. We hear 'two white sheep in the meadow' and have no idea what it means. Arthur will be able to tell us if it means two ships out at sea or two battalions on their way. It's called code breaking.'

'Is that what they say? Sheep in the meadow?'

Vasilis laughed. 'I was just giving you an example. I've no idea what they say, but Arthur seems to understand.'

'Does he speak German as well as the English?' asked Manolis.

Vasilis nodded. 'German, French and Italian. Pity he concentrated on the modern languages. Greek would have been more useful to him at the moment than French.'

'How did he lose his leg?'

'A car accident, years ago. Are you ready?'

'I wish I'd brought my clean clothes ashore with me,' complained Manolis. 'It hardly seems worthwhile to have had a bath when I have to put these filthy rags back on.'

'You've always got something to complain about! If it isn't lack of food it's dirty clothes! Be thankful your body is clean.' Vasilis said the words mockingly, but Manolis felt a pang of guilt. How often had the inhabitants of Spinalonga gone hungry and worn nothing but dirty rags for months on end? He had only been uncomfortable for a few weeks, and as Vasilis had said, he was always complaining.

'It's a bad habit of mine. Ignore me.'

Vasilis grinned at him. 'Don't worry. I do.'

They sat in the monastery and ate the bowls of lamb stew the priest brought to them, grateful for the hot, sustaining meal and unlimited amount of bread to go with it. All three men wiped their bowls with the bread and announced they were satisfied.

Vasilis held a quiet conversation with the priest and learnt that Douglas had decided to return to the mountains where he would organise the groups of andartes and, hopefully, stop them from fighting between themselves. Arthur opened his book again and Manolis wandered around the church, examining the icons and painted screen. He had never taken a lot of notice of the artefacts when he had attended church in Aghios Nikolaos, accepting them without question, but now he admired the delicate and dedicated work.

As the time passed Vasilis became more uneasy. 'Yiorgo should have been here hours ago, before us in fact. Something must have happened.' He began to pace up and down the nave. 'If he isn't here in another hour we'll go back to the boat and spend the night out at sea. We'll be safer there.'

'We're in a church,' Manolis pointed out to him. 'A church is a sanctuary.'

'It should be, but unfortunately our conquerors take no notice of such ethics.'

'Should I go back and fetch the guns?'

Vasilis shook his head. 'That could endanger our host and certainly would not guarantee our safety. If Yiorgo has not arrived by tomorrow we'll make for Analipsi and hope all is safe there.'

The priest hurried in, his face white. 'Yiorgo has arrived. You must leave immediately. The Germans are almost here. Can you take Yiorgo with you? He's exhausted and I have nowhere to hide him.'

'Of course,' answered Vasilis without even glancing at Manolis. He picked up the water bottles and a bundle of food and thrust them at Manolis. 'Take these, I'll help Arthur.'

Holding the unwieldy bundles close to him, Manolis sprinted through the village and down to his boat and scrambled aboard. He raised the anchor and held the boat steady with the help of an oar whilst he waited for Vasilis and Arthur to arrive. He watched in admiration as Arthur kept pace with Vasilis. An unknown man with a sack tied to his shoulders was trying hard to catch them up and he finally threw himself into the boat, sending the small and overloaded craft rocking dangerously.

Manolis used his oars to manoeuvre them away from the beach and began to raise the sails. 'Leave those,' ordered Vasilis. 'Use the motor.'

The engine spluttered into life, coughing and threatening to die intermittently as they drew away from the jetty.

'Keep down,' ordered Vasilis. 'I expect them to shoot at us.'

Manolis dared to glance back and he could see soldiers on the path leading down from the village.

Arthur, Vasilis and Yiorgo lay flat in the boat and Manolis ducked down as far as he dared whilst steering their course away from the shore. As Vasilis had predicted shots rang out, narrowly missing the fishing boat and Manolis said a silent prayer of thanks to Doctor Stavros for the engine, despite the problems he was experiencing with it. From a safe distance they could see the soldiers had given up and were resigned to their quarry escaping. Manolis cut the engine and raised the sails under Vasilis's direction.

'What will happen to the priest?' he asked fearfully.

Vasilis shrugged. 'They won't find Yiorgo there and the soldiers may have thought we were just arriving. Hopefully he will get no more than a beating.'

'Where now?'

Vasilis ignored his question and turned to Yiorgo. 'Have you got the spare parts with you?'

Yiorgo nodded. 'They're in the sack.'

Vasilis turned back to Manolis. 'We'll make straight for Matala. When we have made our deliveries we shall once again be innocent fishermen going about our business.'

'How far is Matala?' asked Manolis.

Vasilis shrugged. 'About three day's sailing I reckon.'

Yiorgo curled up with a blanket beneath his head, thankful to be able to get some rest after walking for two days over rough terrain. Arthur unstrapped his wooden leg and massaged his lower leg, which looked red and sore.

'That stump was not designed for running,' he declared to Vasilis ruefully. 'I'll have to leave my leg off for a while until it's less tender.'

'Would a bandage help?' asked Manolis. 'I've bandaged an amputation before. I know how to fold it so that it stays on.'

Vasilis relayed the message to Arthur who shook his head. 'If it's bandaged the leg harness won't fit. It's better that I leave it. I may beg a pad to put between the stump and the base if I think it will help.'

As the sun began to sink into the sea, Vasilis ordered Manolis to make for the shore. Once there Manolis lowered the sails and all four men sat quietly, listening for any sound that could mean the Germans were in the area. Finally declaring himself satisfied, Vasilis told Manolis to continue rowing.

'There should be an inlet around that we could hole up in for the night. I don't know the coastline and nor does Yiorgo. We'll keep a lookout for submerged rocks and you take it slowly.'

'With the weight I have on board now I can't row anything but slowly,' muttered Manolis.

'Arthur could help,' Vasilis offered and spoke to the Australian, who smiled and nodded, taking his place beside Manolis.

They moored a short distance from the shore and in the last of the light Vasilis showed the map to Manolis. 'I reckon we're here. Assuming I'm right, we'll go round the headland tomorrow and then it's a straight run up to Matala. No more than a couple of days.'

'What happens then?'

'We'll leave Arthur and the spare parts. Yiorgo may be asked to take a message and we might be able to give him a ride to save his legs. After that, it's just you and me.'

'What does that mean?' asked Manolis suspiciously.

'That means we wait and see what happens. Take each day as it comes'

'Would there be anywhere in Matala where I could sell fish?'

Vasilis shrugged. 'I'm sure they'd be grateful for a catch.'

'I want to sell it,' insisted Manolis. 'I'd like to buy a new shirt and trousers and I've nothing warm to put on when the weather turns. My old clothes are like rags. At least I can wash these out if I've something else to put on.'

'You're very fastidious suddenly.'

'I'm used to changing my clothes every week. No one will want to buy my fish if they see me looking like this. They'll think I'm a gypsy and stolen it. They won't believe that it's fresh,' protested Manolis.

Yiorgo grinned at the exchange that was taking place. 'I don't think you need to worry about your fish being fresh. I came past Alithini. I reckon they would have been grateful for anything. The fields and orchards were stripped bare. I didn't even see any sheep or goats.'

Vasilis frowned. 'They may have hidden them away or let them loose.'

Yiorgo shrugged. 'They can't keep them hidden all the time. If they've let them loose they'll come back when they're hungry. They're not used to fending for themselves if they've been tethered or penned since they were young.'

'Did you see any food in the shops?'

'I didn't go through the village itself. I skirted round.'

'That's the answer, then. They'd moved their animals and probably picked all their produce themselves.' Vasilis chuckled. 'I don't think they'd want Manolis's fish anyway. By the time he'd walked there from Matala they'd smell him coming. The villagers would be hiding from him!'

Manolis smiled with them. It was true. Unless you had access to ice, as they had at the fish market, within an hour or so the fish would be uneatable if it was carried in the hot sun.

Yiorgo was allowed the pick of the food from the package the priest had prepared for them. 'We had a good meal whilst we were waiting for you,' explained Vasilis. 'You have whatever you want and we'll share it our properly tomorrow.'

Manolis's mouth watered. Despite the meal he had eaten, the sight of the olives, tomatoes, bread and chunks of goat meat, made him feel hungry again. He did not begrudge Yiorgo his share, but he hoped the man would not be greedy. After all, the priest had allocated food for three people, not four.

Arthur offered to keep awake for the first part of the night. He brooked no argument from Vasilis. 'I've not walked for a couple of days like Yiorgo, nor rowed for any length of time. I'll wake you about midnight and snatch a few hours before the morning. Trust me. It will be too dark to read so there's no chance that I'll become engrossed in my code book,' he chuckled.

Vasilis agreed. Arthur was more vulnerable than they were. With only one leg, he would not be able to swim as fast as they could, nor run as quickly over any distance. His chance of escaping if they were ambushed was very slim.

The night passed peacefully without incident. They shared some more of the food, keeping a small amount of goat meat and some olives. Manolis placed it in amongst the remaining two rounds of cheese and tied the mouth of the sack tightly. He did not want a fly to gain access and lay its eggs on the meat.

Just before mid-day a brisk wind had sprung up and Manolis scanned the horizon warily. 'I need to get closer to the shore. If this wind gets any stronger we'll probably capsize.'

Vasilis nodded. 'You're the sailor. You know best when it comes to the weather.'

Carefully Manolis changed course, running before the wind at speed. Vasilis held on to the mast, whilst Arthur and Yiorgo sat as low down as they could, all of them shielding their faces from the spray that flew over the boat periodically.

'We're going to have to find somewhere to shelter,' announced Manolis. 'I can't sail in this. It's too dangerous.'

'Where do you suggest?'

'I've no idea,' replied Manolis angrily. 'I don't know where we are.'

Vasilis smiled at the fisherman's anger. 'I meant did you want to find a harbour or were you willing to anchor in a cove?'

Manolis shrugged. 'I really don't mind, but we need to get somewhere safe before the worst hits us.' He pointed to a dark smudge on the horizon. 'I reckon we have a meltemi on the way.'

Vasilis nodded. 'Wherever you think is suitable. I'm in your hands.'

The coast seemed to loom up at them and Manolis lowered the sails carefully, then detached the motor from its mounting. He took the oars and called above the noise of the rising wind to Vasilis and Yiorgo. 'Keep a look out. I'm just going straight ahead. Hopefully we can beach safely and then drag the boat up above the water line.'

The boat grounded with a rush on the shingle, the waves that had increased in strength, slewing it to one side and pushing it deeper into the loose stones.

'Can you help me?' asked Manolis. 'We need to get further in.'

Vasilis and Yiorgo jumped overboard. 'Tell me what to do,' said Yiorgo.

'Wait for the next wave. As the boat lifts pull with all your might.'

Vasilis did not remind Manolis that he had an injured arm that would have very little strength. The three men heaved and the boat shifted slightly, before settling back down again.

'Arthur will have to get out as well. Ask him if he wants me to make a pad for his stump.'

Manolis steadied himself against the mast, picked up a bandage and offered it to the man who shook his head and pushed his stump into the leather socket, wincing as he did so. He buckled the cup firmly to his upper leg, then placed the harness over his shoulders.

'Good as new,' he grinned and Manolis smiled back, having no idea what the man had said.

Vasilis spoke to Arthur who climbed over the side and stood a short distance away. He knew he could not be of any help to the three struggling men.

'Hold on. I'll be back.' Manolis climbed back on board and picked up the mooring rope that was firmly attached to the side of the boat. He rejoined Vasilis and Yiorgo and passed the rope to them. 'Put that over your shoulder and pull when I say. We'll have more leverage.'

Vasilis and Yiorgo followed his directions, pulling and trying to struggle forwards in the swirling water each time Manolis called 'pull'. Gradually the boat was inched further ashore. 'Now we unload,' ordered Manolis. 'If it gets swamped we'll lose everything.'

'Including the boat,' remarked Vasilis grimly.

'I can bail it out and refloat it when the wind eases. We might even be able to drag it a bit further in without the additional weight.'

'Pass out the sack with the spare parts first. I don't want that to get wet. I'll take it up the beach away from the water. You and Yiorgo bring the food and the rest of our meagre cargo.'

Manolis followed Vasilis up the beach with the heavy motor over his shoulder. It took all three men a number of trips back and forth before the sack containing the rifles, the bundle of blankets, box of bandages, bale of material and buckets were on the shore. Vasilis looked at the motley assortment and laughed.

'We look like travelling tinkers.'

Manolis grinned with him. 'I don't think we'd make our fortunes with that little lot. Can you come and help me move the boat again?'

Now the boat was lighter they managed to move it a short distance further up the beach until Manolis declared himself satisfied. He threw the anchor overboard and looked for somewhere to attach the mooring rope. Finally he gave up.

'I'll wind it round my leg,' he announced. 'If you see me being dragged down the beach come and help me.'

Vasilis raised his eyebrows. 'Is that likely?'

'If the wind changed direction and the anchor gave, the boat could move swiftly. I might not be able to untangle myself before being dragged in with it.'

Vasilis looked up at the darkening sky. 'How long do you reckon this will last?'

Manolis shrugged. 'I've no idea. Could be a couple of hours or a couple of days.'

'In that case food is rationed. We'll just eat the meat tonight.' Vasilis looked around the deserted beach. 'I'm going for a walk. I'd like to see if there's anyone around. If I can find a house nearby I could beg some food and water from them.'

'Do you know the area?'

Vasilis shook his head. 'I know roughly where we are.' From his pocket he took the map wrapped in oilskin to keep it dry. 'It's pretty sketchy. There's no scale to it.' Vasilis spread it out before them and anchored the corners with pebbles. 'We left Kapsa yesterday and sailed in this direction,' he traced their route with his dirty finger. 'I think we've beached about here.' He pointed to a spot. 'If I'm right we're a short distance from Koudouma Monastery. We could make for there when the weather improves and I'm sure they would provide us with some food.' Vasilis folded the map carefully and replaced it in his pocket. 'I'm off. I should be back in an hour or so.'

Manolis, Arthur and Yiorgo each wrapped themselves in a blanket to protect them against the wind and gazed morosely at the sea. Manolis was particularly concerned. No one sailed when there was a meltemi and he had a feeling he could be asked to put to sea again before he considered it safe.

Vasilis returned more quickly than they had expected. He shrugged his shoulders. 'I couldn't find anyone around. There's no sign of habitation, but people must be living fairly close as I found some orchards. They're not very large or ripe, but it's the best I could do.' He passed each of them a couple of apples and took a bite from one himself. 'Any change in the weather?'

Manolis shook his head. 'The wind is as strong as ever. I think we shall be staying here for the night. Can I have another look at the map you have?'

Vasilis pulled it from his pocket and passed it to him. Manolis studied it carefully. 'You think we are about here?'

Vasilis nodded.

'And you say we are only a short distance from Koudouma?' Vasilis nodded again.

'So why don't we walk along to wherever it is and bring some food back with us? suggested Manolis.

Vasilis sighed deeply. 'I only think this is where we've landed. We may have travelled further than I calculated in that wind. We could walk in the wrong direction and end up anywhere. Besides, Arthur can't walk too far over rough ground and we can't leave him here alone.'

Manolis looked at the map again. 'Where's this place we're taking him?'

Vasilis traced a route along the coast to where the island widened out, then once again the land began to narrow forming a large open bay.

Manolis frowned. 'I reckon that could still be two day's sailing.'

'Why so long?'

'It's a fair distance. Even when this wind dies down there could be a strong swell. We ought to stay as close to the coast as we can. There's no guarantee that we won't run into it again and we have four men aboard weighing us down.'

'Suppose we used the motor?'

Manolis shook his head. 'I'm not sure how much petrol we have, besides you told me that was for emergencies.'

'I might be able to get hold of a bit more later on provided the Germans haven't taken it for their vehicles.' Vasilis folded up the map. 'I suggest you all try to get some sleep. If the wind drops I'll wake you. I can always sleep on the boat.'

'You say there's no one around so why don't you try to get some sleep also?'

Vasilis gave a wry smile. 'Just because I didn't see anyone around doesn't mean someone isn't watching us. I don't fancy waking up to find a gun pointed at me.'

Manolis rolled himself around in the blanket and tried to ignore the buffeting of the wind that howled and shrieked around him, the continual pull of the mooring rope around his leg and the pangs of hunger that were assaulting his stomach.

At first Manolis did not know what it was that had woken him, then he realised all was quiet. The howling wind had died down and now was no more than a stiff breeze. He lifted his head and looked at Vasilis. He sat with his chin on his hands, looking out to sea and Manolis wondered what thoughts were going through the man's head. Arthur and Yiorgo still lay huddled in their blankets.

'Ready to move on now?' he asked Manolis.

Manolis shook his head. 'I need to check the boat over. There's a chance she could be holed where we ran aground or where she's been moved around. I'm not prepared to sail until I'm sure she's seaworthy.'

'By the time we've loaded it will be daylight.'

'Do you really want to put your precious spare parts into a pool of water? The chances are I'll need to bail out and I can't do that in the dark.'

Vasilis frowned. He could not argue with the fisherman, but

they had already spent hours lying idly on the beach. No doubt those who were waiting for Arthur at Matala would realise he had been delayed by the weather. He took another apple from his pocket and handed it to Manolis.

'Breakfast,' he said with a wry smile.

Both men sat and watched the sky until the inky blackness gave way to a haze of grey where the sun was rising and Vasilis woke Yiorgo. As soon as he was able to make out the outline of the boat Manolis rose, picked up the buckets and walked down to the shoreline. The prow of the boat had been buried deep into the shingle and would need to be dug out before there was any chance of floating her off the beach.

Manolis climbed aboard, the water coming half way up his calves. The boat rocked gently with his movement, the water inside her slopping against the sides. He sighed deeply. They would have to bail her out before they could attempt to dig her out from the shingle.

'First we'll have to bail her out. Once we've removed as much water as possible we'll use the buckets to move the shingle.'

'How long is this going to take?' asked Vasilis.

Manolis shrugged. 'Probably an hour or so.'

'Why don't we load up first, then when you've checked her we can get on our way?'

Manolis shook his head. 'If she is damaged we don't want to be away from the shore with everything on board. If she sunk we'd lose everything, including the spare parts,' he reminded Vasilis.

The three men stood in the boat, scooping the seawater up in the buckets and throwing it overboard. Arthur walked up and down the beach, carrying their belongings as close to the water as he dared ready for them to commence loading. To Manolis's relief the water level was dropping and he felt fairly confident that no damage had been done to the hull. When it was no longer possible to remove any more water they climbed back onto the beach.

'Could we try pushing her?' asked Vasilis.

Manolis shook his head. 'Not until we've loosened her. We'd be wasting our time and energy.'

He set to energetically clearing the small stones and throwing them a short distance away and Vasilis and Yiorgo followed suit. By the time Manolis declared himself satisfied the sun had risen and he examined his boat carefully. The remaining water did not appear to be any higher and he could not see any holes in the wooden planking. There were a number of gouges made by sharp stones, but they did not appear to have penetrated.

Manolis straightened up and took a drink from his water bottle. He shook it and frowned. 'Will we be able to get some more water soon? I've only got a little left.'

'Not until we reach Koudouma. Are you satisfied now that your boat is in one piece?'

'Help me push her off. I won't know for certain until she's fully afloat.' Manolis pulled up the anchor that had been stretched to the limit of its rope and placed it close to his feet. The men put their shoulders to the prow and strained to move the unwieldy vessel. Inch by inch they pushed it further into the sea, finally sending them both toppling into the water as it no longer met with resistance and moved easily.

Manolis watched anxiously, but the water level did not increase and he finally declared himself satisfied that the boat was safe to sail. He mopped the residue of the water from the hold with one of the blankets and Vasilis placed the sack containing the wireless parts inside, packing it round with the remaining blankets. The bale of material they placed on the top with the sack containing the guns to one side. A round of cheese remained and Manolis eyed it hungrily. The meat and apples for his evening meal and another apple for breakfast had done little to satisfy his hunger. He fixed the motor back into position and declared himself ready to leave.

He rowed a short distance out to sea; then shipped his oars. 'I want to test the motor before we go any further. We need to know that we can use it in an emergency.'

Vasilis curbed his impatience as Manolis had a number of attempts at coaxing the motor into life until he was eventually rewarded with it spluttering before it died again. Cursing, Manolis waited, then tried again, this time it continued to run, sending out a plume of acrid blue smoke.

Manolis shut it down and shrugged. 'It's working, but I'm not sure how long it will last before it burns itself out.'

'Can't you adjust it or repair it?' asked Vasilis.

Manolis shook his head. 'I don't know anything about motors. I'm a fisherman, remember, not a mechanic. Would Arthur know about motors?'

'Possibly. I'll ask him. Are you ready to sail now?'

Manolis pulled a round of cheese from the sack. He hesitated before breaking it and looked at Vasilis. 'I'm hungry. Why didn't we eat some cheese last night and this morning?'

'We ought to keep the cheese as emergency rations. We've got to sail to Matala, remember.'

'You said we would be able to get food and water at Koudouma,' Manolis replied sulkily.

'We will, but whatever they are able to give us will have to last us until we reach Matala. You reckoned it could take a couple of days. We might be able to make a stop at Kali Limenes. If that's not possible we'll just have to manage on what we have.'

'Let's hope we don't run into another storm, then.' Manolis reluctantly replaced the cheese in the sack and turned his attention to the sails.

They sailed out of the inlet and around the headland at Vasilis's instruction. 'It should be safe enough to sail straight up the coast,' he announced. 'This whole area appears totally deserted. The Germans may have been here, but they'd have no reason to stay.'

Manolis nodded. He hoped Vasilis was right when he said it would only be a couple of hours sailing time before they reached Koudouma. He was feeling very thirsty.

It was no more than an hour when Vasilis directed Manolis to sail in to the shore. 'You three stay here. Give me your water bottles. I'll go up to the monastery and see if I can obtain some food for us. If I'm not back within the hour sail away and make for Matala.'

Manolis frowned. 'If you're not expecting to return, can I have your map?'

Vasilis grinned at him and withdrew it from his pocket. 'I'm certainly planning to return and I shall want the map back when I do. If by any chance I walk into a load of Germans or Italians I don't want them to find you all sitting here waiting for them.'

The hour was almost up when Manolis saw Vasilis walking down the path accompanied by a priest. He was carrying a bundle and Manolis hoped it contained both food and water. His tongue felt swollen and his lips were sore and cracking from the sun. He wished it had rained whilst the meltemi blew. At least they would have been able to catch some of the rainwater and he could have eased his thirst.

Vasilis threw the bundle to him and Manolis waited until he climbed aboard and handed it back. Vasilis untied the neck and handed a water bottle to each man, half a loaf of bread and six olives. He eyed Manolis sternly.

'Before you complain about the paucity of the food, I'll just tell you that the priest has given us his supper and probably tomorrow's also.'

Manolis dropped his eyes and looked embarrassed. 'I would be happy just with the water,' he mumbled. 'Here's your map.'

Vasilis replaced the map in his pocket. 'Whenever you're ready, Manolis. We'll make for Kali Limenes.'

It was late afternoon when Vasilis directed Manolis to head for land. In the bay a couple fishing boats were hauling in their nets. A small village could be seen, dominated as usual by the dome and cross of a church, the Greek flag flying proudly. A small wooden jetty projected from the beach and Manolis tied up to it, thankful that he was not expected to run his boat ashore again.

Arthur pulled himself to his feet and Manolis wondered how he would manage the ladder. He watched in surprise as Arthur supported his weight with his arms and hopped up the rungs until Vasilis was able to take his arm and help him ashore. The man must be immensely strong in the upper part of his body.

The four men walked into the village. The women were sitting outside their doors chatting to a neighbour in the last of the sunshine, whilst the children were playing in the village street. They eyed the unkempt men warily, calling their children closer to them. At the church Vasilis knocked and they were ushered inside by the priest, who scrutinized them carefully with rheumy eyes.

'We are not vagabonds,' Vasilis assured him. 'We have been travelling by sea with important messages. We had hoped to reach Matala by today, but we had to shelter from the meltemi. We have come to beg a little food from you and then we will continue on our way.'

The priest frowned. 'Can you tell me what is happening? We've seen aeroplanes in the distance and have heard rumours that foreigners have invaded our country. Is this true?'

Vasilis nodded. 'The Germans have taken control of the towns on the northern coast. Many of the townsfolk have fled to the hills for safety.'

'Will they come down here?' asked the priest anxiously.

'I don't know, Father. I know they were at Sitia and a small detachment arrived when we were at Kapsa Monastery. I can only imagine they are making their way along the coast. It should take them some time before they reach here.'

'I will pray that they do not arrive.' The priest spread his hands. 'We have nothing here for them. We are a poor village. The people live by farming and fishing.'

'All we are asking for is a little food and shelter for the night.'

The priest regarded the four men dubiously. 'I will ask the

women for some food,' he said finally. 'As for shelter,' he shrugged, 'there is only the church.'

'We'll be grateful,' Vasilis assured him. 'We have some blankets on the boat. Yiorgo and Manolis can collect them whilst I go for a walk in the village and speak with the men. I'll not be long.'

Vasilis spoke to Arthur, who settled himself on a chair by the door and took out his little book. Manolis and Yiorgo, at a nod from Vasilis, began to walk back down to where the boat was moored at the jetty. The fishermen had returned and eyed the new comers suspiciously.

Manolis asked if their catch had been successful and assured them he had not come to fish in the area, just to have shelter for the night. Once they knew he was no threat to their meagre livelihood they relaxed and began to question him about the sparse news that had drifted into the village over the past weeks. He answered them as best he could, not mentioning the assassination of the government in Aghios Nikolaos. He was unable to reassure them that they would be safe and untroubled in their village and was relieved when they reached the church and he was able to make his excuses to leave them.

The priest returned, assuring them that food was being prepared for them, but it would be simple fare. Manolis assured him that whatever could be spared they would be grateful for. His stomach was rumbling unpleasantly and he hoped the women would not be too long in their preparation.

The men looked up as Vasilis slipped back inside the church, a satisfied smile on his face and a petrol can in his hand. 'I found some supplies,' he grinned.

'Where?' asked Manolis.

'A couple of farmers have motorised carts. They were willing to let me have a little. Give me a couple of your drachmas and we'll leave it for them as recompense. Look after it.' He handed the can to Manolis who accepted it dubiously and placed it beside him.

'I don't know how much longer the engine will work. Do you think one of the farmers would have a look at it? They might know about motors.'

'I doubt it, but I'll ask them when we've eaten,' Vasilis promised.

Vasilis spoke to the farmers who had agreed to part with some of their petrol and they accompanied Manolis back down to his boat and climbed aboard. Manolis removed the top cover and a man stepped forward and sniffed. He beckoned to his companion who did the same, placing his nose even closer to the outlet. When he lifted his head he rubbed his nose and wiped his eyes.

'I reckon you've got some sea water in there,' he told Manolis. 'It should be washed out, but we haven't any facilities for that. The only alternative would be to run the engine dry to try to get rid of it. It might not work and the engine might blow.' The man shrugged. 'The choice is yours.'

Manolis groaned. 'It must have been when we ran into that storm.'

They entered the hook shaped bay at Matala and Manolis looked around warily. If a boat load of German snipers sat in the middle of the entrance to the bay it would be most unlikely that they could evade them, even with the help of his motor. Vasilis directed him across to where the cliffs fell sheer into the sea and cave entrances at various levels were evident.

'Go in to the beach. I'll go ahead and see who I can find. Yiorgo needs to know where to take the spare parts and Arthur's going to need some help on this sand. His wooden leg will sink!'

Vasilis returned, two ragged and unkempt men with him. They helped Arthur from the boat and directed him to place an arm around their shoulders. He kept his wooden leg above the sand and hopped, with their help, until he reached the rocky path that led up to the caves. Once there he turned and raised his hand to Manolis and Vasilis who waved back. Yiorgo followed them into the cave and returned empty-handed moments later. Swiftly he ran down the path and vaulted aboard the boat.

As Manolis was about to raise his anchor and pull away he saw Arthur and his companions waving wildly to them to return.

'Has he forgotten something?' asked Manolis.

'Probably his precious code book,' grinned Vasilis. 'I'll go and find out what the problem is.'

Manolis watched as Vasilis once more scaled the cliff path to the cave. Once there the two men and Arthur were very soon in a deep conversation with him and he continually looked back at Manolis's boat. Finally he nodded and walked back down the beach with one of the men to where Manolis and Yiorgo were waiting.

'We've a passenger and we're collecting some more,' he announced as he climbed aboard and signalled to his companion to do the same.

Manolis looked at him. 'How many?'

'Only a couple. They're badly wounded and need to get to Preveli.'

'Shouldn't they go to a hospital?' asked Manolis.

'And wait for the Germans to come and check on the patients? They're just as likely to get shot in there as on a battlefield. Once we get them to Preveli they'll get some proper medical attention and be shipped over to Alexandria to a hospital.'

'Where've they come from?' asked Yiorgo.

'Rethymnon,' answered Makkis, the man from the cave. 'They were told to make for Sfakia, but they followed the main road and ended up at Spili. They were told if they continued they would reach the coast. Just outside Agia Galini they ran into a patrol and were gunned down. Fortunately for them they were found by a man with a donkey and cart and he hauled them into the back and took them to his farm where his wife is looking after them. I was asked to come down here to intercept you and get you to take them up the coast to Preveli.'

'How safe is Agia Galini?' asked Vasilis.

'The Germans are there.'

Vasilis frowned. 'How are we going to get them off? Is the harbour being watched?'

'Of course. You'll have to sail past Agia Galini to Agios Georgios. There's a beach there with a cart track leading down to it. If you think that's too vulnerable you can sail on to Agios Pavlos. I'll go up to the farm and bring them down to you on the cart. The first route is easier, but I leave the final decision to you. Whichever you think could be safer.'

Manolis looked at the men in exasperation. 'Just tell me which direction I'm supposed to be sailing in now.'

Vasilis placed the map before him. 'There's Matala. Straight out to sea from here are a couple of islands. We'll do as we did before. Anchor between them and run in towards the coast in late afternoon. You can do some of your obsessive fishing on the way.'

Manolis scowled. He never knew when Vasilis was being sarcastic or joking. He shrugged and concentrated on steering the course that Vasilis had indicated to him.

Vasilis turned back to Makkis. 'Is that a small island?' he asked, pointing to the map.

'More like a large rock.'

Vasilis nodded. 'We'll make for Agios Pavlos. If anyone is using binoculars we could be visible at Agios Georgios. We'll aim for the rock and creep round the coast from there. You can go ashore and make your way to the farm. Will you be able to bring them down over night?'

Makkis nodded. 'Once I'm over the first couple of hills it's not so bad.'

'Why don't I come with you?' offered Yiorgo. 'You know what donkeys are like. They have a mind of their own and move at a snail's pace. If we placed a rope round each shaft and round ourselves we'd be able to move much faster than a donkey.'

Makkis considered. 'That's a good idea. I don't want to be stuck out anywhere in the open with two wounded soldiers during daylight.'

'That's settled, then.'

Manolis frowned. 'It's all very well, but I've only got a small boat. If these men are wounded they'll have to lie down. It's going to be very cramped.'

'That's no problem,' Makkis assured him. 'Once we've brought the men to you we'll take off. You won't need either of us any more.'

'I've a couple of rifles hidden away,' Vasilis confessed. 'Do you want to take them with you?'

Yiorgo shook his head. 'If we're caught with rifles we'll be shot immediately. If we're not carrying any arms we have a chance of talking our way out of trouble.'

Manolis and Vasilis watched as the two men waded the last few yards to the shore.

'What happens after we've taken these men to Preveli?' asked Manolis.

Vasilis shrugged. 'I'm sure they'll find a use for me. What do you plan to do?'

'I don't know. I only thought I'd be away for a short while and then return to Aghios Nikolaos. I hadn't planned to get mixed up with delivering wireless sets and carrying wounded men.'

'You've been invaluable,' Vasilis assured him. 'Can you imagine what it would have been like trying to find a new boatman at every stage of our journey? We'd probably still be at Toplou.'

'How did you become involved?' asked Manolis.

'I received a rather strange message from an old friend. I went up to Rethymnon to visit him and he had been shot. I travelled on to Heraklion to see if another acquaintance there could explain why he had wanted to see me. I saw the treatment the Germans were meting out to the Cretans first hand. I met some of the allied troops who'd been forced to retreat. They were injured and exhausted, but quite prepared to go back the following day and continue to try to defend us. If they were prepared to do that for us surely I should be willing to leave the comfort of my farm and help in any way I could.'

'How do you know English? Did they teach you that at school?'

Vasilis threw back his head and laughed. 'I am English. I came over here as a young man and loved the history and archaeology of the island. I'd learnt some Greek whilst I was studying history at University and I volunteered to work on one of the sites that was being excavated by the British. I'd planned to return to England at the end of the season, then I changed my mind. I stayed doing a bit of work here and there, getting to know people. Then I met a girl.'

'You're married?'

Vasilis smiled. 'I met Katerina and her parents finally allowed us to get married. They were very worried that I would take her off to England and they would never see her again. That was when I agreed to become a farmer.'

'You must miss her.' Manolis spoke sadly, thinking of Flora.

'I certainly do. I miss my son also. He's only a baby, but I'd like to be there to see him develop a little more each day. If I'm away too long he'll forget I'm his Pappa. What about you? Have you got a girl waiting for you?'

Manolis nodded slowly. 'We're not allowed to get married.'

'Her parents don't approve?'

'We're not allowed by law.' Manolis dropped his voice. 'She lives on the island.'

Vasilis frowned. He looked at Manolis in surprise. 'You mean she's a leper?'

'Yes.'

'That must have been very hard for both of you when she was diagnosed.'

'I didn't know her before she went to the island. I didn't even realise how much I cared for her until the doctor had to operate.' Manolis smiled ruefully.

'What did he do?'

'Amputated her arm. She had developed gangrene.'

'So that explains how you know about bandaging.'

Manolis shrugged. 'I used to bandage it for her if necessary. She trusted me not to hurt her and it meant the doctor could be treating someone else.'

'It doesn't concern you that she's sick?'

'I'm not frightened of catching it, if that's what you mean.'

Vasilis sat in silence, considering the information the boatman had imparted to him. 'You say you were trying to make your usual delivery to the island when the Germans shot at you?'

Manolis nodded.

'When we get to Preveli I'll see if I can find out for you what they're up to in that part of the island. It may not be good news.'

'I'd rather know now if something has happened to her. She had recovered from her operation, but there's always a chance the doctor hadn't managed to remove all the infection and it will return.'

Vasilis glanced at the young man keenly. He thought it extremely unlikely that he would be able to find out the fate of the sick girl, but he should be able to ascertain if the Germans had occupied the island.

It was daylight before they were alerted to the creak of cart wheels and Vasilis ordered Manolis to lie flat in the boat, whilst he crouched with his revolver in his hand. At the edge of the beach the cart stopped and Vasilis was relieved to see both Yiorgo and Manolis slide a rope over their heads and walk towards him.

'We can't bring the cart any closer,' explained Yiorgo in a low voice. 'The wheels would sink into the shingle. We'll have to carry them.'

'What are their injuries?' asked Vasilis.

Yiorgo shrugged. 'I don't know. One has a head wound and is semi-conscious, the other has a shattered arm and leg.'

Vasilis nodded. 'I'll get Manolis to spread some blankets and make them as comfortable as we can. Did you have any problems?'

Makkis shook his head. 'It was heavy going in parts. I'm glad I had Yiorgo to help me. I'd not have made it otherwise. The farmer said he would start riding out at dawn and meet us on the road as we return. If we run into a patrol we'll abandon the cart and he'll find it eventually.'

'The farmer gave us some food and we filled some water bottles for you.'

'Thank you, Yiorgo.' Vasilis looked up at the sun. 'We ought to move. I'll cover them in a blanket and get Manolis to drape a net overboard. If we're seen I hope we'll pass off as a couple of fishermen.'

'It could be a dangerous run to Preveli.'

Vasilis shrugged. 'It should only take about an hour. We'll take the chance and hope our luck holds. I'll get Manolis to bring the boat in as close to the shore as possible and when I give you a wave you'll know we're ready to receive passengers.'

'Are those rifles still on offer?' asked Makkis. 'I'd like to accept them now.'

AUGUST 1941

Vasilis directed Manolis to sail across the open bay to Preveli. He continually scanned the coast line for any sign of movement, wishing he had some binoculars. Manolis found the journey difficult. Each time he needed to adjust the sails he had to be careful to step over the injured men. Vasilis had spoken to both of them, telling them of their intended destination and assuring them they would have their wounds tended to and be made more comfortable as soon as they arrived.

'Thanks, mate.' The man with the shattered leg and arm spoke for the first time. 'How's Eddie doing?'

'He's alive, more than that I can't say,' replied Vasilis as he removed the cap from a water bottle and placed it in the man's hand.

Mick looked over at his companion. 'I'd like him to make it. He's got a wife and couple of kids back home.'

'Where's home?'

'I'm Australian, Melbourne. I'm a banker. What about you?'

'I'm English.'

'I'd guessed that by your refined accent. What do you do?'

'I was a history teacher.'

'Yeah? You teach in London?'

Vasilis shook his head. 'I didn't enjoy teaching.'

'How come?'

'I found the children difficult. I came over here for a holiday, liked the country and decided to stay.'

'So you're a fisherman?'

'No, I'm a farmer. I just happened to meet up with this young man who owns the boat and was able to persuade him to give me a ride.'

'Are you planning to leave when they send the ships to take us off?'

Vasilis smiled at the idea. 'I can't leave. I've a wife and child over here now. Where were you fighting?'

'We'd fallen back from Chania. We'd been ordered to march down to Rethymnon and defend the town. Our battalion was ambushed. When the commanders realised our position was hopeless we were told to make for Sfakia where they said we'd be rescued. They told us to follow the road as far Spili, then make for the coast. No one told us how far away it was.'

Vasilis frowned. 'You should have had a guide with you. What happened to your companions?'

Mick compressed his lips. 'There were ten of us when we started out. We'd decided it would be safer to travel in small groups, rather than march as a unit; less easy to be detected and easier to hide. The Germans were bombing any troop movement they saw. We were all pretty exhausted by the time we were about half way, I reckon.'

Vasilis allowed himself a smile. 'You walked about twice as far as you needed. You ended up at Agia Galini.'

'We couldn't read the signs and just kept on walking. Eventually we could smell salt in the air and saw a town in the distance. We thought it must be Sfakia. As we reached the outskirts the Germans came out of nowhere and fired at us. I'm pretty sure I was unconscious and I've no idea how long I lay there before a farmer arrived. He loaded Eddie and myself onto his cart and left everyone else. I reckon they were all dead. He took us back to wherever it is he lives and he and his wife cleaned us up and did what they could for us. How did you know we were there?'

'We were just leaving Matala when a message came to us. We were told there were two injured men and we were asked to take them to Preveli.'

'Is that where you're stationed?'

Vasilis shook his head. 'I'm not stationed anywhere. I'm just doing whatever I can to help.'

Mick took another drink of water. 'Are the rest of my battalion at Preveli? Did they make it?'

'I've no idea. We've been sailing round the coast from the eastern side. We've sailed considerably further than you walked.'

'Yeah, well, I reckon my walking days are over now.'

'Don't be pessimistic. I had to offload a passenger at Matala and he's had a wooden leg for years. Once they get you to a hospital you'll be as good as new.'

Mick gave Vasilis a sour glance. 'I'm not sure I want to be. They might expect me to come back here.' He tried to shift his position. 'God, my leg hurts.' His face screwed up in pain and beads of sweat stood out on his forehead.

'How about your arm?'

'Can't feel a thing there.'

Vasilis nodded sympathetically. 'I need to have a few words with my companion. Just call me if you need anything.'

'What's your name?'

'Basil, but I'm called Vasilis over here.'

'And your mate? What's his name?'

'Manolis, but he only speaks Greek.' Vasilis rose from where he had been kneeling beside the man and sat beside Manolis. 'We're nearly there. I'm hoping we can sail in to the river mouth, but you'll have to watch the depth at this time of year. It could be pretty low. I'll go up to the monastery and see if someone can help us with the men. I'll leave my revolver with you.'

'What for? I don't know how to use it,' protested Manolis.

'It's easy enough. Point at your target and pull the trigger.'

'One revolver won't do much good against an army of Germans.'

'I'm not suggesting you fight an army. If by any chance there are Germans here and they come down to the boat shoot the injured men. They'll have no mercy on them. They'll just leave them out in the open to die. They don't need to suffer like that.'

Manolis swallowed hard. He felt sick. 'Where should I shoot them?' he asked.

'The head or the heart. Just make sure it's a fatal shot. Now, sails down. You'll have to row from here. Just keep an eye on the depth. We don't want to get grounded and have to wait until it rains to float off.' Vasilis turned, took his revolver from his holster and began to scan the low sand banks as they made slow progress.

Manolis had covered very little distance when he stopped rowing. 'I can't go any further. I can feel the keel scraping on the sand.'

Vasilis sighed. 'Go back a few yards until you've some water beneath us. We'll be lighter when we've disposed of our passengers, but I don't want to take a chance. If the Germans have reached here we will have to move fast. There won't be time to dig the boat out.'

Carefully Manolis propelled the boat back a few yards until Vasilis declared himself satisfied.

Manolis took the revolver from Vasilis with a shaky hand.

'The safety is on. If you have to fire remember to take it off. It's a last resort, only shoot if you have to. I may be gone a couple of hours or more, keep moistening Eddie's lips. Mick can manage to help himself to a drink.'

Manolis sincerely hoped he would not have to use the gun, but resolved that if he needed to shoot the two injured soldiers he would shoot himself also, rather than be taken prisoner by the Germans.

Vasilis disappeared amongst the palms that grew along the river banks and down towards the shore and Manolis smiled nervously at Mick. The man grinned back and saluted him with the water bottle.

Vasilis was gone for considerably longer than he had estimated. It had taken him some time to climb up the exceedingly steep cliff path to get to the monastery and once there he had to gain admittance and request an urgent audience with the Abbot. It was late afternoon when Manolis saw a small procession of men advancing towards him. He levelled the revolver and slipped off the safety catch. If they were Germans he would at least shoot some of them first and save three bullets to use on Eddie, Mick and finally himself.

As they came closer, he could see they were wearing cassocks and he slipped the safety catch back in place. He would not tell Vasilis of his intention. He now felt rather embarrassed. He had never handled a gun in his life and he had proposed shooting Germans from a distance and then turning it upon his companions. He continued to watch until he was able to recognise Vasilis amongst them and he felt able to relax.

Whilst he and Vasilis held the boat as still as they could, four monks lifted Eddie from the boat by the corners of the blanket and began to walk back the way they had come. The other four did the same with Mick, and Vasilis signalled to Manolis to accompany them. They took a longer, but less steep route back up to the monastery, to enable the monks to carry the injured men safely.

To Manolis's surprise, the monastery was a vast building. He was used to seeing the tiny, white washed buildings on top of the hills where a monk would go and spend some time meditating, sometimes living there in solitude for years. This was a community.

The injured men were taken away and Vasilis and Manolis were taken to a bath house where they were able to strip off their soiled clothes and wash thoroughly. Both Vasilis and Manolis were given a robe to wear whilst their own clothes were washed.

'I suggest you sit in the courtyard whilst I have an audience with the Abbot. I doubt I'll be that long, it will soon be time for their evening service.'

'Are we expected to join in that?' asked Manolis.

'You can if you wish.'

'I'd rather have something to eat.'

Vasilis shook his head in despair. 'All in good time. They will eat a meal after their service and we shall be amply fed.'

They joined the monks in the refectory for a meal, sitting at the end of the table, curbing their appetite until more prayers had been said and the Abbot gave the signal that the men might commence eating. The food was plentiful, but plain and the monks ate in silence. Manolis scraped his plate clean with his bread, belched discreetly, and finished the last of his glass of wine. He felt considerably better than he had during the last few days. Their meal over, Manolis returned to the courtyard with Vasilis joining him and they sat in the last of the sun. Vasilis smiled contentedly at Manolis.

'Thank you,' he said. 'You've been a tremendous help. Without you, those poor men would still be languishing at that farm. I don't know if the one with the head wound will pull through, but the other one stands a good chance now.'

'I'm glad I didn't have to shoot them.'

'I'm glad about that too. If that had been necessary, no doubt I would already have been dead. That doesn't fit in with my plans.'

'What are your plans?' asked Manolis.

Vasilis shrugged. 'The Abbot has asked me to stay and act as an interpreter for the men who had to be left behind.'

Manolis frowned. 'I haven't seen any troops around here.'

'After Rethymnon and Heraklion fell the British tried to take the troops off from Heraklion, but it became far too hazardous. The Germans bombed the ships and they lost those along with the men. Mick told me that was why they directed the remaining troops to make for Sfakia. I understand that some thousands were taken off by ship, but there are hundreds of allied soldiers still in the area. They're spread about in the villages or living rough in the countryside. There are far too many of them for the monastery to accommodate.'

'What's going to happen to them? Are they going to regroup and fight the Germans?'

Vasilis shook his head. 'They're in no fit state to fight anyone. They're exhausted, and have little ammunition left. The Germans haven't reached this area of the island yet. They're concentrating on the main ports and towns. There's nothing down here to interest them.'

'Surely they must know they've come this way. Hundreds of soldiers don't just disappear.'

'They know. They're not stupid. They also know there is no way the men can leave the island without the help of the navy and as they managed to inflict such heavy losses before it's doubtful that the allies will attempt another operation. They probably assume the men are living rough and it will only be a matter of time before they flush them out or they die from starvation or the result of infected wounds.'

Manolis considered his companion's words. 'So are we just going to sit here and wait for the Germans to arrive?'

Vasilis shook his head. 'We're waiting for Yiorgo. What we do next will depend upon the news he brings.'

He felt apprehensive when Vasilis announced that Yiorgo had arrived bringing the news that the German army had joined up with the Italian forces. The Germans had left areas under Italian supervision and control to enable them to move deeper into the countryside. Yiorgo brought tales of heroism and atrocities with him. Any villagers found helping the remnants of the allied forces were severely punished, many of them rounded up and shot. Their crops and animals had been taken to feed the army and they were left to feed themselves as best they could with whatever they could find.

'Where are they now?' asked Vasilis anxiously.

'Making their way towards Matala.'

Manolis frowned. 'What will happen to Arthur if they find him there?'

Yiorgo shrugged. 'I expect he will be shot. Unless he's willing to change sides and become a code breaker for the Germans. Then they will shoot him when they have no more use for him.'

Vasilis rose to his feet. 'I'm going to speak to the Abbot. Don't go away, Manolis.'

Vasilis returned far more speedily than Manolis had expected. He squatted back down beside him. 'Are you willing to make another trip to Matala?' he asked.

Manolis nodded. 'When do we leave?'

Vasilis clapped the fisherman on the back. 'Tomorrow.'

'Same way as before; out to the islands and then over?'

'Unless you want to try for a direct run?'

Manolis shook his head. 'I'd rather not try that until the motor's been fixed.'

Vasilis considered. 'There must be someone around here who knows about motors.' Vasilis rose to his feet again. 'I'll ask around and see what I can find out.'

Vasilis returned half an hour later. 'I've found a couple of men who reckon they know everything there is to know about motors. They'll go down to the boat with you now and have a look.'

Manolis looked at his companion doubtfully. 'I won't know what they're saying.'

'I'll come with you,' Vasilis assured him. 'I'd like to know the motor will work if we encounter an emergency.'

'Doctor Stavros won't be very pleased if I've ruined it. He only bought it for me to use when I took him out to Spinalonga. Have you found out any news of the island?'

'Give me a chance. I've got to find out first if any of the troops who are here were in that area originally. Be thankful I've found you a couple of mechanics.'

'What will you do when we've brought Arthur back?' asked Manolis.

'Whatever is asked of me. I'm married to a Cretan girl and I consider myself a Cretan now. Every Cretan must do whatever he or she can to regain the island.'

Manolis frowned. 'I don't know what to do. All I want is a quiet life. I suppose I could sail back to Aghios Nikolaos if I watched the coast all the time. I wouldn't dare to go out to sea on my own.'

'Remember the stars.'

Manolis pursed his lips. 'That's all very well, but suppose I decided to follow the wrong one? I could end up anywhere. I don't know where it would be safe to land and get supplies.' He sighed deeply. 'Maybe the monastery would like me to supply them with fish?'

'I think the Abbot would appreciate it if you stayed here. I know he needs someone to deliver supplies to the surrounding villages. There's no knowing how long they will have soldiers to feed.'

'So I could catch fish and sell it to them?'

Vasilis laughed. 'You must widen your horizons beyond fish! Supplies have been dropped to help feed the troops. The monastery will provide sacks of flour and anything else they have available to the villagers. On your way to make deliveries you can catch as much fish as you want, but you'll be expected to give it away. In return you'll have a bed and your food provided here.'

Manolis looked doubtful. 'Will I be expected to live like a monk? All those prayers and chanting all the time?'

'Not unless you want to take Holy Orders. A bit of lip service doesn't hurt anyone, even if they're a non-believer.'

'I'm a believer,' Manolis hastened to reassure him. 'I just don't want to spend all day saying prayers.'

Vasilis grinned at him. 'Provided you join them in a Grace before you fall on your food they'll accept that. Shall I tell the Abbot he has a volunteer?'

Manolis nodded slowly. 'I've nothing better to do. I suppose I could stay here and deliver supplies until the war is over and then make my way back round the coast.'

'A wise decision, and one that will be appreciated.' Vasilis rose. 'I'll let the Abbot know you're staying.'

Manolis nodded sombrely. 'I'm willing to help, if I can.'

Manolis watched whilst the two men removed the motor from his boat and began to dismantle it. They laid each piece out in order until they had a collection of nuts, bolts, and tubes spread out before them. Meticulously they cleaned every piece with a rag, removing every vestige of grit and sand that clung to the metal. Finally they re-assembled the motor, filled the tank with fresh petrol and re-mounted it on the boat.

'There y'are, mate. Should be good as new now.'

Manolis smiled, not understanding the man.

Vasilis leaned forward. 'Is that all it needed? A good clean?'

'I reckon. Tell 'im to start it up an' we'll 'ear 'ow she sounds.'

Vasilis relayed the message to Manolis, who looked annoyed. He had never been told that he needed to clean out the motor. 'Why should it get dirty?'

'Probably blew in from the meltemi. You only need one bit of grit in the feed pipe to give you a problem.'

'The men at Kali Limenes reckoned it had sea water in it.'

Vasilis shrugged. 'Probably got in with the muck the meltemi blew in.'

'That's what I meant,' Manolis declared defensively. 'Sea water and dirt must have got in and contaminated the petrol.'

The two men waited patiently until Manolis climbed aboard and started the engine. To his delight it sounded smooth and efficient, much as it had when the doctor had first had it fitted for him. He had become used to the noisy, intermittent spluttering that it made and had never considered that it might need some maintenance.

'With it working like that we could try a straight run,' he said to Vasilis, who nodded and thanked the men on Manolis's behalf.

Vasilis sat with Manolis and traced the route on the map he had decided for Matala. 'We'll go along the coast to Aghia Galini, then cut across the bay. We should be there by the early afternoon. We can spend the night moored between the islands as we did before and return here in the morning.'

'With enough food and water,' added Manolis.

'Thinking of your stomach again!' laughed Vasilis.

Manolis shook his head. 'If we are delayed on our return we shall have Arthur to feed. We need to remember that.'

They sailed into Matala Bay where all appeared to be quiet and deserted. Vasilis looked around apprehensively. 'I would have expected them to have been looking out for us. We'll give it half an hour, then we'll leave.'

'Maybe they're waiting for you to go ashore and let them know we're here,' suggested Manolis.

Vasilis shook his head. 'Something tells me I'm safer where I am.'

Both men sat and waited, Vasilis scanning the entrances to the caves. There was no sign of anyone.

'Right,' said Vasilis finally. 'We're leaving. Use the motor and get out of the bay as fast as you can.'

Manolis looked at him in surprise. 'What about Arthur?'

'Forget Arthur for the time being. We're leaving.'

The engine spluttered into life and Manolis turned the boat in an arc and began to head out of Matala Bay. Gun fire broke out immediately, men emerging from the caves. Manolis swung the boat from side to side, desperate to avoid the bullets that were hailing down around him and get out of their range.

He was sweating with fear as they finally reached the safety of the open water and he cut the motor. 'Where's Arthur?' he asked Vasilis.

'How do I know? I just hope the men had some advance warning and were able to get away.'

'Where will they have gone?' asked Manolis.

Vasilis shrugged. 'Probably hiding up somewhere in the hills. Go in a bit closer to the coast. I want to see if there's any movement.'

'Which direction?'

'Up towards Kalamaki. There's just a chance the villagers may have some information.'

Manolis sat and watched the shore as they sailed along. If the men had not received a warning about the impending arrival of the enemy forces there was little hope that Arthur had managed to escape. He felt scared and depressed, wishing with all his heart that he was back in the comparative safety of Preveli and that the Germans had never invaded.

As they arrived at Kalamaki, Vasilis directed Manolis to sail in to the beach. 'I'll go up to the village and see what I can find out. You stand off and if there's any sign of trouble make a run for it.'

'What about you?'

Vasilis shrugged. 'I must take my chance.'

'How long should I wait for you?'

'Dawn tomorrow. If I haven't returned or sent you a message by then you must return to Preveli and tell them that Matala has been taken.'

Vasilis checked his revolver one more time, placed it between his teeth and slipped overboard with his boots in his hand. Manolis nodded sombrely as he watched him wading towards the shore. He rowed back out to sea until he gauged he was out of range of anyone who decided to shoot at him, but would still be able to see Vasilis clearly when he returned.

He rummaged in the sack that held the rifles and brought out the one that had been given to him by the old man in Aghios Nikolaos. He had never handled a rifle before and he inspected it carefully. It looked simple enough to use and he decided he would ask Vasilis to give him a lesson. There could be a time when knowing how to shoot a gun would be useful to him. Inadvertently he had become involved with the resistance or the andartes he had heard about and he was not sure whether he should feel proud to be one of their number or frightened.

Vasilis walked openly up the path. There was no point in trying to hide and arrive secretly if the Germans were in possession of the village. Everywhere appeared peaceful and quiet, but there was no one around. Either the village was deserted or the people were hiding behind their doors in fear. He knocked gently on the first door, convinced he was being watched, but no one answered. It was not until he reached the fifth house that a window opened a crack and a voice asked his business.

'Is the village priest around? I would like to speak to him.'

'Why do you want to see him?'

'I have just come from Matala. The Abbott at Preveli asked me to collect a man with a wooden leg from there. The only people I saw there were Germans. Can you tell me the fate of those who were living in the caves?'

'What's your name?'

'Vasilis.'

The window closed and Vasilis heard the sound of bolts being withdrawn on the door. He stepped inside, wrinkling his nose and gagging on the foul odour. Arthur was sitting up in a bed, a glass of raki in his hand.

'You old devil!' exclaimed Vasilis. 'There we were thinking the worst and you're sitting here drinking.'

Arthur raised his glass and chuckled. 'I'm glad you've arrived. I thought I could be stuck here for months.'

Vasilis turned to the man who had admitted him who had a broad smile on his face. 'The men who brought your friend here told me that a man named Vasilis would come for him.'

Vasilis sat down in the chair that was indicated and held out his hand. 'I'm very grateful to you for looking after him. Did the Germans not come here?'

The man's smile became even wider. 'All they found was a man who'd had his leg chopped off. All he could do was groan – you can do that in any language.'

'Didn't they want to know how it had happened and examine it?'

Stelios winked. 'Cut it off with his scythe. By the time they arrived it was pretty smelly.' Stelios winked again at Vasilis. 'Goat dung beneath the bandage is enough to deter anyone from investigating.'

Vasilis slapped his leg and laughed at the man's ingenuity. That accounted for the foul smell in the house. 'Wait until I tell Manolis,' he wagged his finger at Arthur. 'He'll refuse to have you on his boat if you smell like a goat.'

'He probably won't realise it's me. He's not always that fragrant,' observed Arthur. 'Please give my heartfelt thanks to the gentleman here. Without his help I would certainly have been discovered.'

'What happened to your companions?'

Arthur swung his legs over the side of the bed and began to attach his false appendage. 'They've disappeared round and about or up into the hills as far as I know. It was a damn nuisance. We'd got the wireless running sweet as a nut and Jacob was listening in. He was taking down everything he heard. At first the transmission was pretty broken and we were missing bits, then it became clearer and clearer. They were obviously closer to us than we had realised. He kept passing it over to me and I couldn't make head nor tail of it, then I realised, fool that I am, they weren't using any codes. They are so confident they were making open broadcasts to their troops.'

Arthur stood up and delved beneath the bed cover, pulling out a sack. 'Wireless parts,' he explained. 'We dismantled whatever we could. Didn't want to leave it for the Germans to use.'

Vasilis took the sack from him, anxious to hear the rest of Arthur's story, but also impatient to return to Manolis. 'Tell me the rest as we go down to the beach. Manolis's waiting and the sooner we depart the better.'

Arthur swallowed the last of his raki and clasped Stelios to him. 'Thank you, my friend. I wish there was some way I could repay you.'

Vasilis reiterated the thanks. 'Suppose the Germans come back and look for him?' he asked Stelios, concerned that the man would suffer reprisals.

Stelios shrugged. 'My poor brother died. You could tell by the smell emanating from him that he was decaying. Very sad.' He shook his head mournfully.

Vasilis hoped the Germans would have no reason to disbelieve the story.

Vasilis hurried Arthur through the village and back down to the beach. He waved to Manolis, who immediately set sail for the shore. 'Tell me the rest of your story,' Vasilis urged as they waited for the boat to sail in close enough for them to board.

'Not much to tell. I realised the Germans had reached Mires, only a day's march away, maybe less. They had picked up on a signal from Matala and were making their way down there. We packed up and were ready to leave within half an hour. I was their problem. They knew I wouldn't be able to keep up with them and I had no hope of masquerading as a Cretan. One of them went into the village and found a barrow. I was ignominiously loaded on to it and a couple of them pushed me until we reached Kalamaki. Not the most comfortable of rides, I can assure you.'

'I'm sure it was better than the Germans would have provided for you.'

Arthur nodded soberly. 'I really am indebted to them and that man Stelios. The villagers here were frightened half to death. The Germans rounded them all up and held them in the square whilst they searched the houses. They threatened to shoot all the men if they found anyone hiding there.'

Vasilis helped Arthur aboard and then had to regale Manolis with the story of Arthur's escape from Matala.

Manolis held his nose and smiled. 'I ought to throw him overboard until he smells better. We are going to suffer all the way back to Preveli.'

'You'll soon get used to it,' Vasilis assured him. 'In view of Arthur's information that there are Germans around we'd do better to make for the islands and return to Preveli once it's dark.'

Manolis nodded. He had learnt to trust the judgement of the Englishman.

Manolis loaded up his boat with sacks of flour and vegetables before consulting the rough map that had been given to him. The Abbot had marked various places with a small cross to indicate where Manolis was to make his deliveries. Each sack had a label with the name of the village and the number of sacks that were to be left there. He had offered to fish and supply the monastery, but the Abbot shook his head.

'We are able to look after ourselves at present. It would be better if you fished on the way to make your deliveries and gave your catch to the villagers. You can store the fish in a bucket and tip them into an empty sack when you deliver the flour. The people will be grateful for them.'

'Why don't they do their own fishing?'

The Abbot gazed at him sadly. 'Most of the men have gone into the hills to join the andartes. Some have taken their families with them, but there are many who could not go. They are too old or sick to make such a journey, or the women did not feel they could expect their children to suffer such deprivation. They have stayed behind, but life is becoming hard for them. They have no men folk to do the heavy work on their farms and at the moment they have extra mouths to feed.'

'What will happen in the winter?'

The Abbot shrugged. 'We are in God's hands. If these infidels have left our shores by then we shall be saved. If not,' he spread his hands, 'then may the Lord have pity on us.'

Manolis felt a shiver go down his spine. 'I'll stay to help,' he promised. 'I'll be here as long as you need me.'

The detachment of Germans walked into the village. As they walked down the street they banged on the doors and demanded that the occupants came out and assembled in the square. Frightened women appeared, the young children holding on to their mother's skirts. They were ordered to stand there in the sun whilst their houses were searched.

Eleni looked at the young German who had his rifle trained on them. He was tall and fair and really very good looking. Heinrich eyed her up and down and she looked back at him unflinching.

The soldiers returned, reporting they had found nothing and asking if their commander wanted them to ransack or burn the houses.

Heinrich shook his head. 'I think there could be an easier way to extract information here,' he smiled. 'Return to camp. I will join you shortly.'

The soldiers marched down the road and Heinrich turned to the villagers. 'Return to your houses. Go about your business. You were fortunate that we found nothing.'

Eleni turned to follow the women, but Heinrich touched her shoulder with his rifle. 'You, girl. I want to talk to you.'

Eleni stood where she was. Despite being alone in the centre of the village with a German pointing a rifle at her she was not afraid. She knew that if he laid a finger on her the women would rush out with whatever they had to hand and beat him until he cried for mercy.

Heinrich moistened his lips. He had to win her confidence and then her allegiance. He smiled.

'I only wish to speak with you. I'll not hurt you.'

Eleni waited for him to continue.

'You care about your country?'

'Of course.'

The young man smiled thinly. 'I admire your patriotism. To be a good patriot you need to have trust. Do you agree?'

Eleni nodded.

'So do you trust me?'

'No.'

'Why not?'

'You are a German.'

Heinrich smiled. 'Of course I am a German, but that is no reason not to trust me. I have only the welfare of your village at heart.'

Eleni smiled at him coyly. 'I'm not sure I understand you.'

'Then let me explain. We know there are a number of soldiers hiding in the area. They must be suffering. We want to find them so we can help them. Would you be willing to help them?'

Eleni stood silently.

'I have been sent to this area to explore the villages. I have to send back a report. How many people are living here, their occupations. When we have this information we will be able to help you,' Heinrich continued patiently. 'In my country all the roads are surfaced which makes travelling on them easy, the people have plenty of food, everyone has work and they have as much money as they need to live comfortably. We want to bring these benefits to you.'

'You don't have farmers?'

Heinrich smiled. 'Of course, but they have machinery to help them in their fields. That means they can grow more crops. They have plenty for themselves and are able to sell the remainder. The money they have they spend in the towns. There are shops there that sell pretty dresses for pretty girls.'

'I don't need a pretty dress to work on the farm.'

'But you would not have to work on the farm. You would be able to work in one of these shops if you wanted. Even if you preferred to work on the farm when you went up to the town you would have money in your pocket and you could buy whatever you wished. Have you ever been up to the town?'

Eleni shook her head. She had never been further than Lefkogia.

'The nearest large town to here is Spili. It is a beautiful town. In the square there are lions' heads and from the mouth of each one water gushes down from the mountain side. It is the purest, coldest water you have ever tasted. Everywhere there are large buildings and shops selling a greater variety of goods than you could never imagine. It would take you all day to travel there at the moment. When we have made a road out of your cart track we will be able to provide you with a bus. That will call at all the villages and collect people, take them up to Spili and bring them back to their homes. If your mother wants a new cooking pot she will not have to wait for the travelling tinker to arrive. She can visit Spili on the bus and buy exactly the size she wants. You understand that all we wish to do is help you to have a better life?'

Eleni nodded. The life the German was describing sounded attractive.

'But before we can start all these improvements we have in mind for you we need to find these soldiers who are hiding and being a nuisance to us. Once we have removed them from the area and sent them safely home to their own countries we can begin to help you.'

'Why can't you do it whilst they are here?'

Heinrich shook his head sadly. 'They do not want you to have the benefits. They want to keep you as a poor country, always asking other countries to lend you money. It is to their advantage. When they ask for the money to be repaid they ask for double the amount they loaned.'

Eleni frowned. She no longer understood what he was talking about and Heinrich realised this.

'If you ask me to lend you a drachma.' He pulled one from his pocket and held it out to Eleni. 'Take it,' he said and she took it tentatively from his fingers. 'Now I ask you to return it to me.' He held out his hand and she placed the coin on his palm. Heinrich shook his head. 'That is not enough. I expect two drachmas in return.'

Eleni's eyes opened wide. 'I haven't got two drachmas. You only gave me one.'

Heinrich smiled. 'This is the problem that your country is facing. They ask to borrow one drachma and they are asked to repay two drachmas. They do not have it. We would give you money to build the roads and buy machinery for your farms. The countries who are lending you money at the moment do not want this to happen. They would no longer be making money from you.'

'When will you start to make the road?' asked Eleni. She did not understand why someone would lend you one drachma and then ask for two in return, but she did understand about a road going to this wonderful town of Spili he had described to her.

'Immediately we have cleared this area of the soldiers,' he promised. 'If you are able to tell us where they are hiding it would save us so much time hunting for them. If you help us I promise you will be the first person from this village to travel to Spili on the new road. I will take you myself.'

'I don't know where they are,' answered Eleni honestly and wishing she could give him the information.

'Maybe you could find out? Maybe your mother or one of the other women would know?'

Eleni shook her head. 'I don't think they know. I've never heard them talking about them.'

Heinrich smiled at her, inwardly annoyed that he had spent so much time trying to gain her confidence for nothing. 'Never mind. I shall be coming back to this area in a week or so. If you have found out anything you could tell me then. Of course, in the meantime, we may have found them.'

Eleni's face fell. She could see her promised visit to Spili disappearing. 'I'll see what I can do,' she promised. There was just a chance that the boatman who delivered food supplies to them from Preveli would know about soldiers hiding in the area.

Penelope was waiting for her daughter as she entered the house. 'What did that German want with you? What were you talking about?'

Eleni tossed her head. 'He was telling me about Germany.'

'Why should he do that?'

She shrugged. 'Why shouldn't he? He was telling me how much better it is over there than it is here. They have proper roads everywhere and everyone has plenty of money.'

Penelope sniffed derisively. 'You don't want to believe everything you hear. Keep away from him. He's German.'

Manolis delivered sacks of flour and fish and within a few days the villagers began to look for his boat and come down to greet him, thankful for the supplies he was bringing that were keeping them fed and providing food for the number of soldiers hiding locally who were dependant upon them. Each day the women would ask if he had any news and he would shake his head sadly.

The Abbot would acknowledge him with a nod of his head if they happened to meet, and the other monks were sociable and friendly, but he felt nervous when he was amongst them. He was sure they thought him bad mannered due to his ignorance of the protocol of the life in the monastery.

Vasilis entered the room they shared with a triumphant smile on his face. He had a pair of binoculars slung around his neck and he pointed them out to Manolis.

'I've managed to get some. They'll be invaluable.'

'How did you manage that?'

'Mick gave them to me. He asked what he could do to thank us for bringing him and Eddie here. I said I'd like a pair of binoculars. He promised to see what he could do and here they are.'

Manolis frowned. 'He didn't have any with him.'

Vasilis smiled. 'I expect he asked someone who did possess some to give them up. All the men will do whatever they can to express their gratitude.' Vasilis leant forward to Manolis and spoke quietly. 'There's a little job for you tonight.'

Manolis raised his eyebrows and Vasilis continued. 'Contact has been made with a submarine. They're planning to send someone ashore tonight. You'll be asked to go out to collect him.'

Manolis pursed his lips. 'I'm not sure if I'll have enough petrol.'

'If the wind is right you'll be able to sail most of the way.'

Manolis frowned. 'Suppose the Germans find out there's a submarine standing off in the bay?'

'It could turn – nasty.'

'Yes, and I'd be the first target with white sails standing out like a beacon!'

Vasilis shook his head. 'You have a bale of black material. Couldn't you make some sails from that?'

'I've never made sails before. I don't know if that material will be strong enough to withstand the wind. It was meant for trousers.'

Vasilis ignored his objections. 'It can't be that difficult. If you take down those you have we can cut the material to the same shape.'

'How long is that going to take?'

Vasilis shrugged. 'I don't know, but I suggest we go and get the sails now and make a start. If the new ones get blown to bits and you run out of petrol then you'll have to row all the way or risk using the white sails. Surely it's worth a try?'

Manolis considered. It was an ingenious idea and could make his journey safer. 'How many trips will I be making?'

'Just out to the sub a couple of times. Collection one night and return the next,' replied Vasilis cheerfully.

'Then all the work of making new sails will have been for

nothing,' grumbled Manolis as he pulled on his boots. 'Come on, then. I'll need some help. Sails are not light items to carry around.'

Manolis stood by his boat in the darkness. He felt sick. 'How will I know when I'm there?' he asked hoarsely.

Vasilis placed his hand on Manolis's shoulder and pointed to the sky. 'Use that star. Keep it straight ahead and slightly to your left. Every so often the sub will send out a signal.' Vasilis removed his hand. 'Good luck.'

Although there was a slight breeze, Manolis rowed to speed the boat along. He would save his petrol for the return journey. Manolis kept turning his gaze on the star that Vasilis had indicated to him. He did not want to lose his way and be marooned out at sea when daylight came. If the Germans flew a reconnaissance flight he would be spotted immediately and he was certain he would be blown out of the water. He tried to calculate how long he had been sailing, but gave up the effort and took a brief rest from his exertions, leaning on his oars. To his relief he saw a light flick on and off in the darkness and made his way towards it.

He lowered his sails and rowed the last few metres, making for the point where he had seen the light. The light flickered again and for a second he could make out the enormous bulk of the submarine. He nosed his way gently forward until he was able to grab at a rope that was thrown over the side.

Without hesitation a man swarmed down the rope and landed in Manolis's boat. Manolis released his grip on the rope and started the engine. He breathed a sigh of relief as it turned over the first time and the boat sped over the water. He remembered Vasilis's instructions about the stars and checked that he had the star above him and slightly to the right for his return journey.

Vasilis helped his passenger ashore and shook his hand. 'We'll take you up to the monastery and introduce you to the Abbot. Once you've spoken to him someone will take you to meet the men who contacted you. When you're ready Manolis will take you back out to the sub. No doubt you'll have some arrangements to make.'

The man nodded. 'We were surprised when we picked up their signal. How many of them are in this area?'

'No idea. Probably some hundreds.'

The man frowned. 'We only have very limited facilities. We hadn't planned for passengers.'

'If you could take some maybe a couple of ships could be sent for the others,' suggested Vasilis.

In the darkness the man nodded. 'We'll see. After what happened at Heraklion we don't want to take any chances.'

Vasilis turned away. He had made the suggestion, it was up to others to make a decision. 'Follow me,' he said. 'It's pretty steep, but quicker than the easier route.'

Manolis slept restlessly. He dreamt he was out at sea, no idea of his direction and all around him bombs were dropping. He moved this way and that, finally being thrown into the sea. He landed on the stone floor of the cell and woke up abruptly. He lay there, bathed in sweat, relieved to find that he had been dreaming and the event was not real. It occurred to him that if he could suffer a nightmare after an event that had not incurred any danger, the men who had been under fire, watching their comrades fall around them, must be suffering terribly.

He picked himself up and dressed swiftly. He would be far too late to breakfast with the monks and would only be able to have some bread and water. He had not delivered to the villagers the previous day and they would be waiting anxiously for him to arrive with their food supplies. Hastily he made his way down to his boat and then realised he would have to remove the black sails and re-rig his white ones before he left. Cursing and sweating profusely, he struggled for an hour before he was able to load his boat.

Thoroughly bad tempered he sailed out of Preveli and began

the journey to the various drop off points he had marked on his map between Preveli and Plaka Bay. He no longer needed the map. He had memorised any small landmark and was able to sail in to each of the stops and would be unloaded and on his way within minutes.

This morning he did not stop to fish, but proceeded immediately to Skinaria Bay, a tiny inlet where a road ran down to the beach from a cluster of houses. The beach was deserted and he thought the villagers had probably given up hope of him delivering that day. He scratched his head. Should he leave the three sacks of flour and sack of potatoes laying on the shore and hope someone came down later in the day?

Finally he decided he would leave them. He would continue on to his other destinations and on his return journey, if they were still laying there, he would make his way to the village and alert them. He hoped he would not find his other delivery places deserted and have to search out the villagers in the area.

The other half a dozen places that he stopped between Skinaria and Koraka he found a child sitting on the shore looking out for him. In each case they waved to him, then ran back to their home to inform their mothers that the boatman had arrived. The women hurried down to the shore and Manolis helped them to load a sack on their shoulders and apologised for his late arrival. As he watched them trudge back up the hill he felt a pang of guilt. Women should not be expected to carry such heavy loads.

He sailed back towards Skinaria, hoping he would find the sacks had been removed by the time he reached there. To his dismay they still sat beside the rock where he had left them. He would have to walk up and find an inhabitant of the village and he had no idea how far away it was. He hoisted a sack onto his shoulders. At least that would be one less for the women to carry.

Manolis had only walked a short distance from the beach when he saw a girl lying in the grass on the bank. He drew in his breath sharply and moved closer. He saw her chest moving rhythmically and to his relief he realised she was sleeping. He lowered his sack to the ground and looked at her. She reminded him of Maria, the chemist's daughter, for whom he'd had such a longing. He gazed at her hungrily, longing to take her into his arms and feel her soft breasts in his hands. Her skirt had risen up to show an expanse of leg that excited him.

As if she knew she was being watched the girl opened her eyes and saw Manolis standing there. She sat up and pulled down her skirt.

'Who are you?' she demanded.

'I'm the boatman who delivers to the village.' Manolis held the sack of flour in front of him, not wishing for her to see the effect she had had on him. 'Who are you?'

'I'm Eleni.'

'I'm pleased to meet you, Eleni. I left the sacks on the beach earlier and they were still there when I passed on my way back. I thought I ought to tell the villagers. I've brought one up with me.'

Eleni nodded. 'I can see that.'

'Could you pass the message on to the village, please? I need to get back to my boat.'

'What is so urgent about returning to your boat?'

Manolis felt at a loss for words. 'Well, nothing really. I just don't know my way to the village.'

'It's only up the hill. If you follow the path you'll not get lost.'

Manolis frowned. 'Surely if you live in the village you could go and tell them?'

'I could, but it seems rather a waste of time. I would have to walk back there and then return to collect them. If you left that one here I could walk back down with you and then you could help me to carry them back.'

'The women usually come down for them.'

Eleni shrugged. 'There was no sign of you when they went down. They've gone off to the fields and told me to look for you and bring them up. Why were you late?'

Manolis was about to say that he had been out the previous night helping soldiers to escape from the island and searching for survivors but thought better of it. 'I overslept, then I had some jobs to do before I could leave.'

'Lucky you to be able to oversleep.'

'You were asleep when I found you.'

Eleni opened her eyes wide. 'I was only resting,' she protested.

Manolis laughed. 'You were fast asleep. I could have walked past you, robbed your village and walked back again and you would not have known.'

Eleni dropped her eyes. 'You won't tell them, will you?'

Manolis grinned at her. 'What's it worth?'

Eleni eyed him speculatively. 'I'd have to think about that,' she said. 'I don't know you.'

'What do you want to know?'

Eleni continued to sit on the grass and Manolis placed the sack to one side and sat beside her.

'What's your name?'

'Manolis.'

'Where have you come from?'

'Aghios Nikolaos.'

'Where's that?'

Manolis waved his hand airily. 'The other side of the island.'

'So why are you down here?'

'I was asked to take a message to someone. Each time I thought I'd found them they'd moved on. I eventually ended up at Preveli.'

'How long are you here for?'

Manolis shrugged. 'I don't know. I'll stay whilst they need me to deliver supplies to the villages.'

'Then what will you do?'

'Go back to Aghios Nikolaos, I suppose.'

'What will you do there?'

'Become a fisherman again.'

Eleni leaned closer to him and sniffed. 'You don't smell like a fisherman.'

'I haven't done any fishing today.'

'Is that why you're in a hurry to get back to your boat?'

Manolis shook his head. 'I'm not really in a hurry. I was just concerned about leaving the sacks down on the beach.'

Eleni lay back on the grass and placed her hands beneath her head, her bodice straining over her taught breasts. 'I'm not in any hurry to get them. They'll be safe enough there.'

Once again Manolis felt an overwhelming desire rising in him. He ran his finger down her cheek. 'You're very pretty,' he said.

'Do you think so?'

Manolis nodded.

'Why don't you lie down and have a rest as well?' suggested Eleni.

'I don't think I'd be able to rest.'

Eleni moved one hand out from beneath her head and ran it down his arm. 'Why wouldn't you be able to rest?'

Manolis licked his dry lips, not sure how he could answer her. Eleni sat up abruptly and leant over him. 'You've got very broad shoulders,' she observed as she ran her hand across his chest. 'Are your arms as strong and muscular?'

'Of course. I row a boat for my living.' She nestled closer to him and Manolis lifted his hand and cupped one of her full breasts, feeling her nipple harden. She did not resist him as he touched her and he slipped his free hand beneath her skirt.

'Oh, Manolis,' she murmured, 'we really shouldn't.'

'I want you,' he said, burying his face against her chest.

'I know that,' she said and placed her hand on his very evident erection, making him groan. 'My Pappa would kill you if he thought you had taken me against my will.'

'Where is your father?'

'In the hills with the andartes, so he won't know,' she giggled as she ran her hand provocatively down the bulge in his trousers

'I wouldn't force you,' Manolis was struggling to regain control of himself.

Eleni pouted. 'I think I'd like to be forced. I could fight you and pretend to be frightened. Why don't you try to force me?' She held Manolis firmly, feeling him throbbing beneath her fingers.

Manolis pushed his hand further up her skirt and Eleni opened her legs. 'Oh, Manolis, I am so frightened,' she murmured. 'You are forcing me to succumb to you.' Her hand was on his belt, undoing the buckle.

Manolis threw caution to the winds and tugged at his trousers to release himself.

Manolis would have liked to confide in Vasilis, but felt too ashamed to take the man into his confidence. He felt guilty about his association with Eleni. At night Flora's tear streaked face would rise before him and he would vow not to touch Eleni again; but as soon as he saw her he pushed the guilt to the back of his mind, excusing himself by saying he was a man with a man's appetites.

Manolis had changed his routine. Each morning he would load his boat and fish on his way to Koraka. He now made that village his first stop rather than his last. By the time he reached Skinaria the women had left Eleni to watch for him whilst they went to the fields to harvest whatever they could find to supplement their diet and provide food for the troops hiding nearby. Manolis would carry the heavy sacks to their meeting place and they could be certain of an undisturbed hour together, leaving Eleni to carry them into the village when he left.

Every time they met she asked him what was happening at Preveli and he answered honestly that all was quiet and life there was progressing normally. She wanted to know if there were many troops stranded there and Manolis replied that he had no idea of the number. He saw them lounging around, but they all looked the same to him in their ragged uniforms. She seemed annoyed and tried to press him for different answers, but he remained adamant.

'I cannot tell you what I don't know. Why are you interested anyway?'

'I'd like to know when my Pappa might come home.'

'When he does it will mean the war is over and we'll have to stop meeting like this.'

'You could ask his permission to court me.'

Manolis hesitated. 'We'll see when he returns.' He knew he did not love Eleni; her attraction for him was her voluptuous and willing body. He loved Flora and he would never be able to admit to her that he had been unfaithful, knowing how hurt she would be. Once they left Preveli he would have to go to confession and ask to be excused for his sins of the flesh.

In the inky darkness, the sound of men scrambling carefully down the precipitous and dangerous cliff path came to their ears. The soldiers gathered on the beach in small groups their weapons and boots lying in an untidy pile to be removed and distributed between those who were left behind.

They stood for over an hour on the small beach and waited for any sign that a submarine was in the bay. Manolis strained his eyes continually, but could see nothing beyond a few yards from the shore. A light winked out at sea and the men shifted restlessly. They began to remove their boots and jackets, place their rifles beside them on the ground, and wade into the sea.

A dozen men were directed over to Manolis's boat and four more joined them. Manolis frowned. He could not accommodate sixteen passengers, however short the journey to the submarine. He allowed the first eight on board, then held up his hand.

'I can't take any more, Vasilis. I'll come back for another load.'

'I'll tell them.'

The men appeared to accept the decision as Manolis drew

away from the shore. As he neared the submarine he could see its dark shape looming up in the water and shuddered. He was quite at home on the sea, but he had no desire to travel beneath the waves. The nearest man clutched eagerly at the rope ladder that had been thrown over the side and climbed up, ignoring the pain it caused to his already sore and tender feet. He was no more than half way when the next man began his ascent. All along the hull of the submarine men were doing the same, willing hands helping them aboard.

The whole operation was over within a matter of minutes and Manolis turned and made for the shore to repeat the journey. Along with the eight that were waiting for him another four had joined the group. He sighed. That would mean two more trips. The men were no longer standing in line on the beach, but had entered the water and were swimming strongly towards the direction of the light from the submarine.

His two other journeys complete Manolis put the engine into reverse and began to draw away from the dark, menacing hulk, until he was able to thrust the control into the forward position and make a wide arc before heading as speedily as possible for the safety of the shore. He had no wish to be dragged beneath the water as the submarine dived.

'No problems?' asked Vasilis as Manolis climbed ashore.

Manolis shook his head, relieved that the night's work was successfully completed.

Heinrich entered Skinaria and called the villagers from their houses as he had done before. Their properties were searched; the people sent about their business and Eleni told to remain in the square. She stood there unconcerned, staring boldly at the German.

'Have you any news for me?' he asked.

Eleni smiled. 'Not really. I asked my mother and she told me not to be silly. A boatman delivers supplies to us from Preveli monastery and I asked him if there were any soldiers there. He said there were some, but he didn't know how many.'

'At the monastery? Are you sure?' Heinrich frowned.

Eleni pouted. 'That's what he told me.'

'You can trust this man?'

'Oh, yes. He's in love with me.'

Heinrich raised his eyebrows. 'And are you in love with him?'

Eleni smiled triumphantly and shook her head. 'Of course not. I let him think I like him so he will answer my questions.' She moved a step closer to Heinrich. 'When you take me to Spili I shall have nothing more to do with him. I don't want to marry a boatman.'

The reconnaissance flights made by the Germans across the area were erratic. Twice Manolis had had to delay his delivery to the villages until the afternoon and he had left Eleni pouting disconsolately at his brief visit. He noticed that there was less food available at their meals in the evening and the atmosphere in the monastery seemed to be one of tense expectation.

He wondered if he was going to be asked to raise his black sails again and make a night time trip out to a waiting boat. Vasilis had told him that many allied service men were still on the island, some as prisoners of the Germans or Italians, others had fled to the mountains to join the andartes and formed resistance groups, whilst many were still living rough in the vicinity, hoping a ship would be sent to rescue them.

The monks would continually glance up at the sky or out to sea and Manolis wondered if they were expecting the Germans to arrive by either route. If that was the case he would have no chance of escape by boat and had to hope that the Germans would respect the sanctity of the monastery and leave the monks unmolested. He would willingly slip on a robe and hope to pass as one of them.

'There are some ships coming in tonight to take off some more men,' Vasilis informed him.

'Will I have to help?' he asked.

Vasilis shook his head. 'It shouldn't be necessary. You'll only be asked to stand by. I understand they're going to send landing craft in for them. They should be able to come right in to the beach and the men can wade out.'

Manolis drew a breath of relief. He had no wish to make trips in the darkness with an overloaded boat.

The men stood in lines, a hand on the shoulder of the man in front. All of them were straining their eyes looking for the first sign that a landing craft was heading towards them and a collective sigh of relief was expelled as they heard it grind to a halt. Manolis admired their discipline as they marched aboard, there was no rushing or attempt to be the first man on. When the loading was complete those left behind did not push or fight to be included, but stood and waited patiently to be directed onto the next craft.

Finally the beach was cleared and Manolis and Vasilis began the climb back up the cliff. Before they reached the shelter of the monastery the drone of aircraft overhead could be heard. Vasilis placed a firm hand on Manolis's shoulder. 'Lie flat,' he ordered and pushed the fisherman to the ground as a bullet shot through his hat.

'My hat!' exclaimed Manolis in surprise.

'Keep down or it will be your head next time,' warned Vasilis.

Manolis lay there, his ears ringing from the sound of the explosions and he was sure he could hear screams coming from the direction of the sea. He longed to look up and see what was happening, but Vasilis's hand was planted firmly in the small of his back. He realised he was trembling and hoped Vasilis would not brand him a coward.

The encounter seemed to continue for hours, before the sound of the aircraft grew fainter and Vasilis relaxed his pressure and sat up cautiously. 'Back to the beach,' he announced.

Manolis rose and followed in his wake as he scrambled back

down the steep cliff path from the monastery, both men missing their footing on a number of occasions and sliding some way before they were able to regain a foothold. The beach was dark and silent when they reached it. Small groups of men sat shivering in the darkness. The few survivors who had managed to swim to shore.

'We'll take them back up to the monastery and as soon as it's light we'll take your boat out and see if there's anyone who needs to be picked up,' decided Vasilis, although he felt anyone who had been caught directly in the onslaught would have perished.

Manolis nodded in the darkness. He felt sick and had no desire to be out on the sea. He realised there could be dead bodies floating out there and there was the added hazard that the Germans might return. 'I'll wait whilst you take them up,' he said. 'There's no need for both of us to go.'

Manolis sat on the shore in silence, recalling the events of the evening. Had the Germans come by chance or had someone told them there would be an evacuation attempt from Preveli? If that was so the area was no longer safe for anyone, least of all the soldiers who were hiding there. Manolis shivered intermittently. If he had been asked to transport any of the men he could have been out in the bay when the bombing took place. It was unlikely he would have survived.

As the dawn lightened the sky he walked down to the sea. He wandered disconsolately along the shoreline, examining the miscellany of items that littered it. There was a broken chair, papers, clothing, odd boots, some broken china, glass, wood and twisted metal. Of the ships that had stood off earlier there was no sign and he hoped they had managed to clear the area before the bombing had started and this was just debris thrown up by the explosions.

Vasilis returned, carrying his binoculars.

'How are the men who went up with you this morning?' asked Manolis.

Vasilis shrugged. 'Shocked; a few bumps and bruises; but no real injuries. They were the lucky ones who hadn't reached the ship. The blast simply threw them into the sea. Now they're only concerned about their comrades. I just hope we're able to find a few more.'

Manolis was not sure he wanted to find anyone. No doubt they would be badly mutilated, even if they were still alive. He rowed away from the shore, whilst Vasilis stood with one arm draped around the mast, the glasses to his eyes, looking for anything he thought should be investigated more closely.

'Go further out,' he ordered.

Manolis complied and something bumped against the boat, surprising Manolis so much that he nearly lost the oars. Vasilis bent over the prow and then shook his head. 'Debris,' he announced. 'At least we're in the right area.'

Manolis rowed back and forth at Vasilis's direction. They examined more debris, but they could find no sign of anyone surviving in the bay. Vasilis refused to give up. He continually asked Manolis to row further in each direction, lowering his glasses and closing his eyes periodically to rest them. Just as Manolis was about to declare that he could row no longer Vasilis gave a shout.

'Over there.'

Manolis headed in the direction he indicated and Vasilis relinquished his grip on the mast and bent over the side.

'Come and help me,' he ordered and Manolis scrambled across to join him. The boat rocked dangerously and both men clutched at the sides.

Manolis moved back into the centre of the boat. 'We'll sink if we're both on that side and you haul him aboard also.'

Vasilis was gripping the man's wrist. 'What do you suggest, then? Sail away and leave him?'

'Of course not. Tie my mooring rope round you and go into the water and hold him up. I'll drag you both back in.'

Vasilis released his grip on the man and struggled to tie the thick mooring rope around himself. Manolis was tempted to laugh at his clumsy efforts.

'Let me do it.' He seized the end, wound it twice round Vasilis's waist and looped the end through. 'I've left you enough slack, just let yourself down over the side.'

'If this works loose make sure you come back for me.'

Manolis grinned. 'I'll think about it.'

He watched as Vasilis removed his boots before climbing over the side of the boat and lowering himself into the sea. Vasilis placed one arm around the man and pried his fingers loose from the piece of wood he had been clinging to for hours.

'Ready,' he called up to Manolis. 'Use the motor. I don't want you hitting me with the oars.'

Vasilis felt the rope tighten round his waist as Manolis began to slowly make his way towards the shore. The man was heavy and appeared lifeless in his arms, but Vasilis had felt the pulse in his neck and knew that whatever his injuries, he was alive.

Vasilis pushed himself as far ashore as he was able, holding the man's head above the water, until Manolis had moored the boat and was able to help him onto the beach. Manolis shuddered as he looked at the survivor. His clothes had been blown to shreds, his back, chest and arms were red raw with shrapnel embedded in them.

'I'll go up and get some help,' said Manolis. 'He'd be too heavy to carry up the cliff path between us.' He gave his feet a cursory wipe on the sleeves of his shirt and pulled on his boots. He had no wish to stay on the beach looking at the injured man.

'Pass me a water bottle before you go. I'll see if I can get him to drink a little.'

Manolis detached his own from his belt and handed it to Vasilis. 'I'll be as quick as I can,' he promised.

By the time Manolis had scaled the cliff path to the monastery he was regretting his decision to leave his water bottle with Vasilis.

He entered the courtyard and ducked his head under the pump to drink and cool himself. From there he accosted the first monk he encountered and requested help for the injured man on the beach. Without questioning him the monk hurried away and returned moments later with three companions and a blanket. They followed Manolis back down to the shore where Vasilis still sat with the man cradled in his arms.

As the monks lifted him gently onto the blanket he whimpered in pain and Manolis winced at the sound. He vowed never to complain again about any hardship he had to endure. As he made the vow his stomach rumbled and he realised he had spent almost twenty-four hours without food.

'I'm hungry,' he said automatically to Vasilis.

'Well you'll have to put up with it a while longer. We haven't finished yet. We found one man. I want to go out and check again. There could be someone else clinging to a bit of debris.'

Manolis sighed. Not only was he hungry he was extremely tired.

The two men searched the area for a further three hours, but no more survivors were found clinging to debris and they had no sooner returned to the shore when the drone of aeroplanes could be heard overhead. They ran for cover and sat beneath the low trees that boarded the river whilst the Germans made pass after pass across the bay.

'Are they looking for survivors?' asked Manolis.

'I doubt it,' replied Vasilis. 'If they did see anyone they're quite likely to shoot them. They're probably looking for the ships that were here last night, hoping to catch them limping back to Egypt and wanting to finish them off.'

It was late in the afternoon when the aeroplanes finally gave up their search and disappeared over the horizon. Manolis and Vasilis rose to their feet and continued the arduous climb back up to the monastery and Manolis retrieved his damaged hat. Vasilis went to enquire about the injured man they had rescued and Manolis collapsed thankfully on his bed, his tiredness overcoming his hunger.

Vasilis shook him awake when it was time for the evening meal. 'Come on. If you sleep any longer you'll miss your meal. I don't want you keeping me awake all night complaining that you're hungry.'

Manolis grinned sheepishly, once awake conscious of the hunger pangs that were assailing him. 'How's that man?' he asked.

'He'll live. He'll probably end up badly scarred.' Vasilis shrugged. 'What's a bit of scarring compared with your life? It was lucky we found him when we did. He'd not have lasted much longer out there, particularly when the sun was full.'

'Do you think the others arrived back safely?'

'Who knows? Hopefully we'll get a message at some time.'

'Will they send it in code?'

'No idea. You'd have to ask Arthur.'

Manolis did not remind Vasilis that he could not communicate with Arthur and that he had hardly seen the man since they had brought him to Preveli.

Manolis was not relishing his trip to the villages that morning. He was concerned that if the aeroplanes came over they would shoot at him and was pleased when Yiorgo arrived and he had an excuse to delay his departure whilst he heard the news he brought.

'I've heard the Germans are fanning out and planning to surround Preveli. They know the allied troops were told to make for this area and they suspect a good many of them are still hiding down here. Wherever possible the locals hinder them. They've blocked roads and the andartes have come down and picked them off whilst they were trying to clear them.' Yiorgo flicked his worry beads. 'Then the Germans go back to the village and shoot any men they find there. If they don't find any men they rape and beat the women. I've heard that they've picked up radio signals and know about the food drops.'

Manolis felt sick. He would have to warn Eleni and her village. 'How would they find out?' he asked.

Yiorgo shrugged. 'Not everyone is loyal to Crete. Some people think they will be safe if they help the Germans. They will ask questions that appear to be quite innocent, but the answer can be just the information the Germans have been waiting for. It's best to plead ignorance if you're asked anything.'

Manolis nodded and began to rack his brains. Eleni had asked him questions. Surely she was not going to tell anything to a German? He had not given her any information, of that he was certain. He had none to give. Besides, the villagers were helping to hide and feed the refugee troops.

Yiorgo turned back to Vasilis. 'Not content with that,' he added, 'they're stealing whatever they can find of any value in the houses and they've robbed some of the churches. Sometimes they just destroy the icons, but if there's gold or silver around they take it. We ought to warn the Abbot to hide the relics safely away.'

'I always thought Germans and Italians were Christian people.' Vasilis spoke bitterly. 'They sound more like animals.' He shook his head. 'No, animals behave better.'

'The ordinary soldiers just obey their masters. They carry out their orders in fear of reprisals from their commanding officers. When they took Heraklion they were told they could do whatever they pleased for ten days. Some people lost everything they owned, others have disappeared and their families have no idea where they are or if they are still alive. If they gave them that freedom there I expect they did the same in the other towns.'

'What's happening in Aghios Nikolaos?' asked Manolis. 'Have you any news of that area?'

Yiorgo shook his head. 'Nothing definite, but I expect it's much the same down there. The town is under the control of Italians.'

'Do you think my aunt and uncle are safe?'

'I've no idea. I've not been that far down. It appears that people are left unmolested provided they do as they're told and obey their new masters.'

Manolis nodded. He could not imagine his aunt or uncle rebelling. They would be only too relieved to be left in peace to continue with their humdrum life. 'What about supplies going out to the island?'

'What island?' asked Yiorgo.

'Spinalonga. I used to take the doctor out and deliver their supplies.'

Yiorgo shrugged. 'I told you, I've not been that far down. It's only what I've heard in the villages.'

Vasilis sat deep in concentration. 'You say they're on their way to Preveli?'

'I heard they'd reached Spili.'

'I think the Abbot ought to disappear for a while. When they find there's nothing and no one here they'll move on.'

Manolis frowned. 'Won't they think it strange to find a monastery without the Abbot?'

'Better for them to think he has fled than for them to find him.' Vasilis rose. 'I need to speak to him. Wait here until I come back, Manolis. I may need you.'

Manolis scowled. 'What about my deliveries?'

'The villagers can manage for twenty four hours.'

Yiorgo stretched out on Vasilis's bed and was soon snoring gently, whilst Manolis sat in a sulky silence. No doubt it would take Vasilis all day to convince the Abbot that he must leave the monastery. Much as he had dreaded making his deliveries earlier, he now wanted to visit Eleni and warn her of impending danger and also the other villages. He played with his worry beads, checked the amount of drachmas he had in his pocket and reverted again to his beads.

Vasilis returned just before mid-day and shook Yiorgo awake, beckoning him outside. Manolis felt aggrieved that he had not been present at their conversation. Did Vasilis no longer trust him? Vasilis returned alone and Manolis looked at him curiously.

'Where's Yiorgo?'

'He's taking a message. I suggest you get some rest. We've got a busy night ahead of us.'

'I've been sitting around all morning,' protested Manolis. 'I could make the delivery and have a rest when I get back.'

Vasilis shook his head. 'You need to check your motor and fill up with petrol.'

Inwardly Manolis groaned; what hazardous activity was he going to participate in that night?

'We're going up the coast to Aghios Georgios. The Abbot should be safe enough there in the church for the night. The next day we'll take him to Sfakia. Yiorgo has gone on ahead to tell them and we can give him a ride back.'

'When are we leaving?'

'As soon as it's dark.'

With Vasilis's help Manolis pulled his boat off the sandbank and out from beneath the bushes where he hid it regularly. He poled it down to a reasonable depth of water, checked that the boat would not be grounded with the additional weight of the Abbot and rigged his black sails. He was not at all sure that he would have enough petrol to make the journey and there was no more available at the monastery.

They helped the Abbot aboard and Vasilis folded a blanket for him to sit on. 'A little more comfortable than sitting on the wooden planking for a few hours,' he smiled.

'Thank you.' The Abbot smiled back gratefully. 'There's not a lot of flesh on these old bones now.'

'Have you sailed before?' asked Vasilis.

'In my youth, but not for many years now. I have to warn you, I am not a good sailor. I shall pray for a smooth journey.'

'I shall pray for an uneventful one,' replied Vasilis grimly. 'Are you ready, Manolis? If so, we'll be off. We'll use the sails unless we have to make an emergency run in to the shore.'

The prayers of both men were answered, the sea was calm and no aeroplanes were heard. Manolis sailed steadily until Vasilis decided they should stop and anchor until dawn and they could ascertain there exact position.

'If I've calculated correctly we should only be about half an hour's run from here.'

Manolis nodded. 'Do you want me to use the motor to run in?'

Vasilis nodded. 'Yiorgo should have reached the village and they will be expecting us. We don't want to alarm them by arriving with black sails.'

They motored as far into the beach as possible, before Manolis took to the oars and rowed as close to the shore as he dared. He felt the boat ground and stopped immediately.

'This is as far in as I can go. I'm sorry,' he apologised to the Abbott, 'you will have to get your feet wet.'

Vasilis jumped overboard and offered his hand to the Abbot who gathered his cassock up as far as he could, exposing his skinny legs. Manolis steadied him as he swung first one leg and then the other over the side and waded the short distance to the shore. He resisted the urge to laugh at the spectacle the normally dignified Abbot presented.

Manolis followed them up the beach and onto a grassy track. A cluster of houses came into view, with the church, flying the Greek flag, predominating. As they walked along the village street the women stared at them in surprise and Father Philippos hurried from his church to greet them.

He kissed the Abbot's hand and welcomed him, obviously flustered by his arrival. 'I had no idea you were making a visit. We have nothing prepared for you. I will ask the women to make some food. It will only be plain fare. Please, come in and have some wine. I have only a humble house, but it is yours for the duration of your stay.'

The Abbot followed Father Philippos into his house and Manolis stood back hesitantly. Why should the priest be surprised by their arrival? Yiorgo had come on ahead to notify him.

'Come on,' urged Vasilis. 'We deserve a glass of wine as well.'

Manolis grinned. He would rather have had some breakfast. He pushed his worries concerning Yiorgo to the back of his mind and sat at the table with the men, trying to stifle his yawns. The wine had gone to his head and he hoped the women would not be too long in preparing food for them. He turned thankfully when the door opened.

'Father, there are Germans on the way. Andreas saw them from the hill. They are driving along the road in a truck.' The woman wrung her hands in distress.

Father Philippos frowned. 'Return to your home and continue with whatever you were doing.' He rose from his chair. 'We will go to the church,' he announced.

Manolis found his legs were shaking. He very much doubted the Germans would respect the sanctity of the religious building.

Father Philippos strode to one side and began to move the chairs from an area of the stone floor. He lifted a section easily and revealed a dark pit. The Abbot immediately let himself down, grunting as he landed on the earthen floor and Vasilis pushed Manolis to follow him. Manolis hesitated.

'Get down, man,' Vasilis spoke roughly and Manolis hesitated no longer. Vasilis jumped in after him.

'Not a sound,' Father Philippos warned as he threw a water bottle down to them. 'As soon as it is safe I will return.'

The priest had no sooner replaced the chairs than the sound of tramping feet came to the hidden men. It was pitch dark beneath the floor and Manolis was petrified. He drew his legs up to his chin and sat, his whole body trembling. Either Vasilis or the Abbot patted him on the shoulder to reassure him. Manolis strained his ears to hear the exchange between the priest and the unwelcome soldiers.

The priest rose from before the altar and held up his hands. 'Please, this is a place of God. If you have come to worship you are welcome.'

The two soldiers holding Yiorgo released his arms and he dropped at the feet of the priest, the man's face a mass of pulp and blood. Father Philippos gasped in horror. 'What has happened to this poor man?' he asked, knowing that the man had been interrogated unmercifully.

'Where are you hiding them?' asked their commanding officer.

The priest frowned. 'Who am I supposed to be hiding?' He swept his hand around the empty church.

The commander moved closer, the white scar on his face showing up clearly. 'We know this man arranged to meet partisans here. Why was he meeting them and where are they? If you do not hand them over you will suffer the same fate as he has, but we may take our time with you.'

Father Philippos shook his head. 'I fear your information is incorrect. As you can see I am alone in my church.'

'Then where are they hiding in the village? Someone will tell us if you do not. Those that keep silent will regret their decision.'

'I have not heard of any strangers in the village. Please, allow me to attend to the injuries of this man.'

The officer gave an order and two soldiers walked around, examining the walls, searching behind the screen and the altar, knocking over the candles, one of which set the altar cloth burning. Father Philippos hurried forward and patted the flames out with his bare hands, leaving a smell of smouldering in the air. The soldiers shook their heads and went through to the empty wash house at the back. They pulled the robes belonging to the priest to the ground, tipped up the tin bath and looked in the cupboard. There was no one hiding there.

The commander gave the priest a steely glare. 'Why should this man finally say the name Aghios Georgios?'

'He lives in this area. He was trying to tell you that to deter you from beating him further. He no doubt wished to be brought to my church for sanctuary, expecting to be safe from your rough treatment.'

The officer looked at Father Philippos venomously. 'My men will search the village, and you will come with us. When we find these men you will wish you had disclosed their hiding place more quickly.' His eyes roved around the church, taking in the icons inlaid with silver, the candlesticks, and the lectern.

They left Yiorgo lying where he had fallen, took the priest by his arms, and marched him from the church.

'I will be back,' Father Philippos called loudly, hoping the men hidden below the floor would hear him.

Once outside the church the commanding officer pointed his revolver at the priest. 'This is your last opportunity to tell us where these men are hidden.'

Summoning up his courage, Father Philippos looked into the man's cold, blue eyes. 'You have searched my church and found no one. Shoot me if you wish, but you will not find any men hidden in the village.'

The commander looked around. 'Why is the Greek flag flying from your church?' he demanded.

'It is our national flag. Why should it not fly from our churches?'

'It is no longer your national flag. You are under our command now. Remove it.'

Father Philippos looked up at the cupola surmounted by the cross where the flag fluttered. 'I am not able to reach up there.'

The commander turned, aimed his revolver at the cross, and fired. The metal bent and he fired again, causing the adornment to crumple sideways, pinning the flag beneath it.

'Now, we will see who my men have found hiding.'

Slowly the soldiers returned, shaking their heads and standing in a group awaiting further orders. The commander tapped his revolver against his hand. 'So, they have found no one. Where are you hiding them?' he barked.

'I told you they were not here and you have found no one.' The priest shrugged. 'Now maybe you will believe me.'

By way of an answer, the commander hit the priest on the side of his head with his revolver. Father Philippos fell to the ground unmoving.

'We will be back.'

The commanding officer signalled to the soldiers who returned to the truck they had been travelling in and climbed aboard. Father Philippos lay where he was, the dust from the wheels of the truck covering his face and hair. Horrified villagers emerged from their houses and a woman knelt beside him.

Father Philippos opened his eyes cautiously. 'Have they left?' he asked.

The woman nodded and crossed herself. 'Are you badly hurt?'

Father Philippos gave a wry smile. 'A bump on the head. It is nothing. I thought it better to pretend I was unconscious or they might have decided to damage me further. Help me up. I have necessary jobs to attend to.'

Once on his feet the priest swayed. The blow had been more vicious than he had realised. He allowed the woman to help him over to the church and sank down in the first chair. He touched the swelling with a trembling hand. A cold compress was needed, but first he must ensure the brutalised man was attended to and release the Abbot and his companions from the hole in the ground.

He pointed to where Yiorgo still lay on the stone floor. 'Find someone to help you and take that man into my house where you can attend to his wounds. I will stay here and say a prayer for our deliverance and his recovery.'

Father Philippos waited impatiently whilst Maria hurried away and she seemed to return with most of the women from the village. They helped Yiorgo to his feet, almost carrying him from the church, then the others began to fret over the priest, arguing about who should have the honour of attending to him.

He waved them away. 'I have told Maria I wish to stay here and pray. I have some important guests. Go and argue about women's business whilst you prepare some food for them.'

Father Philippos waited until the last of them had left the church, then he closed the door. He did not trust gossiping women to know about the cavity he had created beneath the church floor. He moved the chairs back and lifted the first slab. As soon as he had done so, Vasilis and Manolis pushed up the others, climbed out of the hole and bent down to assist the Abbot.

Manolis took a deep breath of relief. He had heard the shots and was petrified that the priest had been shot and no one would know where they were hidden. They would be condemned to die by suffocation and starvation.

'Who did they shoot?' he asked.

'The Greek flag was flying. They asked me to remove it. How am I supposed to climb up there?' asked Father Philippos. 'They shot it down.'

'What happens now?' asked Manolis.

'The Abbot is insisting on continuing to Sfakia. He doesn't want to endanger the priest and the villagers further.'

'So we're taking him?'

Vasilis nodded. 'It's his decision.'

'What about Yiorgo?'

'We'll leave him here to be looked after. When he's recovered he can make his own way to wherever he wishes to go.'

'Suppose the Germans catch him again?'

Vasilis shrugged. 'We can't prevent that. He knows the risks he runs. He'll probably make for the hills and stay there for a week or two with the andartes. It could be more dangerous for him if we took him back to Preveli with us.'

Manolis nodded soberly. He had thought to evade any threat of danger, but it seemed he was more vulnerable on this coast than he had been at Aghios Nikolaos.

In the late afternoon Manolis and Vasilis walked down to the shore accompanied by the Abbot and Father Philippos. The priest held a cold cloth to the side of his painful face. It was purple with bruising, his eye half closed, and his jaw hurt whenever he spoke.

Manolis stopped abruptly. 'My boat!' He ran forwards to the heap of timber that lay on the beach, smashed beyond repair.

Vasilis hurried after him. Manolis was touching the broken timbers, tears streaming down his face. 'My boat,' he kept saying.

Vasilis did not know how to console the distraught young man.

'It was my father's boat. It's all I have.'

'You can get another.'

'What with? I have no money; and who would sell their boat to me? No one.' Manolis sat down in utter despair beside the wreck.

'Maybe there is an old one here that you could repair?'

Manolis looked at him scathingly. 'Have you seen any boats here? I haven't.'

Father Philippos patted Manolis's shoulder. 'I am truly sorry that such a thing should have happened.'

'It's not your fault, Father,' Manolis managed to say. He scrubbed at his face with his sleeve. 'How are we going to take the Abbot to Sfakia now?'

The Abbot looked at the young man sadly. 'Had I not asked you to bring me here this would not have happened. I feel responsible.'

'It could have happened anywhere,' Vasilis observed philosophically. 'How are you going to reach Sfakia, Father?'

The Abbot looked down at the ground. 'I have two legs and two feet, thanks to the Lord. I shall walk.'

'That is a day's walk!' Father Philippos was horrified.

The Abbot shrugged. 'It will take as long as the Lord decides. He will look after me. If I leave now I should reach the village by this evening and be able to beg a bed for the night.'

'Please, stay here. You can have my bed,' offered Father Philippos.

The Abbot shook his head. 'I have endangered you enough. The Germans could well pay a surprise visit here during the night, hoping to find me comfortably asleep. I prefer to disappoint them.'

Vasilis nodded, realising the sense of the Abbot's words. If the Germans returned and found any of them in the village the whole community would suffer their vengeance.

'We'll walk with you, Father,' he offered. 'I would like to know you were safe.'

'That is a thoughtful gesture and appreciated, but not necessary. You and your boatman friend must look to your own safety.'

Vasilis shook his head. 'I insist that we walk with you to Sfakia, Father. We cannot stay here. As you so rightly pointed out the Germans could return during the night hoping to catch us unawares. That excellent hiding place will not remain undiscovered for ever.'

Manolis shuddered. He had no wish to return to the underground hole for an indeterminate amount of time. He took a last, long, look at his wrecked boat and followed Vasilis and the priests back up to the village.

Vasilis insisted they used the path over the hills rather than the road. He continually strode on ahead of them for a considerable distance to ensure the area was safe and Manolis found the slow, measured pace of the Abbot frustrating. He hoped they would not be escorting him any further than Sfakia. It was dark by the time they saw the first few buildings that made up the hamlet and Vasilis had raised the occupants of a house and begged shelter for the Abbot.

Willingly the woman gave up her bed. 'We were searched

earlier yesterday. They should have no reason to return here tonight.'

She was about to move her children from their mattress when Vasilis stopped her. 'It is a warm night. We will come to no harm sleeping outside.'

She shook her head. 'You are visitors. I cannot allow that.'

'I insist,' said Vasilis. 'We are more used to sleeping in the open air in rough conditions than inside on a mattress. It will be no hardship to us. In fact we will sleep better.'

Without any more cajoling on Vasilis's part the woman capitulated and the two men returned to the rough road.

'Why did you refuse a bed for the night?' asked Manolis.

'I want to listen out for troops moving in this direction. If we're asleep in a bed we'll not hear a thing. You can sleep first. I'll wake you' he looked up at the sky and pointed, 'when the moon is there.'

Vasilis woke Manolis who blinked the sleep from his eyes. 'Wake me as the sun begins to rise,' ordered Vasilis and curled up on the hard ground.

Manolis sat with his back to a tree. At first every slight rustle of leaves or creatures going about their nocturnal business made his hair stand on end, then he began to relax, identifying each sound as he heard it, until his ears picked up a low rumbling in the distance.

He placed his mouth close to Vasilis's ear. 'Vasilis. Wake up.'

Without moving Vasilis answered him. 'What is it?'

'I don't know. A noise. It could be a truck.'

Vasilis sat up, placed his finger to his lips to silence Manolis, and listened intently. Vasilis rose and signalled to Manolis to do the same. 'Into the scrub and hide,' he said quietly.

Both men pushed their way through the low bushes and scrub to lay flat. The noise grew louder and a truck loaded with soldiers rumbled past them on the road. Once it had passed Manolis made to get up and Vasilis stayed him with his hand and shook his head.

'We will be safer to stay here.'

'What about the Abbot?'

In the darkness Vasilis gave a shrug. 'If a couple of soldiers come back and search the house I will deal with them. I cannot fight a truckload.'

They stayed in their uncomfortable hiding place amongst the scrub, thorns penetrating their clothes, thistles scratching their hands and faces, low branches digging into them, and whichever way they turned they were unable to avoid the discomfort. Both men were thankful when the truck returned and drove on down the road. Eventually Vasilis decided it was safe for them to emerge and they crawled out.

'I need to know if the Germans found whoever they were looking for last night.'

'We'd know if they'd found the Abbot,' pointed out Manolis.

'They may not have been looking for him. I'll speak to the Abbot and his host. It could be safer for him to stay with her than the church. Wait here until I return.'

Manolis nodded. Where did Vasilis think he would go?

Vasilis was absent most of the morning, but he looked cheerful when he returned. 'The Abbot should be safely on his way to Egypt tonight. Once we know he has left we can return to Aghios Georgios. I want to check that Father Philippos and Yiorgo are safe. We will then return to Preveli.'

'Why are we going back there?'

'They will wish to know the fate of the Abbot, besides we can be of more use at Preveli than staying here. The people of Sfakia have more than enough mouths to feed.'

They entered the small village of Aghios Georgios and walked up to the church where the doors stood open. Father Philippos was on his knees, but he looked up fearfully at their arrival.

'The soldiers came back,' he stated simply.

Vasilis nodded. 'Did they hurt you again?'

Father Philippos began to shake his head, then stopped, it was too painful. 'They took the valuables from the church and destroyed things they considered of no value.' There were tears in his eyes as he looked around. The candlesticks, lectern, and silver incense container were missing. The icons had been slashed and the Bible lay on the floor, its pages torn out and trampled.

Manolis gasped in horror. He was resentful and angry about the destruction of his boat, but to rob the church and destroy religious artefacts was indefensible.

Vasilis helped Father Philippos to his feet. 'Is there anything we can do to help?' he asked.

The priest tried to shake his head again. 'Pray that they will now leave us in peace,' he said.

'How is Yiorgo?'

'The women are looking after him. I fear he has some broken ribs and his jaw is definitely fractured.'

'And yourself, Father? How are you? I can see how very painful your face has become.'

Father Philippos shrugged. 'It is just bruising, nothing compared with Yiorgo's injuries. It will heal. My church will never recover from the desecration that has been inflicted on it.'

'When these barbarians have been driven from our country no doubt the artefacts they have stolen will be recovered and returned to you.'

Father Philippos shook his head sadly. 'I fear not. The icons can never be repaired. I should have placed everything of value in the hole. That may have saved them from their fate.'

'They knew they were here. They had seen them earlier. Had they been missing when they returned they would know you had hidden them and beaten you until you revealed their hiding place. You are more valuable to the community than the artefacts.'

The priest looked at Vasilis doubtfully. 'I am sure you are right,' he sighed. 'What news of the Abbot?'

'He had a good night's rest at Sfakia and continued his journey last night.'

'May God protect him.' Father Philippos crossed himself. 'And you two men? What are your plans now you no longer have a boat?'

'We are returning to Preveli.'

Manolis and Vasilis bade the priest farewell and Vasilis took the road to Komitades.

'Why are we going this way?' asked Manolis after they had been walking further into the countryside on a well made road for an hour.

'I decided I wanted to return to my village and see my wife and son. I should like to know they are safe and unmolested.'

'But you told Father Philippos that we were going to Preveli,' protested Manolis.

Vasilis nodded. 'If the Germans visit him again and manage to extract information from him he believes that is where we are going. If I had told him I planned to visit my home he would have asked, quite naturally, the name of the village. I do not want to draw the Germans' attention to the area.'

'Is it close by?' asked Manolis.

Vasilis shook his head. 'It is almost at Chania.'

'Why are we using the road? If any Germans drive down this way they will see us immediately. Isn't there a safer way across the hills?'

'I am taking the easiest route,' explained Vasilis patiently. 'If we went along the coast or tried to cut across the country we would end up at the mouth of the gorge. It is deserted and we would have to climb the steep sides, scrambling up and down rocks, some of them loose and dangerous. We could well have to walk a couple of days or more without replenishing our food and water. We would bake during the day and freeze at night. Trust me.'

'So what do we do if the Germans do come this way?'

'We should hear them and then we will go into the fields and hide or pretend to be working.' Vasilis reassured him. 'We will stay on the road until we reach Alikambos, then we can take to the country paths.'

'How long will that take?'

'I hope to reach there tonight. It is no great distance, but we have to cross the mountains. The road is steep and twisting. That will slow us down.'

'How far is it from there to your village?'

'Another couple of days.'

'What will you do when you reach there?' asked Manolis curiously.

Vasilis shrugged. 'If all is quiet in the area I could stay and help on the farm. If there are soldiers around my family would probably be safer if I went elsewhere. What about you? I can put you on the road to Filippos and it is only a short distance from there to the main road down to Rethymnon. If you stay on the coast road you'll end up in Aghios Nikolaos.'

'What will I do if I go there? Even if I was allowed to fish I have no boat,' Manolis said morosely.

'You can come to my village with me if you want,' offered Vasilis.

Manolis considered. 'What I would really like to do is visit the churches.'

Vasilis raised his eyebrows. 'Has living at Preveli influenced you?' he asked.

Manolis smiled and shook his head. 'It was when I saw what they had done to Father Philippos's church; the robbery and needless destruction. He said he should have hidden the artefacts. I'd like to go to the churches that haven't been robbed yet and warn them to hide their precious objects.'

Vasilis stopped and regarded the young man. 'You're serious?'

'Very serious.'

'Where would they hide them?'

Manolis shrugged. 'I don't know. How many priests have thought to make a hole under the floor of their church? Maybe they could dig a hole in a field somewhere, or find a cave.'

Vasilis nodded slowly. 'I think that's quite a good idea.'

'Would you come with me? You seem to know everywhere.'

Vasilis laughed. 'No promises. I'll be quite happy to stay at home if all is peaceful there.'

'Vasilis!' A young woman straightened up from where she was bending over, lifting a small, wet baby from the bath. Vasilis took no notice of the wetness of the child as he encircled her with his arms before dropping a kiss on the curly head of the small boy.

'Manolis, meet my wife, Katerina, and my small son, another Vasilis.'

'I'm pleased to meet you,' mumbled Manolis.

'Now, Katerina, let me look at you. Yes, you are more beautiful than ever. I have missed you. Have you missed me?'

'Of course I have. Let me go, now. I must see to Vasilis.'

'Wrap him in a towel and let me cuddle him. Whilst I do so, you can make us some coffee. We are in need of sustenance. Bring us some food also; we haven't had a decent meal in days.'

Manolis shifted his feet uncomfortably. Vasilis sat down on a chair and looked at his son. 'You've grown since Pappa last saw you.' Vasilis sighed deeply. 'All too soon you will be a man, with all the trials that brings with it.'

The small boy gurgled happily as he struggled to get out of the towel that was wrapped around him. Vasilis seemed to remember that Manolis was there and smiled at him.

'There's a pump a short distance along the street if you want to wash.'

Manolis nodded. 'You ought to have a wash yourself.'

'Later, later. I want to enjoy my child whilst I can.'

Manolis looked at Vasilis enviously. He wished with all his

heart he could be with Flora and they had a child. He recalled his fleeting affair with Eleni and felt even more ashamed and guilty. That had been the momentary madness of a lonely man. He loved Flora.

Eleni woke up feeling sick again the moment she attempted to rise from her mattress. This week she would know for certain if she was pregnant. She had missed her last period and prayed fervently this one would appear at the appointed time. She was cross with herself. She had been stupid to continue meeting Manolis in the hope of providing the German with information and gain his affection.

She would not be able to keep her condition hidden from her mother for much longer. It was doubtful if Heinrich would want to take her to Spili now. She had liked Manolis, but Heinrich's blonde looks had captured her fickle heart.

Manolis had not appeared for over a week. He had probably found a girl in another village, she thought resentfully. It would serve him right if she accused him of raping her. Her mother would want to know why she had said nothing at the time and she could say she was scared that Manolis would hurt her if she told anyone how he had forced her to succumb to him.

She swallowed the bile back down her throat and made her way out to the yard, hoping her mother would not come out at the same time and see her retching.

Heinrich appeared alone in the village at mid-day. He placed his hand on the horn of the jeep he was driving to attract the attention of the villagers. Despondently they left their farm implements on the ground and walked slowly back to the square. He looked them over contemptuously. The only one who had any semblance of good looks was the girl. He beckoned to her and she walked over to him, a smile on her lips.

'Get in,' he ordered. 'The rest of you get back to your work.'

'In the jeep?'

'Where else.' He opened the door and she slid into the seat beside him.

'Where are you taking me?'

'It's a surprise.'

Eleni smiled delightedly. 'Are we going to Spili?'

'You'll see.'

Eleni looked around her in delight as they drove along. She had never been in anything more than a motorised cart before and the jeep went much faster. They passed through the next two villages and out into the countryside where Heinrich drew up before a collection of tents. He sounded his horn and men appeared from beneath their canvas shelters.

Heinrich opened the door and pushed her out. 'She's all yours,' he announced. 'I'll take her back this evening.'

The men surged forward eagerly and Eleni felt the first prickling of fear. What were they going to do to her?

Eleni lay on the ground where Heinrich had thrown her. She had been raped continually since arriving at the soldiers' camp. At first it had not been too objectionable, then she became sore and finally she was in agony and screaming each time a man thrust himself inside her. When it was dark, Heinrich returned to her.

'I hope you have enjoyed your day. I will take you back to your village now.'

Eleni attempted to stand, but it was impossible. Two soldiers pulled her to her feet and dragged her to the jeep where they tossed her into the back and gave her a towel.

'Make sure you do not bleed in my jeep,' ordered Heinrich and Eleni stuffed the towel between her legs. She would do anything to prevent any of the men from touching her again.

Her head banged continually on the floor of the jeep as it jolted over the rough road to reach her village. By the time Heinrich drew up on the outskirts she was only semi-conscious. He pulled her out unceremoniously and left her lying on the ground, the bloodied towel beside her.

Eleni did not have the strength to move or even cry out as he drove away. Hot tears trickled down her cheeks. No one would want to marry her now, certainly not Heinrich. Her dream of going to Spili and becoming rich was shattered. Her only consolation was the unlikelihood that she was still pregnant with Manolis's child.

Manolis watched Vasilis playing with his small son. He had not felt so comfortable for a long time. Sleeping on the boat or out in the open had been hazardous and unpleasant. Even sharing a room with Vasilis at Preveli, despite being warm and dry, had been Spartan in the extreme, no rug on the stone floor and only one chair on which to place their belongings. This was a home.

Vasilis junior was eventually laid on his mattress to sleep, and Vasilis joined Manolis at the table. 'We'll move on tomorrow.'

Manolis looked at him in surprise. 'I thought you wanted to stay here with your family.'

'I would love to stay with them, but I'll not endanger them. Haven't you noticed; there are no young men around in the villages. According to Katerina, the Germans pay unexpected visits and search the houses. If we are found here she will be accused of harbouring andartes or resistance workers.'

'So where will we go?'

'We'll go back to Preveli. The soldiers that weren't evacuated and haven't been taken prisoner are forming resistance groups. We could be useful to them.'

Manolis looked at him sadly. 'I no longer have my rifle.'

Vasilis laughed. 'You didn't know how to shoot it anyway.'

'I was going to ask you to teach me.'

SEPTEMBER 1941

Manolis and Vasilis left the village during the morning. Vasilis was carrying a sack that held two thick jumpers, spare socks, some underwear and three clean shirts. Katerina had tears in her eyes as she bade her husband farewell, knowing it could be months before she saw him again. She held up little Vasilis's hand and waved it to his father as the men turned for one last look back.

'Which way are we going?' asked Manolis.

'We'll keep to the back roads and go through the villages until we reach Georgioupoli. From there we can begin to make our way over to the other coast and we'll be back at Preveli.'

'I hope it will be easier than when we walked here.' Manolis looked down at his boots. 'My boots are so thin I can feel every stone.'

'We can try to find a cobbler in one of the villages and you can get them repaired.'

'What am I going to pay them with?' asked Manolis. 'I've only a few leptas in my pocket and there's no way I can catch any fish.'

'You could offer to do some digging for them, or repair a wall. Something the women are finding difficult to do.'

Manolis looked at him sceptically. 'I've never repaired a wall.' As he said the words he felt guilty. The inhabitants of Spinalonga had not only repaired walls, but also built new ones with no previous building knowledge.

Vasilis grinned at him. 'It's not that difficult.'

'Could we ask at the church to see if they want their artefacts hidden?' suggested Manolis. 'Maybe the priest would pay then to have my boots repaired.'

Vasilis shook his head. 'I think we're a bit late offering in this area. The Germans have beaten us to it. When we get further down, provided they haven't visited those villages we can ask.'

'I shall be walking in bare feet by then,' grumbled Manolis.

The road they had travelled had snaked up low hills that turned into steep, stony inclines that wound their way higher and higher, before beginning an equally hazardous descent. The area was devoid of villages, even when they reached flatter countryside, and Manolis was relieved when Vasilis took a detour to the village of Embrossneros and Vasilis called a halt.

'It will be safer to stay here for the night. We don't want to be too close to the road in case the Germans decide to use it. We can make an early start.' Vasilis pointed to the map. 'We'll aim to be in that area by tomorrow night and then it's only a short hike down to Preveli.'

Manolis snorted. 'Your idea of a short hike means another long walk! I still haven't managed to get my boots repaired.'

'I can't help it if the cobblers haven't any leather.'

Manolis shrugged. He was tired, hungry and his feet hurt. Vasilis had not suggested they stop and eat during the day. He hoped Katerina had managed to pack sufficient to satisfy his rumbling stomach.

They filled their water bottles from the village pump and walked away into the countryside. 'We'll be safer sleeping out,' announced Vasilis. 'If they're making unexpected visits to the villages we don't want to be found there.'

'What about some food?' Manolis suggested longingly.

'When we stop for the night,' Vasilis promised him and with that Manolis had to be content.

The following day Vasilis led them back to the road and across the rough countryside covered with low scrub and thistles until the reached Lake Kournas. Manolis looked at it in wonder.

'I didn't know we had lakes in Crete.'

'I believe there's only that one,' replied Vasilis.

'Are there fish in there?' asked Manolis.

'No idea,' replied Vasilis cheerfully. 'And if there are we're not stopping whilst you do some fishing.'

Manolis grinned. 'Have you ever tried to catch a fish with your bare hands? It's difficult enough when you're taking them from the net. They manage to wriggle and slip through your fingers.'

As they skirted the lake he watched the waters carefully for any sign that fish might live there. He dabbled his fingers and licked one of them. 'It's fresh water.' He shook his head. 'I can't see any fish living in that.'

They moved deeper into the countryside, moving more swiftly as they saw a couple of small villages in the distance.

Father Theopolis listened politely as Vasilis suggested he should hide the church artefacts from marauding soldiers, and shook his head.

'Sadly you are too late. They have already visited me.'

'What about the other churches in the area?'

'I know Father Alexandros's church was robbed.' He spread his hands. 'As for the others in the vicinity, I could not say. Before these barbarians arrived we would visit each other in our respective villages. Now we do not leave the shelter of our homes unless it is necessary. The Germans view everyone with suspicion. I have to warn you, they are forever making unexpected forays into the countryside. They terrorise the people, insist on searching their homes, causing damage heedlessly. No one is safe.'

'Why do they keep returning?' asked Manolis. 'If they have found nothing, why should they come back?'

'They say they are searching for allied soldiers they believe the villagers to be hiding.' Father Theopolis shook his head. 'I do not think they would be so foolish as to try to hide so close to where the Germans occupy the towns. It is my belief that any men who are hiding are doing so in the mountains.'

'Have you told the Germans this? If you did they might leave your village alone,' suggested Manolis.

Father Theopolis regarded him sternly. 'I would not tell a German soldier what time of day it was. If I said there were men hiding in the mountains they would probably take me for interrogation thinking I knew their exact whereabouts. I saw the allied troops when they were forced to retreat. We gave them food and the women tended to their wounds as best they could. Where they went from here I do not know.'

'What now?' asked Manolis as they left the village.

'We'll speak to the priest each time we reach a church, but I fear Father Theopolis was right. The Germans will have searched this area thoroughly and probably taken anything of value they could lay their hands on.'

By late afternoon the two men had visited four more churches. In each one the priest had shaken his head and shown them his desecrated building. One even had swastikas daubed on the stone walls and the Germans had declared the pages they had torn from the Bible would be used as toilet paper. In one church the priest accused them of being Germans in disguise and threatened to have them arrested. Vasilis admired his courage. Had they really been German soldiers it was unlikely he would have survived the threats he made to them.

Manolis looked downcast. 'Maybe it was a foolish idea of mine. Let's just get to Preveli.'

Vasilis shook his head. 'Don't be defeatist. You're tired and no doubt hungry as usual. We're still too close to the coast. We'll try again tomorrow when we're further inland. The Germans haven't had time to penetrate all the inland areas yet.'

Father Elias was sceptical when they approached him. He was adamant that the Germans would not penetrate that deeply into the countryside and certain they would not desecrate his church if they did reach the village. Patiently Vasilis explained to him the ravages that had taken place in other villages on Crete.

Father Elias pursed his lips. 'How do I know you are not robbers? You could persuade me to hide these artefacts, then come and help yourself later. No, my church artefacts will stay where they are and I know they are safe.' The priest sat back and folded his arms defiantly.

'Very well. It is your decision. We'll trouble you no further.' Vasilis rose and held out his hand. 'I assure you we are not robbers,' he smiled. 'It was just an idea we had when we saw the damage that had been done elsewhere.'

The priest waved them away and watched until they were out of sight. It was a good idea to hide the artefacts, but he would do it himself, without anyone else knowing where they were.

'An obstinate man,' said Manolis dispiritedly.

'Obstinate and foolish.'

Manolis shook his head. 'No, it is us who are foolish. Why should the priests believe us? We could well be planning to return later and retrieve them for ourselves.'

Vasilis pulled out the creased map that he carried with him. He pointed to a spot with a dirty finger nail. 'We're here. Just a short distance away is Lapa. I worked there for a short while doing a bit of digging for the archaeologists. If Father Nicolas at the church remembers me he'd give us a reference I'm sure.'

Father Nicolas in the village near Lapa did remember Vasilis and was more than willing to write a short note assuring anyone who read it that the two men were trustworthy. He pulled at his beard and considered. 'To prove my trust in you I will ask your advice. I would like to conceal a couple of items in my church.'

Manolis sat forward eagerly.

'I have been robbed of the gold artefacts of course, but they have not touched the icons. They are so old they thought them worthless. Where can I hide them safely?'

Manolis sat and thought the problem over. 'Could you not move them into your own house? You could hang a mirror or picture in front of them. They wouldn't exactly be hidden, but they'd be less obvious.'

Father Nicolas nodded slowly. 'That could be an answer.'

Manolis and Vasilis shared a meal with the priest and accepted his offer of a bed for the night before setting off early the next morning. Each village they entered they sought out the priest, showed the letter Father Nicolas had written and suggested he hid any valuables. The priests listened carefully, some insisting they were capable of defending their churches.

Father Pavlos, crippled with arthritis, shook his head sadly. 'I cannot dig a hole. When old Penelope died I had to ask the village women to dig her grave.'

'That's the answer,' Vasilis smiled. 'We can dig a hole at the foot of her grave. We can bury anything you want and no one will be any the wiser.'

Father Pavlos crossed himself. 'I'm not sure the grave should be disturbed.'

'I promise we will be very careful. The grave will be just a little larger than before. We will have no need to interfere with her resting place.'

Despite his misgivings, Father Pavlos eventually agreed. He wrapped the candlesticks, lectern and incense burners carefully, the icons having to remain in the church. Manolis and Vasilis looked at the large collection. This church had been much richer than they had anticipated. There was far too much to hide at the foot of a grave.

It took them most of the night to dig a hole deep enough to take a coffin with the religious artefacts packed inside. Father Pavlos had insisted it should be accomplished without the knowledge of the villagers.

'Won't they be curious and ask who the new grave belongs to?' asked Manolis.

Father Pavlos shrugged. 'I will just have to hope they do not notice.'

'Why don't we move the marker?' asked Manolis. 'If the people think that Penelope's grave is the last one dug in the churchyard they are certainly not going to notice the one before hers.'

Vasilis nodded. 'Manolis is right. Relatives will be looking for Penelope's and take no notice of one they think has been dug earlier.' He pulled the wooden marker from Penelope's grave and forced it into the loose earth at the head of the one they had so recently dug.

Vasilis frowned. 'I feel you should confide in someone. You are not a young man, Father. You would not want these precious items to be lost for ever.'

Father Pavlos smiled benignly. 'If they do not know they cannot give the secret away. I trust when the war is over you will return to visit my village one day. If I am not here and the items are not in their proper place in the church then I am relying on you to retrieve them on my behalf.'

Vasilis and Manolis exchanged glances. This was something they had not foreseen.

'Would it not be better if we passed the information to another priest in the area?' suggested Vasilis.

The priest shook his head. 'Once they heard I was dead the graveyard would be dug up like a ploughed field. There are a number of churches in the vicinity who would like to possess the priceless relics I have in my care. Sad to say I am not able to trust the other priests in this area not to claim them as their own should the opportunity arise.'

Manolis swallowed nervously. 'I promise I will come back to visit you.' Despite his vow, he did not relish ever having to return and dig in the graveyard. He had spent a good deal of time looking over his shoulder during the night, concerned that a ghost might appear.

Three weeks after leaving Katerina, Manolis was feeling happier. At the village of Velonado he had managed to get his boots repaired. A woman had produced an old pair belonging to her husband. They were too small for Manolis to wear, but an old man who claimed to be a cobbler, managed to prise off the soles and reattach them to Manolis's boots and patched the sides with the surplus leather.

Manolis asked how he could pay him for his services and the old man sighed. 'Shoot a German for me. That would be the best payment I could have.'

Vasilis and Manolis walked down the road towards the village of Gianniou. From there it would take them under an hour to reach Preveli. They should arrive before it was fully dark and be in time to share the evening meal with the monks. As they turned a bend on the road they found their way blocked by a German jeep.

Manolis threw his arm around Vasilis's shoulders and bumped against him, making Vasilis almost lose his balance.

'Pretend to be drunk,' Manolis said as he lurched against Vasilis again, pushing him closer to the edge of the road and the ditch that ran alongside. 'When I push you again fall into the ditch. I'll do the same further down the road.'

'I'll fight you,' muttered Vasilis and Manolis was not sure if his companion was serious. They moved apart, weaving unsteadily across the road, both balling their fists and taking wild and inaccurate swings at each other.

The Germans occupying the jeep were watching them, amused at the two drunkards trying to keep their feet. They began to laugh when one threw a punch at the other, missed wildly and tumbled into the ditch. Manolis continued to totter from side to side, he seemed to be making a conscious effort to keep his feet and walk in a straight line towards them. His legs buckled and he rolled into down into the ditch some distance from Vasilis.

'Shall we pick them up?'

The second soldier shook his head. 'Leave them. We'll wait until they sober up and climb out. Time enough to question them then.' They relaxed back into their boring surveillance duty, chuckling to themselves intermittently as they recalled the scene they had witnessed.

Vasilis and Manolis lay where they had landed, not daring to move. Vasilis tried to calculate the time, hoping the soldiers would soon return to wherever their base was or it would become dark enough for them to continue on their way without being seen.

As it became dark the soldiers switched on the lights of the jeep, floodlighting the road, and both men knew they had no hope of climbing out of the ditch undetected. Manolis began to wriggle slowly and carefully along in the gully until he reached Vasilis.

'What now?' he asked.

'We'll wait a while longer; then we'll have to crawl across the field and hide up for the night. We don't want to be found here tomorrow morning.'

Their journey on their stomachs across the rough ground was painful and slow. They stopped continually, expecting a soldier to have noticed their movement, order the jeep to be re-positioned and have the lights trained on the field. Manolis cursed as he fell into a hollow in the field and Vasilis landed almost on top of him. They rested for a while; then Vasilis declared they must move further on.

'Once it becomes light they'll probably come looking for us. We're not that far from them and there doesn't appear to be any cover.'

'Can we take a chance and walk?' asked Manolis. 'It will be quicker than all this crawling.'

Vasilis shook his head. 'Not yet, besides, think how you're saving the soles of your boots.'

Manolis snorted in disgust, but began to crawl dutifully at Vasilis's heels.

Both men were relieved when they were able to regain their feet and the first houses that made up the village of Lefkogia emerged from the darkness. Quietly they walked through the dark village street and into the countryside beyond.

'We'll wait here until dawn. I'll go into the village and see if anyone knows about that jeep. I can't believe they were there by chance. That was quick thinking on your part.'

Manolis shrugged off the compliment.

Vasilis returned from Lefkogia with the disconcerting news that the Germans had occupied Preveli. The two lesser bishops had been arrested and taken to Firkas Prison where Vasilis guessed they would be interrogated brutally for any information that could be extracted from them, either about the Abbot or any allied soldiers in the area.

'Any news of Arthur?' asked Manolis.

Vasilis shook his head. 'That was all I could find out. The priest said they were guarding the roads and no one is allowed in or out of the area.'

'Pity we didn't make a stop in Lefkogia last night,' remarked Manolis morosely. 'That information could have saved us a long crawl over the fields.'

'Well, if we don't want another one I think we should move away from here now. Once those soldiers find we're no longer in the ditch they're going to realise we tricked them. There's no point in going to Preveli if the Germans are there, so it's the mountains we'll have to make for.'

'How far away are they?'

Vasilis shrugged. 'No more than two or three days to reach the foothills.'

Manolis rose to his feet. 'We'd best make a start then. Any chance of breakfast on the way?'

September 1941

Vasilis's estimate of two or three days had been optimistic. They retraced their steps until they reached the low mountain range and Kotsifou Gorge that they had negotiated only a couple of day's earlier. Manolis sighed. He had not enjoyed climbing over the lush, but treacherous land the first time. Thorns snagged at their clothes, the grass became slippery and frequently their feet went from under them, only by clutching at handfuls of fern and low branches were they able to make any progress.

They were hot and exhausted by the time they reached the summit, both of them appreciating a rest beneath some small trees. Manolis turned to his companion.

'When we reach the foothills will it be climbing like that?' he asked.

Vasilis shook his head. 'For a short while, then it becomes scrub land. A bit higher and that disappears and you just have outcrops of rock.'

'It seemed more difficult climbing up this time.'

'Probably because on the way to Preveli you climbed down this side and you were looking forward to a hot meal and a comfortable bed. Either that or it's your imagination.'

Manolis grinned at him. 'Do you think it would work if I imagined a flat road?'

'You can try, but I fear you will be disappointed. Are you ready to tackle the downward side? I'd like to try to reach Kanevos tonight.'

Reluctantly Manolis rose to his feet.

The walking was reasonably easy the following day as they took the country roads until once again they were close to the main road from Rethymnon to the coast. They hid in a vineyard, watching and listening for any sign of troop movement, ducking down and lying flat on the grass each time a lorry passed. Finally they took a chance that the road was going to be clear for a while, emerged from the vineyard and sprinted across the open ground to throw themselves hurriedly behind another wall.

'We'll need to stop in the next village and see what we can get in the way of food. Unless we make long detours there's an area without any habitation except monasteries and they are high up on the hills. We don't want to spend more time than we have to climbing.'

'It doesn't look very far on the map,' frowned Manolis.

'It isn't, but it will be hard walking. There are no roads or cart tracks, only goat trails. The hills are not particularly high, but they're steep.'

'Wouldn't it be quicker to use a cart track and walk further?' asked Manolis.

Vasilis shook his head. 'If we used the cart tracks we'd be doubling back on ourselves. We've already had to do that once and lost a couple of days. We should be able to reach the Amari Valley tomorrow and there are plenty of villages in that area.'

They reached the village in the late afternoon and Vasilis did not want to risk moving into the countryside during the hours of darkness due to the ruggedness of the terrain.

'We don't want to fall into a hole in the night and damage an ankle. We'll ask if we can use an outhouse. If the Germans decide to pay a surprise visit the villagers can deny all knowledge of us.'

The villagers were good to them. No one refused to share their sparse meals or turned them away, and they were offered a barn in which to spend the night. Manolis shivered. He was cold even with the blanket around him and wished he had some thicker clothes. Vasilis rummaged in his sack and pulled out two jumpers, passing one to Manolis.

'Good job we're near enough the same size,' he grinned as Manolis pulled it over his head thankfully.

They left the village just as the inhabitants were rising and Vasilis struck off across the fields. In a very short time they were climbing up and down inclines studded with rocks and hollows, using the tracks left by the goats. Some outcrops of rock were too steep to climb easily and they had to make a detour to avoid them and find an easier route. If it was like this climbing in the hills what would it be like when they reached the mountains? Manolis appreciated that they had not tried to negotiate the terrain during darkness.

As the sun sank lower in the sky there was no sign of the villages that Vasilis insisted were in the area and they dared climb no longer once it was dark. The moon played tricks with the landscape, casting deep pools of shadow that could hide crevices or deep holes. With their blankets wrapped around them and pulled up over their heads both men resigned themselves to spending the night in the open. They huddled behind an outcrop of rock, their bodies close together for warmth. At intervals one or the other would rise and crawl a short distance away where he would stand flapping his arms and stamping his feet to bring some warmth back into his body.

Cold and stiff they walked in silence as they continued to negotiate the rocky, undulating terrain, thankful that the warmth was returning to their bodies. It was a relief when the ground became a grassy slope and in the distance they could make out the dome of a church. It galvanized both men into making further exertions and they hurried towards it. The priest welcomed them, but warned them that there was little food in the village.

'The Germans are blocking the main roads. They have taken all the petrol for their own use and supplies are having to be brought in by donkey. Sometimes they refuse to let them pass, other times they just take the produce for themselves. There is no flour for bread, no rice. We hid our harvest of potatoes, but even those are dwindling now.'

'We will be grateful for anything,' Vasilis assured him, and even more grateful for some shelter over night.'

'That can be arranged. You should be safe enough here. The Germans are not confident enough yet to drive over the mountain roads. Once they start to come this way we will send a message to the andartes and ask them to ambush their vehicles. I do not think they will be so anxious to investigate our villages if they find they have to walk back to their bases.' The priest chuckled at the idea.

Vasilis smiled and stored the idea away. That could certainly be a job for him. He was an excellent marksman.

They spent the night in a village house. The woman insisting she gave up her bed for them and they both revelled in the luxury of a mattress beneath them and blankets above. In the morning she heated water for them and both men stripped and bathed, not knowing when they would be able to do so again.

As Vasilis packed his sparse belongings, his binoculars on top, the priest arrived with two of his own blankets as a gift. As recompense, they offered to hide his church artefacts for him, but he had winked and said he had already hidden them away. As Manolis folded his and slung it over his shoulder he wished he still had the bundle of blankets that had been destined for Spinalonga.

Vasilis was secretly pleased by the priest's refusal. He did not want to delay their arrival in the mountains for any longer than necessary. Snow often arrived early in the area, even in the foothills and he did not relish trying to negotiate the steep inclines with snow underfoot. He knew if it rained the water could run down the hills in torrents and he did not relish the thought of sleeping out exposed to such harsh elements. There was no guarantee they would find a convenient cave in which to pass the night.

After being in the hills, the walking that day was relatively easy. They were able to use the road that ran through the Amari Valley connecting the hamlets and monasteries. It was quiet and peaceful, the buzzing of bees the only sound to break the silence as they searched for pollen. As the sun rose it beat unmercifully on their backs. They removed their pullovers but neither man took off his shirt, not wishing to be bitten by insects and spend the night scratching.

'I thought we were making for the mountains,' observed Manolis.

'We are,' Vasilis assured him, 'but I thought we'd take the easiest route available. We don't need to scramble over mountains unnecessarily. If we can keep up this pace we'll be nearly there this evening. We can spend the night in a village and tackle the climb tomorrow.'

Low hills rose up in the distance that loomed larger as they reached them. Dense thickets of bushes and small trees covered the lower slopes and they had to force a way through them until they thinned to scrub. The tough grass gave up its struggle to cover the rock face and large, exposed faces of white rock seemed to be all around them reflecting back the sun to dazzle them and hurt their eyes. Frequently they had to make their way over or around rock falls, the boulders slipping and sliding beneath their boots. They found that carrying a sack of clothes or the rolled up blankets pulled them off balance and they began to pass them to each other as they scrambled their way across.

From the summit, the village where they had passed the night began to look like a collection of dolls' houses. As they climbed higher the wind increased. At first it was a cooling breeze that they were thankful for, then as they descended steeply and were in the shade it became chill and began to cut through their clothing like a knife. A black gash across the hillside announced the presence of a cave and they stumbled over the last of the rocks and sat thankfully in its dark mouth, the wind no longer whistling around them.

Vasilis peered into the dark interior of the cave. 'We stored our gear in here when we were excavating nearby. At least it's dry. We'll spend the night here and go further into the mountains tomorrow.'

'How far back does it go?' asked Manolis.

Vasilis shrugged. 'Quite a way. The Minoans treated it as a religious site and used to leave offerings here for the gods.'

'Pity they didn't keep up the practice,' grumbled Manolis. 'They could have left us some food.'

'Be careful or I'll make you leave yours for them. An offering to ask for fair weather again tomorrow and meeting up with the andartes.'

Manolis nodded. 'Do you know where they are?'

'No,' replied Vasilis cheerfully, 'but if they're in the area I'm sure they'll soon find us.'

Despite the cave being dry it was cold, the sun never penetrating more than a short distance into the mouth. Manolis felt thoroughly miserable, wishing with all his heart that he still had his boat and could be out on the sea.

The mountains rose higher the next day and seemed even steeper when they had to descend. The most difficult time came when the solid rock turned to shale and small loose stones. Any purchase they tried to make with their hands gave way as they clawed their way up the loose scree, often they slipped backwards and had to allow their bodies to relax and go with the rock slide, then commence the climb all over again. The muscles in their legs ached, their hands were sore and had numerous small cuts that became more painful each time they slipped and tried to stop themselves. It took them twice as long to cover the same distance as they had travelled the previous day. Wearily they sat in the shelter of a stony outcrop and ate the remains of their food.

'What happens if we don't meet up with the andartes? We've no food left and very little water.'

'If we've not joined forces by tomorrow we'll go back down to the last village.'

Manolis looked at his companion in horror. 'That's two days walk away!'

Vasilis nodded. 'You'll have the choice. Sit here and freeze, die of thirst and starvation or climb back down and move to a different area to look for them.'

Manolis gave him a venomous look and rolled himself up in his blanket. He knew he had no choice but to follow where Vasilis led. Left alone he would not have known if he was walking in the right direction to reach the village or penetrating deeper into the mountains.

Vasilis lifted his binoculars to his eyes and scanned the surrounding area. He thought he caught a glimpse of movement and trained the glasses in that direction. He spun round in amazement when he heard a voice behind him.

'Who are you and where have you come from?'

Vasilis looked up into the barrel of a rifle and smiled at the ruffianly looking man who held it.

'I'm Vasilis and this is my companion, Manolis. We've come to join you.'

The man nodded without lowering his rifle. 'Why didn't you come before?'

'We were at Preveli, helping out there. Manolis had a boat, but it was destroyed by the Germans. We began to return to Preveli on foot and found the monastery had been occupied. We've walked for more than a week to get here.' Vasilis deliberately omitted that they had visited his own village.

'So what use do you think you can be here?'

Vasilis shrugged. 'We're willing to do whatever we can. I'm a good marksman.'

'Where's your rifle?'

'I only have a revolver. Douglas, the Englishman gave it to me. Do you know him?'

'I know of him. How do you know him?'

'We worked together some years ago. He trusted me to deliver a wireless to Toplou.'

Manolis listened to the interchange between the two men. He sincerely hoped this man was one of the andartes and not one of the bandits who were known to prey on unwary travellers and some of the villages, retreating from their forays into deserted areas of the country.

The man slung his rifle onto his back. 'I'm Stelios. You'd better come with me and meet the others.'

Vasilis replaced his binoculars into his sack. 'I thought I saw some movement over there,' he indicated with his hand.

'You were meant to. You were so busy watching them you had no idea I was creeping up on you.' Stelios began to stride away, Vasilis following him. Manolis hastily gathered up his blankets and hurried after them.

They passed a large cave entrance and continued on around the side of the mountain to where a series of smaller caverns yawned. Stelios beckoned them into the second dark opening and they bent almost double as they followed him inside.

'You can stand up now,' he announced.

Vasilis lifted his hand above his head and felt for the roof. He was taller than the other two men and did not want to crack his head. Manolis reached out his hand to find the wall, grazing his knuckles as he was far closer to it than he had realised.

'Wait here for me,' said Stelios and both men stopped in their tracks.

Stelios returned within a matter of minutes, a wooden torch in his hand that gave off a feeble, flickering light. They followed him along a winding passage until the cave widened out to form a vast space. Unerringly Stelios led the way across to a fold in the rock on the far side and inched his way through; again they were in a narrow passage, openings leading off into darkness. Manolis shuddered. They would never find their way out of this place if their guide abandoned them.

Muted voices, the sound of laughter, the click of beads, the slapping of hands on thighs or boots and the constant drip of water came to their ears. The passage widened out and they could see men sitting and lying around in the cave. The talking stopped as the occupants became aware of their presence and curious eyes turned towards them.

The men rose to their feet and surrounded Manolis and Vasilis. Manolis raised his hands in the air, bringing forth a gale of laughter from the men. One of them slapped him on the back.

'There's no need for that. We just appreciate seeing a new face. Where've you come from?'

Before Manolis could answer a cry came from one of the men. 'Basil! It is you, isn't it? What the devil are you doing here?'

'Douglas! I could ask the same of you.'

'Did you deliver that wireless?'

Vasilis nodded. 'That was no problem once Manolis and I met up. We ran into a few difficulties a bit later on when we were collecting Arthur. Any chance of a drink and I'll tell you what happened.'

'Sure. What would you like? We've raki, wine or whisky.'

'What! I was thinking of water. Where did you get those supplies from?'

Douglas grinned. 'The villagers. Which would you like?'

'Just water for now. I'm sure Manolis would like some too, and probably some food if you have any. He's always hungry.'

'Help yourself. It drips through into the bowl over there. We're never short of water, but we all eat at the same time. That way everyone gets their fair share.'

Vasilis nodded and turned to Manolis. 'There's plenty of water over there, help yourself. We'll eat later.'

Manolis nodded. He had not understood the conversation between Vasilis and Douglas any more than the other occupants of the cave and wished they would speak in Greek.

They sat on Douglas's mattress and he lit a cigarette, blowing the acrid smoke into the air around him. He offered the pack to Vasilis and Manolis who both shook their heads.

'I haven't had one for weeks now. I'll not bother, thanks,' said Vasilis.

'We ought to speak in Greek,' said Douglas as he blew out another swirl of smoke. 'They're a suspicious lot and they'll think we're plotting something if they can't understand what we say. Tell me about Toplou and then I want to know what brings you up here.'

Manolis listened as Vasilis told Douglas of the events they had experienced over the last four months. His days as a simple fisherman seemed to be a life-time ago.

1942 - 1944

Flora sat on the jetty at Spinalonga and looked out towards Plaka. Little seemed to have changed in the village. She could see someone working in the fields above the farm that Yannis said was his home and intermittently she caught the flash of sunlight reflected on the lens of binoculars. Anna came down and joined her, a pad of paper and pencil in her hand.

'What are you doing, Flora?'

Flora smiled at her. 'Just looking out for a boat. Hoping someone will come.'

'Surely Manolis will come soon. He'll come to see you.'

'I wish he would.' Flora sighed deeply. 'I'd be happy if he just sailed past and waved to me. I don't know where he is or what has happened to him.'

'Why should anything happen to him? He's a fisherman, not a soldier. Can I draw you sitting there? I'll put a boat in the picture and you can pretend it's Manolis coming. You can smile and raise your hand.'

Flora shook her head. 'I don't mind you drawing me, but don't put any boats in the picture.'

Anna settled herself beside her. 'When someone does come could you ask them to bring me out some more paper and some pencils? I'm sure Yannis will pay for them and my Pappa will pay him back later.'

'I don't think anyone will be coming.' Flora spoke sadly. 'You heard what that German man said. Any boat that tried to come here would be shot at.'

'I wish the doctor would come.'

'Aren't you feeling well?' asked Flora anxiously.

Anna shook her head. 'I feel all right. It's Phaedra. I know Yannis is worried about her. He's sitting with her now.'

The Germans had finally braved the mountain roads. The andartes constructed hideouts amongst the rocks at the base of the mountains and some men began to live permanently in the lower cave. If a message came that the Germans were on their way they would take up positions outside the villages and ambush the vehicles as they tried to pass through. The Germans would leave their vehicles and take cover, trying to flush their assailants out by firing back at them. Whilst they were occupied those men who had stayed quietly in hiding would move forward and sabotage the jeeps, piercing their tough tyres with their hunting knives or pushing stones into the exhaust pipes.

Any Germans who were killed during the skirmishes and not removed by their companions were robbed of their weapons and ammunition. The andartes would turn out their pockets and remove any cash they found in their wallets, but never touched their personal possessions. The first time Manolis searched a dead soldier and found photographs of the man's family he felt guilty. He replaced them in the man's pocket and pushed the feeling aside. No one could afford to be sentimental.

The soldiers were not deterred. After the first few sorties they sent extra troops who would go into the hills searching for the snipers whilst the others continued to the villages where they stripped the occupants of whatever produce they could find hidden away along with their sheep, goats and chickens.

The Germans knew the andartes were living in the vicinity and would spread out, searching for their hideouts. Lookouts were posted at strategic points and Manolis took his turn with the others.

He knew now how to shoot a rifle and he also knew he would not hesitate if a German soldier came within range. He hated them with a bitterness that he did not know he possessed.

The first snow arriving made them feel more secure. There was no way the soldiers would be able to penetrate the area, but it did not make living amongst the mountains any easier for the men. They moved closer to the villages and joined the inhabitants in their search for anything they could find that was edible, resorting to snails and leaves to sustain them. Manolis had never felt so hungry in his life, but he did not complain. The other men were suffering equally as badly as he was. Their bodies had little defence against the bitter cold they experienced whenever they left their shelters and they often stayed down in one of the village houses for the night, rather than face an arduous climb back. All the men spoke longingly of their homes, but no one considered leaving.

With the onset of spring the German patrols returned, determined to search out and eliminate the men who dared to oppose them. Lookouts were posted permanently on the mountain side. If a signal came that Germans were approaching each man took cover and ensured his rifle was loaded, willing to give up his life to prevent the discovery of their hideouts and where the wireless was hidden.

The other benefit of the better weather came from the parachute drops of food, clothing, money and other supplies from the allies. Once again the men were able to use a battery torch to make their way through the cave complex, rather than having to rely on a flickering flame that had a tendency to blow out. Spending hours on lookout duty was not so cold and they were able to stay in their positions longer before having to be relieved.

More radios were received, and they were carried to other parts of the mountains where a base was made and communications extended. Having the radios meant the men were also able to follow the war as it was progressing in Europe, rather than just having the ability to transmit and receive messages. They listened in horror as they heard the Germans had moved deeper into both Egypt and Russia and the Japanese had occupied further territory in the east. They passed the melancholy news on to the villagers, who shook their heads and asked when the andartes would bring them good news and they could celebrate.

A semblance of normality returned to the towns. Despite being under a curfew, the populace were permitted to continue with their occupation provided they did not enter any of the restricted areas. No one was allowed to go down to the shore or the harbours and many of the fishermen had been forced into labouring work, repairing the roads whilst the Germans stood and watched their efforts, ensuring they did not slack. Bakers worked around the clock to satisfy the needs of the army and the shoemakers were in continual demand to repair their boots. The buses ran regularly along the main roads, even the cinemas in the large towns had been re-opened, but they were for the entertainment of the German soldiers only.

Occasionally a man would leave their number for a week or more whilst he made the journey back to his home village, wanting to visit his family and confirm they were still alive. They would return elated at having found them safe and well, but despondent about the deprivation they were suffering. Some returned with their bitterness etched in their faces. Members of their family had been imprisoned, beaten or shot.

Vasilis made the long journey back to his village, offering to take Manolis with him, but Manolis refused. He did not relish the arduous walk there and back. He would have preferred to return to Aghios Nikolaos and visit Flora. The men who came from the area and had returned to visit their families assured him that no boats were allowed out and his journey would have been in vain.

During the summer months they suffered as much from the heat as they had earlier from the cold. If they removed their shirts they risked becoming sunburnt and would be attacked even more viciously by insects that left them itching madly. They kept their heads covered and always filled two water bottles to carry with them.

Messengers arrived on foot from across Crete to inform them of proposed plans to ambush and avenge themselves on the Germans, often asking for volunteers to return with them to swell the numbers in the area and ensure success.

Manolis was always the first to offer. He hated the long hours he spent laying on the hillside looking for infiltrators. He disliked staying in the cave even more. He was used to being out in the open for most part of the day. At first he had enjoyed being able to play cards, gossip with the other men, listen to Makkis playing his bouzouki, and discuss the latest news that had filtered through to them. Now tempers were fraying between all of them. A discussion would turn into an argument that could quickly end up as a fight. Manolis was much happier if he was away from the close confines of the community. Vasilis usually offered to go with him. He felt responsible for the young man's welfare and had become fond of him during the time they had spent together.

They climbed from their mountain cave down to the lower levels along with the other men who had volunteered to join with them in an unknown mission. Despite Vasilis telling Manolis they were taking the shortest and easiest route he was not convinced. The mountains stretched out before them, as fast as they descended they were climbing towards another peak again. They spent the night in a cheese hut, thankful for the protection it gave them as the nights were still cold, and Manolis was pleased it had not fallen to his lot to stay up on guard. It would probably be his turn the next night and he sincerely hoped by then they would be in a more hospitable area of the country.

That morning two of the men, who knew the area well, were sent ahead to scout for any evidence of German soldiers in the vicinity. The rest of the contingent followed at a safe distance to the agreed signalling points, crouching behind rocks until Vasilis declared he had seen the signal through his binoculars. Moving so slowly and cautiously it took them all that day to reach the lower ground and enter the first of the villages.

They rested overnight, courtesy of a villager, in a barn. Manolis and two of the men spent half the night patrolling round and round the building, their eyes peeled for any movement in the shadows. Relieved that nothing had happened to raise an alarm, they woke the men who were to take over from them and rolled thankfully into their blankets.

They walked on towards the coast, the highest mountains behind them, but another low range lay ahead. The scouts began walking half an hour ahead of the main body of the men, checking it was safe for them to move through the village. It was rare to see such a large group of andartes together and the villagers looked at them in surprise.

'Where are you going?'

'What's happening?'

'Are the Germans coming?'

The questions came at them frequently from the apprehensive villagers.

'We're taking part in a training exercise,' they replied. 'Nothing to worry about.'

The men had been told to make for a gathering point between Rethymnon and Heraklion and the operation would be explained to them when they arrived. They knew they were not informed of the details deliberately. If any one of them fell into enemy hands they would not be able to reveal their final destination or objective. Vasilis was feeling particularly cheerful. If they were staying in that area for any length of time he might have the opportunity to visit his wife and child again. Little Vasilis now nearly four years old, had been running around and talking when he last saw him. Sadly Vasilis acknowledged that he would be a virtual stranger to him when he finally returned home permanently.

When they reached the agreed rendezvous they were surprised to be met by a member of the British resistance, and when they were told the nature of their mission they were even more amazed, yet each man hoped they would succeed. Now they stood in their appointed places and waited.

The car rounded the corner and the driver came to an abrupt halt. Immediately the men surrounded the car, their rifles at the ready. Roughly the General was bundled out and the car turned and sped back down the road. The German had his hands firmly bound and a gag across his mouth. With a pistol in the small of his back, he was forced to start walking into the countryside. Scouts went ahead, allowing the General a few moments in which to draw as much breath into his lungs as he could through his nose.

They continued to walk away from the main road and the villages until they came upon a horse tethered to a farm gate.

'There's your transport for the next few days, General.' Willing hands seized the German and hoisted him up into the saddle. 'We will release your hands so you can use the reins, but one false move from you and I assure you that my men will not hesitate to shoot. There will come a time when the horse will no longer be able to cope with the terrain and you will have to walk. I suggest you enjoy the ride whilst you can.'

The General pointed to the gag on his mouth and the British officer removed it. He sucked air gratefully into his lungs, then began a tirade in German at his captors. The gag was immediately replaced and the British officer stood in front of him.

'We are travelling a considerable distance and you are coming all the way with us. I will remove your gag so that you can breathe more easily and also drink occasionally provided you do not make a sound. The first time you raise your voice the gag will be replaced and only be removed again if I decide to give you a drink and a morsel of food. Do you understand?'

The General nodded and glared balefully at his captors.

'Not a word,' he was reminded as the gag was removed a second time.

A water bottle was held to the General's lips and he drank gratefully. 'Where are you taking me?' he asked.

'You'll find out. If it's any consolation to you we don't plan to kill you, provided you behave yourself. Any attempt on your part to escape and we won't hesitate to shoot you.'

'My men will soon find you and you will all be shot.'

The Englishman shook his head. 'I don't think so. Now, you've had a drink. We'll move on.'

Muttering curses under his breath the German had no choice but to continue his ignominious ride into the hills with the andartes and British resistance.

They climbed all day, all the men were tired, but determined to reach a safe hiding place before stopping to rest. The higher they went the more the temperature dropped and Manolis hoped they would not be spending the night in the open.

The next three days followed the same pattern, climbing all day, forcing the General to ride with them. At night four men sat guard over him whilst he was allowed to sleep. On the fourth day as they neared their final destination for the night, they began to see movement as German soldiers penetrated higher into the mountains as they searched for their General. The General was bound and gagged again, the Englishman apologising as he tied the knots firmly.

'We shall be hiding up here for a while and I can't risk you calling out to them or attracting their attention so I'm afraid you will have to suffer this inconvenience again.'

The andartes spread out, finding vantage points from where they could watch the movement of the soldiers. Despite having their rifles trained on the men, they had no intention of firing and giving their position away unless it became essential. As darkness fell the soldiers were called together and their flickering torches could be seen as they retreated from the inhospitable hillside.

As soon as the lights from their torches were no longer visible, the General was hauled to his feet and his hands untied.

'You know what will happen if you make any sound,' the Englishman warned him. 'We should reach our planned resting place for tonight in about an hour.'

The General did not answer. He was cold, hungry, and exhausted. How much further was he expected to go into these mountains with this gang of ruffians?

Each day as they moved further into the mountains, more men joined them, scouts moving ahead, checking there were no German soldiers scouring the hillside. At night they hid in a cave or deep hole, men keeping watch and two standing guard over the General whilst the others snatched a few hours sleep. Their pace during the day was more leisurely now, and Manolis wondered where they would eventually end up and what they would do with their captive. Surely they could not keep him with them indefinitely.

Unable to ride any further due to the terrain, the General seemed to have finally accepted his plight. He no longer protested when he was told to rise and start walking each morning, complain about his meagre food and water ration or the heat of the day and cold at night and the Germans appeared to have given up on their search for him.

They reached a cleft between the mountains, making a camp there at midday and Manolis wondered if this was where they planned to stop permanently. The Englishman disappeared out of sight and returned two hours later, his face grim. He ordered the General to be bound hand and foot, and called the men to gather out of his hearing.

'Everything was going to plan from our end and I had thought we could have a couple of days' rest. Unfortunately the radio transmitter here is out of order. Lakkis, you know this area better than anyone so I am sending you as a messenger to let them know how far we are. That means we will have to move on tomorrow. We need to be able to communicate by wireless.' He beckoned Lakkis to one side and they sat out of earshot of the others, a map spread out before them and their heads close together.

They were aroused as dawn broke; the Englishman called the men together. 'We are retracing our steps.'

The men groaned.

'Not all the way,' their Commander assured them. 'I have agreed a new rendezvous point with Lakkis. Unfortunately it means we have to return to the Amari Valley area and cross the road where the Germans are patrolling. We'll keep to the hills for as long as possible. Scouts will go on ahead. When we reach the road there will be a diversion that should keep the Germans occupied whilst we get the General across. He will be bound and gagged, of course. Any questions?'

The men shook their heads. They might argue amongst themselves, but they did not query decisions made by the Englishman. He was their leader. The men slung their blankets over their shoulders, attached their water bottles to their belts and took up their positions circling the General.

'What about some breakfast?' he asked.

The men with their rifles trained on him shrugged. 'What makes you think you deserve any?'

Once again they were able to spend the night in a barn, but Manolis did not mind taking his turn on guard duty. The weather was warmer, the night sky was cloudless, and the moon lit up the area so that anyone trying to move towards them would be seen immediately. He wondered what kind of a diversion would be created the next day to enable them to cross the road.

Before it was light they began to walk across relatively flat farm land. As they drew closer to the road the General was once again gagged. The men were given an order to spread out and take advantage of whatever cover they could find. They were not to shoot unless it was unavoidable. The object was to get across the road with the General undetected and regroup on the other side.

The rumbling of vehicles could be heard and the men crouched lower. Just before the vehicles finished negotiating the first bend, a bus pulled out of a side road and stopped, effectively barring the way and cutting off the view of the road round the bend.

'Now!'

The General was seized bodily, propelled across the road and pushed into the bushes on the other side. Men took their chance and followed him. The German convoy had halted when they realised they were unable to continue on their way. The bus driver was making a great show of changing and grinding his gears, explaining that he had a problem with his engine and he was doing his best. At intervals he would take his hands off the wheel and pound his forehead.

Finally exasperated, the German in charge of the convoy called his men to him and ordered them to push the bus out of their way. As they arrived a plume of evil smelling exhaust fumes were emitted and the engine sprang back into life. The driver grinned widely.

'It is fixed. No more problem now.' He gave a cheery wave of his hand and drove off down the road, leaving the soldiers to return to their vehicles.

The bus travelled a short distance further down the road and stopped again. This time the driver climbed out and opened up the engine cover. As the German convoy passed him they made rude signs and jeered about the inefficiency of his vehicle. The driver waited until they had gone on out of sight, made an equally rude sign towards them, climbed back into the driving seat, and started the engine. He turned his bus easily and began to drive back to Rethymnon.

The contingent moved on and within an hour they were once again amongst the foothills of the mountains and climbing steadily. They were lower than the mountains the andartes were used to living in but the climbing was no easier, despite there being grass underfoot and a dense foliage of saplings and larger trees that they could use to haul themselves up the steep hillside. They stubbed their toes and barked their shins on hidden rocks, following goat trails whenever they could, that wound around the hillside in meandering circles.

They reached the village in the mountains and the residents looked at the large contingent of armed men. The andartes dispersed amongst the narrow streets asking the villagers for access to their houses and the use of their roof where they could look out across the countryside. They were welcomed, despite the fear of an impending full-scale battle where they would be trapped in the midst of the fighting and suffer.

Andreas arrived bringing the news that there was a radio in perfect working order hidden only a short walk away and they were in communication with Cairo. The beach selected originally for a boat to come into the shore and collect the General was no longer viable. The Germans had vast numbers guarding the area and a new rendezvous had to be arranged rapidly.

During the night messages passed back and forth between the radio station and the contingent in the mountain village. Manolis was shaken awake and informed that they were moving, despite it still being dark. The men gathered together and marched openly down the road away from the village with the General in their midst. By dawn they were in a valley with a vista of mountains ahead of them.

Throughout the day they climbed steadily, stopping only briefly for a rest and some food, until they had crossed the range. They finally halted at a small village and Manolis could smell salt in the air. He was directed, along with the others, to make his way down to the beach and ensure that it remained deserted. He stood listening to the soft lapping of the waves and a deep melancholy overtook him. He would love to feel the movement of the sea beneath him again.

A signal came from out at sea and a lookout immediately returned to where the General was being held prisoner. Still under guard, he was escorted down to the beach and helped aboard a small boat. Four men climbed in after him and the boat sped out to sea. The men on the beach turned and grinned at each other, slapping each other on the back before returning to the hills behind the village to spend the rest of the night reminiscing over the previous three weeks and congratulating themselves on their success.

Vasilis and Manolis made ready to return to the mountains with their companions. Such a large body of men would be an easy target for the German soldiers who were still searching for their General and the sooner they dispersed into small groups the safer they would be. They thanked the villagers and began their hike back over the Rhodakino Mountains. Despite feeling confident and moving at a leisurely pace they still sent scouts ahead to look for any sign of German soldiers.

Yiorgo came running back to the main body of the men, waving his arms and gesticulating. Immediately every man unshipped his rifle from his back and had it ready to fire. He shook his head.

'They're burning the village.'

The andartes looked at him in disbelief.

'Why should they do that?'

'Someone must have told them we were there with the General.'

'Are they hoping they will find him hidden there?'

'We have to go back.'

The men conferred together, grim faced. They spread out across the mountain, taking advantage of the cover it gave, and retraced their steps until they could smell the smoke and see the flames rising from the houses. From their vantage point they watched whilst the Germans divided their forces. Some took the road towards the shore and the others began to follow the trail that led into the mountains that the andartes had so recently left behind.

The andartes waited until the Germans had passed their observation point. At a signal from Yiorgo they opened fire from all directions on the unsuspecting soldiers. Finally satisfied that not one of them remained alive, they added rifles and ammunition to their own and continued their climb, intent on reaching the village in the mountains to pass the night.

The following morning many of the andartes parted company. Those who had been living in the mountains above the Samaria Gorge bade farewell to their compatriots who were returning to the Ideon range. Vasilis took the opportunity to visit his family again, promising Manolis that he would return.

Manolis waited anxiously for Vasilis's return to the mountains. He wanted to discuss the latest news of the war with him and also to be reassured that his friend was safe. At last the British forces seemed to be having success, they had occupied Rome and invaded Normandy, but not before the Germans had burnt many more of the mountain villages.

Vasilis returned as news came through that someone had tried to assassinate Hitler. The failure of the attempt brought derision from the men. They would have accomplished the task. They had succeeded in capturing the German General and moving him from one side of Crete to the other. They would certainly have managed to annihilate the megalomaniac who had thrown the world into such agonised turmoil.

Vasilis listened to them with a certain amount of amusement. Without the Englishman to lead and command them they would probably have spent so much time arguing about the route to take that they would still be sitting in the mountains with the General as a companion. Manolis was more interested to know about conditions in the towns and villages along the coast. Were the fishermen allowed out again yet?

Vasilis shook his head. 'The towns are still under a curfew. If your papers don't give you permission to move from one prefecture to the other you are taken for questioning. There are checkpoints everywhere along the main roads. They stop anything that moves, even their own vehicles.'

'Why do they stop their own men?' asked Manolis puzzled.

Vasilis chuckled. 'It's been known on more than one occasion for them not to be full of German soldiers. If the andartes have captured a vehicle they will make use of it. They have plenty of German uniforms, identity papers and permits. Once it runs out of fuel they set it on fire and continue on foot. Overall we're giving our invaders quite a headache.'

'How is your wife and son?' asked Manolis, realising he should have asked after Vasilis's family first.

'They're well. Each time I see little Vasilis he seems to have grown bigger. I stayed for three days. By then he had lost his fear of me and was happy to sit on my lap whilst I read to him. He calls me Pappa, but I'm not sure if he really knows what a father is. There are two old men still living in the village, the others have taken to the hills and visit infrequently. He's surrounded by women most of the time.'

Manolis nodded sympathetically. There were going to be many boys in the country who did not know what it was to have a father.

The news they heard continued to cheer them. The Germans were retreating in Normandy and Paris had been liberated. They continued their sorties, targeting the German forces, but there seemed less soldiers around. They watched as armoured vehicles, trucks, jeeps, and men moved along the main roads from the countryside towards the north-eastern coast.

During their retreat, the Germans continued to take their revenge upon the villagers. Any village they suspected to have sheltered the resistance fighters who had abducted the General they burnt to the ground. Sometimes the inhabitants were allowed to leave the immediate area, other times they were gathered together and shot. Their bodies left piled up in the square for the fire to turn them to ashes. The andartes followed them, and although often hopelessly outnumbered, they would try to engage them in battle to give the villagers time to escape from the area and only lose their homes and not their lives.

Daily the andartes found hiding places lower down the mountains until they were finally able to take shelter again in the villages that nestled in the foothills. The feeling between the men was one of cheerful confidence. No matter what they had suffered, they had succeeded in driving their captors back towards the sea. In each village the black crosses on the doors of the houses showed how many family members had been lost during the struggle and Manolis gave up trying to count the total.

The news filtered through to them that the allied forces had landed in Greece, then that they had entered Athens. The war could not last much longer now. As they moved across the countryside and entered villages they saw no sign of German soldiers, they were welcomed and hailed as heroes, much to Manolis's embarrassment. He began to think longingly of returning to Aghios Nikolaos, at the same time he dreaded visiting Spinalonga and finding Flora was no longer there for him.

'What do you plan to do when you return home?' asked Vasilis.

Manolis shrugged. 'I'll have to see. I'm still the book-keeper for the island. I'm sure someone has been taking out the doctor and his supplies so I shall just have to ask them to take me with them in future. I can't afford to buy another boat for myself.'

'You're welcome to come back with me and be a farmer,' offered Vasilis.

Manolis shook his head. 'I probably know less about farming than you do about fishing. No, I need to live by the sea. The smell and the sound of the waves were the things I missed most up in the mountains, apart from Flora, of course.'

'Well, at least when I do go home I won't have to walk this time. I'm planning to go up to Heraklion and from there I can catch a bus most of the way.' Vasilis smiled happily.

'Would I be able to catch a bus to Aghios Nikolaos?'

'No reason why not. The buses have been running between the towns regularly. There may still be checkpoints, but they'll be looking for Germans now. We'll be able to move around freely again.'

Manolis frowned. 'I'll have to see Father Andreas before I go down to Aghios Nikolaos, if he's still there, of course. I need to find out if there's any money left from the amount Father Minos deposited with him.'

'I suppose I should also visit him and let him know I delivered the radio safely. It was his idea to place it in a coffin and walk openly through the streets under the nose of the Germans.' Vasilis chuckled at the memory. 'I can thank him on behalf of all the men who managed to evacuate from Preveli.'

'What do you think has happened to the Abbot? And Arthur? Do you think they captured him?'

'Once we reach Heraklion we can try to find out. Someone is bound to know.'

It was a week later when the two men reached the outskirts of the city and made their way to the church where Father Andreas was the priest. He answered their knock, a puzzled look on his face when he saw the two dirty, unshaven men, both smiling broadly at him.

'May we come in, Father?'

'Certainly. My door is never closed to supplicants. You would like a meal, no doubt, when you have had a chance to wash.'

Manolis grinned at him. 'You don't recognise us, do you? I can't say I blame you. I'm Manolis, the boatman from Aghios Nikolaos and this is Vasilis who carried the radio to Toplou.'

'Manolis? I would have passed you by in the street. Come in, come in, both of you. You are welcome.'

Father Andreas led them into his small parlour and indicated that they should sit whilst he busied himself fetching glasses and a bottle of wine from the cupboard.

'To your good health, gentlemen.' He raised his glass. 'Now, I would like to hear your account of the past three years and then you must tell me the purpose of your visit.'

'I'm sure Vasilis could tell you better than I.' Manolis suddenly felt shy before the priest.

Vasilis launched into a description of their journey to Toplou, on to Kato Zakros, collecting Arthur and finally ending up at Preveli. He told how they had taken the Abbot to Agios Georgios and Manolis had lost his boat, their decision to join with the andartes in the mountains, the skirmishes and fights in which they had participated and their journey escorting the General across Crete.

'The way you tell it you make it sound like an adventure,' observed Father Andreas. 'I am sure you all suffered. How you must have missed the comforts of your homes.' Manolis looked around the small room. It was almost as Spartan as the caves where they had hidden. Apart from the cupboard, the only furniture was a table and four upright chairs with a rug before the empty fireplace.

'That's in the past,' smiled Vasilis. 'Poor Manolis has suffered most. He has lost his boat and subsequently his livelihood.'

Manolis shifted uncomfortably in his chair. What was a boat compared with the losses others had sustained. 'I'm sure someone will take me out to the island. Do you know if the villagers are still receiving their pension and is there any money left from the amount Father Minos entrusted to you?'

Father Andreas nodded. 'There is money from Father Minos, but I know nothing about their pensions. I am sure Doctor Stavros will be able to enlighten you about their condition.' He crossed himself and the action was not lost on Manolis.

'What do you mean, their condition?' he asked, his throat dry with fear.

Father Andreas regarded him sympathetically. 'I understand they were cut off completely from the mainland. No one was allowed to visit or take supplies to them.'

'What about their food?'

Father Andreas shook his head. 'I know you had made many friends over there and I feel I must prepare you for the worst. I think it unlikely many of them have survived the ordeal.'

Manolis looked at him, wild-eyed. 'Flora. What's happened to Flora?'

'I cannot say. You have to understand that communication between the prefectures has been difficult. It is only during the last two weeks that life has begun to have any semblance of normality. I am sure the doctor will have visited the island at the first opportunity and in time will advise me. We have to be patient.'

Manolis bowed his head. He did not trust himself to speak. Tears flowed unchecked down his cheeks and into his beard. 'Flora, oh, Flora,' he moaned.

Father Andreas patted him on the shoulder. 'You must not despair. I have prayed for their well-being, along with many other of my countrymen. My first prayer, to be rid of these invaders, has been answered. As for my other prayers, we will have to wait and see.' He poured Manolis a second glass of wine. 'I am sorry to be so pessimistic. I pray that I am wrong in my assumptions. Please, take some time to compose yourself, then I wish to speak about the loss of your boat.'

'I don't care about losing my boat! I care about Flora,' answered Manolis angrily.

'Of course, I understand, but think for a moment. You do not know the fate of Flora. You do know the fate of your boat. How do you plan to earn a living? Do you plan to become a beggar on the streets?' Father Andreas considered the distressed young man before him. 'I can provide you with a boat.'

'How? Will you pray for one to appear?' answered Manolis scathingly. 'All I want is Flora.'

'And how will you visit her as you please without a boat? Listen to me, Manolis. I cannot replace Flora if you have lost her, and I pray that is not so, but I can replace your boat. My father's boat has been sitting at the harbour ever since he left for America. I do not want it. It is yours.'

'You're giving me a boat to replace my wife? I don't think that is a fair exchange.' Manolis spoke bitterly. 'I would have risked the German bullets to take food to the islanders. Why wouldn't they let supplies out to them? They're sick people. They were no threat to anyone. I should never have left Aghios Nikolaos. I should not have listened to Father Dhakanalis.'

'My cousin is over there and I do not know his fate yet. I pray for strength to face whatever news comes of him. You must do the same. I can assure you that staying in Aghios Nikolaos would not have helped the islanders. As it is, you helped to save many lives. That is why I am giving you my father's boat.'

Manolis shook his head. 'I can't accept a boat. I did less than many others.'

'You did not run away and hide.'

Again Manolis shook his head.

Vasilis touched him on the shoulder. 'I can vouch for your bravery. You should accept the offer of the boat. Whatever fate has befallen Flora you will still have to make a living and you have the rest of your life ahead of you. Think of yourself and be grateful that such an offer has come your way.'

Manolis looked at his companion. 'I can't accept it as repayment for Flora,' he said stubbornly.

'No one is asking you to. It is a replacement for the boat you lost whilst helping the resistance.' Vasilis sighed. 'If I was in your position I would accept thankfully.'

Manolis frowned. 'What about the people who lost their homes? You can't offer them all new houses.'

'The government will recompense most of them, but it will take time. They have to prove ownership and the fact that their property was lost due to enemy action. No doubt a number of people will put in false claims. Such is human nature.' Father Andreas sighed. 'I am in a position to offer you a boat immediately. It could take years before your claim headed the queue and there is no certainty that you would be paid sufficient to buy another boat even then. They would want to know how old it was, the state of repair, they could even claim that as you left it on a beach you acted irresponsibly.'

Manolis looked at him puzzled. 'I appreciate the offer, but don't you want to sell it?'

'If you do not accept it I shall simply leave it there to continue to rot, but that seems a rather wicked thing to do to a serviceable boat.'

'You'd leave it to rot?' Manolis could not believe his ears.

Father Andreas smiled. 'I have no use for money. I have sufficient for all my immediate needs.' He cast his eyes around the sparsely furnished room as if he saw a palace.

'But what about your father? Doesn't he need the money?'

'He has sufficient. He left me his boat to dispose of as I saw fit. I want to give it to you.'

Manolis sighed deeply. 'You leave me no option but to accept,' he said. 'I am truly grateful.'

Father Andreas sat back and smiled. 'I will give you the ownership papers and also the key to the padlock so you are able to release the mooring chains. As from this moment it is yours. I would prefer that you did not mention the amount you paid for it.'

'But I have paid you nothing,' protested Manolis.

'Exactly. Now that we have concluded our business would you care to eat with me? I would like to hear a good deal more about your time in the mountains.'

Manolis stowed the papers giving him ownership of Yiorgo's boat into his pocket. He felt elated with his new possession, but it did not take away the feeling of fear in the pit of his stomach. What would he find when he finally managed to visit Spinalonga?

Vasilis took his leave of Manolis the following morning. 'I shall miss you, Manolis. We may never meet again, but I wish you well.'

'You could always visit me in Aghios Nikolaos,' offered Manolis.

Vasilis nodded. 'I may well do that. I hear the Germans are still holding out in Chania. If I decide it still isn't safe to live in the area I shall come looking for you. Remember, you're always welcome to visit me. This is the name of my village,' he handed Manolis a slip of paper. 'If ever you are there you know you'll receive a welcome and a bed for the night.'

'Can you travel all the way there by bus?' Manolis remembered the village as being in the depths of the countryside.

'I'm not sure. I know I can ride as far as Rethymnon. I may be able to catch another bus there, but if not I can always walk.'

'Why don't you come to Aghios Nikolaos with me and then I could take you down by boat?' Manolis was suddenly loath to be deprived of the man's company.

'I would have just as far to walk! No, Manolis, this is where we have to part company and go our separate ways.'

The bus for Aghios Nikolaos drew onto the piece of waste ground that served as a terminal. Manolis rose and the two men looked at each other, unsure how to say goodbye. Vasilis opened his arms and embraced the young man and Manolis clasped him back, surprised to find that he had tears coming to his eyes.

Vasilis left the bus just before Souda Bay. He did not want to run the risk of being stopped by the Germans who had retreated into Chania and were still holding the city. At the first cart track he saw he turned off the main road and began to walk his familiar route towards his village. He sniffed the air. He could no longer smell the salt from the sea; instead the air seemed thick, almost sticky, as he tried to breathe. He had been aware of that smell before. It was the smell of burning and death. He quickened his pace down the country road, anxious to get to his home yet dreading what he might find there.

He passed two villages, their ruins still smouldering and no sign of the inhabitants. He did not stop to investigate further, but hurried on. He turned the corner, and stopped in his tracks, his worst fears realised. His house was no more than a charred ruin. He looked around wildly. Where was Katerina, where was Vasilis? He began to circle the ruined building calling for them until his voice was hoarse from shouting.

The church. Of course, they would have gone to the church for shelter. Shaking from head to foot he forced himself to walk on into the village and stopped aghast at the devastation. There was not a building standing intact. The white stone walls were blackened by soot, anything that had been made from wood or anything else combustible had been burnt to a cinder. Door and window openings gaped at him mockingly, the debris from the roofs littering their floors. He reached the church and saw to his relief that the building had been spared. The doors stood open and he entered timidly, hoping with all his heart that he would find his wife and child sheltering there along with the other villagers.

The church was empty. He stood in the doorway of the ravaged building, surveying the vandalism that had taken place inside. Swastikas had been daubed across the icons, the altar was smashed and the windows broken. Vasilis fell to his knees, tears in his eyes, as he prayed fervently for the safety of his family. Where should he look now? Would they have been taken to Chania or had they fled into the countryside to hide? He needed to find someone – anyone – who could give him some information.

Despondently he retraced his steps through the village until he reached his farmhouse and pushed his way inside, walking over the ashes and debris that littered the floor. Below his feet he heard something crunch and he bent down to examine it further.

Sticking out from beneath the ashes was a bone. He felt the bile rising in his throat and passed a trembling hand over his head. It could not be. Carefully he pushed the ashes to one side, revealing more bones, and finally a skull. Was it Katerina? He dug down again into the debris, unearthing a further collection of bones jumbled together along with three more skulls.

Shaking from head to toe he stumbled from the building. Tears were leaving streaks down his dirty face and he tried to think coherently. He tried to convince himself that the bones and skull did not belong to his wife. He sat on the grass opposite the blackened ruin, the pain in his heart so great that he could not move. As darkness fell he was still sitting there, his eyes staring blankly into the distance.

Cold and stiff, he finally rose to his feet at dawn and retraced his steps down into the village. The scene had not changed over night. He moved slowly from house to house, looking for any sign that there was an occupant hiding fearfully inside, until finally accepting that the village was deserted. Intermittently he called his wife's name, although he had little hope of hearing her answer him.

Slowly, his feet dragging with every step he took, he turned his back on the area and began to walk towards Chania. There had to be someone somewhere who could tell him the fate of his family. In each village he entered the ruined buildings and stopped at the church, hoping he would find someone there to help him, but each one was a replica of the one before, empty and desecrated.

It was late in the day when he caught a glimpse of someone hiding behind a wall and his hopes soared. He strode over purposefully to find a priest cowering behind it. On seeing the dirty, dishevelled man, the priest raised his hands.

'Please, spare me. I have nothing.'

'Father where is everyone? Where's my wife and my son? Where have they gone?'

The priest regarded Vasilis warily, his hands still held aloft. 'I have nothing to give you,' he repeated.

Vasilis shook his head impatiently. 'Where's my wife? Where has everyone gone?'

The priest finally lowered his hands and crossed himself. 'There is no one left. The Germans came. They insisted the villages in the area had harboured andartes and resistance workers. They did not believe the protests of the people. They gathered them together, old and young alike, all in one house, then they shot them and burned the house down.'

Vasilis felt the bile rising in him. He groaned. 'My wife. My son.'

'No one was spared. At least they had the grace to shoot them before they incinerated the building. I have prayed long and hard for their souls.'

'Where were you when this happened?' asked Vasilis harshly. 'How is it you have survived?'

'I was at Profitis Ilias when they came this way. I can only think they saw it as a short cut to Chania and revenged themselves on the villages as they passed through.'

Vasilis buried his head in his hands. The tears ran unchecked down his cheeks. He had thought his family safe, and they had been until the withdrawal of the troops. This had to be the Germans' revenge for their defeat.

The priest touched his shoulder. 'I have nothing to offer you, except prayer. We can pray together and I hope I can bring some comfort to your troubled heart and mind.'

Vasilis shook off his hand. 'I'm leaving now.'

The priest shook his head. 'I do not think that is wise. Where will you go?'

Vasilis shrugged. 'Where I go is of no importance. Thank you for telling me.' He turned his back on the priest and continued along the road towards the deserted countryside.

As he walked he gave free rein to his grief, sobbing unashamedly until he could cry no more and only a dry retching came from him. He curled his body into a foetal position and lay on the hard ground, oblivious of the cold. The question went round and round in his brain – why them?

The morning found him cold and wretched. Despite being tempted to lie there, he forced himself to his feet. Suddenly he felt alone in an alien country. He wished he was still in the mountains fighting with the andartes and had no knowledge of the events that had taken place in the area. He had been able to rely on his comrades for help and support during difficult times, now there was no one he could call on.

Manolis alighted from the bus and walked straight to the harbour. Yiorgo's boat sat exactly where he had seen it last. It was larger than his had been and he hoped he would be able to manage it. Yiorgo had often employed a rower. He would not be in a financial position to do that for a considerable amount of time. He decided it was too late that night to visit the Town Hall and register his claim on Yiorgo's boat and trudged along the main road until he reached the outskirts where he had always lived with his aunt and uncle.

He knocked politely on the door, not liking to walk in unannounced and startle them. His aunt Eirini was spooning something into the slack mouth of her husband and looked at him with a puzzled frown as he entered.

'Yes?' she said. 'Who are you and what do you want?'

'It's me, Aunt Eirini. Manolis.'

'Manolis?' she peered at him. 'What are you doing here?'

'I've come back to Aghios Nikolaos now the Germans have left.'

'We had Italians here. Not that you would have known that as you ran away.' She sniffed derisively and pushed another spoonful into her husband's mouth.

'I didn't run away, Auntie. I've been with the andartes in the mountains.'

Eirini eyed his unkempt appearance up and down. 'You look like a tramp.'

Manolis ignored the remark. 'What's wrong with Uncle?'

'He was hit over the head by one of the soldiers. They didn't believe him when he said he hadn't any more leather to repair their boots.'

'When?'

Eirini shrugged. 'A couple of years back now. The doctor says he has brain damage.'

Manolis shook his head sadly. 'I'm sorry to hear that. Will he get better eventually?'

'More likely to get worse. What do you want anyway?'

'I thought I could come back here and live. I'm going to be a fisherman again now the war is over.'

Eirini calculated rapidly. 'The rent will be double now. Your uncle can't work and nor can I. I have to stay here to look after him.'

Manolis nodded. 'I understand. I may need a week or two to become organised but I'll make up anything that I owe you.'

'You need a wash. You stink.'

Manolis was taken aback. He had washed that morning before leaving Heraklion, although he had to admit that he had worn the same clothes for months on end. 'I could do with a bath,' he admitted.

'You'll have to heat the water. I have your uncle to see to. I'll use the water after you've finished to give him a wash. You can help me.'

'Yes, Auntie.' Manolis felt his heart sink. He had hoped for a warmer welcome.

Manolis was on the doorstep of the Town Hall when it opened the next day. He had bathed and shaved off his beard the previous night. Despite being clean he knew by the way people looked askance at him that his clothes were disreputable. Once his business at the Town Hall was completed he would visit the bank.

He was amazed at the amount of money that had accumulated in his account. He drew out more than enough to buy some new clothes, leaving a generous amount to give to his aunt. He debated whether to buy Flora a present and decided against it. He needed to ascertain if she was still alive first.

He returned to the harbour and unlocked the padlock that held Yiorgo's boat chained safely to the jetty. He stood on board with a feeling of disbelief. This was his boat. He was tempted to sail immediately out to Spinalonga, but his caution as a sailor stopped him. He must make a trip out into the bay first and be sure he could handle the craft safely. He raised the sails, the ropes creaking from long disuse and he made a mental note to bring some grease with him to oil the pulleys. Inside the small hold were some folded fishing nets that he shook out and examined for holes. They could be mended later.

Remembering his experience with his previous motor he decided to have this one checked by a mechanic before he tried to use it. Hurriedly he chained the boat to the bollard again and almost ran down the harbour road to where the ships' chandlers had their stores. He insisted the motor had to be checked immediately. He offered the mechanic twice as much as he usually earned in a day to return with him. Sighing deeply the mechanic collected his tools together and returned to the boat with Manolis.

'This is Yiorgo's boat,' he remarked.

'It was Yiorgo's boat. It's my boat now,' announced Manolis proudly.

The mechanic shrugged. If the fisherman could afford to buy Yiorgo's boat he could easily afford to pay him double the usual rate for his work.

Manolis fretted with impatience as the mechanic stripped down the motor, checked the parts, oiled and greased them and finally reassembled the engine. 'All you need now is some petrol and you can be off.'

Manolis looked at the sun. It was too late now to visit Spinalonga. He would have to wait until the next morning and it could be advisable to let Doctor Stavros know he was back. He would just go for a short trip out into the bay and back to familiarise himself with the handling of the boat.

He rose early the next morning and looked for Doctor Stavros at his house. There was no sign of him and Manolis debated the wisdom of waiting around. The doctor could be anywhere, even out into the countryside for a couple of days or more. He went down to the harbour and gazed lovingly at the boat. He would take her out a short way, then see if the doctor had returned.

He was not far from the jetty when he thought he saw the doctor turn into a seafront taverna. With alacrity, Manolis started the motor and headed back to the harbour. He sought the doctor out, slid into the seat opposite, and called for a beer.

Doctor Stavros scowled at him. 'So where have you been?'

Manolis swallowed hard. Now the time had come he dared not ask the doctor about the fate of Flora. Surely if the news was good he would have greeted his former boatman in a more friendly fashion.

'I went down to Preveli and helped out down there for a while. I ferried soldiers around and took supplies to the local villages until they smashed my boat up. Then I went up into the mountains and joined up with a resistance group. I'd never handled a rifle until then, but I became quite a good shot. What about you?'

'My usual duties and tending to wounded resistance workers.'

Manolis could put the moment off no longer. 'How's Flora?' he asked, his throat dry and his fists clenched at his side.

Doctor Stavros shrugged. 'As well as can be expected under the circumstances. She's still alive.'

'What do you mean?'

'She suffered from starvation the same as everyone else. No one was allowed to go out to Spinalonga.'

'I heard that a couple of days ago. I never thought they'd stop the food going over.' Manolis swallowed the rest of his beer. 'Are you going out today? I could take you over. I'll be leaving in about ten minutes.' Now he was desperate to make the journey to the island.

'I can't be ready that quickly. You'll have to give me an hour to get my medical supplies together. Nothing will have changed in an hour. You can tell me more about your experiences on the way over and I'll tell you what to expect when we arrive.' The doctor spoke grimly.

Manolis waited in a fever of impatience for the doctor to arrive. 'I'm going through the canal,' he announced. 'It will be quicker.'

'You've got a new boat,' observed Doctor Stavros. 'Is the canal deep enough to take it?'

'It should be,' Manolis replied confidently. 'Yiorgo used to go that way sometimes. Now, tell me exactly what happened on the island whilst I was away.'

Manolis scanned the jetty eagerly as Spinalonga came into sight. He had still expected to see Flora waiting there for him as she had for so many years.

'Where is she?' he asked as he tied his boat alongside two others that had arrived before him.

'Probably up at the hospital.' Doctor Stavros climbed ashore. 'Is she that sick?'

'They all are,' he replied tersely.

Manolis hurried along the path to the hospital, leaving the doctor to trail behind him carrying his own bag. He entered apprehensively and waited for his eyes to become accustomed to the dim interior. He cleared his throat.

'Flora?' The word was a whisper and he looked around to see if he could espy her. 'Flora?' he said again more loudly and this time a head turned in his direction.

'Over there.'

Manolis stepped over mattresses to where the man had pointed. Curled up on a mattress, looking no bigger than a child, Flora appeared to be asleep.

Manolis felt his throat constrict and tears filled his eyes. 'Flora, oh, Flora.'

Flora's eyes flickered open, closed, and then opened again. She frowned. 'Manolis?'

Manolis placed his arms around her, holding her gently, his tears falling onto her unkempt hair. She felt so thin and fragile he was afraid she would break beneath his touch. She reached out her skeletal fingers and touched his face.

'It is you, Manolis?'

Manolis could only nod his head and bury his face deeper into her hair. Sobs racked his body. He felt a hand on his shoulder and tried to shake it off. He did not trust himself to speak to anyone.

'It is good to see you, my son.' Father Minos spoke in a trembling voice. 'Why don't you take Flora outside where you can talk together quietly? The fresh air will do her good and I will make sure her soup is brought out to her.'

Manolis lifted Flora gently from her mattress and carried her outside to the daylight. He cradled her gently in his arms like a baby, taking in her ravaged features, her cheek bones standing out prominently in her thin face and was wracked with guilt. How many times had he complained that he was hungry? His hunger had been nothing compared to what the islanders had suffered.

'Where have you been, Manolis?' asked Flora, her voice hardly above a whisper.

'In the mountains. I'll tell you all about it later, when you're stronger.'

Flora closed her eyes and relaxed back into his arms. 'I never thought I would see you again.'

'When I heard they had stopped sending you food I thought everyone would be dead. I hardly dared to ask Doctor Stavros.'

'Many of my friends have died. Poor Yannis, he lost Phaedra and Anna. He has nothing left to live for. I wanted to see you again before I died.'

'You're not going to die, Flora. I won't let you die.' He tightened his grip on her as if his strength could stop her life from slipping away.

Vasilis stepped off the bus in Aghios Nikolaos and walked to the harbour. A few boats had already returned from a day's fishing but he could see no sign of Manolis. He sat on the wall and gazed steadily out at sea, willing the fisherman to return. The remainder of the afternoon passed slowly and it was almost dark when Manolis finally arrived and moored his boat carefully. He noticed the dirty man sitting dejectedly on a bollard and ignored him as he unloaded his buckets. As he placed the last one on the jetty the man rose and Manolis drew in his breath.

'Vasilis! What are you doing here?'

Vasilis shrugged. 'I didn't know where else to go.'

'I thought you were going back to your farm.'

'I have no farm. I have nothing.'

Manolis threw his arm around his friend's shoulders. Something drastic had obviously occurred. 'Come with me.' He led the way to the nearest taverna, hoping they would not refuse entry to his companion. 'What are you drinking?'

Vasilis shrugged. 'Anything.'

'When did you last eat?'

Vasilis passed a shaking hand across his forehead. 'I'm not sure, yesterday maybe.'

Hardly liking to leave Vasilis alone, Manolis walked up to the counter. 'A bottle of wine and two bowls of kleftiko as fast as you can. My friend has not eaten since yesterday.'

The taverna owner looked suspiciously at the bearded, unkempt man who sat staring vacantly into the distance. He would certainly serve them quickly and hope they would depart as soon as they had eaten. The dirty beggar would not encourage any other customers to eat there.

Manolis returned to the table carrying the wine and glasses. He poured for both of them and pushed the glass into Vasilis's hand.

'Can you tell me what happened?'

'Every house had been burnt to the ground, the church had been defiled. It was the same in each village. I spoke to the priest at Agios Georgios. He told me there were no survivors. They shot them and then burnt their bodies.'

Manolis felt a lump come into his throat. 'Are you sure? They're not in hiding somewhere?'

'I thought they would be safe. I would never have left them if I had suspected they would be attacked.' Vasilis slammed his fist onto the table.

'You could not have prevented it. You would have been one against many. You would have lost your life as well.'

Vasilis shrugged. 'My life means nothing without Katerina; and Vasilis – what had he done? He was four years old, a baby, and they shot him.'

Manolis shook his head, he had tears in his eyes on behalf of his friend. 'Tell me exactly what happened.'

'I can't. I don't know. I don't know if they suffered. I wasn't there to help them.' Vasilis's anguish was evident and tears coursed their way down his cheeks as he spoke.

Manolis stretched out his hand and covered Vasilis's. 'What can I do for you? How can I help?'

Vasilis withdrew his hand. 'You can't help me. No one can.' He passed a trembling hand over his face, wiping away the tears and streaking his face further. 'I had nowhere else to go.'

'Eat,' commanded Manolis as the bowls of food were placed in front of them and was relieved to see Vasilis pick up his fork and spear a piece of meat.

They ate in silence, until Vasilis finally pushed the empty bowl away from him. He poured himself a second glass of wine and leaned forward to Manolis.

'May I spend the night on your boat?'

Manolis looked at him in surprise. 'Of course, but why should you want to?'

Vasilis smiled thinly. 'I would feel more comfortable there than inside a cottage. I was never on a boat with Katerina. There is nothing to remind me.'

Manolis nodded understandingly. 'You may stay as long as you wish, but first we have to get you cleaned up. When we've eaten we'll go to my aunt's cottage and you can have a bath and a shave. I've some clean clothes you can wear.'

Vasilis shrugged, but to Manolis's relief did not argue.

Eirini looked at the dirty man who accompanied her nephew with distaste. 'He's not welcome in my house looking like that,' she declared. 'He smells worse than you did when you returned.'

'I'm going to heat some water for him to have a bath. When he's clean and shaved he'll look considerably better.'

Eirini sniffed. 'Where did you pick him up? This is a respectable house.'

Manolis looked at her with a hurt expression. 'We spent the war years together; either on my boat or living in the mountains. He and his wife made me welcome at his house. His wife was shot during the Germans' retreat to Chania, along with his son.'

Eirini's expression softened a little. 'He won't have been the only one who suffered. Why has he come down here?'

Manolis shook his head. 'I'm not sure. He said he had nowhere else to go.'

'Well there's no room for him here.'

'He's not stopping here. He'll spend the night on my boat and then I'll find out what his plans are tomorrow.'

Vasilis sat out in the yard whilst Manolis heated water for him to have a bath. Now Manolis's uncle had ceased working at the tannery the stale urine was no longer saved, but the smell still emanated from the surrounding houses and Manolis wrinkled his nose in disgust. He was ashamed that Vasilis should have to sit in such surroundings.

He stropped his razor and watched whilst Vasilis shaved off his beard before stripping off his clothes and stepping into the hot water. Under Manolis's direction he soaped his body clean and waited whilst Manolis poured a fresh bucket of water over him before handing him a rough towel to dry himself.

Manolis disappeared up to the loft and collected the new pair of trousers, shirt and jumper he had bought earlier in the week. He laid them on a chair for Vasilis whilst he collected the man's earlier discarded clothing and pushed it into a corner with the rest of the rubbish that had accumulated there.

Once shaved, bathed and dressed Vasilis looked a different man. The blank look remained in his eyes and Manolis was seriously worried. Where could he turn to get help for his friend? He pushed Vasilis back into the living room with his aunt and uncle.

'I have to go out for a short while,' he announced. 'I'd like my friend to stay here until I return.'

Eirini pursed her lips in disapproval as Manolis set a glass and bottle of wine at Vasilis's elbow. 'How long will you be gone?' she asked.

'No more than half an hour, if that.' Manolis closed the door behind him, hoping that Vasilis would be there when he returned.

Manolis knocked on the door at Doctor Stavros's house and was relieved when the doctor looked out. He frowned. 'What brings you here, Manolis? Not an emergency on the island at this time of night I hope?'

Manolis shook his head. 'I need your help, doctor. A fellow resistance worker has arrived at my house.'

'Is he injured?'

'His wife and child were killed a short while ago. He's behaving strangely. I don't know what to do.'

'How am I supposed to help?'

Manolis shrugged hopelessly. 'I thought maybe you could talk to him.'

Doctor Stavros sighed. 'I would have thought a priest would have been more helpful to him. Have you been to see Father Dhakanalis?'

'I thought you might have a medicine that would help him.'

The doctor laughed mirthlessly. 'If I had everyone on Crete would want a dose! I can give you something to help him sleep. That's the best I can do.'

Manolis nodded eagerly. 'I'm sure that would help him.'

Doctor Stavros unlocked the cupboard in the corner of his room and removed a small bottle. He decanted half the contents into an even smaller bottle and handed it to Manolis. 'Put some in his wine if he resists taking it.'

'Thank you, doctor. I'll see you tomorrow and tell you how he is.'

Doctor Stavros shrugged. The man was not really his concern if he had no physical injuries.

Manolis rolled up his mattress and collected his blankets, the sleeping draught safely in his pocket. 'We're going down to sleep on the boat, Aunt Eirini. I'll see you tomorrow.'

Eirini looked after the two men as they left the house. She had thought her nephew would eventually get married, but he seemed to have an attachment to this strange man. She was relieved they were not going to be sharing a mattress above her head, but she did not approve of them going off to sleep on the boat together. What were they going to get up to?

Vasilis was still snoring gently when Manolis awoke. He sat and watched as the harbour area came to life, the fishermen climbing aboard their boats, the traders opening up their shops in preparation for the morning's trade. As soon as the taverna keeper appeared Manolis stepped carefully ashore and returned a short while later carrying a jug of coffee. He shook Vasilis awake and handed him a cracked cup, full to the brim.

'What do you want to do today?' he asked.

'Do? What is there to do?' Vasilis's eyes were still blank, his whole body appearing limp and lifeless.

'I need to go out to the island. You can come with me.'

Vasilis shrugged. He did not care what he did or where he went; then he remembered. Manolis had said his wife was on the island and he had been so concerned with his own feelings of despair that he had not even asked if she was still alive.

'Your wife?'

'She survived – just. Many of the islanders starved to death. The doctor says she'll recover given time.' Manolis felt unreasonably guilty that Flora should still be alive. 'She seems to get a little stronger every day.'

'I'm pleased for your sake.' Vasilis managed to utter the words, as once again a feeling of utter desolation washed over him.

Each day Vasilis accompanied Manolis on his journey to Spinalonga, waiting on the boat until Manolis was prepared to leave and go fishing for the remainder of the day. Once back at Aghios Nikolaos, Manolis would take his catch to the fish market, return to the boat and insist Vasilis went to the taverna with him for a meal. Manolis tried to curb his impatience with his companion. Vasilis showed no inclination to do anything. Manolis knew how devastated he would have been had Flora died and tried to excuse his inactivity. He spoke to Spiro, hoping he would know how to tackle the problem.

Spiro shrugged. 'I don't know how to help. Look at Yannis. He refuses to leave the hospital and return to his house although there's no need for him to be here. He spends all day sitting in the taverna drinking himself senseless.'

'I'm sick of sleeping on the boat. Once the war was over I

was looking forward to a bit of comfort. It's cold and wet and the cabin is only large enough to hold one of us. I don't like to leave him down there on his own over night.'

'Why don't you ask your aunt to take him in?'

Manolis shook his head. 'She thinks there's something more than friendship between us. She won't have him under her roof if she can help it. I insist he comes for a bath each week, but he's not allowed in past the kitchen.'

'Maybe Father Minos can help?'

'Maybe,' answered Manolis dubiously. He was not sure how much longer he could be patient with his morose companion.

The weeks Vasilis had spent travelling backwards and forwards to the island with Manolis had done a little to ease the pain he was suffering. He knew he could not spend the remainder of his life in limbo, being no more than a parasite to Manolis, and when Father Minos climbed aboard the boat he agreed to say a prayer with him and talk with him afterwards.

Vasilis made no mention of their conversation during their return journey and Manolis knew better than to ask. They ate their meal in their customary silence, but on this occasion Vasilis drank more sparingly and appeared more thoughtful. Finally he pushed his chair back from the table.

'I won't be coming out with you tomorrow. I have some jobs to do,' he announced. 'I shall be away all day and maybe the next.'

Manolis raised his eyebrows, but Vasilis was not forthcoming. He must find out how quickly he could leave Crete, the country he had once loved and now hated. Every blade of grass seemed to remind him of his beloved Katerina.

Vasilis caught the bus to Heraklion, changed onto the one for Rethymnon and finally arrived in Chania by early evening. He handed his papers over for inspection at the checkpoint, suppressing the desire to put his fist into the soldier's face, and walked to the outskirts. There was bound to be a derelict building somewhere that he could spend the night.

Unkempt and uncaring, Vasilis walked to the bank where he kept his account, only to find that he had an hour to wait until it reopened. He forced himself to drink two cups of coffee, sitting alone, trying to ignore the German soldiers who were also patronising the cafe, despite hating them with an intensity he did not know was in him. He wished he still had his revolver with him. He would have shot dead as many as possible before they killed him.

At the bank it took some time to convince the cashier that he wanted to withdraw all his money immediately. The manager was called, and Vasilis tried hard to curb his impatience as he told him he had to travel back to England immediately on urgent family business and did not know when he would return. The manager was unsure if they would have that amount of drachmas on the premises and asked Vasilis to wait a few days. Vasilis refused.

'I need all my money now. I know how banks work and if you do not have enough cash on the premises you can give a promissory note to the nearest bank and make up the difference. I'm not moving until I have it down to the last lepta.' He glared at them balefully and defiant. 'I also need my British passport. It's in a strong box here. I know the code, but I no longer have a key.'

The manager sighed. 'I will see what I can do, sir, but it will take a little while.'

Vasilis nodded. 'That's quite all right. I'll sit here and wait.' He folded his arms and leaned back in the chair. The manager scowled. It would have been so much easier if the customer had been willing to wait a week. He could have visited the taverna and negotiated with the manager of the bank across town. As it was, if he put in an official request, the manager would have every right to charge him for a courier to bring the money and he had a feeling that the man before him would not be prepared to pay for the service.

When the money finally arrived, Vasilis sat and counted it slowly. The manager fidgeted. He hoped there would be no discrepancy. It was almost time for the bank to close for the day and he did not want to be late leaving and have to explain why he was out after the curfew.

Vasilis piled the wads of notes together, folded them, and placed them in his pocket. He could see he had plenty there for what he had in mind and did not really care if the figure was accurate. He had only counted it because he knew it was expected of him and it would annoy the manager further.

'And my passport, please.'

The manager withdrew it from a drawer and pushed it across the table.

'Thank you.' Vasilis pushed his way out of the door without bidding him farewell and went immediately to the bus station. He hoped the bus for Rethymnon was still running. He did not want to pass another night in the town.

'We won't be returning tonight,' the driver warned him and Vasilis nodded.

'I won't be returning either,' he said.

Vasilis spent the night behind the wall of a ruined house in Rethymnon. He had forced himself to eat, not tasting the food as he swallowed it. He then sat at the table, paper and pencil at hand and written down the names of all the people who had lived in his village, Katerina and Vasilis heading the list. At first light he rose, checked he had his money and the list safely in his pocket, along with his old British passport, and caught the bus that would take him to Heraklion.

Father Andreas was surprised to see him, but one look at the man's ravaged face told him he had received bad news. He held out his arms.

'What can I do for you? How can I comfort you?'

Vasilis shook his head. 'No one can comfort me. My wife, my child,' his voice broke and he struggled to regain his composure. 'They were shot along with the other villagers and their bodies burnt.'

Father Andreas sucked in his breath. 'That is monstrous.'

Vasilis banged his fist against the wall. 'I wish we had killed every single one that ever set foot in our country.'

'I can understand your anger and bitterness, but it will do no good. I pray that in time you will be able to forgive them for their wickedness. If you do not, it will eat into you like a cancer and destroy you. Do not give them the satisfaction of adding you to their list.'

'I am going to make sure that their evil deeds are known for ever more.' Vasilis pulled the money from his pocket. 'I want to have a memorial erected to them. I want their names engraved on it and the message telling everyone that they were shot by the Germans in cold blood so anyone who passes can see and read it. I have made a list of all the villagers who perished.'

Father Andreas frowned. 'So why have you come to me?'

'I trust you, Father. I am leaving the money and the list with you. Please do this for me.'

'Why do you not arrange this yourself?'

'I am returning to England. I plan never to set foot in Greece again.'

'To England?' Father Andreas was puzzled. Why should the man wish to go to a foreign country?

'I am English, despite having lived over here for many years and considering myself a Cretan. I cannot stay here now.'

'You are English?' Father Andreas had assumed the dark haired man who spoke the language so fluently to be a Greek.

'I am as English as you are Greek. Will you do this for me, Father?'

Father Andreas nodded slowly. 'I am honoured by your trust in me. It may take a little while. We have to return to our normal way of life and that will take time. As soon as it is possible I promise I will see that the memorial is built.'

'I want it built where my farm stood. I own the land. I do not want it hidden away.'

'As you wish. Write down the name of your village and indicate where your farm stood and I will ensure your wishes are carried out.'

'It's all on the paper.' He handed the sheet over to the priest. 'Thank you. I will leave you now. I have to return to Aghios Nikolaos. I need to see Manolis one more time.'

Manolis was relieved when he saw Vasilis waiting for him. It had been pleasant to spend the day without him, able to stay as long as he pleased with Flora without feeling a nagging anxiety about the man.

'I've just come from Heraklion,' Vasilis announced. 'I saw Father Andreas. He will have a memorial erected, to Katerina, little Vasilis and the other villagers. I've left the money and a list of names with him. It will be on the land where our farm stood. It has to be there.' Vasilis looked at Manolis intently. 'Will you make sure it's placed there? You know where our farm was, Father Andreas does not know the area.'

Manolis nodded sombrely. 'Of course. Would it not be better if you stayed and supervised it yourself?' he suggested.

Vasilis shook his head. 'I have no reason to stay in Crete without Katerina.'

Manolis did not have an answer. He would have had no option but to stay in Aghios Nikolaos if Flora had died, but this man came from another country. He could return to his native land and try to put the agonising memories behind him.

'Tomorrow I will return to Heraklion,' continued Vasilis. 'I have a passage to England arranged for two day's time.'

Manolis raised his eyebrows. 'What made you decide to do that?'

'I have to go somewhere and start again. Where else can I go?'

'At least stay here with me tomorrow,' urged Manolis. 'I will take you to Heraklion in the evening.'

Vasilis hesitated. He had no wish to be alone and he did not wish to impose on Father Andreas.

'We can sail up in the evening, you can spend the night aboard again, and you will be in time to catch your boat.' Manolis pressed home his suggestion.

'What about your island deliveries?'

Manolis shrugged. 'They can wait a day. They waited long enough before.'

Manolis insisted on going ashore with Vasilis when they reached Heraklion. He was still not convinced that the man would not do something stupid due to his misery and despair. He accompanied Vasilis on board, making the excuse that he wanted to see what an ocean going ship looked like, despite Vasilis's protests that it was unnecessary.

Manolis finally clasped Vasilis to him and bade him farewell with tears in his eyes. The man's grief over his lost family was tangible and Manolis knew there was nothing he could say or do to give him any solace. Before finally parting company Manolis asked if there was an address in England where he could send a letter to say the memorial had been completed, but Vasilis shrugged.

'I could be anywhere. I trust Father Andreas to commission it and you to make sure it is erected where I stated.' Vasilis pressed some money into Manolis's hand. 'That's for all the meals you bought for me.' Vasilis turned and walked away without looking back.

Manolis sailed back to Aghios Nikolaos, stopping at Spinalonga on the way. He held Flora in his arms, his hot tears dropping onto her hair as he wept unashamedly for his friend's loss. He knew he would not have wanted to continue with his life if Flora had not survived the war years.

Eirini looked at her sombre faced nephew. 'Where've you been for the last couple of days? Out on that new fancy boat of yours with your friend again I suppose.'

Manolis shrugged. 'I took him up to Heraklion to catch a ship for England. He lost his wife and child during the war.'

'A lot of people lost their loved ones. Look at your uncle. He's nothing more than a vegetable. I have to do everything for him.'

Manolis had heard her lament on a number of occasions since his return. 'He's fortunate to have you to look after him.' He tried to placate her.

'You want to think about a wife now you're back, Manolis. I won't be here to look after you when you're old. You should get married.'

Manolis smiled. 'I'm happy as I am.'

'Maria's looking for a husband.'

'What happened to Phoebus?'

'He didn't come back. She's looking for someone to take his place.'

'She'd not look at a fisherman, and I'm not interested.'

'You ought to get married,' persisted Eirini. 'People will begin to think you're not – right.'

'I'm perfectly all right. I just don't want to marry a local girl. People can think what they like.'

1945 – 1954

Manolis was unhappy. With so few islanders still alive after the war his requests for purchases dwindled. He was still paid his usual sum for being the book-keeper, but he was worried that when the authorities saw how few purchases he had made they would decide he was no longer necessary.

Those who had survived tried to return to their previous life, but it was difficult. The barber, who had sent for new scissors, combs, razors, and mirrors on a regular basis, had only asked for replacement articles twice during the year. Despina, who had previously had a thriving dressmaking business, now had bales of cloth sitting on her shelves and her treadle machine would sit idle for weeks at a time.

The gardens had been dug over and re-planted; their produce now was more than enough to feed the villagers during the season. Building materials were not requested as Yannis spent his days sitting in the taverna drinking and no one seemed to have any desire to repair the derelict houses. Spiro still asked for mattresses, blankets, but they were not forthcoming and bandages were taken over by the doctor when he made his regular visits.

Manolis took over food supplies as before, but far less was needed and the consignments were shared out amongst the other boatmen. Where he had earned at least thirty drachmas a week he was now thankful if he earned ten. At least the fish seemed plentiful, although the price for his catch did not increase.

Father Minos was also concerned. Everyone seemed apathetic and although he went amongst them trying to encourage them to paint their house or repair a shutter, his words seemed to be ignored. He reminded them that the Germans had not been able to break their spirit when they tried to starve them, but now they were free again they seemed willing to sit and do nothing until the end of their days.

One or two took his words to heart and made an effort, but many of the men would spend their time in the taverna playing dice, backgammon or cards, whilst Yannis sat in a morose silence and drank himself into oblivion. The pride the women had had in their houses was diminished, although they continued to cook and clean in a desultory manner.

Father Minos sought out Doctor Stavros when he visited and asked if there was anything the man was able to do to help the villagers.

Doctor Stavros shook his head. 'There is no miracle cure. They are all suffering from a reaction to the war. They are all mentally exhausted and many of them are no longer strong enough to work as they did before. They are no longer starving and having to think of ways to survive. Thanks to Yannis's previous efforts they all have a serviceable house to live in and the hospital is here if they need your attention. They need something to give them an interest in life again.'

Father Minos walked from his church down the main street to the small square. Some of the houses were already beginning to show signs of dilapidation and he was concerned that when new sufferers were sent out to the island there would be nowhere for them to live. He shuddered at the thought of newcomers having to live in the tunnels as the original lepers had done for so many years.

From the square he made detours into the side roads, noting how many of the walls were crumbling and in places a roof had been partially blown away. The doctor was right. Even if the men had the inclination to work, they would not have the physical strength. Without Yannis to encourage and inspire them the island would return to the state of neglect he had found when he had made his first visit so many years ago.

He sighed deeply and returned to his church. Life here had been no different from any other village until the war. His mind went back over the time when George Pavlakis had visited and their pension from the government had finally been granted. That had given all of them an incentive. What would restore their enthusiasm and energy now?

Father Minos was surprised when Manolis delivered a letter to him from Heraklion. He opened it with trepidation. Were the authorities revoking his permission to live on the island? He sighed with relief when he saw it came from Andreas. He read it through carefully and realised he would need to reply, thanking him for recovering the money that had been stolen by the doctor. A germ of an idea took hold and he was suddenly anxious to start the missive.

The priest wrote at length, describing the deprivation they had suffered and the number of unnecessary deaths that had occurred, leaving no more than a hundred survivors, all of whom were weakened by the experience. Surely they were entitled to compensation from the government.

Andreas replied that the government was unable to compensate them financially. If they agreed to do so for the islanders all Cretans would consider themselves eligible as so many of them had suffered under the hands of the brutal invaders.

Father Minos tried again. He understood the financial position; but would the government at least send some builders to repair the houses? The inhabitants were no longer strong enough to do the work themselves. There was also the question of the hospital. It needed to be properly modernised and equipped, staffed with trained medical personnel, rather than sick people taking responsibility for their fellows.

The letters went back and forth between them, until Andreas was finally convinced that he should approach the government. Andreas presented his case for the islanders carefully and logically, but the men shook their heads and refused. Why should a hundred or so people have preferential treatment when there was so much needed for the population as a whole? Andreas was enraged. Had they not listened and understood? He continued to harangue them until a compromise was reached. He was to visit the island and compile a report of the most urgent repairs needed and they would then consider his request. With that he had to be content.

Father Andreas stepped ashore and made his way to the taverna where he had been assured he would find his cousin. Andreas looked at Yannis in disgust. His glazed eyes and shaking hands showed that he was already far from sober, despite the early hour.

'I want to ask your opinion about the repairs Father Minos says are needed over here.'

Yannis shrugged. 'Why should I know?'

'You organised the rebuilding. You're in a better position than anyone else to assess the condition of the houses.'

Yannis lifted his eyes from his glass. 'I don't seem able to concentrate these days.'

'I'm not surprised. You're a drunkard, Yannis. I'm disgusted with you. I never thought you would turn your back on the people here. I thought you cared about them. Just because you have somewhere warm and dry to live you're willing to let the others suffer.'

Father Andreas returned to the square and began to examine the houses, noting a shutter that was hanging by one hinge and a couple whose walls looked distinctly unsafe. The rest of the houses there looked reasonably sound, but when he began to examine those in the side roads he saw the extent of the disintegration.

Under Yannis's direction the men had piled up stones to form walls, covering some of them with a cement skin for a modicum of stability. Without foundations and continual repairs they were now unstable and dangerous structures.

He made copious notes, finally returning to the taverna, where Yannis still sat with a glass in his hand. Andreas ignored him. He would not be able to get any sense out of him, of that he was certain. He continued up to the hospital where he found Spiro and Father Minos waiting for him.

'So? What do you think?' asked Father Minos. 'Are we being unreasonable in asking for help?'

Andreas shook his head. 'I'll need you to tell me if any one is living in some of the houses. If so, they should be moved immediately. It could be dangerous to walk past them if there was a high wind. The walls could collapse at any time.'

'How sound is the hospital?'

Spiro shrugged. 'The roof is leaking in one corner. That will obviously get worse. It needs enlarging. Everyone here is older and the privations they have suffered will take their toll. I'm expecting to have more patients as the time goes by and I'll not have the space for them or the people fit enough to nurse them. I've already asked for more blankets and mattresses and they haven't been sent out.'

'I'll make sure you get those as soon as I return,' promised Andreas.

'What about the generator? George Pavlakis agreed to send that to us when he was in office. There are also the beds he promised me. That would make nursing easier. We wouldn't have to spend all our time on our knees.'

Doctor Stavros nodded in agreement. 'We could do with some arc lights so I can see what I'm doing when I operate and an X-ray machine is essential. How do I know how far to amputate a limb if I cannot see how much bone has been destroyed?'

Andreas turned the page of his notebook and added the

requests. He thought it very unlikely that their demands would be met.

Manolis was feeling happier. Flora appeared to have completely recovered her health, along with many of the other islanders, although Doctor Stavros was convinced it would only be a matter of time before they relapsed.

The generator had been delivered to the island and he had ferried men across to install electricity to the island. He had been as fascinated as Flora the first time a light was switched on inside a dark house. It had encouraged the villagers to take a pride in their homes once more and paint and brushes were a regular order, along with material for new curtains. The doctor requested that he take a bundle of medical periodicals to the island and deliver them to Yannis, and Manolis had queried the doctor's decision, checking that he did not mean Spiro.

The doctor shook his head. 'It's just something to keep Yannis occupied. Now he's ceased drinking to excess he's bored. I've just asked him to check through them and let me know of any new drugs that are advertised. I've no time to read them myself.'

Manolis was sceptical that such a mundane activity would relieve Yannis's boredom, but to his surprise, after a few weeks Yannis sought out the doctor and was soon in an impassioned conversation with him. He had then demanded that Manolis take him copious supplies of paper and was now busily employed writing letters, the medical periodicals pushed to one side and forgotten. As Manolis delivered letters to the post office to be forwarded to Father Andreas, he wondered how the man found so much to write about. Manolis was even more surprised some months later when a parcel from America arrived for Yannis and the man seized upon it as if it were gold.

Manolis looked warily at the doctor who had arrived from Athens and announced his plans to visit the island each day. Flora was waiting for them on the quay. She greeted the doctor with a smile. 'Welcome,' she said. 'I'll take you to met Yannis. He always greets the newcomers.'

'I'm not stopping,' Nikos said firmly. 'I have been asked to come here to examine you all.'

Flora looked at Manolis, who shrugged. 'You'd better take him up to Yannis. Where do you want this lot, doctor?'

Nikos looked at the pile of boxes. 'I'm not sure. Could I just leave them here for the time being?'

Manolis nodded. 'They'll be safe enough.

Flora led to the way to Yannis's house and knocked on his door. 'Yannis, there's a visitor for you. He says he's a doctor from Athens.'

A broad smile crossed Yannis's face. 'And about time too.'

Nikos travelled over to the island every day and at the end of a week he returned to Heraklion with the samples he had taken from the inhabitants of Spinalonga. He was relieved that the job was over. It had been a shock to find that his school friend of so many years ago was amongst the islanders and was also the man who had been such a nuisance to the government with his demands.

He was disconcerted when he met with Dimitris and was told he had to take the samples again as Athens were not satisfied with the results. Twice more Nikos visited the island, having to placate Yannis each time regarding the delay there was in providing the new medication. Yannis threatened, and Nikos shrugged. He knew the government wanted him to take as long as possible examining everyone and taking the samples.

Finally he was able to delay no longer and arrangements were made to fly some of the inhabitants of Spinalonga to Athens for further medical tests. Yannis was elated. At last they were going to be given the treatment he had been demanding for the last two years.

Flora was not so happy. 'No medicine they give to me will make my arm grow again. They should take someone else rather than me. I'd far rather stay here with you, Manolis.'

Manolis placed his arm around her thin shoulders. 'I'll be here waiting for you when you return. They say you should only be away a few weeks. If they keep you too long I shall sail over in my boat and bring you back,' he promised rashly.

Flora looked at him with wide eyes. 'You mustn't do that, Manolis. It's miles and miles away.'

'I sailed miles and miles with Vasilis, probably twice as far. Sailing over to mainland Greece would not be a problem to me,' he boasted.

'We're going to fly in an aeroplane.'

Manolis felt his heart lurch. He wished they were going by sea. It was far safer than being up in the air. He had seen the wrecked aeroplanes during the war – few people had walked away from those.

'They say that some of us will be told we don't have leprosy any more,' continued Flora. 'What will happen if I'm not sick?' She looked at Manolis fearfully.

'What do you mean?' Manolis frowned.

'Where will I go?' asked Flora in a small voice.

'Go? You won't have to go anywhere you don't want to.' He held her tighter. 'If they confirm you don't have leprosy any more we'll get married, properly married. We'll have a service over here in the church and invite people from the mainland, like Marisa had when she got married.'

A tear ran down Flora's cheek. 'But you still can't live over here, Manolis.'

Manolis wiped away her tear with his thumb. 'You won't have to live over here either. You can come and live in Aghios Nikolaos with me.'

Flora looked at him wonderingly. 'Do you mean that, Manolis?'

'Of course I do. If you come back with a clean bill of health no one can stop you coming to live with me. We'll have a little house of our own, just you and me.'

Flora's lips trembled and Manolis kissed her gently. 'I love you, Flora. You're my wife.'

Manolis watched as Flora, along with the other patients who had been selected to go to Athens, boarded the bus for Heraklion. He wished he could go with her. He was convinced she would be frightened up in the air without him to hold her hand. Doctor Stavros had assured him she would be gone about six weeks, certainly no more than two months, and the time already seemed to stretch ahead of him interminably. He shook his head sadly. How must Flora have felt during the war, watching and waiting for him to return day after day? He would pay a visit to the church and say a prayer for her safe journey and swift return.

As he received a blessing from the shaking hand of Father Dhakanalis he was reminded of Father Pavlos. Was the elderly priest still alive? Had he retrieved his church treasures from the impromptu grave he and Vasilis had dug? Manolis gave a groan. He had not asked Father Andreas if he had arranged for the monument to be erected in memory of Vasilis's wife or checked that it had been situated on the site of his farm.

He lit a candle in memory of his father and made a decision. Whilst Flora was away it was the ideal time to travel around and fulfil his obligations, he might even visit Preveli and see if he could find out the fate of Arthur.

Manolis alighted from the bus at Heraklion and made his way to the small house where Father Andreas lived. The priest was surprised to see him on his doorstep and crossed himself.

'You bring bad news?'

Manolis shook his head. 'Not that I know of. Some of the islanders have left for Athens, but then I expect you knew that.'

Father Andreas nodded. 'So what brings you up here?'

Manolis dropped his eyes. 'I should have asked when you were down at Spinalonga and I forgot. Have you arranged the monument Vasilis wanted in memory of his wife and child?'

Father Andreas smote himself on the forehead. 'It is me who had forgotten! I meant to tell you and I became so involved with the plight of my cousin that it went out of my head. Come in and I will show you how it looks.'

Manolis stepped into the tiny parlour and Andreas busied himself searching in a drawer, finally withdrawing a large sheet of paper. He handed it to Manolis. 'What do you think?'

Manolis looked at the drawing in surprise. He had expected to see a stone, probably granite, engraved with the names of the dead villagers; instead there was a statue of an angel with a child in her arms. Where her skirt flowed out, the stone had been smoothed and the names carved, Katerina and Vasilis heading the list. At the base was inscribed:

'INNOCENT VICTIMS
OF GERMAN SOLDIERS'

Manolis felt a lump come into his throat.

'Is this what Vasilis asked for?'

Father Andreas nodded. 'He drew the design sitting at the table here.'

'And it has been completed and erected?'

'It has. I wish I knew his whereabouts. I'm sure he'd like to see the result. I also have some money belonging to him. He left me more than enough to cover the cost.'

Manolis drew in his breath. Vasilis must have been a very rich man to have paid for such a memorial and still have enough to pay for his passage back to England. The amount he had pressed into Manolis's hand before leaving had been more than generous, amply covering the food and clothes Manolis had bought for him. He shook his head.

'Sadly I have no idea where he is. He decided to return to England and left me no address.'

Father Andreas frowned. 'What should I do with his money? It does not belong to the church and it certainly does not belong to me.'

Manolis hesitated. It was not his money either. 'I am sure he would not object to the church having it. Maybe it could be used to help those who suffered during the war?'

'You are thinking of the inhabitants of Spinalonga?' Father Andreas raised his eyebrows.

Manolis shook his head. 'I am thinking of children. Many would have been orphaned and I'm sure their relatives are caring for them. This can cause hardship if they already have a family of their own.'

'I cannot travel all over Crete looking for deserving orphans!'

'Of course not, but in your own parish you would know if there were families in need.'

Father Andreas nodded slowly. 'I see many around me who do not know where their next meal is coming from.' He did not add that it usually came from him. 'They would be grateful for any help that I was able to offer them.'

'Then do so, Father. I am sure Vasilis would approve, particularly if it helped children.'

Manolis looked at the drawing of the memorial again. 'May I keep this? I plan to visit the memorial and it will enable me to check that all the names are spelt correctly.'

Father Andreas shrugged. 'Certainly. It is of no further use to me.'

Manolis stood hesitantly at the bus station in Chania. He wished he had sailed up, convinced it would have been a quicker journey, and he would have had somewhere to sleep at night. From his pocket he drew the piece of paper he had written his proposed itinerary on. Firstly he had to ascertain if there was a bus that travelled close to Vasilis's farm. He was not averse to walking, but doubted he would find his way without Vasilis as a guide.

He was fortunate. There was a bus due in an hour that would travel down the main road depositing those who had visited the town back close to their villages. It would return two hours later and if he wished to catch it he should be on the main road waiting in good time. Manolis purchased his ticket and pushed himself onto the wooden bench along with the other waiting passengers.

The bus arrived on time and Manolis spoke to the driver, stating his ultimate destination and requesting that he should be allowed to leave the bus as close as possible to the village.

The driver scratched his head. 'Why do you want to go there? There's no village there any longer. The Germans burnt it.'

'I know,' replied Manolis patiently. 'I understand there has been a memorial erected there and I want to see it.'

'Oh,' enlightenment spread over the bus driver's face. 'You can see that as we go past on the bus.'

'Really?' Manolis was delighted. 'I shall still want to get off, though.'

The driver shrugged. 'Up to you. If you want a ride back to town be waiting there when I make my return journey. There's not another bus for a couple of days.'

'I'll be waiting,' Manolis assured him.

Manolis stood before the memorial erected at Vasilis's instructions in memory of his wife and son and the other villagers who had lost their lives. The drawing Vasilis had made had not prepared him for the size and he felt completely over awed. It towered above him, both the angel and the child twice life size. He read their names sadly, tears coming to his eyes as he remembered the few happy days he had spent with them during the war and Vasilis's devotion to them.

It seemed no time at all to him before the bus driver hooted to attract his attention and he climbed aboard, taking a seat at the back, hoping no one would notice that he had tears running down his face intermittently.

By the time the bus reached Chania he had composed himself, but he also realised he had no idea where to find Father Pavlos. All he could remember was that they were making their way towards Preveli and had passed Lake Kournas, but where amongst the cluster of villages that lay in that area the church was situated he did not know. He cursed himself as a fool for not asking Father Andreas when he was with him.

As fast as he berated himself he also realised that Father Andreas would probably not have known which church Father Pavlos served. The area was too far away from Heraklion for him to have any contact with the parish.

He looked at the map of the bus routes that was pinned to the wall beside the ticket office. There was the bus that went to Rethymnon, and then you had to catch another if you wished to travel to Spili. Manolis considered carefully. It was too late to travel any further that night. Tomorrow he would make for Rethymnon and ask at the main church in the town if they could help him. With this comforting thought, he made his way to a cheap taverna that was also offering rooms.

Manolis entered the ornate church and looked around in awe. Icons and richly embroidered hangings decorated the walls, the candlesticks were so highly polished their brightness dazzled him, silver incense burners hung from the ceiling and in a bowl of sand small candles burned continuously. He selected two small candles, placed his lepta in the box, and lit them in memory of Vasilis's family. It seemed a small and insignificant gesture on his part, but once again it brought tears to his eyes and he brushed them away impatiently.

The action was not lost on the young priest and he hurried forward. 'Can I help you, my son?'

Manolis looked at the man, his obvious youth taking him by surprise. 'I'm not sure. I'm looking for someone.'

'Do they live in this area?'

Manolis shook his head. 'I'm not sure where they live. I am trying to find Father Pavlos.'

The priest frowned. 'There is no one of that name here.'

'I did not expect to find him in Rethymnon. During the war I was travelling to Preveli with a companion and we visited Father Nicolas at Lapa. The following day we met Father Pavlos, but I cannot remember the name of the village. He was an old man and I realise he may no longer be alive.'

'Sadly I cannot help you. No, wait,' he held out his hand as Manolis prepared to leave. 'If you care to come with me I am sure one of the older priests would have knowledge of Father Pavlos. They should at least know if he is still alive so you would not make your journey in vain.'

Manolis followed him from the church to a large house opposite. The priest opened the gates, strode across the courtyard and entered, beckoning Manolis to follow him. Manolis stood just inside the door. This house was unlike the Spartan interior of Father Andreas's house in Heraklion. There were rugs on the tiled floor; soft chairs were spread about and with small tables beside them.

'Please take a seat. I will speak to my superiors and see if one of them can help you.' With a smile the young man disappeared through a door and Manolis was left alone. He looked at the chair, debating whether he dared to sit down. He would not want to break or soil it. He decided to stand until the priest or one of his number returned. These surroundings were very different from those at the monastery at Preveli.

'I am Father Achilles. How may I help you?'

Manolis whirled round. The priest had entered the vestibule from another door.

'I am sorry if I startled you,' he smiled. 'I was told you were enquiring about Father Pavlos – is that so?'

Manolis nodded. 'His church is somewhere near Lappa. I was hoping you could tell me the name of the village.'

The priest smiled sadly. 'I can tell you the name of the village, but I am afraid that Father Pavlos is no longer with us. He died shortly before the end of the war.'

Manolis crossed himself in unison with the priest.

'I believe he may have a cousin living in the village if that is any help to you?'

Manolis shook his head. 'I really wanted to know if he had recovered the church artefacts.'

The priest raised his eyebrows and scrutinized Manolis carefully. Was this man a treasure seeker? 'Unfortunately his church appeared to have been stripped bare.' He spread his hands. 'Some very rare relics were stored there, along with items of monetary value.'

Manolis nodded. 'He told us that. Has anyone looked for them?'

'Where are we supposed to look? The Germans shipped anything of value back to their own country. No doubt they melted down the gold and probably threw away the relics as of no consequence.' Father Achilles shook his head. 'No, they are gone for ever.'

'I know where they may be.'

'You? How would you know?' Father Achilles looked at Manolis sceptically.

'My companion and I hid them for him. The Germans may have found them, but if they didn't and Father Pavlos did not retrieve them they should still be there.'

Father Achilles hesitated. 'Come with me,' he said finally and led Manolis from the vestibule into a room that appeared to be a library. 'Please wait here. I need to speak to my colleagues.'

This time Manolis did sit down on the soft chair that was indicated and waited until Father Achilles returned with three other priests. They sat opposite and regarded him gravely.

'Father Achilles tells us that you have knowledge of the treasure that disappeared from Father Pavlos's church.'

Manolis nodded eagerly. 'I told Father Achilles that we hid everything except the icons.'

'And where did you hide these valuables?'

'We dug a hole in the graveyard.'

The priests looked at each other. 'And you were planning to go down and retrieve these items for yourself?'

'No,' Manolis shook his head vehemently. 'I wanted to see if Father Pavlos had recovered them. I promised him I would return after the war was over, but I couldn't remember the name of the village,' he ended lamely.

'Your companion did not remember either?'

'He has returned to England.'

Father Achilles sat forward. 'The war has been over for a considerable number of years. Why did you not visit Father Pavlos immediately?'

'I returned to Aghios Nikolaos and forgot about it.'

'You forgot?'

Manolis nodded miserably. 'My wife was barely alive. My friend was distraught over the loss of his family. My promise to Father Pavlos went out of my mind.'

Father Achilles looked at him dubiously. 'So what finally brought your promise back into your mind?'

'My friend, Vasilis, had arranged with Father Andreas to have a memorial erected to his family and the villagers who had perished. Vasilis had entrusted me to make sure it was on his land. Talking to Father Andreas about that reminded me of Father Pavlos.'

'Where is this memorial?'

'In a village south of Chania.' Manolis pulled the piece of paper from his pocket with the drawing of the monument. He passed it to Father Achilles. 'It's beautiful. I saw it yesterday.'

Father Achilles studied the drawing and passed it to his colleagues. 'Excuse us for a few moments.'

The priests withdrew to the far end of the room and conversed in undertones whilst Manolis sat uncomfortably. He sighed. 'You don't believe me, do you? Thank you for your time. I'll go now. I have told you where we placed the items. If Father Pavlos is no longer alive there is little point in me going to the village with the idea of helping him.'

Father Achilles shook his head. 'Please, we do not disbelieve you. We would like to ask you to stay in Rethymnon tonight and we will accompany you to the village tomorrow. You can show us where you buried the items and we can retrieve them safely and bring them back to the church with us.'

Manolis shrugged. 'What time do you want me to be here?'

Manolis arrived at the church in Rethymnon well before the appointed time. He entered and sat at the back, waiting for the time to pass. He had been foolish to arrive so early, but he had been unable to sleep any longer. Having walked along by the harbour he could think of nothing else to do to pass the time and began to wish that he had not agreed to the journey in the company of the priests. He should have made his own way to Lapa and asked Father Nicolas for directions. Sighing deeply he crossed the road and entered the courtyard to the house where the priests appeared to live in luxury.

Within a short while, a private car appeared at the gates and hooted to attract attention. Father Achilles opened the door and waved to the driver. Manolis smiled at him.

'I'm not late, am I?'

Father Achilles shook his head. 'Father Stergios and I will be with you in just a few moments.'

The driver opened the door of the car and Manolis was ushered into the back with Father Achilles whilst Father Stergios took the front seat next to the driver. Manolis sat nervously, he had never ridden in a car before, and the awful thought assailed him that someone could have discovered the hidden artefacts and retrieved them already.

They left the main road for a secondary road that began to

lead into the countryside and then on to smaller, unmade tracks. They bumped over the rough ground, holding on to the straps that hung down from the roof to avoid being thrown around. The area became familiar to Manolis and he forgot to be nervous as he looked out of the car window. Villagers stared at them curiously as they passed, unused to seeing people, particularly priests, travelling in a car.

The car did not stop at the church where Father Pavlos had been the priest, but continued on a short distance to the graveyard. Manolis hoped he would be able to remember where he and Vasilis had hidden the coffin containing the church artefacts. He racked his brains to remember the name of the woman the villagers had dug a grave for when the priest was unable to do the manual labour. They had dug their hole next to her.

He led the way to the furthest grave and looked desperately at the headstones to give him the name of the occupants. He was sure they had visited Father Pavlos before the dates that were recorded on the most recent stones. He walked slowly along the row, and then he saw it. A low mound in the ground with no headstone or memorial and next to it was the grave for Penelope Spanakadis. He drew a breath of relief, convinced he was in the right place and the ground looked undisturbed.

'I think this is the spot,' he said to Father Achilles. 'The villagers had recently dug the grave for Penelope Spanakadis and we dug one next to her.'

Father Achilles nodded and Father Stergios returned to the car and opened the boot, removing a pickaxe and spade and carrying them back to the waiting men. He handed the pickaxe to Manolis.

'I'm sure you will be more adept at using the implement than I,' he smiled.

Manolis thought the observation was probably true when he looked at the soft, white hands of the priest and compared them with his own calloused and scarred hands.

'Stand back,' he said, and swung the pickaxe down into the hard earth.

The priests stood and watched him labour whilst the driver of the car sat reading his newspaper and smoking. Manolis felt resentment rising in him. It would not hurt any of them to take a shovel and help to clear the earth away.

It was late in the afternoon when the coffin was finally exposed and Manolis stood back. 'Are you going to lift it up?'

Father Achilles shook his head. 'You need to clear enough earth at the side to go down to open it.'

Manolis compressed his lips. Had they told him that when he first started digging he would have sloped one side. Now a good deal of loose earth would fall back into the hole and he would have to shovel it out again. He took up the pickaxe again and attacked the earth viciously. He had been digging for hours, with only a short break for a snack and frequent mouthfuls of water, whilst the other men stood and watched. He knew if he had been with Father Minos or Father Andreas they would both have done their share of the work.

Finally Father Achilles peered into the hole and declared Manolis would be able to stand close enough to prise off the lid. Manolis licked his lips nervously. He dreaded that he had made a mistake and when he lifted the lid they would find a body inside.

The priests were obviously of the same mind as both of them crossed themselves and muttered a prayer before Manolis stepped cautiously into the hole and began to insert the claw of a hammer under the nails that held the rotten lid in place. The wood splintered and Manolis began to pull the pieces away, tossing them up onto the mound of earth that he had created.

He finally gave a sigh of relief. Wrapped, just as they had placed them lay the items they had buried for Father Pavlos.

'What do you want me to do now?' he asked.

'Pass them up, then you can fill the hole in again,' ordered Father Achilles and stretched out his hand.

Dutifully Manolis lifted them and passed them to the priest until he finally reached the box that contained relics the priest had kept hidden from them. As he pulled it from its resting place the bottom fell out, rotted over the years. A collection of wrapped items fell at his feet and he heard the priests draw in their breath.

Father Stergios knelt down on the grass and held out his cassock. 'Place them in there,' he ordered and Manolis hastened to comply.

Manolis climbed back out of the hole and began to shovel the earth back in. The priests stood together, examining each piece reverently and rewrapping it again. Father Stergios returned to the car, taking with him the pickaxe and chisel and bringing an empty box back with him. Carefully the priests placed the smaller items inside the box. Once Manolis had finished filling in the hole Father Achilles lifted the box, Father Stergios hung the incense burners over his arm and lifted the lectern, leaving Manolis to carry the candlesticks and the spade.

The large items were packed into the boot, but Father Achilles sat with the box of relics on his lap. His mission accomplished Manolis felt more at ease and was able to enjoy the journey back to Rethymnon, revelling in the novelty of riding in a car.

Once back at the church Father Stergios hurried inside and returned with willing helpers to carry the items safely inside. Manolis hovered beside the car, uncertain whether he was expected to stay with the priests or go his own way.

Father Achilles beamed at him. 'I apologise for doubting your word. I had to make sure you were not asking for a reward by claiming to know a hiding place.'

Manolis frowned. 'I don't understand.'

'The church gives a reward to anyone who finds and returns something that belongs to the church. So many priceless items went missing, so much was destroyed.' He shook his head sadly. 'Unfortunately we have had people come forward declaring they knew where items were hidden and claiming a reward. When we examined the area there was nothing and the informant had disappeared. I was encouraged this morning when you arrived as arranged and prayed that you would be able to unearth these treasures.'

Manolis shrugged. 'I promised Father Pavlos I would retrieve them if he was unable to do so. I keep my word,' he added stiffly.

'I appreciate that you are a very honourable young man. Come inside. You have worked hard and we can offer you refreshment and a bed for the night.'

'I really need a wash.' Manolis looked at his dirt begrimed hands and clothes. He did not feel he could walk into the opulent house in his present dirty state. 'Maybe if I returned to my lodgings and cleaned myself up first.'

Father Achilles shook his head. 'You can have a bath here and I am sure we can find you something to wear temporarily. You are close to Father Stergios in size.'

Manolis hesitated. He was now feeling incredibly tired and ravenously hungry. The effort of returning to his lodging house and persuading them to heat water for him was not appealing. He would then have to replace his soiled clothes and find a taverna where they would be willing to serve him a meal.

'I would be grateful,' he said humbly.

Manolis sat on the bus for Heraklion. He could hardly believe it. He kept taking the piece of paper from his pocket and looking again at the amount written on it. He was used to handling coins or drachma notes and this piece of paper with a vast sum written on it meant nothing to him. Father Achilles had instructed him to take it to his bank and present it to them along with his passbook, assuring him that it was the same as having money in his pocket. Within a week the money would be available to him and he could withdraw as much as he wanted.

He gazed out of the window and wondered what he could buy with it. He had his fishing boat, a home with his aunt and more than enough for his daily needs. He must not waste it, but nor did he want to leave it sitting in the bank forever. He would be able to buy something special for Flora when she returned home. As he thought about a present for her, a smile spread across his face. If she was given a clean bill of health from the hospital he had promised her a little house of their own once they were officially married. That was how he would spend the money.

Once he had thought of the idea, it began to take hold. He did not want anything luxurious like the priests' house in Rethymnon. He had felt uncomfortable in there. Flora was certainly not used to luxury, but he wanted to provide something more spacious and comfortable than where she had been living on the island.

In his mind he envisaged the buildings in Aghios Nikolaos, discounting immediately the houses on the hill with a panoramic view of the sea. He did not want to live in an apartment on the main street with the traders below, and the houses where the tanners lived he would not consider. He wanted to be near the sea, just a short walk away from his boat, one of the fishermen's cottages would suit him very well. He pulled the cheque out of his pocket and looked at the figure again. He wondered if the amount would be enough for him to rent Yiorgo's empty house or was he dreaming in vain?

Flora was elated. She was going home and most importantly of all she was no longer classed as a leper. When the doctor had first broken the news to her she had not believed him, then she had cried, finally she felt resentful. She and Manolis could have been married years ago and her continual worry that she would infect him had been unnecessary.

Her eyes glowing with pleasure she sought out Yannis and begged him to write a letter for her. 'I have to let Manolis know I'm coming home. We're going to be married, properly married like Marisa was on the island. Manolis is going to give me a house in Aghios Nikolaos and I'm going to live in the town.'

'I'm pleased for you, Flora. At least you know what your future holds.'

'So do you, Yannis. You're not infectious now either.'

Yannis sighed deeply. 'They won't let me go home yet. They want me to stay here and help the next batch of patients to settle in. It's an excuse. I know it's an excuse. For some reason they want to keep me here.'

'I'm sure they don't really, Yannis. You know how to talk to people, to give them confidence. If you're here they know they can trust you.'

Yannis shook his head. 'I can't help feeling there's more to me staying here than they've told me. Who shall I write this letter to, Flora? I think Doctor Stavros would probably be best. He'll pass it on to Manolis.'

Flora nodded eagerly. 'Tell him I'm clean and I shall be back on Spinalonga when the authorities go over again. I hope I shall go up in an aeroplane again.'

Yannis shuddered inwardly. He had no wish to repeat the journey in the sky. When he returned he would insist he went over by boat.

Manolis took the letter from Doctor Stavros and opened it with trembling fingers. He recognised the writing as belonging to Yannis and dreaded the news the envelope contained. What if they said Flora was incurable and would have to stay in Athens for treatment? What if Flora had died in Athens without him at her side?

'You read it,' he said and pushed the sheet of paper into the doctor's hands.

Doctor Stavros scanned the words quickly. He cleared his throat.

This is Yannis writing to you on behalf of Flora.

I am pleased to say that she has been given a clean bill of health and will be returning to Spinalonga within a few weeks.
   She is looking forward to seeing you again.

'Is that all?' asked Manolis. 'Is that all it says?' He took the sheet of notepaper and read the words for himself.

'What more can you ask for?'

'I need to know when she's arriving. I have arrangements to make. I want everything to be ready for her. I have to see Father Minos about the service. Despina must make a special dress for her. I have to get the house prepared. I need to go to Heraklion and see Father Andreas.' Manolis groaned. 'She could arrive tomorrow and nothing's ready.'

Doctor Stavros looked at the man in amusement. 'Provided you are here to greet her when she arrives I doubt that she'll worry about anything else. I'm sure you'll have plenty of time for all these arrangements you seem to have to make.'

Manolis shook his head. 'I must go to Heraklion today. I should have gone weeks ago, but I was frightened.'

'Frightened of going to Heraklion?' The doctor looked at the boatman in surprise.

Manolis shook his head. 'Frightened that if I made arrangements Flora wouldn't have been allowed to come back. It would have been tempting fate.'

Manolis fretted with impatience. He had visited Father Andreas to ask if he could rent Yiorgo's derelict cottage and to his amazement the priest had immediately offered to sell it to him. He declared he had no need of it and his father had died. Tentatively Manolis had asked how much he would have to pay and was pleasantly surprised to find that, with the addition of the cheque from the church, he had more than enough in his bank account to purchase the small property.

Once he walked inside he realised how much work he would have to do before he would consider it fit for Flora. He paid an extortionate amount to the electricity company for them to install the current within a week, and a further vast sum to a builder to have a toilet built on at the back. There would be no more using of the yard for him or an old soak away toilet for Flora.

He scrubbed the flagstones on the ground floor and the stairs leading to the loft room before replacing the wooden floor up there. He wished the window was larger but dared not knock out any stones, frightened he might send the whole wall crashing down. He bought cans of whitewash and brushes, painting the inside walls, immediately noticing how much lighter and brighter the cottage looked. He replaced the broken glass in the front window and renewed the hinges on the shutters, then painted them blue.

Deciding he could do no more decorating inside he purchased a bed, two chests, table and chairs, two arm chairs, a sideboard, radio, cooking utensils, crockery and cutlery, along with a rug for the floor and curtains for the windows. He spent most of one day moving the furniture around to see where he thought it looked at its most advantageous, finally replacing it in its original position.

He sighed with relief when Doctor Stavros told him the authorities had finally made arrangements to bring back the islanders who wanted to return and collect the next group to go to the hospital in Athens.

Dressed in a clean shirt and new pair of trousers Manolis waited on the quay for the bus to arrive. He had been there since early morning, despite the doctor telling him they could not possibly be there before mid-day. He paced up and down, continually scanning the road across the bridge, hoping for a sight of the hospital bus and when it eventually rumbled towards him he ran towards it, pulling the door open before it had come to a halt.

Flora looked around the tiny dark house that had been her home on the island for so long. It was very different from the accommodation she had been allocated at the hospital. Her room had been light and airy, there was space for an armchair where she could sit comfortably, and she had not had to ask for help to haul a bathtub down to the shore to have a wash.

'I'm so pleased to be home,' she smiled. 'It's horrible living away from the sea. I could never live in a town or the countryside.'

'You'll never have to,' Manolis promised her. He placed her bag on her bed and pulled her towards him. 'We have so much to arrange. I've spoken to Father Minos and he's happy to marry us whenever we please, but I want to do it properly. I want you to have a wedding like Marisa had. One that you can always remember. This time I shall give you a proper wedding ring.'

Flora touched his face gently with her hand. 'Manolis, provided I am married to you I shall always remember it as the best day of my life.'

'Aunt Eirini, I want to invite you to my wedding.' Manolis radiated happiness.

Eirini smiled with pleasure. At last her neighbours would no longer look askance at her bachelor nephew.

'Maria?' she asked hopefully.

Manolis shook his head. 'No, her name's Flora. She's from the island.'

'Marrying a girl from the island! It's out of the question!'

'No it isn't, Aunt Eirini. She's a lovely girl. I'm sure you'll like her.'

'I'm not prepared to meet her. Think of the shame for the family. She's not coming here to live in my house. You can think again there.' Eirini pursed her lips with disapproval and folded her arms, daring Manolis to challenge her decision.

'I have thought. I've bought Yiorgo's house. We shall live there.'

'You've bought a house? Where did you get the money from to buy a house?' Eirini glared at her nephew. She should obviously have asked him for considerably more money whilst lodging with them.

Flora moved slowly around the room, touching the furniture gently and fingering the curtains whilst Manolis looked on anxiously.

'It's a proper house. Is it really ours?'

'It's our home, Flora. I've cleaned and painted it, but you can do whatever you wish, change the furniture, the curtains, whatever takes your fancy.'

A tear ran down Flora's cheek. 'It's the most beautiful house I've ever seen – and we have Yannis to thank for everything. If he hadn't kept on writing to the government I would still be on the island.'

Manolis looked around the small house with pride and held Flora tightly to him. If Vasilis ever came back to Crete he would not be ashamed to bring him to this house. It was also a fitting home where he could entertain Yannis when he returned from Athens – and Manolis was sure he would return one day.

to be continued...

If you have enjoyed reading *Manolis*, you will be pleased to know that the next book – *Cathy* – is a sequel to *Manolis* and is planned for publication in June 2011.

See overleaf for a 'taster' of what is to come.

For up-to-date information, have a look at the author's website:

www.beryldarbybooks.com

CATHY

Basil landed at Southampton when the ship bringing him from Crete docked. He had spent most of the voyage in the cabin he shared with three other men, his face turned to the wall, not sharing in their company.

Now he wandered bemused down the gangplank and looked around. What was he supposed to do?

'Over there, mate.' The man indicated with a jerk of his thumb and Basil walked slowly towards the building.

Once inside he completed the formalities and was directed to the Red Cross room. There a cup of tea was placed before him and he sat staring at it morosely.

'You haven't drunk your tea.' A young woman stopped by the table.

'It's cold,' muttered Basil.

'I'll fetch you another.'

Before he could refuse the offer, she had taken the cup and made her way to the counter, picking up a freshly poured beverage and returned to Basil.

'There you are. That one is nice and hot.'

'I don't want it.'

'We haven't any coffee.'

Basil shrugged.

'Is there something you would like that I can get you?'

Basil shook his head.

The woman slid into the seat opposite him. 'Are you waiting for someone to meet you?'

'No.'

'Where are you planning to go?'

Basil raised his eyes for the first time. 'Wales, I suppose.'

'You have relatives there?'

'Maybe.'

'Drink your tea, then I'll show you where you can get a rail pass for your journey.'

'A pass? Don't I have to pay?'

The woman shook her head. 'Returning combatants are given a free rail pass to travel to their home town. Many of them wouldn't have any money and we can only accommodate the truly homeless here. Even then, we try to find them somewhere to live as soon as possible. We couldn't cope with the numbers otherwise.'

Basil finally picked up his cup and took a sip. It was a long time since he had drunk a cup of tea and he was not at all sure if he liked the taste. He pushed the cup away.

'Show me where I have to go.'

He followed the volunteer across the room and he added himself to the queue of men waiting patiently.

'You shouldn't be too long. They'll give you directions to the station. There'll probably be a bus going there soon. Have you got your luggage?'

'I haven't any luggage.'

'Nothing?'

Basil shook his head and the volunteer frowned again. 'Maybe I should take you to the Red Cross supplies before you get your pass. They can kit you out with the basics.'

Basil stood in line waiting to be given a razor, comb, toothbrush, toothpaste, face flannel, a small piece of soap and a thin towel and a bag in which to place the items. To his surprise a one pound note was placed in his hand along with a temporary ration book.

'What's this for?' he asked.

'Everyone is given a small amount. Enough to cover a bed for a week. You'll need to hand over your ration book wherever you stay. Sign there.' The man pointed to the place on the paper and Basil dutifully signed his name.

To Rebecca's surprise, two weeks later Basil walked into the Red Cross Centre again. He sat down at an empty table and seemed uncertain what he should do next.

'I'll go,' she said to her companion at the counter and poured a fresh cup of tea.

Rebecca sat down opposite Basil and passed the cup to him. 'Hello. I am right, aren't I? You were here a couple of weeks ago, weren't you?'

Basil looked at her. She was vaguely familiar. He nodded.

'My name's Rebecca. Would it help to talk?'

Basil hesitated. He had not held a conversation with anyone for a considerable length of time. He had talked to the solicitor when he had found out his aunt had died and he had inherited her house and a sizeable amount of money. He had talked again with the estate agent as he arranged to have the house placed on the market. He had then returned to the Red Cross Centre as he did not know where else he could turn for help.

'What about?' he asked finally.

'Whatever you wish. English people always discuss the weather.'

'It's damp.'

'And you are used to somewhere warmer?'

'Not always. We nearly froze in the mountains.'

'What were you doing there?'

'Whatever was needed.'

Rebecca was not going to find out anything more about this strange man by asking questions about his activities during the war.

'What do you plan to do now you've returned?'

Basil shrugged. 'I don't know.'

'What work did you do before the war?'

'I trained as a teacher.'

'You're fortunate. You can always go back to that. Teachers are always needed.'

'I don't like teaching and children don't like me.'

'So what else could you do?'

Basil shrugged again and did not answer.

'Have you always been so morose? If you smiled you could find the children you taught did like you.'

'I have nothing to smile about.'

Rebecca rose to her feet. 'I lost my father to cancer three years ago and my older brother is a prisoner of war in Japan. Our house was bombed and my mother and younger brother were found dead in the rubble. My fiancé was in the air force and didn't return after a mission. I have nothing to smile about either, but I try not to inflict my unhappiness on others.'

She walked away, feeling close to tears, leaving Basil alone, staring at his cup of tepid tea. He pushed it to one side, slopping it onto the table and walked out of the building. Rebecca looked after him in annoyance. If he ever returned she would not make any effort to help him a second time.

to be continued...

First book

The compelling story of Yannis, who comes from the village of Plaka on the island of Crete. He attends school in the town of Aghios Nikolaos and gains a scholarship to the Gymnasium in Heraklion.

Whilst in Heraklion, he is diagnosed with leprosy, shattering his dreams of becoming an archaeologist. He is admitted to the local hospital for treatment and subsequently transferred to the hospital in Athens. The conditions in the hospital are appalling: overcrowding, lack of amenities, poor food, and only basic medication. The inmates finally rebel, resulting in their exile to Spinalonga, a leper colony just across the water from Yannis's home village.

The book tells the heart-rending account of his life on the small island, his struggle for survival, his loves and losses, along with that of his family on the mainland from 1918 to 1979.

Second book

In this, the second book in a continuing saga, Anna is left to care for her invalid mother and her sister's children when the Germans invade Crete. A battalion of Italian soldiers is billeted in the village to prevent a seat of resistance being formed on Spinalonga, the leper village opposite the village.

There are resistance workers in the area.

How will she protect strong-willed Marisa from the Italian soldiers, and impulsive Yannis from joining the resistance?

Unwillingly she becomes involved with the resistance and has to draw on all her resources and ingenuity to fool the Italians, finally risking her life to save the man she loves.

Beryl Darby

GIOVANNI

The third book in a continuing saga of a Cretan family

Third book

Yannis has become a successful businessman with a number of hotels. He has taken his resourceful nephew, Giovanni, into partnership. Giovanni is full of ideas to improve the business. He has only one failing – he is susceptible to a pretty face.

His younger brother, Joseph, is resentful of Giovanni's success and determined to avenge himself. With the help of a beautiful woman, he schemes and plans to bring about his brother's disgrace. His final act of revenge has dire results for all involved.

Marianne, Annita's granddaughter, visits Athens with her friend and meets relatives who were previously unknown to her. Elizabeth finds the city romantic in many ways. Later they both visit Crete, which has unexpected consequences for Marianne.

Yannis's loyalty to his extended family saves all of them from shame and humiliation.

Fourth book

Joseph has moved to Rhodes. He lives and works in a warehouse that is a centre for drug distribution and is responsible for taking the money to Turkey each week. He becomes over ambitious and has plans to become a wealthy man.

Sorrell is searching for Joseph to wreak her revenge. She accepts the offer of help from a millionaire hotelier and enjoys a life of idleness and luxury before she finds herself in the clutches of a ruthless criminal. She is both used and abused. Fearing for her life she finally has to ask Joseph for help and protection.

Events take an unexpected turn and a number of people find they are under the scrutiny of the police. Both Joseph and Sorrell are able to evade the law, but they are unable to evade their ultimate fate at the hands of their associates.

Beryl Darby

CHRISTABELLE

The fifth book in a continuing saga of a Cretan family

Fifth book

Christabelle is beautiful and highly successful in her chosen career as a model. She has also inherited her talent for acting from her unknown father. Everyone is charmed by her; but there is an evil side to her nature. Anyone who upsets Christabelle regrets it. She takes her revenge to extremes, becoming more confident in her actions each time. She is convinced she is invincible.

As she travels across Europe a trail of fatal accidents follow her. It finally takes subterfuge and John's talent for photography for justice to be done.

Sixth book

After Saffron's parents separate and divorce, her father brings her to England, where she adapts well and is happy. She achieves her childhood ambition to become a doctor. She falls deeply in love, only to be badly hurt when her hopes for a long-term relationship are cruelly shattered. When she does marry, she finds she has made the biggest mistake of her life.

Over the years she has wished to be reunited with her American family and when she finally contacts them it is with an unexpected and delightful result.

Readers' Reviews

"A remarkable series of books. I have read each book three times."

J. Evans

"One of the best family sagas I have ever read. Please keep writing about this family."

G.. Newman

"The characters are so real that I feel I know them."

D. Mason

"I become so involved in the plot of each book that I await the outcome as anxiously as if the fictitious characters were my own family."

G. King

"Each time I finish a book by Beryl Darby I am eagerly anticipating the next. Please write many more about this family."

J. Wilson

"This series of books is the best I have read in thirty years."

C. Taylor

"These characters have become a part of our family. We talk about them as if they were real."

G. Hiscox

"Thank you for giving me so much pleasure with your writing."

R. Shepherd